INK BLACK MAGIC

TANSY RAYNER ROBERTS

For my kids
who are both artists and superheroes
(mad scientists and evil geniuses)

CONTENTS

You may have read stories about magic with rules —
where good magic and bad magic are easily
distinguishable from each other and the sorcerer saves
the world every single time. Such stories are lies and
fantasies.

Magic does not follow recipes. Magic is not a
natural tool for humans. It cannot be borrowed or
stolen or manipulated. It is a howling random force
that will tear you apart without bothering to learn
your name.

We have the misfortune to live on an island where
magic is commonplace, where the landscape is a riot
of colour and madness, howling spirits and flying fish.

Magic is in the dirt, in the air, in our blood. There's
more around than there used to be. One of these days
our precious Mocklore Empire will surely fly apart in
a cloud of golden smoke and purple sparks. This
future is inevitable.

How do you protect yourself?

Carry a sword, not a wand. Never attempt to use

magic, even if the end seems to justify the means. You will always pay for such use, with a headache or a stab wound or a flying sheep where a man used to be. If you possess natural magical ability, learning how to safely *not* use that power will be the most important thing you ever do.

I will not teach your children warlocklore or witchery. I will teach them to know their unknown enemy, to learn from the catastrophes of our past, to survive the orange mists and silver sparks and refrain from setting the world alight with green demon-fire.

I will teach them not to use magic, and the lesson may very well save their lives.

Yours sincerely,
Mistress Sharpe,
Philosophy of Magic
Department of Highly Improbable Arts

Vice-Chancellor's Note: Mistress Sharpe's Philosophy of Magic course is a prerequisite for many popular Second Year courses including Magic Studies, Alchemy, Neo-sorcery, Practical Mythology, Hedgewitchery and Creative Dance.

MAGIC IS A BAD BAD THING

The dream was about heroes — impossible heroes with rippling muscles, ink-black eyes and amazing powers. They crashed! *and* banged! *their way through the city, conquering villains with a* biff! *and a* thwack! *and a* pow!!! *Good triumphed over evil with swashbuckling ease. The heroes saved the world again and again, pausing only to exchange witty repartee or to redesign their colourful costumes. In a world of heroes and villains, everything was simple.*

Egg woke up, fumbling for a spare piece of papyrus. He scribbled frantic notes with a scratchy pen. The ink in the bottle had scabbed over and made blotchy blobs across the page. Egg barely noticed the mess, too intent on the outline of a new super-villainess, an insect woman with glowing eyes and sensuous hips.

As he squinted to see the page, Egg realised that he was sitting in darkness. Outside, across the cobbled square of the student residence, the clocks struck the hour. Twelve long, sonorous notes drummed out of the tallest clock tower, a frothy confection of ivory spirals, glass runes and marble-white stonework. Three short, piping notes rang out of the middle clock tower, a solid piece of grey granite with gargoyles. Finally, four squeaky pips emerged from the shortest clock tower, a pink assortment of bricks swamped by bright purple ivy. Thirty-four minutes past midnight.

The clocks rang about twelve times a day, never exactly on the hour. When they had first been built they rang constantly, calling out the exact time at every minute of the day. Approximately four hours (and twenty-eight minutes) after the clocks began their noisy refrain, a delegation of students armed with axes, chisels and woefully inadequate padded earmuffs had persuaded Vice-Chancellor Bertie to impose the current restrictions.

Egg lit a lantern and stared at the papyrus, blowing on it to dry the ink. Where did they come from, these pictures in his head? He had never met a super-villainess before — although his mother did have some very strange friends — and yet he knew exactly what one looked like. He also knew which of his heroes would meet her first, and how that tale would tie in to the overall story arc.

What he didn't know was what to do with the story when it was finished. Everyone knew stories were for telling aloud, for spinning over an open fire or singing in a tavern. Hardly anyone wrote stories down, and no one drew stories in pictures like Egg did, with little bubbles to show that people were talking. The closest equivalent were the humorous hieroglyphs that you found scratched on walls, but they tended to be about sarcastic cats and amusing situations involving the workplace. They weren't about heroes.

Someone knocked, banged and thumped on the door. Egg was vaguely aware that they had been doing so for some time. He padded across the room in his pyjamas and bare feet and opened the door.

A girl stood on the other side, her hand raised to knock again. She had the face of a heroine, the kind who gets rescued against a background of flame and intrigue. Her eyes were blue, her ponytail was blonde and her smile was angelic. "Is this Sean McHagrty's room?" she asked.

Egg slammed the door and went back to bed. "Go away!" he shouted as the knocking started up again.

"That's not very polite!" the girl yelled from the other side of the door. "Oy!"

Egg stomped across the floor again, shooting an accusing glance at his roommate's bed. "He's not here," he said as he pulled open the door. "His suitcases are here, but they haven't even been opened. I moved in three days ago and I haven't seen him. The only evidence I have that Sean McHagrty actually exists is that you are the twelfth girl today who has asked after him."

The angel with the ponytail stared at Egg as if he were insane. "I know he's not here," she said slowly. "I asked if this was his room."

"Oh," said Egg. "Yes, it is."

"Good." The girl pushed past him. She was carrying, Egg noticed with alarm, an overnight bag. It was pink. "Is this his bed?" She selected the spare bed and bounced experimentally on it.

"Yes," said Egg. "Um, what are you doing?"

"I'm moving in," said the girl. She took some things out of her overnight bag and headed into the tiny wash chamber. Her towel and flannel were also pink. "Won't be a minute. Feels like I haven't cleaned my teeth in a month." She closed the door behind her.

Egg stared helplessly at the closed door. He wanted to barge in after her and demand an explanation, but an inner voice sensibly informed him that you couldn't do that to girls in wash chambers. Plus, the so-called wash chamber, which

3

he and the mythical McHagrty shared with the occupants of the room next door, was little more than a large cupboard with a copper washtub, a small water pump and a hole in the floor. There wasn't room for more than one person in there.

There was a splash, and some vigorous, frothy, teeth-cleaning noises. "I'm Clio," shouted the girl, indistinctly. "Clio Wagstaff-Lamont. Who are you?"

"Egg," he said, still a little stunned. "Egfried Friefriedsson."

She opened the door and stuck her head out. Her mouth was still rather frothy. "From Axgaard? Awesome. You don't look like a warrior."

"I'm not," he said. "Not a warrior. Or from Axgaard, really. It's just where my dad comes from."

"Oh, okay." A slender arm reached out to grab Clio's overnight bag and then vanished with it back into the bathroom. Egg heard rinsing and spitting noises, and a lot of quiet rustling. He backed away from the door and sat on his bed, sliding his inky papyrus page into a folder full of similar pages. He shoved the folder into a drawer and hovered by the window for a while, trying to look casual.

Clio emerged from the bathroom. "This is how it's going to work, Egg. Your precious roommate has seriously hooked up with my precious roommate, which means I've been locked out of my own room for two days while they discover the wonders of — well, shagging. Apparently it's something special. Who knew? I've tried sleeping in the library tower and I've tried sleeping in the corridors but it's just not working for me. Since classes start tomorrow and I don't want to fall asleep during them, I thought to myself, where is there likely to be a spare bed in this town? Then I said to myself, aha! Sean McHagrty is not in his bed, therefore his bed must be empty. Is any of this making sense to you, Egg?"

"Um," said Egg. He was still trying to cope with the fact that the angelic, ponytailed heroine had unexpectedly transformed into a peculiar creature with pink hair-curlers dotted all over her head and an old-fashioned white nightdress which covered her in lace from neck to wrist to ankle. It gave the overall impression that she was a large, queenly piece of sharp-cornered furniture.

"I live with my grandmother," Clio explained. "She packed this for an emergency, and I'm pretty sure she'd consider sharing a room with a boy to be a complete and utter emergency." She preened a little. "You won't be tempted to ravish me."

"No," said Egg quickly. "Certainly not!"

Clio frowned. "You don't have to be quite so fervent about it!" She climbed into Sean McHagrty's bed and tucked herself up to her chin. "I don't suppose you tell stories?"

"I write stories," said Egg, thinking of inky scribbles. "Sort of. I draw them, like humorous hieroglyphs only without jokes."

Clio yawned and pulled more blankets over her. "Sounds good. Tell me one."

"They're not the kind of stories you just tell."

"Tell me one anyway."

Egg shot an anxious look at the drawer where he had shoved the latest in a large collection of untidy papyrus folders. He tried to think of the right words to explain just how private his stories were, and how they couldn't just be read aloud like any old ballad. By the time he found the words, Clio had fallen asleep.

The Polyhedrotechnical College was the only higher education institution in the little Mocklore Empire. This was unsurprising, as most people still went by the old apprentice system, and actual qualifications were viewed with extreme suspicion. The College itself had only come into existence fifty years earlier because an entrepreneur named Cluft Cooper thought he could make his fortune by selling education. The former Emperor Timregis, then in the early days of his reign, had poured money into the project on the condition that he got to choose the architectural designs.

The result was a town, spilling out on both sides of the Great Mocklore Road. Due to the Emperor's peculiar architectural whims, Cluft was a town like no other. It was crammed with towers, buttresses, mysterious hidden passages, upside down cottages and — due to its student population — lots and lots of taverns. Cluft eventually became an independent city-state in its own right, which was the Emperor's reward to Vice-Chancellor Bertie Peacock for inventing the postgraduate thesis.

The Polyhedrotechnical College was made up of four Departments: Aristocracy, Profit, Certain Death and Highly Improbable Arts. The Department of Aristocracy had only recently changed its name from the Department of Nobility, since there were too many over-literal parents who had questioned whether subjects such as History of Torture, Advanced Posturing and Dictatorship were *noble*, strictly speaking. Aristocratic, certainly.

Egg sat in the draughty Second Lecture Hall, waiting for a lecture. He was quite enjoying higher education so far. He had chosen a general degree, with first year subjects from each department. He was taking Perspectives of the Profithood, Basic Number Crunching, Introduction to Aristocracy, Social Study of Heroes and Villains, Philosophy of Magic and Tavern Skills.

The lecture hall was full of seventeen year olds screaming, gossiping, whispering and laughing. None of them paid attention to anything but each other.

The lecturer walked in from the back of the hall, striding

down the steps in a long, heavy skirt. Her petticoats rustled. Her big black boots made a ringing sound as they struck the floor. She stood at the lectern and arranged her papers, cleared her throat. "Magic," she said in a firm, musical voice, "is bad. Very, very bad. There is a reason that this course, Philosophy of Magic, is compulsory before you take any other magic-related course within the Polyhedrotechnical College. My job is to drill into your sweet little minds the very important fact that magic should never be used unless it is the absolute last resort and sometimes not even then. Magic cannot be safely used At All. It is unreliable, deadly dangerous, and in almost all test cases, more trouble than it is worth. Any questions so far?"

Her audience stared at her. She was a statuesque figure in crimson and black. Her hourglass figure was cinched in by a firm leather bodice and her skirts spread out in a wide, full circle. She had huge golden eyes, a dark red mouth and scarlet hair tied up in an attempt at a respectable bun, though several loose curls escaped around her neck. She was not like the other professors.

Her name, they had been told, was Mistress Sharpe. One look at their scrolls for Social Study of Heroes and Villains told them otherwise. This woman was *famous*. The main topic of gossip among the students was the question of why she, of all people, was here. She had been a pirate, a criminal and a witch. She was young for a professor, but no one doubted her authority. Everyone was terrified of her — or madly in lust with her. There were some seriously kinky rumours about Mistress Sharpe. The latest was that she kept a sheep in her bedroom.

"The trouble with magic," said Mistress Sharpe, addressing the first year class with a steady golden gaze, "is that it doesn't work. This is why witches stick to the milder forms of magic such as herbalism and hedgewitchery, while warlocks rarely resort to magic at all, preferring to spend their time on mathematics and needlework. When you use magic — large or small — something always goes horribly wrong."

Mistress Sharpe's golden eyes changed focus suddenly, staring at a lad in the third row who had been making a disbelieving face. "Yes? Clifford. You have something to say?"

"Well," said Clifford, blushing a little. "You can't say that, can you, miss? You can't say magic never works, that it always goes wrong. It must work sometimes."

"Nope," said Mistress Sharpe.

"But if you follow the rules?"

"Aha," said Mistress Sharpe. She emerged from behind the lectern. "That is a very interesting point, Clifford. The rules of magic. What are they? Can you think of one?"

Clifford, his bravery swiftly departing, slumped in his chair. "Um, harm none, miss?" he suggested, his face blazing.

"That's a good one," said Mistress Sharpe. "Of course, it applies equally well to non-magical activities, we should hope. Yes, Yarrowstalk?"

A girl in the back row lowered her hand. "Please miss," she said. "Don't witches have special categories that make their magic work better? Like hedgewitches, or hearth-witches. Isn't that a kind of rule?"

"Yes," said Mistress Sharpe. "Very good. A seawitch's magic, for example, is intensified by being close to salt water. If she casts a spell at sea, it will be ten times stronger than at any other time. But — and I can't stress this enough — it still wouldn't necessarily work. Even when you do everything 'right', magic does not always choose to obey you. It is a random, unpredictable force of chaos. The seawitch's spell might go wrong. If it went wrong while she was at sea, it might go ten times more wrong. There is no way of guaran-teeing that magic will work, or that it will work in the way you want it to, which is why it is better not to use it at all. Yes, Moonweaver?"

A girl in ribboned pigtails leaned forward earnestly. "What about spells, miss? If you follow a spell exactly, isn't that like following the rules of magic?"

"Nope," said Mistress Sharpe. She grinned widely. "You had Home Economics this morning, didn't you, Moonweaver? With a cake recipe, you know it has been worked out by someone who had an interest in cakes. The chances are, if it's a good recipe, if you follow the instructions exactly, you will get a half-decent cake. If you mess around with the ingredients and make it up as you go along, you also might get a great cake, or you might get a total bloody disaster. But you would think to yourself, that's because I didn't stick to the recipe. Am I right?"

Moonweaver nodded hesitantly.

"Right," said Mistress Sharpe. "With magic, you can follow the instructions of a spell completely to the letter, you can do exactly what the witch or warlock did before you and it can *still go wrong*. In fact, it will almost certainly go wrong if it works at all. Other people's spells are almost certainly doomed to failure. Magic resents any attempt to tie it down. Yes, Friefriedsson?"

Egg hadn't even realised that his hand was in the air. He lowered it slowly. "Mistress Sharpe, this is our first class with you. You haven't consulted a register but you seem to know all our names. Are you using magic to do that?"

Mistress Sharpe smiled a dazzling smile at him. "That's a fascinating question, Friefriedsson." She extended her smile to the entire class. "Any other fascinating questions?"

~

Clio was waiting for Egg as he came out of the lecture hall.

She lay full-length on a park bench, her blonde hair spread out to catch the sunshine. As he approached, she cracked one eye open. "Hi."

"Hi," said Egg, dropping to the concrete and sitting down.

"I'm thinking of taking up Philosophy of Magic," she announced.

"If you'd turned up an hour ago, you could have actually attended the lecture."

"Don't nag," said Clio, yawning. "I really tried with History of Torture, but the lecturer has these horrible green blotches all over his neck and I was so busy staring that I didn't take in a word of what he said. Ugh. After ten minutes of that, I just had to come and lie in the sun for a while to make it up to myself. What's Mistress Sharpe like?"

"Okay, I guess. A bit intense. She has a one-track mind about magical disasters, but at least that should make it easier to predict the exam questions."

"Just as long as she doesn't have green spots," said Clio. She lifted herself up slightly on one elbow. "You know who she is, don't you? Who she really is."

Egg grinned. "Everyone knows who she is. Kassa Dagger-sharp, pirate queen, scourge of the seventeen seas. Well, at least eight of them."

"Oh," said Clio, obviously disappointed at not being the one to pass on this juicy bit of gossip. "But do you know the best bit?"

"You mean how she was at school with the Lady Emperor, or do you mean the time she came back from the dead?"

"Not that," said Clio scornfully. "I mean the love story." She placed her hand against her forehead and swooned back on to the bench. "The horribly tragic, melodramatically romantic and ultimately doomed love affair between Kassa Daggersharp and Aragon Silversword."

"Oh," said Egg. "That."

"*She* was the madcap outlaw pirate queen," sighed Clio, getting into the story despite his obvious lack of interest. "*He* was the famous ex-Champion and traitor of the Empire. They were completely and utterly in love with each other. They had grand adventures together — she rescued him from the Lady Emperor, he rescued her from the Underworld. But one day she woke up and he was just gone. Vanished into thin air. She was *utterly* devastated..."

"Does everyone do things *utterly* in this story?"

"Shut up. Yes. Anyway, Kassa swore off piracy from that day forward, disbanded her crew and dropped out of public sight."

"Until she turned up here," said Egg. "Teaching first years how magic is a bad bad thing."

"She should know. She caused plenty of magical disasters in her day."

"You do know that all this is recent history, don't you? I mean, 'her day' was only a couple of years ago."

"I know," Clio said defensively. "It just seems like it all should have happened once upon a time. Like fairy tales. All the best heroic epics are told hundreds of years after all the characters are dead."

"Why are you so interested in this anyway?" Egg couldn't help asking. "No one cares about who Mistress Sharpe really is." Well, yeah, they all told the stories. He'd never heard them told so lovingly, though.

"I care," Clio said. "I happen to like tragical romance."

"Really?"

"Yes, really. Anyway, Aragon Silversword was my uncle, so it's a family legend."

"Oh," said Egg. There was a long silence. Clio might be sulking, but it was hard to tell. Her eyes were closed against the sun again. "You know," he said eventually. "My father is the exiled prince of Axgaard. He was chucked out and disowned for having an affair with one of his father's Official Wenches."

Clio opened her eyes, staring thoughtfully at him. "My mother died when I was a baby. She was descended from the famous playwright Wilt Wagstaff and his leading lady, Lana Lamont. Wagstaff wrote *Baytriche* for Lana, then she left him because he wrote three plays in a row with no decent female parts for her."

"Well," said Egg, grinning as he saw the competitive gleam in Clio's eyes. "*My* mother is descended from the Silver Warlock, who founded the College of Highly Improbable Arts right here in Cluft."

"My grandmother is Silvia Silversword, who was cousin to the evil Lady Keela of Teatime and looked exactly like her when they were young, so they swapped places and no one noticed for four years."

"When my grandfather died," said Egg, "my aunt Sven-hilda became the first female Jarl of Axgaard. She almost got assassinated for trying to make her subjects shave off their beards and be polite to women, and her husband is made out of clockwork. Also my mother Melinor, before she was the Jarl's wench and ran away with my dad, was sister to the infamous pirate Black Nell, who married Bigbeard Dagger-sharp. I think that actually makes Mistress Sharpe my cousin." He smiled, feeling smug. It wasn't hard to acquire famous ancestors in Mocklore. The island was small, the population was small and everyone got famous sooner or later.

Clio's grey eyes went flinty. "Twelve years ago, my father committed treason against Emperor Timregis and was executed by the Imperial Champion, his own brother."

Egg stared at Clio, too shocked to speak at first. "Is that true?"

"Yep."

"You win, then."

Clio looked a little sad. "I always do."

The door to the lecture hall opened and Mistress Sharpe came out, balancing a teetering pile of parchment and papyrus scrolls.

Clio jumped up from the bench, pasting a cheerful smile on her face. "Mistress Sharpe? I was hoping to have a word about transferring into your class."

Mistress Sharpe looked irritated. "If you'd turned up an hour ago, you could have actually attended the lecture."

Clio's smile brightened noticeably. "Sorry about that. Can I join?"

"All right," sighed Mistress Sharpe. "As it happens, I've had a few cancellations from boys who think my cautious attitude to magic is unnecessary. I expect we'll be scraping them off the walls of your common room in due time. I'll add you to the list. Just remember that lecture attendance does actually increase your chances of passing the exam."

"Yes, miss." Clio hesitated. "Also, I had a message to pass on. From my grandmother."

Mistress Sharpe transferred her pile of scrolls and papers to her hip. Her large golden eyes looked incredibly tired. "Do I know your grandmother?"

"No, miss. But she would like to be remembered to you. Her name is Silvia Silversword."

Mistress Sharpe's armload of papers exploded. Scrolls and parchment scattered on the concrete, where the wind whipped at them. Mistress Sharpe stared at Clio. "Silvia *Silversword?*"

"Yes, miss," Clio said. Her smile faltered a little under the steely gaze of the professor. "She lives nearby, and she was hoping you could come by for tea some time. She would very much like to meet you."

"I bet she would," Mistress Sharpe said grimly. "That would make Aragon Silversword your—"

"Uncle, miss. My father's brother."

"I see. Egfried Friefriedsson, if you touch those scrolls, you will die a horrible death."

Egg paused in the act of attempting to help Mistress Sharpe with her dropped scrolls and parchments. "Yes, miss."

Mistress Sharpe turned back to Clio. "You're Aragon's niece."

"That's right, miss."

It was fascinating to see these two together, Egg thought. Clio was the type who fluttered her eyelashes and bounced confidently through life, but here was a woman nearly a decade older who was far better at it.

"Heard from him lately?" Mistress Sharpe asked.

"Oh, no," Clio protested, her eyes wide. "Not for years."

"That's something, I suppose."

"You must have really loved him," Clio burst out. "I mean, I've read all the ballads. Your story is so romantic."

Egg closed his eyes. He didn't think that Mistress Sharpe saw things the same way at all.

He was right. Mistress Sharpe stared at Clio as if she were some new kind of invading goblin. She snapped her fingers and the scrolls and parchments reassembled themselves, leaping tidily back into her arms. "I don't know about romance," she said. "But next time I see him, I plan to shove a knife between his ribs." She spun on her heel and walked away.

"She did love him," said Clio, sounding satisfied.

Egg frowned. "She used magic to pick up those books. She said that no one should ever ever *ever* use magic."

"I bet she didn't say that at all," said Clio. "I bet she just said that *you* shouldn't."

~

A high, uneven staircase led up to Mistress Sharpe's room. Like everything else in Cluft, these stairs had been designed by a madman. Each step was a different shape and colour. If you climbed them fast enough, they could cause seizures.

Mistress Sharpe climbed the steps slowly. Her feet felt heavy. There was something ridiculously exhausting about the first day of semester. She had only given three introductory lectures so far — second year Practical Mythology and third year Creative Dance, as well as the first year Philosophy of Magic — but her brain and body felt as if she had spent the last ten hours simultaneously ploughing the earth and learning several foreign languages.

It was their little faces that did it, she decided — those bloody first years. They got so much younger every year. Mistress Sharpe was only twenty-six, but the beginning of semester made her feel a century older.

She was five flights up, still climbing the ridiculous stairs. Pink, purple, scarlet, green and yellow flashed in front of her eyes; rectangles, triangles, hexagons. One of the steps, somewhere around the seventh flight, was a perfect sphere. It was single-handedly responsible for 50% of all sprained ankles in the entire Mocklore Empire. When Mistress Sharpe reached it, she stepped over and around it without even looking. Her feet were really hurting now. Maybe it was time to give up her signature black high-heeled leather boots. Time to invest in a pair of flat teacher shoes with sensible padding around the heel.

But, no. That would be the grown up thing to do and, professor or not, Mistress Sharpe was not yet ready to behave like a grown up. It was bad enough that she had a real job, a regular salary and a trusted position in the community.

If her father was alive, he would be disappointed at how respectable she was.

Mistress Sharpe reached the eighth landing. She let herself into her room, closed the door behind her and leaned on it for a moment. Slowly, she removed the two dozen hair pins and the sturdy wire snood which kept her hair in some semblance of order during the day. Her dark red curls tumbled down around her shoulders, and she was Kassa again.

"Remind me, Singespitter," she said aloud. "Why did we pick a tower room for our accommodation?"

Her roommate did not answer. Sprawled out on Kassa's bed with his nose in half a dozen serious academic scrolls, he barely even glanced at her over his little horn-rimmed spectacles.

Kassa knew the answer to her own question. On the far side of the cozy room was a pair of glass doors. She opened them now, and stepped out on to the tiny balcony. The view was spectacular. You could see the sea from here, as well as the misty Middens and the wide spread of the colourful Skullcap mountains.

A breeze rippled through Kassa's hair. She unlaced her leather bodice, tossed the garment into the room behind her and inhaled the cool air with pleasure. Her belt followed the bodice, then several layers of skirt. Still clad in her rumpled chemise and three or four petticoats, she sank on to a stool and began working on her boots.

From up here, you could see the Empire go by. Out to sea, there were several white sails — pleasure yachts, no doubt, enjoying the sunshine. As Kassa watched, several large purple and red sails moved in on the small white ones. Pirates.

"Don't you miss it, Singespitter?" Kassa said wistfully. "All the adventures and escapades and heroic deeds?"

Singespitter snorted. He had settled into academic life marvellously and was halfway through a treatise on the intellectual ramifications of bestial metamorphosis. He was more than happy to leave behind his life as a mercenary and pirate. He lifted a large purple quill with his cloven hoof and scratched a note on one of his scrolls with incredibly precise handwriting.

"Don't get ink on my quilt," Kassa called to him. She wiggled her stripy-socked feet, now free from the heavy leather boots. Finally she could relax.

Out at sea, the little white sails fled this way and that, frantically trying to escape the dread pirates. Kassa watched, and sighed a few more times. She could almost taste the salt from here.

Being an ex-pirate was one thing, but being an ex-witch, an ex-outlaw, an ex-heroine of tavern ballads and an ex-captain of her own ship was an awful lot for one woman to bear. What was worse was knowing why she had given it all up — not for morals or honour, or even because she fancied a quiet life for a change. She had done it for a man. A filthy, stinking, slimy member of the opposite gender.

Kassa managed her most pitiful sigh yet. She had a nasty feeling that giving up her career because of a bloke also qualified her as an ex-feminist. So much for Kassa Daggersharp, scourge of at least seven and a half of the seventeen seas.

Singespitter baaed lightly, reminding Mistress Sharpe that she had essay questions to plan, a lecture to write for tomorrow and a staff dinner for which she had volunteered to contribute a salad.

"Shut up," said Kassa, wiggling her toes and staring out to sea. "I'm allowed at least ten minutes of whiny self-indulgence every evening. Don't spoil it for me."

2

BREAKFAST OF HEROES AND
VILLAINS

*A*fter the initial shock, Egg quite enjoyed sharing a room with a girl. The wash chamber was full of perfumed towels and colourful hair ribbons, but this was a small price to pay for Clio's company. The first week of semester passed in a blur of lectures, essay questions, new friends and long lunches.

Egg hadn't done any drawing or writing since she moved in. He was too self-conscious to do it while Clio was in the room, and without that regular outlet the ideas were building up in his head until he was about ready to burst.

Finally, he got up the nerve to pull out his folders while Clio was washing her hair. She did this every other night, taking about an hour to shampoo, condition, curl and a dozen other mysterious things apparently necessary to keep her ponytail bouncy.

As the flower-scented soapy steam seeped under the wash chamber door, Egg began to draw. He had inked three pages of an action sequence before he realised that the soapy smell was stronger now, and Clio was sitting on her bed with a towel around her head, watching him with interest.

"I, um," he said, blushing wildly. "Sorry, I didn't realise you'd finished."

"Doesn't bother me," Clio said with a grin. She stood up, balancing the wet towel as a turban, and came over to peer at his work. "It's really good. I like the big chap with the muscles. Do you do this often?"

Egg shrugged, embarrassed, and pointed to the folders. Clio opened one and whistled slowly as she saw the sheafs of parchment. "Wow. All this and I haven't seen you pick up a quill since I moved in."

"I don't usually show it to people," Egg muttered. He winced as a droplet of water rolled down from Clio's towel-wrapped hair and dripped into the folder.

"Well, you should," she told him. "You're really talented. Why aren't you studying art?"

"There aren't any real art subjects on offer," said Egg. "Only Improbable Arts. I think the Department of Aristocracy offers Botanical Sketching, but it doesn't appeal. Anyway, it's just a hobby."

"Could you draw a picture of me?" asked Clio. She struck a pose. "I could be a femme fatale."

Egg laughed, relaxing a little. "Okay. But I won't put you into the story. It's weird to do that with real people."

"Forget the femme fatale stuff, then," said Clio. "Wait till I'm in my ghastly night attire. You can do a portrait for my grandmother. I bet she'd really appreciate it." She sat on the end of Egg's bed, bouncing a little. "So now I know all about these heroic drawings and stories of yours, you won't be embarrassed to work on them in front of me?"

"I suppose not," said Egg.

"And you'll let me read them sometimes?"

"Maybe, when they're ready."

"Okay." There was a gleam in Clio's eyes. "While you're in a mood for sharing secrets, what are all those envelopes in the second drawer down? The ones with the green wax seals and magic sigils all over?"

Egg looked at her, aghast. "You've been looking through my drawers!"

"Only a bit. I was bored."

"So you knew about my superhero stories all along?"

"Well, yeah. But I was polite enough to wait until you told me about them."

"Polite?" he said, frantically running through his head to figure out what *else* she might have seen in his drawers.

"Yes, polite!" she insisted. "So what are those envelopes?"

"None of your business!"

"Fine." Clio went over to her bed, pulled her ghastly grandmother nightgown out from under her pillow and flounced into the wash chamber. "Keep your secrets, see if I care!"

"You're just nosy!" Egg yelled after her.

"Did I deny that?"

Ten minutes later, there was a knock on the door of their room. Egg was about to answer it when Clio, all white lace and curlers, swept out of the wash chamber and reached the door first. "I suppose you're looking for Sean McHagrty?" she demanded of the girl who had knocked.

The girl, a brunette in a pink bodice so tight it hurt to look at, smiled radiantly. "Is he here?"

"Oh, yes," said Clio. "I married him this morning. Bad luck." She let the door slam in the girl's face.

Egg laughed. "I'm getting locks for my drawers tomorrow."

"I'd do that if I were you," Clio agreed. "You never know who might be going through your things." She hopped into bed, tucking herself up to her chin. "Will you tell me a story this time?"

So Egg did. He told her about Queenbeetle, his new

insect-woman villainess, and how she received her mysterious powers when she was bitten by a radioactive bug. He didn't even know what radioactive meant, but the word sounded good. It sounded right.

Clio was an appreciative audience, laughing and gasping and sighing at all the right places as Egg described Queenbeetle's tragic and often melodramatic life. As he neared the tricky bit in the story, the bit he hadn't figured out yet, Clio conveniently fell asleep.

Egg slept too, better than he had in ages. It was great to finally be sharing his stories with someone. Maybe this was what he should have been doing all along.

Sometime later, the student clocks struck three hours, twenty-two minutes. There was a soft scrabbling sound as someone entered the room and moved ever so quietly across the floor. Still half asleep, Egg rolled over. He registered the sound, but was not yet awake enough to do anything about it. That is, until there was a twang of bed springs, closely followed by a thump and the unmistakable sound of Clio screaming at the top of her lungs.

Boy, that girl could scream. It was sharp enough to cause spots in front of the eyes. Egg lit his lantern quickly.

Clio was sitting up in bed, blankets clutched around her and an outraged look on her face. A young man sprawled on the floor, his hands pressed to his nose. Blood dribbled from between his fingers. "You *hit* me!" he said indistinctly.

"I don't blame her," said Egg, staring at the newcomer. "Who are you?" But it was obvious, really. Who else would come strolling in as if they owned the place and try to get into bed? "You must be Sean McHagrty."

"Brilliant deduction," said Sean McHagrty, still holding his nose. "If I say yes, will you give me a towel?"

"He's not bleeding on my towels," Clio snapped.

"I'll get something." Egg yawned, getting out of bed and

heading for the wash chamber. Behind the tub, there was a basket of useful things like bandages, safety pins, hangover philtres and spare buttons. Obviously the people responsible for setting up these rooms knew the sort of scrapes students were likely to get into. Egg pulled out a bandage and went back to the room.

"Look — Friefriedsson, right?" said Sean McHagrty, accepting the bandage and pressing it to his nose. "This girl says she's sleeping in my bed!"

Clio pulled the blankets more tightly around her and glared at both boys, defending her territory.

Egg couldn't help smiling. "She is in your bed. Look, there she is, right there. Hard to miss."

"But it's my bed," protested Sean. "Mine."

Clio made a small growling noise.

Egg headed back to his own bed and climbed in. "Be reasonable, McHagrty. You can't expect a respectable girl like Clio to go walking around the corridors in the middle of the night, in her nightgown, just because you've dumped her roommate and are finally condescending to come back to your own bed. She was here first."

Sean stared at Clio. "You're Lemissa's roommate? Actually it would be really helpful if you went back, she was sort of crying when I left."

"Isn't that a shame?" said Clio. "Imagine the sympathy I have for a girl I barely know who made me *homeless.*"

Egg blew out the lantern. "We'll sort it all out in the morning."

Sean wiped the last of the blood from his nose in the darkness. "Where am I supposed to sleep tonight?" he asked plaintively.

There was a soft sound as Clio threw one of her pillows at him. "Count yourself lucky."

As usual, Clio went to sleep quickly. Sean too, despite the

less than ideal sleeping conditions, was soon snoring. Egg stayed awake. An idea for a story had flitted across his brain and he didn't want to let go of it.

He lay on his back, staring at the ceiling. Moonlight streamed in through the uneven curtains. The Cloak, most mysterious of Egg's superheroes, would finally cross paths with Queenbeetle, the insect-woman. They would meet in an alley, surrounded by the blackest of black shadows. She would carry a sleek silver blade, fighting the Cloak with a mad, unrelenting fury. He could counter her attack with ice-cool logic. The tension between them would escalate into restrained passion, and they would kiss...

The curtains moved, shifting as if blown by a gentle breeze. Egg opened his eyes properly to look at them. There was no breeze. The window was closed. Wasn't it?

The curtains parted of their own volition. A leg slid over the window sill: a slender, graceful leg followed by a slender, graceful girl. She landed on the carpet, her feet barely making a sound.

Egg breathed, watching her move across the room. Her hair was a pale, coppery cloud, drenched in moonlight. The girl bent over Clio's sleeping form, then glanced at the young man sprawled on the floor.

Finally, Egg cleared his throat. "Are you looking for Sean McHagrty?" he couldn't help asking.

The girl turned slowly, her eyes wide. "I don't know who I'm looking for," she whispered.

"Who are you?" Egg asked. There was something familiar about her that he felt he should recognise.

"Dahla," said the girl. She looked around, anxious. "Can you smell smoke?"

"No," said Egg, but that wasn't strictly true. There was a scent in the air, something which might have been lightly perfumed smoke. "Actually, yes. Maybe."

23

"I have to get out of here," Dahla said, frantic. "I have to leave." Before Egg could stop her, she ran to the closed door — ran through the closed door — and was gone.

Egg followed her, opening the door to stare out into the corridor. No sign of the ghostly girl.

Too wired to sleep now, Egg went back to his bed. His story folder was still on the bedside table, and he put it away, musing about the possibilities of a character who walked through walls. Ghost Girl? No, she would be too similar to Dream Girl, a heroine he'd been working on for months.

Egg noticed a stray papyrus on the floor. It was his sketch of the nameless city where his characters lived. He picked it up now and stared at it, barely making out the lines in the light that filtered through the curtains. The proportions were all wrong. The walls were too low and there weren't enough towers. It must be an old sketch, from before he had a clear idea of how the city looked.

Egg dug out a new piece of parchment and took it with his pen and ink over to the window where the moonlight was at its brightest. Quickly, he began to draw the city as it should be, with the right number of towers, slitted windows and inky black shadows.

It should have a name, he realised as his hand moved swiftly back and forth across the page. All cities had names. He had never got around to choosing one. It had to be sinister, to convey how dark and dangerous the city was, and why it needed superheroes to protect its mean streets.

Egg's hand moved across the parchment, writing a word in large, imposing script. D-R-A-K.

Drak? What kind of a name was that for a city? Egg gazed at his new picture, and the shadows represented by patches of wet ink. Drak. It had the right kind of sound to it. He left the parchment to dry on top of his chest of drawers and climbed back into bed. Drak, he thought to himself. Oh, well. It would do until he came up with something better.

~

As always, there was breakfast to consider. There were eight dining halls around campus which served breakfast, and there was a fine art in selecting the right one on any given day. The Seaweed Room at the foot of the Mermaid Tower was presided over by Mistress Brim, who was resolute in her aim to maintain an oceanic theme in her menu. Since Cluft was regularly subject to rains of fish, ingredients were never a problem for Mistress Brim. She could regularly be seen pulling lobsters or large trout out of the guttering.

Kassa, as a pirate's daughter, had been wildly enthusiastic about this all-seafood philosophy at first. During her first semester as a resident professor she had consumed many breakfasts of kedgeree, kippers, salmon cakes, tuna steaks or squid porridge. At the end of that semester, her body rebelled. After throwing up five times her body weight, she made a shaky resolution to avoid seafood — and Mistress Brim's cooking — for the rest of her natural life.

It was the second week of the new school year, so Kassa's dining hall of choice was the Majestic, across the square of student residence. With any luck, the first-years would not yet have discovered that this was the only place that provided fresh fruit in the morning, and there might be a free table. Later in the semester, it would be standing room only as the students desperately attempted to ward off scurvy.

To Kassa's surprise, the Majestic dining hall was mostly empty this morning. No students at all. Trays of uneaten breakfasts were littered around the tables, as if everyone had left in a hurry.

Everyone except Vice-Chancellor Bertie, Lordling of the

city-state of Cluft and official administrator in charge of the four Departments of the Polyhedrotechnical College. Vice-Chancellor Bertie was the quintessential absent-minded professor, down to the not-quite-tidy beard and a wardrobe consisting mostly of tweed with elbow patches.

This morning, Bertie sat at a table by himself in the dining hall, chewing his way through one of Mistress Pott's full cooked breakfasts, the kind that came with three kinds of egg plus toast, bacon, sausage, mushrooms, beans, fried bread, more bacon, more sausage and one lone grilled slice of tomato.

Mistress Pott herself stood at the counter with a face like thunder. At this hour, she was usually run off her feet with the extra demand for scrambled eggs and hot toast. But the breakfast troughs had barely been touched and their contents congealed unpleasantly as they cooled.

"Where is everyone?" Kassa asked.

Mistress Pott grunted, and stirred the porridge. She lifted the ladle half out of the cauldron with an expectant look.

"No thank you," said Kassa, selecting a plate of fresh fruit salad and a nourishing muesli yoghurt. After some degree of thought, she added a bacon sandwich to her tray.

"Ah, it's you," said Vice-Chancellor Bertie as Kassa sat opposite him. "Nice and quiet, eh?"

"Without the students, yes." Kassa prodded her bacon sandwich with her fork, trying to decide if she really wanted it. "Where are they all? It's too early in the semester for a hunger strike."

Bertie filled his mouth with three kinds of egg. "Strike? If only! Those were grand days, with student strikes every other week. Marvellous fellows, marching up and down in an orderly fashion with those picket signs of theirs, staying away from classes for weeks at a time. Our lecture theatres never looked so tidy…"

"Where are the students, Vice-Chancellor?" Kassa asked. It was rude to interrupt, but she felt that any rant that used the phrase "grand old days" was fair game.

"Oh, they're all out staring at the thing," Bertie said. "Can't see the point of it myself. Damned warlocks, always showing off, trying to outdo each other. Should have rousted out that local colony years ago."

Kassa blinked and looked down at her hand. Somehow she had eaten the whole bacon sandwich without realising it. She stabbed her fork into the fruit salad, picking up a chunk of pineapple and something pink and squashy-looking. "What thing? What warlocks? I have no idea what you're talking about."

"Oh, I'm sure it's the warlocks," said Bertie, cleaning the juicy remains of his plate with a stiff piece of fried bread. "Who else would magic up a city for no good reason? 'Oh, I've just magicked up a dark and mysterious city, aren't I impressive?' Showoffs, the lot of them." He bit into the fried bread, staring sadly at his empty plate.

"A dark and mysterious city?" repeated Kassa. "Appearing out of nowhere?" She shifted in her seat. "I don't see what's so interesting about that. Really, the students should know better than to go off staring at some magical phenomenon when they could be having a healthy breakfast to set themselves up for the day." She stirred her nourishing muesli yoghurt for a moment. "Actually, I think I'll just — you know, check that the students aren't in any danger."

"Go on," sighed Vice-Chancellor Bertie. "Join the crowd, encourage those warlocks by giving them an audience. Just don't come crying to me when they've turned you into a newt."

Kassa left in a hurry.

Once she had gone, Vice-Chancellor Bertie lifted his

napkin, under which he had secreted Kassa's bacon sandwich. Smiling to himself, he finished his breakfast in peace.

~

Egg woke up, still groggy from his late night burst of creativity. Clio was already up, dressed and packing her nightgowns, perfumed towels and hair ribbons into several small pink bags which fitted neatly into her large pink bag. Sean McHagrty was nowhere to be seen.

Egg sat up. "You don't have to go," he protested, yawning.

"Of course I do," Clio said. "It's time I made friends with my real roommate, cheer her up after her disastrous liaison with the dread McHagrty, that sort of thing. Anyway, all my suitcases are there. You can't expect me to survive the semester with only four changes of clothes, five pairs of shoes and eight nightgowns. I barely lasted the week."

Egg stared at the bulging pink bag and considered the ramifications of 'all my suitcases'. "Well, drop by any time. Where's McHagrty?"

"Breakfast, I suppose. If he's not already plotting to throw some other poor girl out of her room in his mission to get into every pair of knickers on campus. You could end up with a different female roommate every week."

Egg thought about this. It didn't sound too bad. "There are worse ways to meet girls."

Clio threw a pillow at him. "Watch it. You're starting to sound like your roommate."

The door crashed open and Sean burst into the room. He threw open the window and leaned out. "Will you look at that? I knew there'd be a great view from up here."

"Look at what?" said Egg.

Clio was already elbowing Sean out of the way so she could see out the window. Her elbows should be classified as deadly weapons. Once she saw what Sean was so interested in, Clio looked back at Egg. Her eyes flicked to the inked parchment on the chest of drawers, and then back to Egg. "You'd better see this."

Egg got out of bed and went slowly to the window. Every step felt like his legs were full of concrete. He had a horrible feeling about what he was going to see before he saw it.

Even so, it came as a shock.

Drak.

~

Lord Sinistre of Drak liked an elegant breakfast. Quail eggs were a favourite, lightly boiled and served in a frothy cream of lovage sauce. After that, he liked a small piece of toast carved into the shape of a vulture, with a smear of lark's brain paté or walnut jam. He would finish with a thimbleful of jasmine-scented coffee, which he consumed in minuscule sips. "Anything new this morning?" he asked as the last drop melted under his tongue.

The Chamberlain of Drak unrolled a length of parchment. "A few items of interest, my lord. We have possums nesting in the drains again. Apparently they escaped from the Underground Zoo. The City Bailiffs are employing an experimental method to deal with the problem, involving sharp sticks and flamethrowers."

"Good, good," said Lord Sinistre, dabbing at the corner of his mouth with a lime-scented satin napkin.

"Also, I'm afraid two of your poison tasters died last night, my lord. The matter has been investigated."

Lord Sinistre nodded wisely. "The peach souffle. I thought it smelled a little venomy."

"No, my lord. They died in a duel. The first poison taster was caught taking certain liberties with the second poison taster's girlfriend and the matter went to swords. Nothing for you to worry about, my lord."

Lord Sinistre yawned. "Is that all?" Of course it wasn't. There were always exactly three pieces of news, no more and no less. The Chamberlain was a precise sort of man, grading the news from least important to most, just as Lord Sinistre liked it. Some traditions were not only important, they were essential.

The Chamberlain coughed, which meant the third piece of news was of particular interest. "Well, my lord. There is the matter of the wasteland. You know, the vast and treacherously gritty desert of silver sand which prevents us from contact with the outside world?"

Lord Sinistre sighed, examining his black silk sleeves. He had a sneaking suspicion that one sleeve was a touch shorter than the other. It had been bothering him all morning. "What about the wasteland, Chamberlain?"

"It's gone, my lord."

Lord Sinistre's eyes bulged. Had he still been eating breakfast, he would have spat a quail egg clear across the room to make a nasty stain on the tapestry depicting his most famous ancestor, whose name temporarily escaped him. "Gone?"

"Yes, my lord." The Chamberlain consulted his meticulously handwritten notes. "The area formerly known as 'the wasteland' appears to have been replaced with a green and verdant land with multicoloured mountains and pleasant weather. The nearest population centre is a university town which displays some unusually chaotic architecture." He frowned. "Multicoloured mountains. That sounds...familiar."

"Never mind familiar," Lord Sinistre snapped. He strode across the great hall, his velvet cloak swirling around him in a blur of shadows. "I must see this for myself. Lead me to a window, Chamberlain!"

"Yes, my lord."

"And open all the curtains while you're at it. I don't know why it always has to be so dark around here!"

∾

The first thing Egg saw was the skybridge, a glittering golden arch which began somewhere near the sprawling library tower of Cluft and curved gracefully northwards, over the canals and sports field, its far end dipping down into...well, the new city.

The city was the second thing Egg saw. It was a large, menacing edifice with high glossy walls, looming towers, slitted windows and dark gloomy shadows. It was very black indeed. The bits which weren't black were either dark grey, light grey or very dark blue, and those shifts of colour merely served to accentuate the overall blackness of the city as a whole.

It hadn't been there the night before.

"How did you do it?" said Clio.

"Do what?" said Sean McHagrty.

"I didn't do anything, said Egg. "I really didn't."

"It looks just like the picture," said Clio. "Your picture."

"I drew that city this morning," he lied. "Before you woke up."

"Don't give me that. You were just as surprised as I was to see the city just now. What's going on, Egg?"

He considered the possibilities. "There's one way to find out. Let's go down and see what's happening."

"The view's way better from up here," said Sean, but the other two took no notice.

∾

The library tower was one of the outermost buildings of Cluft. It was originally built in the very centre of town, beside the Great Mocklore Road and most of the taverns, but since a certain catastrophic magical event known as the Second Glimmer, the library would relocate every semester. This had not made much of a difference to campus life, except that the number of students who discovered the library for the first time while on their way to a tavern had decreased, while the number of students who ended up in a tavern on their way to the library had mysteriously increased.

There had never been so many students gathered outside the library tower in all of Cluft's history, even during the week that it had actually transformed *into* a tavern.

The beginning of the golden skybridge did not touch the ground but hovered five feet in the air.

Those students who attempted to get up to the bridge were being repulsed by a determined Mistress Sharpe who had stationed herself at the foot of the library tower. She was armed with a stout, bristly broom and had no qualms about smacking anyone who tried to get near herself or the skybridge.

"What is it?" asked Brittany Yarrowstalk, and a few other students took up the cry. "What is it, what is it?"

As Egg and Clio reached the crowd, the door of the library tower opened and Mavis stepped out. A hush fell over the assembled students.

Mavis was a small, unremarkable woman. She wore neat, sensible clothes. She carried a hot water bottle and a handbag full of pink knitting. The heads of two playful kittens poked out from amongst the wool. There were always kittens in the library tower. No one ever questioned this, or why the kittens never grew to be adult cats. The only explanation was that Mavis liked kittens, so there were kittens. Mavis also liked scones and cocoa, so there was a good supply of these in the library tower as well.

Mavis was once the patron goddess of Tidiness Amongst Craftswomen, but the Decimalisation — a process by which an earlier Emperor had reduced Mocklore's vast pantheon of deities to just ten very overworked gods — had given her various extra duties including responsibility for all of Cluft.

The crowd parted as Mavis moved towards the skybridge that led to the new city. Mistress Sharpe nodded to the goddess and lowered her broom. "So what are we dealing with?"

Mavis put down her handbag and hot water bottle with great care, then stepped on to empty air. "Looks like a city to me," she said as her feet landed on the golden bridge.

There were mutterings amongst the students, who had hoped for something a little more profound. Mistress Sharpe craned her neck, looking up at the goddess of Cluft. "What caused it? What brought the city here?"

"Smells rather like Dark Magic," said the goddess.

Mistress Sharpe gave the nearest students a last swat with her broom, then stood on it and floated up to Mavis's level. "I've never heard of Dark Magic," she said. "Magic is just magic."

"You see?" Egg said to Clio. "She does use magic! She uses it *all* the time. How can she tell us never to use it and then go flying around the place on a broom?"

"Shut up, I'm trying to listen," whispered Clio.

Everyone was trying to listen.

"Everything has two sides, a Dark and a Light," said Mavis. Being a goddess, her words floated easily down to the students below. "Trouble comes when the two are separated. The magic of Mocklore has been free of such a division before now."

"So this Dark Magic, it's bad?" said Mistress Sharpe.

"That would be a fair assumption," said Mavis.

"But that means that our magic, natural Mocklore magic, the kind that runs rampant through the cosmos, explodes in people's faces on a regular basis and turns small furry animals into clockwork typewriters for no apparent reason, that's the *good* kind of magic?"

Mavis nodded. "Scary, isn't it?"

3

JUST HOW DARK SHOULD A DARK CITY BE?

*L*ord Sinistre gazed through his spy-glass. "It seems like a very peculiar place out there. Are trees supposed to be that colour?"

"I'm not sure, my lord," said the Chamberlain. "I don't believe anyone in this city has ever seen a tree before." *But I have, haven't I?* He kept that alarming suspicion to himself.

"Hmm, good point." Lord Sinistre twiddled a knob on the base of the spy-glass. "They all seem very young, the natives of this strange country. There's a redheaded woman bossing them around and hitting them with her broomstick. Should we do that when we meet them? It might be a gesture of respect."

"I think not, my lord," said the Chamberlain. "What sort of meeting did you have in mind?"

"A ball, I should think," said Lord Sinistre. "Decadent nibbly things on sticks, elegant music, fabulous dancing. We'll invite everyone who's Anyone in that odd little town, and find out who we have to kill to rule this world that we've landed in." He hesitated. "Do you think I should have laughed maniacally there? I'm never sure if it's a bit too much. Maybe I should just smile and twirl my cape."

The Chamberlain was too distracted to listen. He had to consider the logistics of organising a ball: catering, costumes, re-tiling the ballroom ceiling, cleaning and polishing the chandeliers, not to mention all the windows... "I believe we could whip a grand ball together in time for the weekend," he offered, knowing it would half kill him and his staff to get all the work done by then.

Lord Sinistre did laugh maniacally this time. "Don't be ridiculous, man. That's five days away; we could be at war with them by then. The ball will be tonight. Why have you gone all green?"

"Something I ate, no doubt, my lord."

"Ah." Lord Sinistre nodded. "I knew that peach souffle would get someone in the end."

"Perhaps you could send the invitations out yourself, my lord? While I see to the trifling matter of throwing together a grand ball in less than twelve hours?"

"Very well," Lord Sinistre grumbled. "I always have to do everything around here."

"Yes, my lord," agreed the Chamberlain, bowing low as he left the room. "Your servants are constantly astounded at how well you cope with the workload."

"Sarcasm, Chamberlain?" Lord Sinistre said sharply. "That's not like you."

Isn't it? the Chamberlain thought. He was on the brink of remembering something very important, but there was no time for that kind of self-indulgence now. "I apologise, my lord. If I may be excused? There are quite literally one hundred and one things that I must see to immediately."

Lord Sinistre dismissed him with a wave.

The Chamberlain set off along the corridor. The kitchen staff had only just recovered from the surprise birthday party

Lord Sinistre had thrown himself a month ago, and now there was this.

He paused by the rack of cloaks and boots by the door to the kitchens, listening to the happy chatter from within. It was so tempting to just throw on his cloak and vanish into the night. It was daytime, of course, but that didn't make it any less tempting. The question before had always been *Where do I go?* but now there was a lush land of promise outside the dark city walls.

How long had he worked here, anyway? The Chamberlain couldn't remember. Neither could he remember what he had done before he worked here. Perhaps he had always been a part of Drak, making sure the city and the palace and Lord Sinistre all kept running smoothly. Although…what was it he had thought about earlier? Something about trees?

The Chamberlain sighed. Even as his hand brushed against the fabric of his cloak, he pulled away. *Later.* He would go out later to breathe the air of the city he loved and hated. Right now, he had news to break to his staff.

The Chamberlain took a deep breath, and entered the kitchens.

∾

The faculty staff room for the Polyhedrotechnical College had once been a temple dedicated to Bungo the love god, before he fell victim to the Decimalisation. Amorata, the only surviving goddess of all things lustful, originally claimed the temple for herself, but Mavis besieged her with cups of tea, unsightly knitted garments and kittens until the love goddess fled for her sanity.

The professors of the various Departments had then staked their own claim on the gorgeous marble building, painting over some of the more sordid murals and removing the overly-erotic crockery. They kept the swimming pool, though. And the sauna.

It was an hour after lunch. The professors who were not teaching at this time gathered to relax, drink tea and celebrate the fact that it would be at least four weeks before any of them were required to mark essays. Unfortunately, Vice-Chancellor Bertie had invented something new and wanted them all to admire it.

"I call it the Great Reversing Barrel," he said proudly, smacking the object with a satisfying thud.

"Looks like a perfectly ordinary barrel to me," sniffed Professor Gootch, who taught Assassination and Edged Weapons.

"That's what you think!" said Vice-Chancellor Bertie. "But if I just take this sandwich and drop it into the Great Reversing Barrel..."

"That was my sandwich," said Professor Penelopa Profit-scoundrel. "Really, Vice-Chancellor. It's bad enough that my second year Haggling lectures are scheduled over the lunch hour every day, do you have to rob me of my lunch altogether?"

Lord Ambewine, who presided over the Department of Aristocracy, looked suspiciously at the Great Reversing Barrel. "Is it supposed to be making that noise?"

A squealing sound came from within the Great Reversing Barrel. "Aha!" said Vice-Chancellor Bertie. "You see? A moment ago it was a perfectly ordinary ham sandwich..."

"Roast honeyed ham," sulked Professor Profit-scoundrel. "I had to beg Mistress Pott to save it for me."

"And now, having been Greatly Reversed, we have—" After a suitably dramatic pause, Bertie tipped the barrel over. Something pink rushed out of it, squealing madly.

"A pig!" said Incendia Noir, Professor of Highly Improbable Arts. She lifted her feet out of range, placing them on the coffee table. A moment later, she had to lower them again, because Prince Quenby (History of Aristocracy, Cactus Arranging and Ambitious Empire Building) jumped up on the coffee table and started screaming at a slightly higher pitch than the pig.

"A pig covered in honey," said Lord Ambewine as the pig brushed stickily past his satin academic gown. "Just what we needed."

"A pig covered in honey with a sheaf of wheat in its mouth!" Vice-Chancellor Bertie said proudly. "You see? Great Reversation."

"There could certainly be a market for a method which produces a whole pig from a single ham sandwich," said Professor Profit-scoundrel, her indignation forgotten. She dropped her second ham sandwich into the Great Reversing Barrel. A revolting stench filled the staff room.

"Ah," said Vice-Chancellor Bertie. "There's the trouble, you see. We can't always predict how something will be Greatly Reversed. It's a bit random." He tipped the Great Reversing Barrel over again. A lump of something green, putrid and festering rolled out. "Here we have a perfectly fresh ham sandwich which has been Greatly Reversed into, er, something less than perfectly fresh."

Professor Profit-scoundrel backed away from the Great Reversing Barrel and was promptly sick into the nearest pot plant.

The pig caused a great deal of chaos. After smearing honey and dried wheat everywhere, it ended up in the swimming pool. So did Lord Ambewine, Prince Quenby and several third-year students who had come in to ask about tutorial times.

Some time later, as everyone calmed down and dried themselves off, Mistress Sharpe entered the staff room.

"Ah, there you are!" Vice-Chancellor Bertie called out

cheerfully. "Given up sentry duty over that silly warlock's flying bridge, have you?"

"I made the postgraduate students do it," said Kassa. "They'll take any excuse to avoid working on their thesis. What's going on here?" Her eye fell on the sheep in the corner, who was comforting the traumatised pig. "Singespitter, what are you doing here? You're not staff."

"Actually, Master Singespitter will be handling the third-year Magic Studies tutorials for me," said Professor Noir, her cool gaze chilling Kassa by several degrees. She was the only member of the faculty who had been present for the entire pig incident and had no evidence of honey, wheat or pool water on her clothes. She was that sort of person.

"Magic Studies," Kassa repeated, glaring at Singespitter. He knew how she felt about practical magic being taught to students. "All handled very responsibly, I'm sure." She turned to Vice-Chancellor Bertie. "Communication has arrived from the mysterious dark city in the form of a party invitation. Interested?"

"Not interested in warlocks," Bertie said. "Show-offy show offs." He paused, thinking about it. "On the other hand, could be just the job to demonstrate my Great Reversing Barrel. They'll be green with envy when they see it!"

"Mmm," said Kassa. "Thing is, Vice-Chancellor, I'm not sure that the city has anything to do with warlocks." She handed over a stiff piece of black card embossed with silver borders and squiggly writing. "This was delivered by a large demonic gargoyle that breathed fire at several first-year students, ate three tiles from the library roof and frightened the school mascot into a coma."

"Not Gerald the mouse?" said Bertie, examining the card with some interest.

"No," said Kassa patiently. "Not Gerald. The other school mascot."

"Townhall?" said Vice-Chancellor Bertie. "How could a gargoyle frighten an eight foot long dragon?"

"The gargoyle was nine foot," said Kassa. "In all directions. I really think you'd better read the invitation."

~

Egg was hustled along by Clio. At her insistence, his arms were full of parchments and papyrus: all his maps, inky drawings, character notes and storylines. "I don't know what you think this is going to achieve," he said. "I don't know anything."

"You created that city, Egg, and now it's right here on our doorstep. Don't you think you should take some responsibility? The Vice-Chancellor needs all the information we can give him."

"You just want an excuse not to go to your Basic Poisons seminar," he said. "You got all hysterical last time because Doctor Wampweed demonstrated sulphur and you had to wash your hair six times to get the smell out."

"That's just not true. I'm deeply committed to all my classes, regardless of strange eggy smells. Don't you see what an emergency this is, Egg?"

"It's a city. What harm can it do?" He dreaded confessing the truth to the Vice-Chancellor. "What do I say to him?"

"You don't say anything. I'll explain it all. You just stand there and nod. Here we are."

They were outside a gleaming white temple. Egg looked at it doubtfully. "Are you sure this is the staff room?"

"Yes!" Clio said crossly. She peered in through the marble columns. "He's there all right. Off you go."

Egg stared at her in horror. "You said you were going to explain it to him!"

Clio nodded sympathetically. "I lied. I'll wait out here in the sun."

Grumbling to himself, Egg stomped into the temple. He narrowly missed a collision with Mistress Sharpe as she stomped out, muttering to herself. "Watch it, Friefriedsson," she barked, and continued on her way.

Egg took a deep breath, and went inside. The first thing he saw was a pig in an armchair, being cuddled by a large, bespectacled white sheep. The temple smelled of honey, pig droppings, vomit and some kind of rotting meat. Various staff members were towelling themselves dry or wiping honey from their clothes and shoes.

What did they need the honey for? Egg thought in something of a panic.

Vice-Chancellor Bertie was busy dropping things into a large squat barrel. "And this lovely antique gold fob watch, generously donated by Lord Ambewine over there, has been Greatly Reversed into...ooh look, a broken piece of very modern clockwork!" He waited, as if expecting applause.

"Does anyone mind if I take my bra off?" said Professor Profit-scoundrel. "I think I've got dried wheat in here."

Egg backed out of the staff room before anyone could ask him why he was there.

Outside, Clio and Mistress Sharpe sat on a bench together, talking in low undertones. Mildly traumatised by what he had seen in the staff room, Egg approached the two women. "I was just telling Mistress Sharpe about this city of yours," Clio said cheerfully. "It occurred to me that she might be a bit more useful than the Vice-Chancellor."

"Now you tell me," said Egg.

Mistress Sharpe shaded her eyes from the sun as she looked at him. "Come on, Friefriedsson. Let's have a look at these humorous hieroglyphs of yours."

Reluctantly, Egg handed his armful over. "I really don't

know what happened," he said. "I didn't mean to create a city, and I can't think how I could have done it. Maybe it's just a coincidence."

Clio snorted.

"Coincidence is usually the universe telling you that you've been screwed over by magic," said Mistress Sharpe, leafing her way slowly through the pages. Her eye lingered for a long time over a portrait of Queenbeetle, the insect woman. "Do you have a magical background, Egg?"

"On my mother's side," he admitted. "My grandmother was Buttercup the Witch."

Mistress Sharpe stared at him. "Don't tell me you're Melinor's son? Holy nutmeg, we're cousins!" She grinned broadly. "I don't expect Aunt Mel taught you magic. I heard she gave up the profession to join some harem."

"She was the favourite Wench of the Jarl of Axgaard for nearly a whole year!" Egg said hotly.

Mistress Sharpe seemed to think this was incredibly funny. "Wenching runs in the family, then. I might have known. What happened to her?"

"After her first son was born, the Jarl lost interest in her, and that's when she fell in love...with the Jarl's eldest son," Egg began embarrassedly.

Mistress Sharpe clicked her fingers. "The exiled prince? I thought this story sounded familiar. He was your dad?"

"Yes, miss."

"The weirdest things happen in our family. If we're cousins, you might as well drop that 'miss' stuff and start calling me Kassa." She produced a black card covered in squiggly silver writing. "The people of Cluft have been invited to a grand welcoming ball in this fictional city of yours, Egg. Tonight. I'm thinking that if I stand half a chance of figuring out what's going on, you'd better come too."

Egg looked at Clio. It occurred to him that she hadn't

been included in Kassa's invitation. "I don't suppose—" he started to say.

Kassa turned to Clio. "Do you have a frock you can wear? I'll be relying on you to see that this boy wears a suit."

Clio's eyes gleamed. "Dressing up is what I do best."

"Good." Kassa stood up, handing the sheaf of parchments back to Egg. "I'll want you, cousin dearest, to give me the nitty gritty on everyone in that city — and, if necessary, to write a different ending. Think you can manage it?"

Obviously, his cousin was a crazy person. "No," said Egg. "Not really."

"Excellent," Kassa smiled. "Now I have some incredibly important preparations to make."

"Magical supplies for protection spells?" said Egg hopefully.

Clio elbowed him. "Stupid. She has to decide what to wear."

"Forget that," said Kassa Daggersharp. "I have to decide what my sheep is going to wear."

~

Egg did have a suit. He had fought tooth and nail with his mother about packing it, convinced it wouldn't be necessary. Now he was quite pleased to be able to put on the formal shirt, waistcoat, trousers and sweeping cloak.

Clio, whose roommate Lemissa was useless with fashion advice (apparently the poor girl still spent all her time weeping about Sean McHagrty), brought a selection of dresses to Egg and Sean's room. She occasionally emerged from the wash chamber to display a different gown or hairstyle, and then would whisk away before either of them could venture an opinion.

"Is there a reason she packed twelve evening dresses for college?" Sean drawled.

"I find it best not to ask these questions," said Egg.

A shadow passed over the window. Egg looked up in alarm. For the first time that day, he remembered his ghostly visitor. It was still afternoon, hardly a suitable time for a ghost to make her reappearance.

It wasn't the ghost, though. It was a bat. A large black bat at the window. It wasn't an appropriate time for bats either, Egg couldn't help thinking.

The bat flew straight at the window, its head thwacking the glass. It fell back for a moment, then tried again.

"Is that from the new city?" Sean McHagrty asked. "I heard a gargoyle came out of it earlier and ate the town dragon. Or was it the town hall? Anyway, it breathed three different colours of fire!"

"This isn't from Drak," said Egg, staring at the bat as it lunged at the glass for a third time.

"How do you know?"

"Because it's carrying a letter for me."

Sure enough, the bat held a large envelope in its claws. An envelope covered with magic sigils and sealed with green wax. *Them again. Why won't the bastards leave me alone?*

"So?" said Sean. "The city only just got here. We don't know what they use as a postal system."

The bat's head hit the glass for a fourth time. It was starting to look seriously pissed off. "Could you wait in the bathroom?" Egg asked. "Keep out of sight a few minutes?"

"Sure," said Sean, without asking any questions. He was good like that. "I'm brilliant at sneaking around. Been practising for years." He sauntered into the bathroom.

Clio screamed.

Egg hoped the resulting argument would keep them both

out of the way for long enough. He unfastened the window and pushed it open.

The bat flew into the room, dropping the letter on the carpet. There was a short whooshing sound and several pink sparks. A shadow billowed out of the bat's mouth, whirling and spinning until it formed a set of black warlock robes, decorated with sigils in green, orange and lemon-yellow embroidery. Inside the robes was a warlock.

He was young, not one of the gruff elderly types they usually sent. This one had apricot-coloured hair and a skimpy beard. "Egfried Friefriedsson," he said, bending to pick up the fallen letter and holding it out to Egg. "Due to your distinguished birthlines and ancestry, you are honoured with this invitation to join the Harvestmoon Order of Warlocks. The privilege of education will begin immediately…"

"No," Egg said. It was best to interrupt with his objections as soon as possible. Waiting for a warlock to stop talking was an exercise in futility. "I don't want to be a warlock. I've refused to be a warlock about twenty times since I was fourteen. I've heard from the Harvestmoons, the Silversigils, the Lizardbloods and the Bronzfetishes. I'm not interested in any of you."

The warlock looked at him, astonished. "But how can you refuse? Becoming a warlock is the greatest pinnacle one can possibly aspire to."

Egg sighed. "And my grandmother was Buttercup the Witch and my grandfather was the Silver Warlock, and how can I possibly betray the blood that runs in my veins? Heard it before. You must be desperate for new recruits."

The warlock looked pale. "It is true that warlocklore is a less popular profession than it used to be, but really! Why would anyone not want to be a warlock?"

Egg went to the window. "See that city over there?"

"Oh, yes," said the warlock. "The magical and mysterious Drak. We've been blamed for its arrival." He snorted. "Humph! As if we would ever do anything so show-offy."

"It looks dangerous," said Egg.

"I expect it is," said the warlock. "After all, it has brought an entirely new kind of magic into Mocklore, tainted with darkness. I fully expect, as do many of my order, that this city heralds the end of Mocklore as we know it, possibly the end of the entire world."

"So what are you going to do about it?" Egg demanded.

"Me?" said the warlock.

"You! Why not you? Warlocks have magic, plenty of it. The Harvestmoons, the Lizardbloods, the Grand High Order of Potatomunchers. That city is not supposed to be there and you know it is dangerous, so why don't you do something? Send Drak back where it came from."

The warlock looked horrified. He tugged nervously on his apricot beard. "You don't know what you're asking. To perform such a feat of magic would be demeaning to our elite order. We have far more appropriate things to do with our time and energy."

"And that, right there," said Egg. "Pretty much sums up why I don't want to be a warlock. Magic should be used for helping people. It shouldn't be conserved in little jars. Don't let the window concuss you on the way out."

The warlock threw the letter at Egg and transformed so hurriedly into a bat that his apricot beard was still visible as he flapped out of the window.

"You can come back now," Egg called to the wash chamber.

Clio stormed through the door, carrying the heavy skirt of her latest ballgown. It was less fluffy than the others, built out of pale blue velvet and trimmed with dark blue lace.

"Next time you want to get rid of McHagrty, just throw him out the window, will you?"

Sean McHagrty emerged from the bathroom, sucking a bleeding finger. "I was only trying to zip you up!"

"This dress doesn't zip," growled Clio.

"That's it," said Egg, his eyes on the bat as it flew over the rooftops of Cluft.

"What's what?" said Clio crossly.

"That's the frock you should wear to the ball. It's very pretty."

"Oh. Okay."

～

"I don't care how groundbreaking and innovative that book is," said Kassa, lacing herself into a brilliant green silk gown with three dozen fine petticoat layers. "You're coming to the ball with me. We never go out and have fun any more. You're a grumpy old man with no sense of party."

Singespitter sniffed.

Kassa hauled the sheep off the bed in one powerful movement, plonking him in the middle of the carpet. "Wings out," she commanded. "You'll look dressier that way."

Singespitter made a growling sound and tried to slink back to the bed.

"Don't even think about it," said Kassa, gazing in the mirror. She had temporarily tamed her hair with a few strings of pearls that wove in and out of the mad red curls. "Needs something," she muttered to herself. "Singespitter, wings out! I'm not going to tell you again."

No one could ignore Kassa when she was using her professor voice. Singespitter closed his eyes and concentrated. Two large purple wings unfolded from within his fleece. He shook the feathers into place and flapped the wings experimentally.

"Much better," said Kassa, still staring critically at herself in the mirror. "Aha! Glitter."

Singespitter's eyes flew open in alarm, just in time to see Kassa dump half a container of sparkly green glitter into her hair. He sighed in relief, then coughed wildly as she threw the rest of the glitter over his fleece. "Ptoooey!"

"Don't look at me like that," said Kassa. "We look fabulous and more importantly, we co-ordinate. Shall we go?"

Singespitter gave her a dirty look, trotted to the balcony and threw himself off it.

Kassa could have flown down too — her broomstick was at the ready — but she didn't fancy descending amid the rest of the faculty with an emerald silk gown flapping up around her waist. She took the stairs.

∼

Several members of the faculty assembled at the foot of the golden skybridge.

Professor Penelopa Profit-scoundrel (who against the laws of reason had obtained a tweed ballgown) was attempting to not stand next to D'Arcy Fitzdeath, a thin-moustached flirt who lectured in the less respectable subjects of the Department of Profit: Highway Robbery, Pickpocketing and the like.

Prince Quenby of the Middens and Lord Ambewine of Teatime, representing the Department of Aristocracy, had each attempted to outdo the other. Lord Ambewine wore a silk suit with a high collar to conceal the green blotches on his neck, an after-effect of taking too many antidotes to popular poisons. He wore black gloves, high boots, a glowing diamond medallion and a snooty expression on his foxy face.

Prince Quenby, who was more solidly built, demonstrated his own nobility with an eccentric costume of pink, gold, green and purple velvets, satins and gabardines. His hat was a virulent orange, dotted with topaz buttons. He wore at least three waistcoats, and his overall appearance was something not unlike the multi-coloured Skullcap mountains.

Doctor Mindette Masters of the Department of Certain Death (lecturing in Heroics, Espionage and Piracy) was extremely corseted, her tiny waist exploding out into big scarlet skirts and an over-filled bodice. Her grey hair was pinned up with several brooches made from human bone. Her earrings were small bat skulls. Her boots were so high-heeled that she was in danger of puncturing the pavement. Kassa hoped to look just like her in forty years time.

Also from the Department of Certain Death was Professor Gootch of Assassination and Edged Weapons, who was bleakly certain that as soon as they all crossed the skybridge, they would be met by a hail of arrows. Paranoia went with his position — he had won his professorship by assassinating his predecessor — but he was worse than usual since the appearance of Drak. He wore a protective vest and a large metal diver's helmet, just in case.

Standing with Professor Gootch was a third member representing the Department of Certain Death, Doctor S. Wampweed. He was a large, vegetable-shaped person who smelled of swamp muck, burbled instead of talking and enjoyed cooking with ingredients that most people wouldn't even use to fertilise their gardens. It was suspected that he was not entirely human, but everyone had been far too polite to mention this once he received his Doctorate in Poisons.

Lastly came the team from the Department of Highly Improbable Arts. Apart from Kassa there was Banjo Harper, a lecturer in Tavern Skills who firmly believed his job at any party was to provide the music. To this end, he was carrying at least sixteen separate musical instruments, many of which he could play just by clashing his knees together.

Then there was Professor Incendia Noir, matchstick-thin and perfectly groomed. No matter how much work Kassa put into her appearance, this woman made her feel like a crazy big-hipped scarecrow. Professor Noir wore black as she always did, a long swirling gown that clung to her narrow body with the kind of elegance that costs an absolute fortune. She wore evening slippers that made her delicately tiny feet look even more petite. Her hair was swept up in a style which on anyone else would last two minutes before flopping ungracefully around their neck. On Professor Noir, it would last all night.

Kassa forced a smile as she approached the group. "You look lovely, Incendia."

"I know," said Professor Noir politely. "What an interesting thing you've done with your hair, Kassa. Quite original."

"Right then," said Vice-Chancellor Bertie who had turned up in his usual old tweed suit, both arms wrapped firmly around the Great Reversing Barrel. "Ready for the off?"

Mavis stood beside him, wearing a ghastly pink ballgown that was several sizes too big for her and about fifty years out of fashion. She gestured to the skybridge and several golden steps appeared out of thin air so the faculty could scramble up with a minimum of fuss.

"We who are about to die salute you," grumbled Professor Gootch.

"I hope there's a nice supper," said Prince Quenby.

"Why didn't you tell me you didn't have proper evening shoes," said Professor Noir, gazing at Kassa's big black boots poking out from under the hem of her ballgown. "I would have lent you some. Although — silly me, your feet would be far too large for my shoes, wouldn't they?"

Several postgraduate students hovered at the back of the group, dressed in their best finery and trying to conceal various bottles of alcoholic beverages about their person. One girl had an entire beer keg under her skirt. Clio and Egg stood with them, trying to blend in.

"Off we go, quicksticks, don't want to be late!" bellowed Bertie. The Cluft delegation began to cross the golden skybridge.

It was only when they were halfway across that everything went horribly wrong.

4

POACHED ALBATROSS AND THE
DEMON DANCE

*S*ingespitter flew on ahead of the delegation from Cluft. As he crossed the halfway point of the glittering skybridge, he transformed from a respectable white sheep with purple wings into a dark, snarling beastie. His wings were suddenly bat-like, and his face dripped with fangs.

Kassa stared in horror as her newly monstrous sheep took off towards Drak. "Nobody move!" she called behind her.

"Sorry, what's happening?" asked Vice-Chancellor Bertie, who couldn't see past the Great Reversing Barrel he was carrying. He bumped into Kassa's back

Kassa fell forward, thrusting out her arms as she hit the bridge. She picked herself up and turned to face the others. "What are you all staring at?"

"You, darling," said Master Fitzdeath with what he probably imagined was a seductive smile.

Kassa stared down at her own body. Her red hair was several shades darker than usual, as was her green silk dress. The heels of her boots were several inches higher, the neckline of her dress was several inches lower, and something disturbing had happened to her underwear. She touched her hands to her waist. Her sudden breathing troubles were explained by the fact that she was now tightly corseted, her ribs constrained by the embroidered bones of a large sea mammal.

And, oh yes — thanks to the corset, her cleavage had reached epic proportions.

"Interesting," said Vice-Chancellor Bertie, peering at her. "Shall we get on?" He marched past with his Great Reversing Barrel hoisted high in the air. As he passed the crucial point, his grey beard turned black, debonair and pointy. His usual tweedy suit became something swishy in brown velvet and gold satin. Bertie shrugged, and kept going.

Singespitter circled back towards them, his bat wings flapping. As he passed over Kassa, he transformed back into the usual white woolly Singespitter with purple wings. He baaed happily and flew back, transforming into the black beastie, who made an excited roaring sound and breathed a small amount of pink flame. At least someone was enjoying himself.

"It's not permanent, then," Kassa said. "Come on, you lot."

The staff and students all stepped across the bridge, each of them transforming into a darker and slightly more glamorous version of themselves as they went. Professor Incendia Noir, Kassa couldn't help noticing, remained exactly as she always was. "That look is so you, dear," she commented as she passed Kassa. "The larger woman is always best to expose her more obvious assets."

Professor Gootch refused to go. "There's no way you'll catch me turning into some kind of demonic gigolo," he choked. "I'd rather have baked beans and toast back at the College, thank you very much!"

"I agree with Professor Gootch," said Professor Profit-scoundrel. "Really, this is all quite undignified."

Master Fitzdeath laughed at her. "Terrible, just terrible. A senior professor in Profit passing up a chance to be the first to set up trading deals with a brand new society, just because she's worried about how she looks."

Penelopa glared at him, then marched across the bridge. The tweed ballgown was replaced with…well, technically it was still tweed, only there was a lot less of it. In true story-telling tradition, her spectacles had vanished and her hair tumbled around her shoulders.

Fitzdeath winked at her. "You've got legs."

"What has that got to do with anything?" snapped Penelopa. She marched across the bridge in her tweed stiletto heels and promptly crashed into the railings, almost toppling over the side. "Damn. Where are my glasses?"

"That's Dark Magic for you," said Mavis the goddess. "All aesthetics and no practicality." Her clothes flickered between a silver sparkly mini-dress and something in floor-length black velvet, but eventually reverted to the original oversized pink ballgown. Mavis gazed at the looming dark city. "That was easy. They can't have a god on their side."

"Is that good?" Kassa couldn't help asking.

"Hard to say," said Mavis. "You may not have noticed, but gods aren't what they used to be."

The rest of the staff and students had already gone ahead. Professor Gootch stomped back towards Cluft, muttering to himself. Singespitter flew above them in tighter and tighter circles, happily transforming back and forth from a white sheep to a dark beastie. Clio and Egg were the only ones left.

"I'm not sure about this," said Clio. She looked down at her pale blue velvet gown. "I like this frock."

"I'm guessing the only way into this party is to follow

their dress code," said Kassa. "You don't have to come." She looked hard at Egg. "You do."

Clio bit her lip and stepped over the invisible line. Her gown exploded outwards, the skirt widening even as the neckline plunged and the waist sucked in with a gasp. Clio looked at Kassa with a pained expression on her face. "I think I'm suddenly wearing silk underwear."

"Join the club," said Kassa. "Come on Egg, be brave."

"Just as long as I don't end up with silk underwear," he muttered, and stepped across to Clio.

"Interesting choice," said Kassa, eyeing his new costume.

Egg was clad in a full set of warlock's robes, black velvet with embroidered silver sigils. As he leaned over to stare at his new boots — also black and covered in occult designs — a tall warlock's hat fell off his head and rolled down the far side of the bridge. "Not bloody likely," he said angrily, wrenching the robes and medallions over his head. Luckily, his original shirt, waistcoat and trousers were still underneath.

Clio grinned. "Can we go to the ball now?"

～

The Chamberlain of Drak was a wreck. While Lord Sinistre had spent the day deciding what to wear to his precious ball, the rest of the palace had worked around the clock to make it happen.

The peacocks wouldn't be fully roasted for another hour and the desserts were yet to be assembled, but the trays of nibbly things were ready to go, the salads had been whipped into a frenzy and the fruit punch was bubbling away merrily.

The Chamberlain sank into a kitchen chair and patted the shoulder of one of the assistant cooks, who was in floods of tears. "Mushroom caps," she kept saying in a weepy, stunned voice. "Thousands and thousands of mushroom caps."

Two more assistant cooks had been locked in the dungeons after a violent dispute about miniature pastry cases.

Sherrie the head cook iced sugar peonies with a fixed grimace on her face. No one dared say a word to her.

"You've all done very well," said the Chamberlain. "Lord Sinistre will certainly want me to pass on his thanks for your marvellous efforts."

One of the assistant cooks blew a raspberry, and two more started crying.

"I'll leave you to it, then," said the Chamberlain, making his exit.

They would be arriving soon, the beautiful people of Drak, as well as the visitors from the strange green land. They would come, they would dance, they would flirt, they would stand around saying nothing to each other, and not one of them would notice that the thumbnail-sized honey cakes were glazed with real gold leaf, or that the tiny sausages on sticks were made from minced albatross poached in a delicate love-in-the-mist mayonnaise.

What in the world was he doing? Why did he care so much about double damask napkins and the correct length of toothpicks? Why were his staff working so hard for such little reward? Why did he appear to have no name beyond his job description?

The Chamberlain stood in the doorway to the ballroom and saw that the chandelier was crooked. One more thing to worry about. "Buttons," he called to a passing footman, "fetch the forty-foot ladder, will you?"

≈

The golden skybridge swept into Drak, leading the delegation from Cluft directly to the door of the palace. It was a tall, glossy, black, looming building entirely similar to every other black spiked building in this city that towered around them, crosshatching the streets with shadows.

"At least we're dressed for the occasion," whispered Kassa, tugging at her bodice.

Kassa couldn't help wondering if the costumes were not the only thing changed by Drak's odd magic. Half of the party were acting aggressively, and the others were making flirty eyes at each other. Kassa had never seen so many tense shoulders and arched eyebrows in one place before, including the annual Staff Ball.

Vice-Chancellor Bertie, despite his new pointy black beard, seemed the least affected. "Do you think anyone's going to let us in?" he bellowed in what he probably thought was a tactfully low voice.

Professor Noir shivered, her eyes darting back and forth as she surveyed the dark shadows around them. "Do you hear that?"

They could all hear it. Music. Several long, slow drumbeats pulsed up through the obsidian paving stones, pounding an irregular heartbeat into the soles of their feet.

Egg held hands with Clio, squeezing her fingers tightly between his own.

The doors swung open.

~

"Marvellous," said Lord Sinistre, rubbing his hands together. "Our guests are early."

One of the serving maids squeaked and fainted, her midnight blue satin skirts fanning out as she fell. Two footmen in elegant suits took hold of the girl's feet, dragging her unconscious body under the piano where she would be hidden from sight until she was able to return to work. The Chamberlain nodded his approval. "Perhaps you would like to greet them in the receiving hall, my Lord, to give us a little time to finish in here?"

The footmen moved like an army of clockwork ants, sweeping trays of food on to tables, straightening decorations, and pouring identical measures of ruby wine into minuscule sipping glasses. They couldn't possibly go any faster.

"Nonsense," said Lord Sinistre, preening. "How can I make my grand entrance in the ballroom if I come scuttling to meet them like some over-anxious butler? Be sensible, man."

The Chamberlain sighed and turned on his heel, barking orders as he crossed the ballroom. "You! Clear that away. You! Straighten that up. You! Stop crying!"

Lord Sinistre, oblivious to the frantic work around him, wandered towards the staircase that spiralled around the grand ballroom. *Hmm. A grand entrance.*

The doors peeled back, revealing a high ceilinged foyer. A dozen or so thin and elegant staircases sprouted off a huge and grandiose Great Staircase. The walls and floor of the foyer were lined with silver-and-jet mosaic tiles. Ambient dancing shadows were projected against the walls by a hundred concealed lanterns. In the centre of the architectural marvel was a single dark figure, robed and cowled, shimmering with more sinister physical presence than a thousand warlocks rolled into one.

"Follow me," he said in a sonorous, musical voice so deep that the tiles rattled on the walls. He led the way past the various spiral staircases to a huge set of dark doors engraved with a frieze of bats, gargoyles and other strange and demonic creatures.

"Clio, this is awful," whispered Egg. "We have to get out of this place."

"Don't you like it? You made it."

"I drew it," Egg said hoarsely. "I don't know who made it."

As the sinister butler and the delegation from Cluft approached the doors, they swung open just wide enough to let someone through, a maid with waist-length black hair. She whispered something urgently at the butler, then slid back through the doors, closing them firmly behind her.

"I apologise," boomed the voice of the butler, in a calm and unruffled tone. "I meant to say, follow me this way." He turned on his heel, walked to the foot of one of the lesser spiral staircases and started up the steps. The steps were like slabs of black sugar candy, and they went up so high that you could not tell where the steps ended and the distant ceiling began.

The faculty and students of Cluft followed the dark figure of the butler up the spiral staircase. Kassa looked down at her high-heeled black boots and sighed. "This is going to be painful."

Egg and Clio, still hovering at the back of the group, were the last to go up the stairs. "What about the butler?" Clio said. "Did you design the butler?"

"Yes," Egg said mournfully.

"Why is his voice so deep like that?"

"I used an extra-thick lettering style. I wanted to give him a bit of presence."

"Creepy."

~

The butler was intent on giving them a tour of the palace. They climbed sky-high spiral staircases, promenaded along velvet-draped corridors, tiptoed through a glasshouse of carnivorous plants, got lost in a museum of dark crystalline sculptures and gasped in awe at an indoor hanging garden of sparkling silver stars.

The overall theme of the palace décor was black and silver with hints of blood red and the occasional splash of midnight blue. There were never enough lanterns or candles, unless they were needed to cast long and fearsome shadows.

"This place certainly works at being dark," said Kassa.

Egg, aware of how often he relied on extra-inky shadows to make his drawings look more dramatic, said nothing.

Finally, the butler led them all back down to the ground floor of the palace and into a huge, gleaming, hexagonal ballroom. A thousand candles glimmered in the chandeliers and candelabras around the ballroom, casting flattering light across the trays of delicate food arranged on long, chiffon-draped tables.

The staff and students of Cluft stumbled across the floor. Somehow, their new costumes no longer seemed ridiculous. It seemed unbelievably right to be clad in velvet and silks and elaborate corsetry.

"Where is everyone?" wondered Kassa.

Apart from themselves and the tables of food, the ballroom was empty. Not a footman or a courtier or a host in sight.

Egg tugged at Clio's sleeve, pointing up to the tip-most top of the room. A silvery spiral staircase ran around the walls. At the highest point of the stair, a silver door was just visible. "He'll come from there," said Egg. "That's where he'll make his grand entrance." He had drawn this room fifteen times before getting it exactly right, and used three bottles of high-grade ink on the final version.

"Who?" whispered Clio. It was impossible to talk in anything but a whisper among all this grandeur and silence.

"Lord Sinistre," said Egg. This was the test. This was where he found out if this really was the city he had created with parchment and ink. He had invented Lord Sinistre a week ago, finally choosing which of three prototype characters would rule the city of Drak. And as for Drak itself — hadn't he only made that name up last night? It seemed such a long time ago.

Did the people of Drak know they had only just come into existence? Did they have any idea?

Music filled the room, a thunderous moan of drums, flutes and fiddle strings. A large circle in the centre of the ballroom rose, to reveal an ornate bandstand packed with moody minstrels. Their eyes glowed red as they played. After a final set of dramatic chords, the minstrels abandoned their instruments and stared upwards. Naturally, this encouraged the audience to do the same.

A dark figure stepped through the doorway at the top of the staircase, his cape swirling in a cloud of crimson. "Greetings," he said. "I am Lord Sinistre. Welcome to Drak."

His feet made no sound as he began to descend. His guests looked slowly around the ballroom, eyeing the length of the staircase that wrapped at least six times around the six wide walls.

"It's going to take him months to walk all the way down here," said Clio in disbelief.

The Lord of Drak continued at a regular, unhurried pace, his eyes on his audience.

Kassa rolled her eyes. "He doesn't expect us to stare adoringly up at him the whole time, does he? I'll get a crick in my neck."

The large doors on the floor level of the ballroom — one against each wall — all opened at once to admit more party guests. Peacock feathers, sparkling tiaras, gleaming rubies and antique gold possum fur were the most prominent fashion accessories for the lords and ladies of Drak. Black eyeliner was also very popular. Most of them had long black hair, flashing violet eyes and plunging necklines, even the men.

The minstrels took their instruments up again. This time, the music was smooth and energetic, the kind that made you dance whether you wanted to or not.

One by one, the staff and students of the Polyhedrotechnical College of Cluft were swept into the dance by gorgeous strangers. Even Vice-Chancellor Bertie put down his Great Reversing Barrel for a chance to pair up with a pale-skinned countess in a black lace crinoline.

"I never would have guessed that Bertie knew how to tango," said Kassa. She grabbed an arm each of Clio and Egg. "Come on, kids. Let's check out the buffet."

"Is it safe?" Clio asked. "Should we eat the food here?"

"You're thinking of faeries," said Kassa, striding towards the nearest food table. "I don't know what's going on in this city, but if it was the fey folk we'd be seeing far more in the way of glitterdust and grass stains." She lifted a small sausage, balanced neatly on a fine gold toothpick. "They've gone to a lot of trouble to impress us. Do you have any idea how hard it is to make a sausage out of minced albatross? Not to mention poaching it in love-in-the-mist mayonnaise. They could have substituted chicken and parsley and no one would have known any better." She ate the sausage and tucked the gold toothpick into her bosom. "Ooh, do I see honey cakes?"

"It's not necessarily to impress us," said Egg awkwardly. "It's just — Lord Sinistre only has the best of the best, whether they're catering for him or for three hundred people. It's the way things work around here."

"He's only just started his second circuit," said Clio, glancing up at the descending Lord Sinistre. "Why doesn't he slide down the banisters?"

"Style," said Kassa, licking honey from her fingers. "It's all about style. Tell us more, Egg. What else do I need to know about old Sinistre?"

"He walks slowly," said Egg. "Really, really slowly."

"I'd gathered that," said Kassa. "What else?"

"Um," Egg racked his brains. "That's it. I hadn't worked out any history or personality stuff yet, just — well, the outward appearance."

"Style, poise and velvet." Kassa lifted a silver chalice to her lips and sipped a liqueur so silky that it stroked her throat on the way down. "How challenging."

"I was hoping you would think so," purred Lord Sinistre.

Kassa spun around. Lord Sinistre stood right behind her, his dark eyes boring into hers. She waved a hand in the direction of the staircase. "Didn't you have about four laps to go?"

"Dramatic entrances are such a bore," he said with a slow smile.

Something inside Kassa uncurled. She pasted a bright false smile on her face. "Enjoying the party?"

"I am now," said the Lord of Drak, his eyes moving slowly over her. "Would you like to dance?"

It had to be an enchantment, Kassa decided. A dark enchantment. A dark, insidious enchantment. This wasn't the kind of man she usually found attractive. Okay, that wasn't entirely true. She cast her mind back over her list of ex-boyfriends, trying to find one that didn't have a bit of 'bad boy' in him. Nope.

Damn it, Lord Sinistre was *just* her type. "I don't dance," Kassa told him. The music had other ideas. It tugged at her feet and wriggled around her elbows.

"Really?" said Lord Sinistre. He looked pointedly down at Kassa's high-heeled boot, which poked out from under her sweeping green gown. Her traitorous foot was tapping.

"Well, maybe just one dance," she said weakly. In an instant she was in Lord Sinistre's arms, moving in perfect synchronicity with the otherworldly music, their eyes and hips locked closely together.

Egg and Clio watched them go. "Are they all under a spell?" Clio asked. "Kassa too?"

"I don't know," said Egg. "Don't look at me. There wasn't any music in my drawings. I didn't come up with the minced albatross and love-in-the-mist mayonnaise thing either. I'm *not doing this.*"

"Hmm." Clio surveyed the crowd. "I wonder who is."

The dance was dark and inviting, a mass of beautiful people in spectacular costumes. Even the serving staff moved in time to the music.

Only one person did not. He was an ordinary figure at the far end of the ballroom, dressed in dark grey. He moved briskly through the crowd, stopping every now and then to speak to a footman or maid, or to rearrange a platter.

"Help me up," Clio demanded, bouncing up and down on her toes to get a proper look.

"Up where?" said Egg. He stared at the immaculate buffet table. "Oh, you're not serious."

"*Up,*" said Clio. Egg gripped her uncertainly, and held on as she propelled herself upwards, her feet landing on the table. Her hem fell into the punchbowl and a purple stain spread along the underside of her dress, but Clio didn't even notice.

"What are you trying to see?" asked Egg.

"Get up here," she said in a breathy voice. "Now, Egg."

Egg scrambled up. "I really don't think we're supposed to do this."

Clio gripped his hand and pointed across the room. "This is your world, Egg. Your precious little dark city that you scribbled down in your spare time. So tell me who in the Underworld is *that?*"

Egg stared, and then smiled. "It's the Chamberlain. Wow, it's really him. He looks just like I always imagined. I never could draw his face quite right."

"He belongs here?" Clio asked in a chilly voice. "He's one of your fictional people that you made up in your head?"

"Of course. He runs the place. He's the first character I came up with, you see, because…"

"What's his name?"

Egg looked at her strangely. "What's up? You sound angry."

"I'm not angry, Egg. Not yet. What's his name?"

"He doesn't have a name. He's just the Chamberlain. It's sort of ironic, you see, because…"

Clio pushed him off the table.

Egg landed hard. The impact of the polished floor thudded painfully through every bone in his body. "Oof," he gasped. "What did you do that for?"

"He has a name, Egg," hissed Clio as she climbed down from the table. "Your precious Chamberlain's name is Aragon Silversword."

Dancing, to Kassa, was as natural as breathing. She had been taught a dozen different dances by a dozen different pirates before she was even a dozen years old. When she escaped from her finishing school a week before final exams and resolved never to return to the pirating life, dancing had seemed an obvious career path to take.

She had tapped her way into the Exotic Dancers Union,

cha-cha'd her way into the exclusive Dreadnought Dollies Cabaret Institute, and undulated her way into the Unusual Bellydancer's League, a group so exclusive that only six members were allowed at any one time. Kassa was the only one of the current six who had never been a courtesan, concubine, spy, or all three at once.

Dancing was one of those things (Annual Staff Ball aside) that Kassa had given up in recent years. In truth, she had given it up long before she started at the Polyhedrotechnical College of Cluft. The year that she spent living above the Whet and Whistle Tavern and Grillhouse, happily singing for her supper, felt like several lifetimes ago.

This dance, her expert feet and hips informed her, was *wrong*. Yes, she was in the arms of a gorgeous man with beautiful dark eyes. Yes, the music was exquisite beyond belief. Yes, she hadn't enjoyed anything so much in ages. No, this should not be happening.

Clio and Egg brought her out of her dance-induced daze. They were the only two in the whole ballroom not gliding around to the music. Clio marched along the edge of the dance floor, dragging Egg behind her.

Kassa lay her cheek on Lord Sinistre's shoulder to get a better look. Why weren't they dancing? Couldn't they feel the lure of the music? Her mind was overwhelmed by the trill of the flutes, the twang of the fiddles and the strange plinking of a musical instrument she did not recognise. Still, she turned her head to see where the children were heading.

All she saw at first was a gaggle of footmen who hovered around someone who was giving the orders. As they peeled away to obey those orders, Kassa had her first glimpse of his face.

Eyes so grey you could stab yourself with them...

Kassa's brain came rushing back with a vengeance. What was going on? Why was everyone dancing with dark strangers, their eyes glazed and their choreography perfect? Why was she allowing this complete stranger to press his velvet-clad groin to hers? Where was that horrible music coming from?

And while she was asking questions, what in *the wide world* was Aragon Silversword doing here?

"Let go of me," she said, trying to extract herself from the dangerous rhythms of Lord Sinistre. "Get off!"

She had to peel herself out of Lord Sinistre's arms and shove him away. Then she had to shoulder a path through a web of gliding bodies. "Out of my way, move it!"

Kassa reached the far side of the ballroom at the same time as Clio and Egg. "Where is he? Where did he go?"

"I don't know," said Clio wildly. "I thought he was dead. Everyone thought he was dead!"

"He is when I catch up with him," Kassa snarled. She surveyed the crowd with a steady eye. Lord Sinistre's dark eyes were fixed upon her. He glided towards her, to the rhythm of the music. Everyone else was part of the dance. There was no sign of Aragon Silversword.

"You are not dancing," said Lord Sinistre as he reached them, his voice low and sensuous.

"I'm okay with that," said Kassa. "Carry on without me."

"We're looking for someone," said Clio.

"The Chamberlain," said Egg. "Do you know where he is?"

"You must dance," Lord Sinistre reproached. "All of you must join the dance."

The music swelled, the beat quickened and the hypnotic, dangerous dance reached out to swallow them whole. This time, it was too powerful to resist.

5

JUSTICE AND BLACK LACE

*D*ancing was for people who were not Egg.

The music, though, the music wanted Egg to dance and he did his best to please it. It sang madly in his veins, demanding that he writhe and waltz and shimmy. He didn't even know what a shimmy was, but he was pretty sure he was doing one. His dance partner was a girl with long dark hair, a clinging gown, spiky black eyelashes and lips so dark and promising that you would swear they were stained with blood.

He couldn't see Clio, or Kassa, or even Lord Sinistre. The dance floor was a melting, grooving mass of bodies and sweat and velvet. Nothing mattered but the music, nothing mattered but dancing until your feet bled and your skin wept and your head pulsed with a blinding explosion of pain…

The music stopped.

Someone screamed, and there was a worried buzz across the ballroom. Through the mass of shiny confused people, Egg noticed that interesting things were happening at the bandstand.

A tall, cloaked figure held aloft the body of the fiddler.

The cloak was such a pale and brilliant grey that it seemed to be almost white. He was quite out of place among the dark, sensuous colours of Drak. He ripped the fiddler apart.

As each limb was torn away from the fiddler's body, it transformed into a screeching black demon. There were nine demons in all, clawing creatures with red eyes and shrill voices. As each demon was exposed, it screamed and dissolved into a puff of smoke. Finally, the cloaked figure tossed the fiddler's empty tunic aside and turned his cowled head towards the other minstrels. They all vanished, leaving only their instruments behind.

Egg stared at the pale grey figure. He was real. It was all really real. "You're the Cloak," he mouthed. His hero, the first real superhero he had ever inked on to the page.

The grey figure turned to Egg. His face was hidden within the shimmering shape of his otherworldly garment. "I am the Cloak who Walks in the Night," he said in a clear, hard voice. "I am the Bringer of Order to Chaos. I am the Maker of Justice for All. This city is mine to protect. Demons and creatures of evil intent, beware. The Cloak knows you. The Cloak will find you."

Light flashed against the upper windows of the ballroom. If it had been a stormy night it would have been lightning, a perfectly reasonable visual effect under such circumstances, but there was no storm. The flash of light was a signal for all eyes to look up and see what needed to be seen. All eyes swung upwards.

On the highest landing of the spiralling silver staircase, two masked figures stood in bold poses. One was a girl in a bright white catsuit, her hair a riotous shock of purple curls. The other was a male in a blue and white checked suit. He kept flickering in and out of sight. Egg felt a dull shock of recognition. Dream Girl and Invisiblo the Mystery Man. "The gang's all here," he muttered to himself.

"Drak is under our protection!" called the purple-haired girl.

"Fear not!" added the flickering, half-invisible man in blue and white. "The tyrant's rule nears its end. We are the Heroes of Justice who shall bring the Reign of Darkness to its final conclusion!"

Light flashed again and the two 'heroes' vanished, as did the Cloak.

There was silence for a moment, as the crowd processed what they had just seen. There was a vague sound as if some of them considered applauding, then thought better of it.

Lord Sinistre cleared his throat. He stepped up to the bandstand and nudged the ashy tunic of the demon fiddler with his boot. "Well," he said, clearing his throat for a second time. "That was odd."

~

The crowd moved towards the food tables, tentatively at first, and then in one big rush. The waiters sprang into action, passing trays of drinks and sugary rose petals back and forth at super speed.

"So," said Kassa, stepping up to the empty bandstand beside Lord Sinistre. "Demons."

"Oh yes," said Lord Sinistre, wiping his boot on a stray decorative banner. "We get rather a lot of them around here, I'm afraid. They can be a dreadful nuisance." He sighed. "Too much to hope we could have one ball without someone getting demonically possessed."

"Are you saying you weren't responsible for that whole demon dance mass hypnotism thing?"

"Me?" Lord Sinistre laughed. "I can think of far better ways to ask a woman to dance. No, the demons get into everything these days. We're rather used to it by now."

"Are they responsible for this?" Kassa plucked at her dress. "The costume changes my people went through as they crossed the bridge?"

"You don't say?" said Lord Sinistre, sounding genuinely shocked. "I thought you were all making an effort to fit in with our way of life. It must be Drak itself, I'm afraid."

"The city?"

"It has a mind of its own, and some magic too. We call it the draklight—the creeping magical mind of the city. It gets ideas. It's never actually changed people's clothes before, but then we've never had visitors from outside until today. I hope you weren't put to too much inconvenience."

"Nothing that a good physiotherapist can't fix," said Kassa, tugging at her tight corset.

Lord Sinistre smiled. The gleam in his eyes did something to the pit of Kassa's stomach. Her whole skin was aware of him. *How's a girl supposed to spot the demons around here?*

He extended a hand to hers. "Can I get you some wine, a little supper? Perhaps, if we find some non-demonic musicians to do the honours, we could have another dance? I hardly think the last one counts." Slowly, he lifted her hand to his mouth and kissed it.

"I'm sorry, I can't," said Kassa. There was nothing she wanted more right now than to dance with this man, which suggested that she should do anything but. "I have to look for someone."

Lord Sinistre sighed and kissed her hand a second time, his lips lingering a fraction longer that before. "Later," he suggested.

Kassa shivered, taking back custody of her hand. "Definitely later." As she stepped down from the bandstand, she spotted Egg. "Where's Clio?"

Egg looked around. "I lost her in the dance."

"Well, find her," Kassa snapped, walking towards the

nearest door. "I'm going to look around for those so-called Heroes of Justice. Something very strange is going on around here."

As she left, Banjo Harper pushed his way out of the velvet-clad crowd and climbed up to the bandstand. He grinned wildly as his knees clashed three different sets of cymbals together. He raised his fiddle, cello, drum kit, flute and ukulele, preparing for the performance of his life. "Now we'll hear some music!"

~

The door Kassa chose did not lead into another set of endless dark corridors and staircases. Instead, it led unexpectedly to an outdoor courtyard. Kassa closed the door behind her and breathed in the clear, cold air.

She hadn't lied to Egg. She fully intended to go looking for the peculiar 'heroes' who had interrupted the ball and destroyed the dance-inducing demons. In a minute. Once she had caught her breath.

Ten minutes passed.

It wasn't just the tightly-laced corset that was making it hard to think. There was something strange about this city — something other than demons being commonplace, and an obsessive attachment to velvet. The draklight? It was doing something to her mind, making her think differently. If only she knew what she was trying to think about...

"Hello, Kassa." The voice cut through the silence of the courtyard like an icicle impaling her in the stomach. He had been standing there all along, in the shadows. All this time wondering where he was, and she might have missed him if he hadn't called attention to himself.

Kassa's golden eyes blazed in the darkness. There were a hundred questions she wanted to ask but her pride would not allow her to speak them aloud. Her pride, in fact, thought it would be better if she never spoke to him again. "Hello, Aragon," she managed.

The door opened behind Kassa. Lord Sinistre stepped out, his scarlet cape swishing around his black velvet suit. "Ah, Mistress Sharpe. There you are. You really mustn't worry about those so-called heroes. The city produces them from time to time, I'm not sure why. Rather like rats. Or demons, come to that. Best leave them to their own devices." He extended his hand. "Your lecturer in Tavern Skills? He's producing a sound not unlike twelve musical instruments eating each other, so it shouldn't be long before my own personal musicians — those not possessed by demons, with any luck — throttle him with his own guitar strap and take over. When that happens, I should very much like to dance with you. A dance of the non-demonic variety, obviously."

Kassa turned slowly, smiling at Lord Sinistre. "I'd love to dance with you, your Lordship." She didn't look back at the courtyard. It was very important that she didn't look back.

"Ah, Chamberlain," said Lord Sinistre, over Kassa's shoulder. "There you are. We appear to be running out of candied bat wings, and you know they're the Duchess of Jetside's favourites. Could you inform the kitchens?"

"Of course, my lord," said Aragon Silversword.

~

The evening passed in a blur of fine wine, black satin and candied bat wings. Lord Sinistre was the perfect host, managing to dance with every visiting female from Cluft as well as all the duchesses, countesses and baronesses of Drak. Since every woman of Drak who wasn't a servant was actually a duchess, countess or baroness, this took some time. Somehow, in between all this, Lord Sinistre found time to discuss Vice-Chancellor Bertie's Great Reversing Barrel with tactful interest, and to slow-dance with Kassa twelve times.

Many hours later, as the non-demonically possessed minstrels began to droop with exhaustion, Kassa found herself alone at a table with Egg and Clio. Neither of the two young people had been tactless enough to mention the presence of Aragon Silversword, even when he appeared in the ballroom to whisper some command or question to Lord Sinistre, only to vanish back into the kitchens. Whenever he was in the ballroom, Aragon Silversword's eyes were always on Kassa.

Kassa found herself smacking an elegant silver pate knife back and forth between her hands in a vaguely homicidal way. She lowered it to the table slowly and let go of it. Her hands were shaking. "Come on, kids. Time to go."

Clio yawned. "Already?"

"There's no already about it." Kassa surveyed the room. "You two leave now. Use the door over there, it leads straight outside. Don't call attention to yourselves. Act like you're going out to get some fresh air, or to snog in a corner somewhere. Once you're out, head straight back over the bridge to Cluft. No looking back. I'll grab Bertie and follow you."

Egg glanced around at the various other Cluft residents who were still eating, dancing and chatting with the glamorous people of Drak. "What about everyone else?"

Kassa shrugged. "Mavis is a goddess, she should be fine. I don't particularly like any of the rest of them." She rolled her eyes at Egg's shocked face. "Don't be so stuffy. I can't sneak them all out covertly. They'll have to take their chances. The important thing is that a few of us are on the outside, figuring out what to do."

"So you don't believe Lord Sinistre?" Clio asked. "You know, that the demon dance was down to some random demons outside his control?"

"I don't know who the demons are," Kassa replied. She fixed her gaze on Vice-Chancellor Bertie, at the far side of the room. "Go now."

Clio took Egg's hand, and the two of them strolled towards the door. Uncomfortably, Egg slung an arm across her shoulders. Clio sighed. "At least look as if you mean it."

"I do mean it," Egg shot back. "I mean—" They were outside before he could finish the sentence. The air hit them, cool and refreshing.

"Let's get to the bridge," said Clio. "I want my dress back."

~

"I didn't get to say goodbye," grumbled Vice-Chancellor Bertie as Kassa hustled him and his Great Reversing Barrel across the bridge.

"Plenty of time for that next time we visit," said Kassa. "We don't want to outstay our welcome, do we? And we have classes tomorrow, Vice-Chancellor. I haven't even written my new Philosophy of Magic lecture yet."

"Oh?" he asked with mild interest. "What's it on?"

"Why magic is a bad bad thing, of course."

The Vice-Chancellor chuckled. "I should have known."

Singespitter was fast asleep on the bridge as they passed, the front half of him in Cluft (white, fleecy and calm) and the back half of him in Drak (dark, scaled with claws, twitchy).

Kassa nudged him awake with a well-laced boot. "If the wind changes, you'll stay that way." She crossed the centre of the bridge and breathed out as the corset vanished and the shot-black lines of silk melted away from her loosened dress. Her hair relaxed, and her cleavage thankfully retreated back where it belonged.

Vice-Chancellor Bertie changed too, although again he

hardly seemed to notice the difference between tweed and velvet.

Kassa half-slid down the far side of the skybridge, landing beside a rain barrel that caught the drips from the library tower roof. In one quick movement, she ducked her head into the freezing cold water, submerging her hair and face. She came out sputtering and shivering, her mind mercifully clear.

"What are you doing?" said Vice-Chancellor Bertie as he manhandled his Great Reversing Barrel down from the bridge.

Kassa gasped as she tossed back her wet hair. She could feel her nose turning blue. "Couldn't you sense it?" she demanded.

"You mean the outpourings of dark mystical energy contained within that black and demon-possessed city?" said Vice-Chancellor Bertie with a cheerful tone in his voice. "Oh, my yes. Very interesting. Do you think there might be a paper in it?"

"I think there might be a whole bloody thesis," said Kassa.

~

"I don't believe a word of it," said Sean McHagrty. It was so late that it was early, though Sean, in his striped pajamas, had shown no sign of being asleep when they arrived back.

"No, really," said Egg, sitting on his own bed. "It all happened."

Sean shook his head. "Minced albatross sausages poached in love-in-the-mist mayonnaise? Have you any idea how tricky that would be to prepare? For a start, catching an albatross is no one's idea of fun..."

Clio leafed through Egg's parchments and papyri. She lifted out one of the sketches and stared at it. Slowly, she sank to the floor and crossed her legs under her, still staring at the picture. It was the portrait of the Chamberlain.

"I told you," Egg said apologetically. "I never could get his face right."

"It's good enough," she said grimly. "I never saw this one before, but it's definitely him. Where has he been all this time? He can't have been in Drak, it's only existed since this morning. Grandmother was so worried when she heard he had disappeared. At least when he was in prison we knew where he was."

"Kassa's worried too," said Egg.

"I suppose she misses him," said Clio with a romantic sigh.

"Utterly," said Egg, teasing her a little. "She'll never admit it."

"Speaking of missing things," said Sean. "What the Underworld are you two talking about?"

"Who invited you anyway?" complained Clio.

"This is my room! If you two had a more interesting night than me, it's your duty to entertain me with it."

Clio narrowed her eyes at him. "Which do you think would hurt more, if I hit you with the chair, or with the chest of drawers?"

There was a knock on the door.

"Come in," called Egg.

Kassa pushed the door open. "Hi, all. Have I interrupted an orgy? I hear that's what students get up to these days."

Sean brightened at the sight of a gorgeous older woman in an evening gown. "Only every other day," he said in a flirty tone.

Clio looked at him in disgust and flopped back down on the floor.

Kassa smiled at Sean, sizing him up. "Well," she said with a gleam in her golden eyes. "Sean McHagrty. Back as a first-year student for your...third year, is it? We've never actually met."

"Hi, good-looking," he drawled.

Clio and Egg exchanged looks. "Does that really work on women?" Egg asked.

"Only the desperately lonely and the slightly deranged," said Clio. "Sean, meet our good friend Kassa."

The change in Sean's face was comical. He backed away, tripping over his bed and crashing flat on the floor. "Holy shit, you're Kassa Daggersharp!"

Egg was confused. "What's his problem?"

Clio laughed. "You should read more epic ballads, Egg. The Daggersharps and the McHagrtys have a feud going back generations. Every time two of them meet, they have to fight a duel!"

Kassa smiled at the cowering Sean. "I don't have my sword. Should I come back another time?"

"I heard about you from my brother Finnley," he choked. "You nearly drowned him, then you nearly cooked him, then you turned him into a frog!"

Kassa frowned. "It was a very small frog. I don't know what all the fuss was about. Anyway, he got back to being human eventually. How's he doing these days?"

"He joined the Wandering Monks of Darkness," said Sean, sounding stunned. "He was with them for a year, meditating and eating nuts and seeds, then he had to leave because the lifestyle was too hectic. He says he's allergic to excitement. Now he lives on a remote mountain with no one for company but a herd of homing pigeons and whenever anyone mentions your name to him he *twitches*."

"Excellent," said Kassa. "Sounds like he's calmed down a bit since the last time I saw him. What do you want to do about this duel?"

"Scimitars at dawn?" said Clio eagerly.

Kassa shook her head. "Too messy. Plus I don't think a member of faculty is technically allowed to disembowel a student from a different department." She glanced at Sean. "You are majoring in Profit, right?"

Sean whimpered a little.

"Yup," said Kassa. "So much for that plan. It'll have to be thumb wrestling. Give me a minute and I'll be with you, Sean." She lowered herself to the floor next to Clio and paged through the pictures. "Who were those Heroes of Justice, Egg? In the words of Lord Sinistre, they were odd."

"Oh." Egg leaned over from the bed and pulled out a papyrus from the very bottom of the pile. "Here we go. The Cloak, Dream Girl and Invisiblo the Mystery Man. They're the main characters. The city itself isn't all that important to the stories, it's just the place where the heroes live. And the city needs heroes because it's so dark and dangerous."

"Interesting," Kassa mused. "Judging from tonight, those three didn't seem to be well known to the people of Drak. Lord Sinistre didn't recognise them."

"That's because he hasn't met them yet," said Egg. "I haven't written that story, I was saving it for the big finale. The three heroes band together against the evil tyrant and remove him from the throne."

"Hmm," said Kassa. "What's so tyrannical about Lord Sinistre? Apart from his dress sense, obviously. What has he done wrong?"

"I don't know," said Egg. "Nothing much, I suppose. He's just the tyrant. You know — he wears a lot of black."

Kassa shook her head. "You need to work on your plotting, kid." She yawned and put the sketch down. "It's late. I have an early lecture. Assuming you don't know why your fictional city turned up…"

"No idea," said Egg.

"Well, then. We'll have to see what evidence I can turn up tomorrow."

"What's happening tomorrow?" Clio asked.

Kassa stretched lazily. "I'm having an intimate supper for two with the dread tyrant of Drak."

"What about the Chamberlain?" Clio burst out. "I mean — my uncle Aragon."

Kassa's expression closed over. "I have no idea what you're talking about," she said coldly. She glanced at Sean and an evil grin took over her face. "Now, before I go. Thumbs!"

Kassa and Clio returned to their own rooms a little while later. Egg then had to put up with half an hour of complaining from Sean McHagrty about his injured thumb. The thumb wasn't broken, but Sean maintained that it was severely sprained and would never be quite the same again.

Mercifully, Sean fell asleep before dawn, leaving Egg awake and staring at the ceiling. He wondered if anyone else had made it back from the ball. They should all be fine, it wasn't as if Drak was especially dangerous… He groaned and rolled over in bed. Of course it was dangerous. He had designed it that way. There was no point in telling stories about superheroes if they lived in cozy suburbia. Drak was a nasty, dark, evil death-trap and half of the faculty and postgrad students of Cluft were probably still dancing the night away in the middle of it.

Finally, Egg fell asleep.

When he woke up, it was because of a soft little sound. He yawned and wiped his eyes, sitting up in bed.

Dahla the ghost curled up by the window, weeping. Her cloud of coppery hair was particularly fine and translucent. Egg had all but forgotten about her. "Is something wrong?"

he whispered, not wanting to wake up Sean. If he heard the word 'thumb' again, he really would have to kill someone.

Dahla lifted her tear-stained face. "I've lost something," she said, and her voice was a gentle billow of smoke. "I don't know where it is."

Egg climbed out of bed and went to her. "Don't cry. We can find it. What does it look like?"

"I don't know," she wailed. "It was here. I think it was here. I can't see it any more."

Egg had a thought. "You don't come from the dark city, do you? The new one, across the way? Do you come from Drak?"

Dahla just stared at him, unhappy and confused. "I've lost something," she whispered.

Egg couldn't help himself. He reached out to touch her cheek. Her skin was warm, firm to touch. "I thought you were a ghost," he said in surprise. "You're real."

Dahla smiled sadly at him, and suddenly his hand was pressing against the cold plaster of the wall. She was gone.

Egg was caught by a yawn that almost took the top of his head off. These late nights were getting the better of him. "Why can't ghosts visit during the day?" he grumbled, staggering back towards his bed.

This time, he slept without waking for five solid hours before Clio banged on the door to wake him up for the lecture.

~

Mistress Sharpe stood at the lectern, staring out at the lecture hall full of Philosophy of Magic students. "We have already covered the general dangers of magic. Today we will be examining some practical and historical evidence. I'm assuming you've all read the Peacock and Lacrobius which were set for this week?"

There was a shocked hush as half the students avoided eye contact with each other and the other half frantically flipped through their notebooks, looking for any evidence of instructions.

Kassa rolled her eyes. "Course guides, people. They are there for a reason. Try and catch up by tomorrow, when tutorials begin. You should have already written down your name for a tutorial time — don't panic, the lists are still on the wall outside the staff room, with the words Philosophy of Magic written above them in large neon letters." She glared at them all, her golden eyes flashing. "Note for the future: tutorials are not lectures. I will not be sitting there telling you what to think. You are expected to think for yourselves, and to discuss the issues in the hope that some ideas will still be geographically located near your brains when the exams come around. The best way to be prepared for tutorials is to read the required texts which are listed in your course guide. That's the blue scroll with the large red lettering which you probably all forgot to bring with you today."

She took a deep breath, and began her lecture. "Twenty-four years ago, the Polyhedrotechnical College was rather smaller than it is today. Cluft had half as many taverns, smaller lecture halls and a population of less than a hundred residents, including students, faculty and dinner ladies. However, the people of the Mocklore Empire were still rather distressed when the entire town unexpectedly vanished."

There was a slight buzz amongst the students. Most of them had probably heard the story as children, but being in Cluft now gave it a new relevance.

Mistress Sharpe continued. "There were many theories as to why such an event occurred, but most of the people who had any skill at analysing such theories had vanished along with the rest of Cluft. It was suspicious, however, that the Vanishing of Cluft occurred simultaneously with another major event. The Emperor of the time, generally referred to as Mad Old Timregis, had hired a large group of warlocks to expand the Skullcap Mountains, adding to the instability of that particular region, and entirely swallowing up the mountain-based barony of Eaglesbog."

A student three rows back raised his hand. "Why did he do that, miss?"

"Beethunter, I did say he was mad," said Mistress Sharpe impatiently. "Also, if you read romantic ballads, you'll discover a story suggesting that the Emperor's wife ran off with Baron Eaglesbog. Those of you who like soppy love stories with happy endings will prefer the Muzzlefud song, in which the Empress and the Baron were honeymooning in Chiantrio when Eaglesbog was destroyed, and lived out their life happily under assumed names, as opposed to the more modern Tippett version, in which the tortured ghosts of the lovers are still trapped under the weight of the mountains, along with all the other souls which were condemned to a nasty death because of their illicit love affair." She shook her head. "I don't know what's wrong with that boy; he used to write such nice poems about pirates and kittens. Still, the depressing stuff sells better, apparently. Where was I?"

The students leaned forward eagerly.

"Anyway," said Mistress Sharpe. "The generally accepted theory is that the huge, destructively magical act of getting rid of Eaglesbog sent shockwaves through the land. Cows turned inside out, milk went sour, crop circles turned into crop triangles and Cluft vanished without trace, never to be seen again."

There was silence. Someone coughed.

Mistress Sharpe smiled brightly. "Until it mysteriously

reappeared ten years later, with everyone intact and none the worse for their experience. The point of this story — and this is something you will see echoed over and over in your tutorial readings — is that large, destructive magical activities always have dire, life-changing repercussions. Yes, Yarrowstalk?"

The girl in the front row lowered her hand. "What about small, insignificant magical activities, miss?"

"They have dire, life-changing repercussions too," said Mistress Sharpe. "We just don't get to them until after the mid-semester break. Yes, Almondstone?"

A girl sitting just in front of Egg and Clio lowered her hand. "The mysterious vanishing and reappearance of Cluft, miss. I was wondering if it had any relevance to the recent mysterious appearance of Drak?"

The students buzzed far louder than before.

Mistress Sharpe tried not to smile. Almondstone, as well as all the girls sitting near her, were very self-consciously wearing velvet tops, lots of eyeliner and black wisps of lace in their hair. The dress code of Drak had started a trend among the students. This at least was better than last year, when Kassa had walked into her second week of Philosophy of Magic lectures to discover that every female student was wearing a wench bodice, wide red skirts and big black boots. She had been forced to borrow tweed frocks from Penelopa Profit-scoundrel until the whole thing died down — not an experience she ever cared to repeat.

The students were hanging out for an answer to Almondstone's question — obviously, rumours had flown around campus since the Drak ball the previous night.

Mistress Sharpe cleared her throat. "Shame on you, Almondstone. If you start assuming that what your lecturers tell you has any relevance to real life, you won't get very far." She grinned widely. "Many serious treatises have been written on the ramifications of large acts of destructive magic, particularly in the last few years. I hope you're taking notes on this, since it relates to a particularly evil essay question I'll be setting you shortly."

The students groaned, sensing the fun bit was over, and most of them opened their notebooks.

"Right," said Mistress Sharpe. "Who knows how to spell 'potentialities of pre-apocalyptic catastrophication'? Should I write it on the blackboard?"

6

THE SUMMONING OF GHOSTS

*A*fter Philosophy of Magic, Clio had to run to a Duelling seminar, and then to a Home Economics lecture. Staggering away from the last with her brain decidedly over-stuffed, she went looking for Egg. There was no sign of him in his room or in any of the dining halls, taverns or tutorial rooms.

"What are you doing here?" she exploded when she finally found him in — of all places — the library.

"Sssh," hissed Mavis, who sat in a far corner, reading a long scroll of romantic ballads. She peered suspiciously over her tortoiseshell spectacles at Clio and Egg, then went back to her reading.

"At least she made it back all right," Clio added in a slightly shushed voice. "I hear that none of the Profit lecturers returned from the ball until this morning, and several postgraduate students are still over there!"

"Well, you know what postgrad students are like," said Egg. "Anything to avoid writing their thesis."

The table in front of him was piled with hundreds of

scrolls, many of which had been untied and flattened out to be read.

"What are you doing?" said Clio. "You do know that there aren't any essays due for weeks yet?"

"It doesn't pay to leave everything to the last minute," Egg retorted. "Anyway, this isn't real work. I'm doing some private research."

Clio sat down. "About the Drak situation?"

"No," he said, a little embarrassed. "About ghosts, actually. I think my room is haunted."

"Ghosts? You're kidding, right? There's no such thing as ghosts."

Egg almost laughed out loud, but caught a stern look from Mavis just in time to turn it into a quiet snigger. "Clio, this is Mocklore. We have exploding mountains and goddess librarians and flying sheep. Why would you possibly find it difficult to believe in ghosts?"

"They're silly," said Clio. "What kind of ghost?"

"I don't really know. I've only seen her twice."

"Ahhh," said Clio, nodding her head. "A girl ghost. Now I see why you're so interested."

"It's not that," said Egg, then blushed. "I mean, it was weird. I saw her, and then I didn't see her. I mean, she vanished."

Clio pulled a face. "Sure she wasn't just one of Sean McHagrty's Ladies of Romance Past?"

"Pretty sure. She didn't seem interested in him."

She gasped in mock-surprise. "A woman who doesn't fall at his feet? How could that be?"

Egg pulled out another scroll. "You're not helping."

"Prove to me that you have a ghost and I'll help you." Clio sat quietly for at least three seconds as he started to read through the scroll. "Egg, I'm hungry. I hardly had any lunch.

Come to the Seaweed Tower with me for an early dinner. Mistress Brim is making fish surprise."

"Don't you have any other friends?" he complained, still trying to read.

"Not interesting friends who create malignant dark cities," she wheedled.

"Not funny, Clio."

"Come on. Fish surprise. Surprising food involving fish. How can you say no?"

"All right. But I'm borrowing these scrolls and you can help me find out about the ghost after dinner."

Clio made a complicated salute. "As a former Junior Sparkling Nun, I swear upon what little honour I have."

Egg started stacking the scrolls. "Good enough for me. And that's another story you have to tell me some time."

Mavis only allowed them to borrow four scrolls each, and she wouldn't let Egg take any of the local history scrolls at all unless he promised to not actually read them. While they were negotiating, Clio looked out of the window at the skybridge. "Wow. Mistress Sharpe is really taking this intimate supper thing seriously."

Egg joined her at the window. Kassa, climbing up to the bridge with the assistance of Singespitter the sheep, had dressed with Drak in mind. She was poured into a black leather bodice with silky black skirts, scarlet boots with spiked heels and a selection of bat-shaped silver jewellery. Her dark red hair was mussed and teased out in all directions. Two elegant daggers rested in black leather sheaths at her hips and several more protruded from her scarlet boots. Even the silver clips that kept her madly-arranged hair in place looked as if they might easily be used as stabbing weapons.

"She looks like a pirate queen," Clio breathed.

"A pirate queen out to seduce someone," Egg said darkly. "Do you think she'll be all right?"

Clio elbowed him. "Idiot. She's Kassa Daggersharp. You should be asking if Lord Sinistre's going to be all right."

Flying above the sky-bridge, Singespitter transformed into a slavering black beastie. This time, as well as bat wings, black fleece and fangs, he grew a wolfy tail and silver claws that went *shing* when he unsheathed them. He cawed in exultation, flicking his claws in and out.

Kassa did not visibly change. She nodded as if this was what she had expected and continued along the bridge.

"That's funny," said Egg.

"Something is funny apart from Kassa's outfit?" asked Clio.

"The sheep. It changed *before* it reached the middle of the bridge."

"That's a nasty thought. You think the dress code is spreading? We could be up to our necks in mock-goths by tomorrow morning."

"Maybe it's not just the dress code that's spreading."

Clio looked at him. "You're just full of nasty thoughts today."

Kassa felt the change. Not her clothes — the draklight evidently approved of her choices, all the way down to her silky satin underwear. Her thoughts were another story. Now she was paying attention, it was obvious that her mind had been affected by stepping across that invisible border. She felt sharper, faster, but darker as well. Less controlled. If someone jumped at her out of the shadows, she was likely to slice out his eyeballs without even thinking.

How did people live in a city like this?

Maybe they didn't. Maybe they were all figments of Egg's imagination and they only became animated when an outsider was present. But how did that explain Aragon Silversword?

Kassa's fingers grasped the hilts of her hip-daggers for a brief moment until she forced herself to slowly let go. The so-called Chamberlain of Drak had better not cross her path tonight. Here in this place of dark thoughts and chaotic impulses, she might end up killing him.

The doors of the palace of Drak opened as Kassa approached. The sinister butler bowed deeply to her. "Mistress Sharpe, you are welcome. His Lordship will receive you in the Twilight Supper Room."

"Sounds intimate," said Kassa. "Can you mind my demonic sheep?"

The butler bowed even more deeply than before. "But of course."

~

While Clio lingered to have a lengthy conversation with Mistress Brim about the healthiness of spinach versus seaweed, Egg found an empty table and set his tray down. He had decided against the fish surprise, as there had been enough surprises in his life lately without adding to them deliberately.

The doors crashed open suddenly. Sean McHagrty burst into the dining hall and looked wildly around. It was mostly empty. There was a major party over at the Split Duck Tavern, where some postgraduate students had returned from Drak and were telling salacious and scandalous stories in return for free drinks.

When Sean saw Egg, he hurried over and sat at his table. "Have you seen a girl called Meridia?"

Egg chewed a mouthful of his dinner and swallowed. "I wouldn't know what a girl called Meridia looks like."

"How about a girl called Cerulia?"

"Ditto." Egg grinned through another mouthful. "Sisters?"

"Twin sisters," Sean groaned. "They're both trying to kill me."

"And you said you had a boring time last night."

"Well, you know, compared to a demon party in a mysterious city full of women wearing velvet and black eyeliner... what are you eating?"

Egg looked down at his dinner, which consisted of a mug of spicy hot chocolate and a paper bag full of brown crunchy objects that tasted good. The warm grease was starting to seep through the bag on to his fingers. "I think it's deep-fried lobster bits," he said thoughtfully. "Or possibly something that was once part of a pig."

"Cool." Sean went over to share his winning smile with Mistress Brim.

Clio brought her tray over, glaring over her shoulder at Sean. "We're friends with him now?"

"I have to live with him all year, be nice," said Egg, crunching loudly.

"What *are* you eating?"

"Crunchy fried things in a bag. What's that you're eating? Don't tell me that's the fish surprise."

Clio poked at her plate, which was covered with an unpleasant green sludgy mess. "I decided on the seaweed surprise instead."

"Why would anyone voluntarily eat seaweed?"

"It's a new diet," she mumbled, sounding embarrassed. "Imani Almondstone told me about it. You eat nothing but seaweed and eggs for two weeks."

Egg looked at the plate thoughtfully. "Your hair will turn green," he predicted. "Also, your eyeballs. This could very well explain those blotches on Lord Ambewine's neck."

Clio sighed and picked up her tray again. "Crunchy fried things in a bag, you say?"

"Possibly lobster," Egg said with his mouth full. "Possibly pig."

"Right." She went back to Mistress Brim.

Sean returned, his tray laden with three bags of crunchy fried things. "Where's the gorgeous Daggersharp tonight? Out breaking someone else's thumb?"

"Intimate supper with Lord Sinistre of Drak," said Egg, crunching away. "I think she's either going to seduce him or assassinate him. Thumbs optional."

"Nice."

~

Singespitter escaped the butler quite easily, and set off on his mission: to poke around Drak and figure out what was going on. It was fun being a demonic beastie. The fire-breathing was a definite plus, and his new silver claws had proved more than satisfactory — a cupboard full of velvet table-cloths (now a nice collection of velvet ribbons) was evidence of that.

No more playing, though. Time to get serious. Singe-spitter set his nose into gear. He wasn't endowed with everyday sniffing skills, but ever since he had been irrevo-cably transformed into a flying sheep, he had a knack for tracking the scent of strange magical phenomena.

The trouble with Drak was that the whole city was drenched in Dark Magic, which to Singespitter's nose had a deep, cloying and utterly distracting perfume. He strained to sniff out anything that was slightly more (or slightly less) strange or magical than everything else.

Only two particularly noticeable smells came to nose: the many dangerous animals caged and prowling somewhere underneath the palace itself; and the heady aroma of toasted cheese sandwiches.

After considerable inner debate, Singespitter followed the cheese.

∾

Lord Sinistre waited.

The Twilight Supper Room was high up in the palace, a silvery balcony overlooking the spread of the night-black city of Drak. Pale, glowing moonflowers twisted around the elegant railing. If you sat in absolute stillness, you could hear the petals humming on the softest of frequencies. The tune was too gentle to recognise, but you could certainly dance to it — if it were possible to dance in absolute stillness.

Lord Sinistre had chosen his clothes very carefully for tonight. It had occurred to him that Mistress Sharpe was the kind of person who would like colours, so he searched his wardrobe for something less dark than usual. He didn't have anything.

If he couldn't be colourful — and apparently he couldn't — he could at least be dramatic. Lord Sinistre chose the boldest, most dramatic black outfit he possessed. It was a body-clinging suit of black leather, trimmed with silver and worn with fitted knee boots and a studded collar.

He could not remember ordering it. Why would anyone deliberately choose a costume so outrageous and impracti-cal? The evening was cool, but his skin was already hot and sticky. He considered changing to one of his more usual silk or velvet outfits, but those were almost as bad. None of his clothes were designed for comfort. That was what happened when you hired demons for tailors, he supposed.

Lord Sinistre was looking forward to spending time with this woman of the strange world Outside. The ladies of Drak were all far too aware of his status as their Lord and Master, which made it hard to have sensible conversations with them. He had a deliciously hopeful feeling that Mistress Sharpe had little respect for authority.

A curtain of obsidian beads shimmered, and the moon-flowers changed their pitch by a fraction of a hum. She had arrived.

Lord Sinistre moved to greet his guest. "So pleased to see you, Mistress Sharpe," he said, his voice rolling out the words in a deep, inviting growl. He wasn't doing it deliberately, it was just something his voice did from time to time.

Mistress Sharpe looked first at him, taking in the leather outfit, then quickly turned her eyes to the view of the city. "Call me Kassa. Are you having a candle shortage?"

"I shouldn't think so," said Lord Sinistre with a sigh. "I have a hundred candles in my library and there's still not enough light to read by. Perhaps it's the quality of our wax."

"Lanterns?" she suggested, still gazing down at the pointy dark buildings and long dark streets of Drak.

"Same problem." Lord Sinistre indicated the lantern above them. It flickered gently, barely bright enough to create a shadow. "Mostly at night we see by the light of the full moon."

Kassa looked up to the full white circle in the sky. "What do you do the other days of the month?"

"You mean when the moon goes behind a cloud? We all go to bed early, I'm afraid."

"No," said Kassa. "I mean when there isn't a full moon. Waxing and waning?"

Lord Sinistre frowned. "I'm not entirely sure what you mean. The moon is always full. Would you like to sit? I have a rather excellent supper planned for us."

Kassa sat, her skirts spreading wide and her bodice creaking slightly.

Lord Sinistre sat, his leather suit creaking more than slightly. He passed his hand along the railings, stroking the moonflowers. Their hum increased by a fraction.

In answer to that subtle signal, a manservant swept in, placing a covered tray on the table between Kassa and Lord Sinistre. He lifted the silver lid and moved back discreetly, back through the bead curtain.

"I hope you like violet-drenched oysters and rose-scented wine," said Lord Sinistre.

"Can't live without 'em," said Kassa Daggersharp.

~

"Cool," said Sean McHagrty. "I've never raised a ghost before. Is she pretty?"

"Very pretty," said Egg. "But that's not why I'm doing this." He and Sean sat cross-legged on the floor of their room, lighting a circle of candles around them. Clio was refusing to participate. She lay on Sean's bed with her nose in one of the local history scrolls.

"So," said Sean. "What do we do now?"

Egg produced a vial of purple sand and another scroll. "We're supposed to pour the sand and say the spell. It doesn't raise ghosts, it sort of attracts the ones that are already here."

Clio made a scornful sound. "What do you think Kassa would say if she saw you using magic for no good reason? After all those lectures about how it always goes wrong!"

"Nothing's going to go wrong," Egg said steadily. "This is barely even magic. My mother uses more incantations than this to get bread to rise. It's not a problem."

"Well," said Clio. "It says in here that four years after Cluft mysteriously reappeared, a first-year student tried to use a simple call-home spell using a remnant from the Glimmer and it exploded in his face, turning him and his entire Philosophy of Magic class into a stampede of frightened hedgehogs."

"You're making that up," accused Egg.

"It's required reading for next week's tutorial, actually."

Egg rolled his eyes and opened the vial of purple sand. He poured it on the carpet, nodding at Sean. Together, they recited, "Spirits of the walls and stones, spirits of the hearth and broom, spirits of the earth and sky, please be welcome in this room."

"I wonder how many ghosts are stored up in the walls and stones of Cluft," Clio said thoughtfully. "A lot of people must have died here over the last hundred years, and you've just given all of them an open invitation. Hooray."

"Are we going to be able to get that out of the carpet?" asked Sean, looking at the heap of purple sand. "We paid a cleaning bond for this room."

Egg stared up at Dahla. She stood with her bare feet on the purple sand, looking confused. "Don't either of you see her? She's right here."

"Right where?" asked Sean and Clio in unison.

~

The cheesy, toasty smell led Singespitter directly to the kitchens, and to Aragon Silversword.

The Chamberlain of Drak sat at a large table, about to start on his supper. Singespitter crawled into a corner where other dark, demonic beasties had gathered to drink from bowls with their names on. Some of the creatures sniffed curiously at Singespitter, but they kept their distance as long as he did not go near their bowls. He settled down to eavesdrop comfortably.

"Thanks, Sherrie," said Aragon, picking up a piece of cheesy toast and then dropping it because it was hot. He blew on his fingers.

"You couldn't feed a spider on the food his Lordship insists on," said the Head Cook, arranging four violet-drenched oysters on a thin crystal plate with a harebell garnish. She slid the plate into a cupboard and rang a small bell. A dark green demon appeared in the cupboard, seized the plate, gibbered briefly and then vanished.

Aragon stared at the cheese on toast. "Do you remember when I started working here, by any chance?"

Sherrie sat at the table opposite him and began to slice peeled prawns into slivers with a wickedly sharp knife. "Bless me, but you've always worked here, haven't you? Like the rest of us." She shook her head and corrected herself. "No, that's silly. I remember your first day. You just turned up, all of a sudden like."

"How long ago?" he asked. "Do you remember?"

"Well, it was before the fancy dress gala, wasn't it. But I don't think you were here for the vampire cotillion..." She counted on her fingers. "Less than half a year, then. Fancy that. It feels longer."

"That's what I thought." Aragon bit into the toast and chewed. "Do you remember me saying anything strange when I arrived? About where I came from?"

Sherrie laughed heartily. "I'll say. You were rude to Lord Sinistre, I wouldn't forget that in a hurry. Although I did, didn't I? Until now."

"He must have forgotten, too."

"Lucky for you! I've never seen him so purple. Don't imagine anyone had been so rude to him in his whole life. I remember you shouting about another world, all bright colours and such. But then you settled down and got on with being Chamberlain. You never mentioned where you'd come from again."

"I forgot," Aragon said softly. "I forgot who I was."

"Funny what you forget, isn't it?" mused Sherrie. "I thought I'd always remember you being rude to Lord Sinistre, but I haven't given it a moment's thought until you mentioned it just now."

"Funny what you forget," Aragon agreed. He stood up, leaving the remains of his cheesy toast. "Sorry, Sherrie. I've lost my appetite. Better go look at the state of the accounts after that damned ball."

"Don't forget that those demons in Brimstone Street are charging extra for violets and nasturtium flowers," said Sherrie. "Honestly, at those prices you'd think they grew the dratted things instead of just magicking them out of thin air."

"I'll have a word with them," Aragon promised. "We'll see if they still insist on the price rise after I tell them the palace demons are close to cracking flower magic. They made half a bluebell yesterday."

"Are bluebells edible?"

"It's amazing how edible people think something is when you coat it in sugar."

"You're telling me," Sherrie giggled. "That's one of my favourite tricks. I say, have you seen his Lordship's supper guest? I had a peek at her when she came in the front door. Such a lovely girl, I hope it all works out for them. It would ever so nice to have a proper Lady of Drak. And a wedding! Wouldn't I just love to get my hands on a wedding feast..."

"Well, now," said Aragon. "That would be an amazing thing."

Sherrie gave him a surprised look. "You sounded almost sarcastic there, Chamberlain. That isn't like you."

"So I hear," he sighed.

After Aragon left, Singespitter slunk out of his hiding

place. He wasn't sure if he had discovered anything useful from that little exchange. Time to see if Drak had a library.

To Singespitter, old parchment was almost as easy to track by scent as magic and cheesy toast. He trotted away from the kitchens, sniffing madly. Aha. That smelled promising. If he didn't discover anything useful, at least he could find something to read until Kassa was finished with her intimate supper. It was a plan with no drawbacks.

~

The violet-drenched oysters with rose-scented wine were exquisite. So were the prawn slivers in hazelnut syrup and the braised peacock's tongues with peach-cantaloupe dressing. Exquisite, elegant, delicate... Kassa was starting to long for steak and mashed potato or a toasted cheese sandwich, something she could wrap her mouth around. At this rate, they could be eating for weeks before she felt full.

Then again, intimate suppers were not just about food. They were also about flirtation, and Kassa was getting extra helpings of that.

Lord Sinistre flattered. He growled compliments in that sultry voice of his, and gazed at Kassa as if she were the most intriguing, fascinating person he had ever met. She knew he was insincere, he just had to be, but the damn man wasn't letting his act slip.

And he was wearing leather. A gorgeous man in black leather, with smouldering eyes and a sexy voice, who just happened to rule a city. Kassa couldn't help enjoying herself.

Except...

He really hadn't let anything slip. Not a crumb, not a clue. No hint about what Drak was, why it was here, or whether Lord Sinistre even knew the answer to such questions. It was difficult for Kassa to justify her presence here at all.

Act like a heroine, she told herself furiously. *Ask the difficult questions, get him angry enough to reveal something. Make him lock you up in his dungeon, villains love to confess when they've got you under lock and key, and this one looks like he might be handy with the handcuffs.*

Mmm, handcuffs. Wait, where was I?

This, of course, was assuming that Lord Sinistre actually was a villain. Was she prejudiced against him, because he wore black leather and made dramatic entrances? Kassa sighed.

The next dish was presented by another effortlessly tactful manservant. It was a rose-shaped plate made from ice, a delicate sculpture scattered with tiny diamonds of sugar. In the centre of the outrageously elegant plate was a single, paper-thin slice of pear. Kassa peered at it in the dim candle-light, hoping to see a drizzle of chocolate or a rosette of cream to liven up the minuscule slice of fruit. There wasn't any.

"Ah, dessert," said Lord Sinistre, his eyes gleaming.

This was ridiculous. She had eaten exactly five and a half mouthfuls of food in the last three hours and they called this dessert? Hunger made Kassa irritable. She flashed her most seductive smile at Lord Sinistre, lifted her delicate flute of lemon-scented wine and clinked it against his.

A second later, she dropped the glass.

It looked like an accident, easy enough to do when distracted by an attractive man in a black leather suit. The crystal was so expensively fragile that it shattered on impact with the ice-plate, which also shattered.

Kassa leaped back, but not before her skirt was soaked with pale wine, ice and glass shards. The slice of pear slid off the table and flopped along the balcony, leaping to freedom beyond the intricate moon-flower railings. She couldn't blame it in the least.

The tactful manservants were instantly there, three of them whisking cloths and brushes and fresh plates of dessert back and forth. The table was immaculate again within thirty seconds. A maid appeared, her gentle hand brushing against Kassa's arm. Before Kassa realised what was happening, she was guided through the shimmering obsidian curtain, down the corridor and into a luscious wash chamber.

When three more maids turned up with racks of fresh clothes for Kassa to try on, she rolled her eyes and pushed them all out into the corridor, protesting that she could towel her skirt dry without assistance. They obeyed without question.

Kassa breathed, glad to be alone for a few seconds. She ran her thumb over the fabric of her skirt, murmuring an incantation and removing all traces of the wine. That done, she was free to examine the wash chamber at her leisure. The tiles, fittings and flickering candelabra were all black, with details and leaf-patterns picked out in gold. She had no doubt somehow that it was gold, not gilt.

More importantly, the wash chamber had doors. Doors other than the door she had entered, which was guarded by the battalion of maids who waited to escort her back to Lord Sinistre and the pear slices.

It would be easy to pretend she had walked through the wrong door by accident and found herself lost in a maze of unfamiliar corridors. With any luck, she would have time to have a good snoop round before one of them caught her.

Kassa opened one of the doors and peered through. This looked promising.

It was a gorgeous corridor, walled in red velvet curtains. Kassa practically drooled at the fabric — she had always wanted red velvet sails for her pirate ship! But that thought belonged to another life. She missed the *Splashdance*, with its flickering silver walls and cheerful crew. Well, not exactly cheerful. To be honest, most of them were miserable half the time, bitching about the dry rations or complaining that Kassa had turned one of them into a frog.

Still, *she* had been happy. Captain of a ship, mistress of all she commanded, even a ragtag crew of reprobates and misfits. *And traitors,* she reminded herself. *Don't forget traitors.*

Kassa pushed open one door and stared at the largest swimming pool she had ever seen, a massive heart-shape glimmering in the moonlight, with dark scarlet tiles that made the water look like blood. She closed the door quickly, moving on down the corridor.

Would they notice if half a hundred-weight of red velvet went mysteriously missing? She was sure they wouldn't go short, there must be an army of velvet makers in this city to supply the demand. The only problem was transporting it unseen back to her room in Cluft, but she was getting pretty good with the flying spells these days, and Singespitter might help out if she promised him a natty red velvet waistcoat in return…

How did you make velvet anyway?

Enough daydreaming, Kassa told herself sternly. *Act like a heroine, damn it. You can't go back to the kids and admit you didn't find out a single clue about the damn city but you're going steady with the Lordling!*

She opened another door. This was a cupboard filled with scrolls. Kassa unrolled one eagerly, but it was a supply list for the kitchens. Apparently they went through a lot of honey, saffron, lovage and smoked parrot livers on a weekly basis. Kassa didn't bother looking at the other scrolls. Housekeeping bored her.

She walked a little further down the velvet-lined corridor, opened a third door and gazed with sudden shock at Aragon Silversword.

He sat at a gleaming mahogany desk, shuffling through

papers. The walls were dark green and lined with shelves of book buckets. The moonlight shone through the window, illuminating his dark blond hair. He looked up and saw her.

"Kassa."

The night before, he had seemed confused, as if he wasn't sure whom she was or even whom he was. Not this time. He leaped up, slamming his hands against the polished desk, scattering papers everywhere. His grey eyes bored into her.

"Kassa, we have to talk!"

She ran. There was no excuse, except wanting very much not to hear the answers to her many questions. She fled down the corridor of red velvet, spun around a corner, found a door and threw herself through it, slamming the door behind her.

Kassa closed her eyes, leaning against the door and breathing. There was no other sound. Was he looking for her? Was he even bothering?

A quiet swishing sound alerted her to the fact that she was not the only presence in the room. Kassa opened her eyes.

It was a perfectly ordinary room. Ordinary for Drak. Gold wallpaper, blood-red furniture, a few portraits of grim-looking lords and ladies, a fireplace that looked as if it had never been used, a spiralling vortex of darkness where a window should be...

Kassa stared into the depths of the vortex. She could see light within its darkness, shimmering colours that she could neither name nor recognise. They whirled invitingly at her. She felt a seductive pull that urged her to step a little closer, let herself be swallowed whole by the spinning, sucking force of shadow. She could even hear something like a voice in her mind. *Step inside, feel our power, taste the light and darkness of the universe...*

Kassa Daggersharp had never wanted anything so much

as she now wanted to step inside that spiralling vortex and lose her mind and body within its dark layers.

Needless to say, she kept her distance.

~

Dahla was weeping. Her tangled, coppery hair was a mess around her face and shoulders. The tears fell fast and hard as she sobbed, her body crumpling up on the floor as if she had been given the worst news of her lifetime. She looked human, and broken.

"I still don't see her," said Clio, as if she thought he was making it up.

"Where is she?" asked Sean, waving his hand dangerously near Dahla's head.

Egg reached out and stopped him. "Don't do that. You might hurt her."

"That's right, McHagrty," said Clio. "Mustn't hurt Egg's imaginary friend."

"She's crying," said Egg furiously, trying to comfort Dahla. "You're upsetting her."

Dahla's tears spilled down, splashing on to Egg's outstretched hand. They looked so real. How could she be a ghost?

"Oh gods," said Sean, staring down at Egg's hand. "Tell me that's you sweating really hard."

Egg thrust out his hand. "You can see them? These are her tears. Taste them and see."

Sean stepped back quickly. "No thanks!"

Clio sat up, looking strangely at them both. "I will," she said.

Egg stretched out his hand, holding it steady. Whole tears still glistened on his skin. "Can you see them?"

"I don't see anything," said Clio. She ran her finger along

the back of his hand and put it in her mouth. Her eyes widened. "Those *are* tears!" She looked closely at his eyes. "Not yours."

"Hers," said Egg, indicating Dahla.

Clio knelt down, gazing at the empty space. "I'm sorry if I upset you," she whispered.

Dahla stopped crying and looked at Clio. She pushed her tangled coppery hair back out of her wet face, her eyes fixed on the other girl.

"It wasn't you," said Egg. "At least, not just you. Maybe it's because you couldn't see her. No one would enjoy being invisible."

"Then it's my fault, too," said Sean, crouching beside Clio. "Sorry, babe," he added to the invisible presence of Dahla.

Dahla did not even seem to register Sean's presence. It was Clio she was fascinated with.

"What's her name?" Clio asked.

The door banged open, revealing Kassa Daggersharp in all her Drak-inspired black and scarlet finery. "You will not believe the evening I have had!" she announced. Singespitter landed on the window sill and spat a fat scroll of parchment on to the carpet.

Clio looked quickly at Egg. "She's gone," he told her. "I think loud noises startle her." He wiped the last trace of Dahla's tears on his trousers and looked up at Kassa. "What's the news on Drak?"

Kassa flopped on Egg's bed. "The news is, we're in trouble. Why are you all sitting on the floor?"

7

CLOAK AND DAGGER

"*T*he first thing to worry about," said Kassa, "is that the draklight is spreading. When did this happen in those stories of yours, Egg, and what can we do to stop it?"

"It didn't," said Egg. "I didn't! There wasn't any draklight in my stories, there was hardly any magic at all." He hesitated. "Well, there were demons doing everything, and since there weren't any farms I suppose there must have been magic to produce food and so on, but I never really mentioned it. There wasn't magic spreading all over, making people dark and mysterious. There was nowhere for it to spread."

Kassa frowned. "Why not? Where was Drak, in your stories?"

Egg shrugged. "Just in a wasteland, really. The city was cut off from everywhere else by this desolate wasteland of grit and rock and…"

"Sand?" Kassa suggested. She stuck out her boots. Fine flecks of silvery sand were encrusted around her heels. "On my way home, I started wondering why we crossed to Drak by the skybridge when we could just as easily walk there from here. So I walked back at ground level. This stuff—" she picked at the silvery grains, "—is everywhere outside the paving stones of Drak, until the draklight ends and the green grass starts up again."

"That's worrying," said Clio.

"It's bloody frightening," said Kassa. "Drak is attempting to recreate its natural environment. At this rate, the draklight could reach Cluft in less than a week. Within a month or two, Mocklore may no longer exist. We'll all be living in... Drakland." She sighed. "Why a *wasteland*, Egg? Why not rolling meadows and verdant fields?"

Egg didn't say anything.

"So what did you discover in the city itself?" Clio asked Kassa.

"Nothing entirely useful," Kassa admitted. "Lord Sinistre's idea of an intimate supper wouldn't keep a gnat alive, they have more red velvet than any one city strictly needs, and their candles don't work very well. Oh, and it's always a full moon over there."

"That's impossible," said Sean. "Isn't it? Why would they have a full moon over there when we have an ordinary moon over here?"

Everyone looked at Egg.

"It's easier to draw," he said, staring at his feet.

"What a fascinating new world we're going to find ourselves in," sighed Kassa.

Singespitter snorted loudly, tapping the large scroll he had brought with him.

"I see your snooping produced more tangible results than mine," said Kassa. "Anything good?" She reached for the scroll, unrolling it.

A movement caught Egg's eye, and he looked at the window. "The Cloak!"

Kassa whirled towards the window. "What? Where? Was

he that pompous costumed one who vanquished the musician demons?"

"Um, yes, him. He was at the window just now," said Egg. "I think he was listening to us."

"Interesting." Kassa went to the window, flung it open and climbed out. "I want a word with this Cloak person."

"She does realise this is three floors up, doesn't she?" said Sean.

By the time the three of them reached the window, Kassa was clambering down the face of the building with apparent ease, her skirts hitched up around her waist. "What should I know about this bloke?" she called up to Egg.

"I told you, he's the Cloak," he yelled down. "Bringer of order to chaos, maker of justice for all!"

Kassa landed neatly on the ground. "No, I mean who is he under that cloak of his? What sort of person?"

Egg hesitated. "I hadn't worked that out yet!"

"Oh, fine," Kassa muttered. "You'd think if the powers that be wanted a fictional city brought to life, they'd find one that was finished!" She ran off across the courtyard, in the direction of Drak.

Clio reached out and slammed the window closed, almost catching Egg's knuckles. He drew his hands back quickly. "What's your problem?"

"You were lying," she snapped. "You just lied to her, Egg. I don't believe you haven't figured out every single detail about those heroes of yours. You keep telling us that it wasn't the city you were interested in, it was the characters. So what are you hiding about this particular character?"

The cloaked figure ran over the skybridge. Kassa thought she was being clever to take the other route, running hard across the grass in an attempt to get to Drak before he did. It meant taking a detour to hop over the canals, but she was still gaining on him. As she passed into the draklight, her mind came alive with dark impulses and morbid thoughts. Sand crunched under her boots, and although she felt strong enough to run forever, the sand slowed her down.

By the time she reached the firm paving stones of Drak, the cloaked figure was nowhere in sight. Kassa stood for a moment, breathing hard. She had come too far to just wander back and get on with her evening.

If the Cloak was a true hero of the city, the bringer of order and maker of justice as Egg claimed, a little injustice might just bring him out of the stonework.

Time to do some damage.

~

Clio ran to the chest of drawers, thumbing her way frantically through the inky parchments and papyri.

"It's not there," Egg told her. "My note tablet is in my book bag over there."

Clio turned on him. "You're carrying it around with you? *Are you still writing the story?*"

Egg bit his lip. "I couldn't help myself after the ball. Seeing Drak for real. I didn't draw anything else, I just made a few notes. And maybe Kassa's right — an unfinished story is more dangerous than a finished one."

"And maybe Kassa really needed to know who was under that cloak," Clio hurled back. "Tell me, Egg!"

He took a deep breath. "I think you already know who it is. You wouldn't be so pissed off, otherwise."

~

The park was beautiful, just like everything else in this city. The shadowy statues and fountains were exquisitely sculpted and shaped. Glowing moonflowers illuminated the delicate paths. The whole gorgeous display was lightly dappled with silvery light from the full moon.

A perfect, blood-coloured marble rendition of a bird of paradise shattered against the whispering fountain. A dark marble peacock soon joined it, spraying stone chips into the water.

Kassa Daggersharp was on the rampage.

A pretty young couple, interrupted from their romantic walk, stared in horror at the woman who was smashing fine art in front of their eyes. She ran at them, her golden eyes flashing. "Hand over your valuables!"

"A vandal and a thief," gasped the young man. He wore velvet, not surprisingly, and his face was outlined with more white powder and black mascara than that of his girlfriend.

"Absolutely," said Kassa. "If you don't mind, I'm on a tight schedule." She grasped a string of buttery black pearls from around the young lady's neck and tugged.

The string broke. Black pearls flew madly into the air and rained down around them. The young lady fainted and her male companion caught her expertly, glaring at Kassa. A hand smacked down on Kassa's shoulder, spinning her around.

"I am the Cloak, Bringer of Order to Chaos, Maker of Justice for All," thundered the cloaked figure. Even staring directly under the grey hood and into his face, Kassa could see nothing but a haze of grey. "You will cease your criminal activities immediately."

The couple both burst into tears and ran away, their heels clattering against the fine black paving stones of the path.

Kassa grinned. "I was hoping I would run into you."

"You will turn aside from your anti-social behaviour," boomed the hero.

A sudden thought flashed through Kassa's mind. *If he's the hero, am I the villain?* "Make me," she snarled and threw herself at him.

It was a long time since Kassa had been in a fight, not counting the thumb-wrestling with young McHagrty, or the time Master Fitzdeath tried to steal her tutorial room, and she was forced to teach him the error of his ways with a scalding coffee pot and a wooden ruler.

This was different. It was a fight without weapons — a rolling, punching, ducking affair, only a few rungs up from a scuffle. The draklight flooded Kassa's mind, overpowering her. Only by a great force of effort did she manage to not draw any of her silver-hilted knives.

It was unfair, really, because the Cloak did have one weapon, even if it wasn't of the stabbing, slicing, swiping variety. He had his cloak, and the cloak had a life of its own. It was warm and soft to the touch, but also weirdly amorphous. When Kassa hit at it, it made a sucking sound, apparently softening the blow. Every time she touched the cloak, it made her feel less controlled than ever. Drak was taking over her mind.

She couldn't pin him to the ground because his cloak would slide him away from her grip, and he was equally unable to gain the upper hand over her. The fight could go on all night at this rate, and Kassa was tiring.

The nearby fountain was ringed with nasty silver spikes. Kassa heaved against the Cloak's body, trying to catch him off-balance.

Not that I'm trying to impale him, her horrified inner mind insisted, struggling up through the crowding Drak-induced thoughts of darkness and chaotic violence. *I just want to...hook that cloak of his on something sharp. That's a good idea. Something sharp.*

Kassa shoved the Cloak one last time and the sucking grey fabric of the Cloak's cloak caught itself nicely on the silver spikes. Kassa brought her legs up in a sideways scissor kick. The cloak held fast and the man within rolled free.

Kassa threw herself on him, holding his head still so she could see whom she had been fighting. She stared at him, and he stared back at her with cool grey eyes.

~

"I don't get it!" Sean McHagrty yelled as the three of them tore madly across the skybridge that led to Drak. Well, Clio was tearing madly. The two boys were just trying to catch up. "What's the problem with this Chamberlain being the Cloak?"

"No problem," Egg yelled back. "But we found out at the ball that the Chamberlain is Clio's uncle!"

"Right!" said Sean, breathing hard. "What's the problem with Clio's uncle?"

"He's Aragon Silversword," Clio screamed behind her, as she slid down the far end of the golden bridge. Her neat tunic and skirt had become a purple velvet ballgown, and her hair swept itself up into a spiral of ringlets and hairpins. "Don't they have any casual clothes in this city?" she shrieked, stumbling on gold stiletto sandals.

Once again, the city had given Egg warlock's robes. He tossed the pointed hat and dangling charm-necklaces over the side of the bridge. "Silversword and Kassa have a history," he started to explain, but Sean — now wearing a midnight-blue evening suit with satin cape — waved him to silence. "No, I get it from there. I know who Aragon Silversword is.

I'm still not entirely sure why we're running. How much of an emergency could this be?"

"She's a woman scorned," Clio said. "You should know more than anyone how dangerous that is."

"This isn't a tragic romance, Clio, it's real life," said Egg.

Clio scowled at him. "Not tragic yet, you mean. We could have stopped this if you had the guts to tell her."

"You don't think she would have run after him anyway?" Egg snapped back. "I didn't want to be there when she found out!"

"What's the worst that could happen?" said Sean.

"I suppose the shock could kill her," Egg mumbled.

"To hell with that," growled Clio. She picked one of the dark streets and started running again. "I'm more worried that she'll kill him!"

They were both panting from the fight, and their bodies were dangerously close. Aragon pushed himself up on his elbows, looking at Kassa. "What took you so long?" he said breathlessly.

She stabbed him.

It wasn't Egg's idea for them to split up, but he wasn't game to challenge Clio in her current mood.

He walked through a slate-lined street, gazing up at the high walls of the black buildings of Drak. He paused to look at a cathedral that he remembered scribbling in a margin when he was bored. His drawings had become a solid city that you could walk around in.

And get lost in.

Egg wasn't rushing. None of them had any idea where Kassa or the Cloak might have gone, and he didn't expect to run into them tonight. Drak was a fair-sized city, and no matter what thoughts Clio had of rushing to the rescue, the chances were that it was already too late.

It was weird to think of the Cloak and the others as being flesh and blood. Egg's favourite storyline had always been that of the Chamberlain, who became a mysterious hero in his spare time. Whenever there was a lull in his palace duties, he would throw on his magical cloak and run out into the night streets of Drak, a shining beacon of hope to the downtrodden citizens. He was Egg's first hero, a character he had been working on since he was twelve years old.

But he was also Clio's uncle, and Kassa's ex-lover. Aragon Silversword was the former Champion of the Empire who had betrayed Emperor Timregis and thrown Mocklore into chaos, before reinventing himself as a pirate and then, a year or two later, mysteriously disappearing. It explained a lot, really. It all fit with what Egg had designed for the Chamberlain — he was supposed to have a mysterious, complicated past.

The Chamberlain didn't belong to Egg anymore. None of them did. It was no longer his story. He wasn't the one deciding on what happened next. He had no control over any of it. But who were fictional characters and who were real people? How could you tell the difference?

A shadow flickered above Egg's head. He craned his neck upwards. Was there someone standing there, up on the spiralling towers of the cathedral? There, between the ears of one of the larger obsidian gargoyles. A man — no, he was gone again.

Of course. Egg groaned. So obvious. It had to be Invisiblo the Mystery Man, who could turn invisible due to a near-fatal wound he had received from the claw of an invisible eagle. Egg stood in the shadows, staring fixedly at the patch of nothing above the gargoyle. A moment later, Invisiblo's body turned visible. He was a slender, slightly muscled man in a blue eye mask, his whole body covered in a tight suit of blue and white checks.

A blur of purple and white flew out of the sky, striking Invisiblo and knocking him off the gargoyle. He skidded across the sloped roof of the cathedral, landing awkwardly between two more shiny black gargoyles. "You!" he yelled.

Egg watched in amazement. This was Dream Girl, who had received her powers of flight and supernatural senses from the exotic tribe who made her one of their own after they rescued her from a shipwreck as a baby. She wore a white domino mask, white catsuit and glossy purple wig. "I can't believe you did that!" she screamed at Invisiblo.

"What?" he said. "What did I do?"

"We were supposed to be fighting crime together," said Dream Girl. "But no, you take on every bad guy yourself. Every time I had one of them cornered, you jumped in and knocked him unconscious."

"That's what we do," said Invisiblo. "We fight the bad guys, leave them unconscious. It's our job."

"Ours, not yours," she said, shaking her bouncy purple wig. "Is it because I'm a girl? You think I'm so weak I can't handle a little action?"

"I'm sorry if you think I hogged all the glory, but you need to get over yourself."

"Me? If you can't trust me to do my fair share of the fighting, this Heroes of Justice thing isn't going to work."

"I thought it was a stupid idea anyway," said Invisiblo. "But you were all, 'Oh yes, Mr Cloak. We'll team up, Mr Cloak. Whatever you say, Mr Cloak.' You make me sick."

"You make me sicker!" She raised her hand to slap him, but Invisiblo caught it.

"For the record," he said in a low voice. "I don't think you're weak. I think you're beautiful."

She stared at him for a long moment. They leaned forward to kiss, but their masks bumped together. They laughed awkwardly, and removed their masks so that they could kiss properly. Which they did. At length.

Egg was still staring up at them from the street below. He couldn't believe it. Every word, every movement of that scene was his own. He had written that dialogue, word for word, and lettered it in precise inky letters. It sounded really stupid when you heard it out loud.

The kiss ended. "Let's go and find some bad guys," breathed Invisiblo. "I'll stand back and watch while you beat them up."

"Sounds like a plan," said Dream Girl. She gripped him around the waist, flying them both down to ground level. They pulled on their masks and ran off down the black cobbled street, hand in hand.

Egg watched them go in absolute horror. Before they replaced their masks, he had seen their faces clearly in the moonlight.

Invisiblo was Sean McHagrty, and Dream Girl was Clio.

~

Aragon awoke. He drifted up from oblivion, hovered for a moment around the thought that he should be dead, and finally crashed into the undeniable reality that *he was not in his own bed.*

He opened his eyes, staring at the ceiling. Ordinary enough. Not black, though. The walls were not black, either. It was a cheery room with sunlight streaming in through the windows. How long was it since he had been this close to sunlight?

The Chamberlain has never seen sunlight.
But I'm the Chamberlain, aren't I?
No, I'm Aragon Silversword.
Can't I be both?
Apparently so.

The quilt on the bed was patchwork, a merry combination of colours and fabrics. He had never seen it before, but it seemed familiar somehow. One rough patch of green lace was particularly striking — hadn't he seen that fabric before? Not in a quilt, though. A long green skirt worn over black boots...

Aragon sat up and looked around the room. It was messy. Dozens of scrolls and papers were heaped over a desk, garments were strewn over all the furniture, and some half-finished sewing projects were pinned to the walls. Several large wooden chests were stacked in one corner, and Aragon didn't have to look inside them to know that one contained the collected memorabilia of a pirate family, another was stuffed full of silver jewellery, and the third held a significant quantity of sexy lingerie.

Once his eyes adjusted to the sunlight that filled the room, he spotted the large white sheep sitting in a deck chair on the balcony. The sheep wore a straw hat and sipped from a beer mug.

"Ah," said Aragon Silversword. This was Kassa's room. If Kassa was living in one of a hundred identical caves, he would be able to tell which one was hers. For a start, it would be the one with the sheep on the balcony.

The thought of Kassa made Aragon frown. Why was she living in a room, and not the cabin on her ship? Why was he lying in her bed and not her hammock? More to the point, how the hell had he gotten here? He tried to think back.

I was in the palace, then I was in the park.
How did I get to the park?

Doesn't matter, move on.

Kassa was there, and...she stabbed us.

What do you mean us, man? Pull yourself together. You are one person.

Which one person are we, Aragon Silversword or the Chamberlain?

Damned if I know.

Aragon pushed back the covers. He appeared to be shirtless, another hint that Kassa was nearby. The skin of his stomach was smooth, without any recent scars or wounds, but he had been stabbed. Hadn't he?

You mean we, right?

Look, I warned you about that...

"You're lucky," said a clear voice. It was not a matter of recognising her. That voice was directly plugged into Aragon's veins. His pulse began to race.

"Lucky," he said. "Care to explain that?"

A door slammed shut and Kassa walked into his field of vision. "Lucky that I've been brushing up on healing spells," she said, her voice even chillier than his own. "The anti-stabbing one is a particular favourite."

"Well now," said Aragon. "I can see how that might be useful."

He just looked at her for a while, trying to figure out what was different. Her hair was just as wild, the same dark blood colour. She wore emerald green skirts over white petticoats, a firm bodice over a floaty chemise, a dozen silver bangles on each arm and a black eyepatch as a hair accessory. Kassa's idea of work clothes — the costume of a pirate queen. There was nothing new here.

Nothing but the look in her eyes, and the way she held herself. *She's grown up*, he found himself thinking. *She's honed that frivolous streak of hers into something dangerous. And I wasn't around to see her do it.*

119

"So," said Kassa, still unfriendly. "You're a Chamberlain now. That's different."

It was coming back to him, how Aragon thought and talked. Being with Kassa made it easier to shrug on the old persona. The secret was to balance out the coldness with the arrogance... "Being second-in-command is my role in life, apparently. A Chamberlain of Drak isn't much unlike a Champion of an Empire, or a lieutenant to a pirate captain. Not so much sword work, of course. And the hours are better."

"Does Lord Sinistre know that you betrayed your last three employers?" asked Kassa.

"Why don't you ask him? The two of you are remarkably intimate, on such short acquaintance. Romantic suppers on the moonflower balcony? You've changed your style."

Kassa grinned suddenly. "You've certainly changed yours, Silversword. The Cloak who Walks in the Night, Bringer of Order and Maker of Justice? It's the funniest thing I've heard all semester. Since when did you play the hero?"

What's she talking about?

Don't look at me!

Aragon tried to disguise his confusion, but apparently he had lost that knack along with his memory and sanity.

"You don't know," Kassa said in amazement. "You really don't know." She snatched up a billowy garment from the nearest chair. A grey cloak with a peculiar sheen to it.

"I've heard of the Cloak, of course," said Aragon, trying to sound calm. "One of those costumed freaks who turned up at the ball and killed those damned demons that slipped through security."

"And I suppose you were in the kitchens when the Cloak and his friends made their dramatic appearance," Kassa said sarcastically.

Aragon straightened the pillows behind him. It was difficult to maintain dignity while sitting up in someone else's bed. He would have got out by now, but he wasn't sure where his trousers were. Difficult to maintain dignity without trousers. "As a matter of fact, I was."

"It's a good alibi," she said. "Lord Sinistre knows you're always off doing the hundred or so little tasks that he needs you to get done. Easy enough to slip out of the city and perform a few good deeds before bedtime."

Aragon was astonished at the very thought of it. "Good deeds?"

Kassa threw the cloak around herself. She seemed taller, more muscular. "I am the Cloak who Walks in the Night," she boomed.

"You look silly."

She whirled the cloak off, becoming Kassa again. "*I* look silly? I wasn't the one patrolling the streets, hero boy. I was the villainess messing up the Cloak's precious city, and when I tore the cloak off him, who did I find underneath?"

We're missing something, Aragon thought wildly. *What happened last night?*

I was reviewing the list of new poison tasters with Lord Sinistre, replied the Chamberlain. *Then I walked down a corridor, then... suddenly we were in the park and you were in control, staring up at Lord Sinistre's new girlfriend and remembering everything about who you were, who she was to you. And then...*

"You stabbed me," Aragon said aloud.

"You left me!" retorted Kassa.

He laughed at that. "For the life of me, I can't remember why."

Kassa's expression hardened, but not before he saw the hurt in her eyes.

I always knew I'd end up hurting her. It never occurred to me that it might be accidental.

"If you'll excuse me," she said stiffly. "I have some investigating to do."

"I have work of my own," he replied. Aragon had no objections to playing the 'who can outfrost the other' game. It gave him time to figure out what was going on. "If you don't mind locating my clothes, I'll be heading back to Drak."

Kassa's eyes gleamed. "I don't think so, Silversword. I want to keep you exactly where you are for the time being."

This was not a game he enjoyed. "How were you planning to keep me here, Kassa?" He swung his legs out from under the quilt, trousers or no trousers.

Kassa's hand moved, and something sparkled through the air between them. Aragon yawned, overcome by a wave of lethargy. "A spell," he whispered. "You swore you'd never use your magic on me again, Daggersharp. You promised."

"We both made promises, Aragon," said Kassa. "Very few of them were kept." A swirl of pale grey passed over her face as she threw the cloak over herself. Her skirts swished as she headed for the door. "Sweet dreams, my hero."

Aragon gave up, allowing his eyelids to droop closed as the enchanted sleep washed over him.

Clio awoke. Her mouth felt gritty and strange. She yawned, stretched, and almost rolled right off the roof. She became fully alert at the last moment and managed to grab hold of a passing chimney before she skidded off the shiny black tiles altogether. Gasping, she stared over the edge of the sloped roof. It was a long drop to the ground. The black, shiny ground that matched the black, shiny roof and the black, shiny chimney.

She was still in Drak.

Clio scrambled up the roof, trying to find somewhere stable (or at least unsloping) to steady herself while she gathered her thoughts. The roof flattened out near the top and she sat there for a moment, trying not to panic.

There was a groan. A tile slid off the side of the roof, shattering below. Sean McHagrty emerged from behind a gable. "What a night. It must have been bloody good, I can't remember a thing and my head's about to fall off."

Clio's own head was pounding, but she had more than that to worry about. "What are you—" she demanded. "No, forget that. What am *I* doing here?"

"Don't ask me, babe. Looks like we shared a wild night on the tiles." Sean chuckled, slapping the side of the roof. "Get it? Tiles."

Clio wasn't laughing. "How could we have fallen asleep on a rooftop? Why am I with you? What happened to Egg?"

"How would I know? Maybe he caught up with Uncle Silversword and Auntie Daggersharp. Gods, I feel bad. We need breakfast."

"We need to get down from this roof," said Clio. "How did we even get up here in the first place? I don't see any ladders."

"Got another stumper for you," said Sean. He pointed across the other rooftops of Drak. They were high enough to have a view beyond the city, of the golden skybridge and the shambling towers of Cluft. "It's morning over there. See the light?"

"So?"

"So, honeybunch, it isn't morning here. Or hadn't you noticed?"

He was right, damn him. It wasn't just Clio's heavy eyelids that made it seem so dark around here. The stars were still sparkling in a twilight sky above them. The moon was full and high. On the far side of the sky-bridge, the twilight was sharply cut off by a blaze of morning sunshine.

It was morning in Cluft and evening in Drak.

8

A COMPELLING PROPOSAL

*T*he Chamberlain was asleep, completely knocked out by Kassa's lethargy spell. This was a good thing, because Aragon was awake. Even with the spell dragging on his body and brain, part of him was alert and himself. More himself than he had been in a long time.

Half a year, Sherrie said. I've been trapped in that damn city for six moons, bowing and scraping to the whims of that posturing idiot of a Lordling. Look out, world. Aragon Silversword is back and he's going to make some changes around here. For a start, he's going to open his eyes.

Painfully, Aragon prised his eyelids apart. Kassa's room was a chaotic blur. He willed himself to get past the restrictions of the spell, to stay awake for as long as he possibly could. Kassa must not be allowed to get away with this. Who knew what kind of trouble she was up to while he snuggled under her blankets?

He managed to raise himself up on his elbows. By the light, he guessed it was late morning. Singespitter was no longer on the balcony. Kassa was gone, too. Aragon was alone — except for the vision that stood beside the window.

She was a wispy figure of a girl with soft, coppery clouds of hair floating around her shoulders. She smelled of perfumed smoke and something else — a familiar scent. Her eyes were red with tears, but she was not crying. She looked at Aragon and attempted to smile.

"Ah," he said softly. "Hallucinations now. Thank you, Kassa Daggersharp. Exactly what I needed."

The resistance left him and he fell flat on the bed. The sleeping spell took over his body again, though his mind stayed alert for longer. Of all possible hallucinations his subconscious could have summoned up for him, why that one? Why now?

It was all too much. Aragon slept again.

~

Clio kept knocking on the door. Her knuckles were beginning to hurt. "Don't you have a key?"

"It must have fallen out of my pocket while we were rolling around on the rooftops," Sean said, still attempting humour.

Clio wasn't in the mood for it. She banged on the door with her palm open, trying to spare her knuckles. "Egg, let us in! We've got something to tell you."

One of the neighbouring doors opened and a bleary-looking young man with mad spiky hair put his head out into the corridor. He was wearing mismatched pyjamas. "Babe, keep down the noise. It's really early."

"It's nearly noon," said Clio impatiently.

The young man looked at her as if she was insane. He didn't quite focus. "Are you students or not?"

"Hey," said Sean. "Your room is connected to ours by the wash chamber, right?"

The other student grinned. "And you must be Sean

McHagrty. One of your girlfriends put a letter under our door by mistake. Very hot stuff."

"Need to get through this way," said Sean.

"Whatever," said the student. He looked hopefully at Clio. "Do you write letters?"

"I don't want to talk to you anymore," said Clio. She followed Sean through the wash chamber to the room he shared with Egg.

"Didn't you hear us knocking?" Sean was saying to Egg, pawing through his clothes in search of something clean. "I have a Profit lecture that started twenty minutes ago."

"There aren't any Profit lectures today," Egg said.

"Well, okay," said Sean. "But I have a lunch date with an amazing redhead, which is almost the same thing." He sniffed a shirt hopefully and held it out to Clio. "How fresh would you say this is? Six out of ten?"

"Get out of here, Sean," she said tiredly.

"Are we forgetting the part where this is my room?"

Clio was busy looking at Egg, who was busy pretending nothing was wrong.

Sean realised he was being ignored. "Fine. I'm having a bath. No peeking."

"I'll try to restrain myself," said Clio.

The wash chamber door closed behind Sean. Clio joined Egg at the window. "What's wrong?"

"You two," he said.

She was mildly surprised at that. "There is no anything about me and Sean McHagrty. Is this because we stayed out all night, because you will never believe what happened…"

"I know what happened," said Egg. "You were possessed by the spirit of Dream Girl, and McHagrty was possessed by the spirit of Invisiblo the Mystery Man, and the two of you spent the whole night running around Drak, fighting crime and righting wrongs while wearing a variety of nifty super-hero costumes."

Clio took a deep breath and let it out slowly. "Okay, obviously you have a better idea than I do about what happened to me last night. It really spoils my 'I woke up on the rooftops with no memory' anecdote, by the way."

Egg said nothing.

"And why are you upset, exactly?"

"You're going to think I'm being all stupid and whiny."

"Only if you whine stupidly."

"I'm fed up, that's all. These are my stories, and everyone else is more involved than I am. Why do I never get to be the hero?"

"There's still time."

"Yeah," he said, not sounding convinced.

"At least you're not the villain," Clio teased, only to see Egg's half-smile vanish entirely.

"Are you sure?" he said.

~

It was easy to enter the palace of Drak without anyone noticing. The Cloak was a pale grey shadow, tall and silent as the grave. Occasionally he passed a servant polishing the stair rail or a group of servants hurrying from one room to another, but they never noticed him. It was as if he didn't exist.

Or, quite possibly, he was such a familiar presence that no one gave him a second glance.

The Cloak went from corridor to corridor, staircase to staircase, looking for one particular room in this polished maze of a palace. Finally, he found it. This was the place where justice would be served. A place of evil that must be banished...hang on, since when had he cared about justice? Come to think of it, since when had he been a 'he'?

Kassa pushed off the hood of the pale grey cloak and took a deep breath. For a while there, she really had believed she was another person. No wonder Aragon was confused, if he was lending out his body to a fictional character on a regular basis. Assuming the Cloak was a fictional character.

She slid the hood back over her hair and face. She really wanted to know what the Cloak thought about the swirly vortex that Lord Sinistre kept in a room just along the corridor. If the Cloak was a hero and he thought the vortex was evil, did that mean it was evil? How did Kassa know the Cloak was a hero, anyway? She didn't think much of the raw material he had chosen to work with — Aragon was not the heroic type.

That wasn't fair. Aragon Silversword had indeed played the hero, if reluctantly, whenever she needed him to. And — damn, she'd missed having him around.

Can we keep our thoughts off boys for one evening, Daggersharp? Kassa had more important things to think about right now. She — *he* was the Cloak who Walks in the Night, Bringer and Maker of Justice. Villains beware.

The Cloak pushed open the door and stepped into the room. His shadowy eyes burned beneath the hood as he looked upon the spiralling vortex of darkness. What powers did it have? What evils did it conceal? How would be he able to restrain himself from throwing himself through the vortex just to see what it did?

Something hard and sharp snapped around the Cloak's throat. He staggered back, put his hand to his throat and briefly felt cold metal there before it burned hot against his fingers.

"Interesting," said Lord Sinistre. He moved around the Cloak, standing now between him and the vortex. "I knew someone had disturbed this room recently. I did not expect you."

~

At lunch time, Egg found Clio on a low brick wall in the square of student residence. She was staring dubiously at some sandwiches that could only have come from the Seaweed Room.

"Ah," said Egg, joining her. "Fish surprise comes in sandwiches, I see."

"It might be fish," said Clio. "Some of it is purple, which concerns me. What have you got?"

Egg unwrapped his own greasy parcel, revealing a slice of meat pie. The brown minced-string filling oozed out of a flaky cardboard crust. "It looked a lot more appetising when I bought it. Maybe we should stop eating altogether."

"Where would be the fun in that?" said Clio with her mouth full. She made a face. "Ooh. Anchovy."

"Good anchovy or bad anchovy?"

"I haven't decided yet." She swallowed quickly. "You seem cheerful."

"I am," said Egg. "It occurred to me that if some of us have to run around Drak in superhero costumes, I'm kind of glad it's not me."

"Very comforting," said Clio. "How nice for you not to be running around strange cities in peculiarly tight-fitting clothes or waking up on rooftops with a whole night's memory wiped from your brain."

"Did I say a little glad? I mean really, really glad." Egg set the slice of pie aside and brought a folio out of the bag he had slung over his shoulder. "I thought you might like to look at these."

Clio put down her last sandwich, and wiped her fingers

carefully on the paper wrapping before accepting the folio. "Dream Girl?"

"Dream Girl."

Clio flicked through the inked sketches. She picked one out. "She does look like me, under the mask and silly wig. Similar build, even the chin looks a little the same."

"I drew that one six months ago," said Egg.

"I hope that doesn't mean I'm a figment of your imagination."

"I've been thinking about that. Is all this happening because I wrote it, or did I write it because it was going to happen? Either way, there's something odd going on."

"Odd things happen in Mocklore all the time," said Clio. "Kassa's lectures have made that perfectly clear."

"But how much power do I have over it? What if I drew something bad — villain bad — and it came true?"

Clio's eyebrows shot up in alarm. "This is not a time for experimentation. You shouldn't be drawing anything!"

"I know," he said helplessly. "It's difficult, though. I'm used to scribbling all the time, little pictures in the margins of my notescrolls, doodles on scraps of parchment. Once I drew a whole story on the back of my arm because there wasn't any paper handy."

"Maybe your pens are cursed," suggested Clio. "Or the ink, maybe it's in the ink. You'd better not touch any writing implements until this is all over."

"How am I supposed to take lecture notes?"

"With any luck you won't need them. Drak will swallow up Mocklore and turn us all into velvet-clad lackeys of Lord Sinistre long before we have to worry about exams."

"That's what you call lucky?"

"I'm really bad at exams." Clio looked through the pictures again. "I'm serious, Egg. No reading or writing. What if you write down something Kassa says in one of her lectures and it comes true? We'd have magical catastrophes up to our necks." She lifted out one sketch and showed it to him.

Egg couldn't help smiling. It was a recent sketch, the one Clio had asked for: a portrait of her with her hair tied up in curlers and ribbons, swamped by a grandmotherly nightgown.

"At least this one isn't Dream Girl," Clio laughed.

Egg picked up his piece of pie again, not particularly hungry. "It is now."

Clio stopped laughing.

~

"Whom were you expecting?" asked the Cloak.

"That's not important," said Lord Sinistre. He was looking particularly lordly today, in a midnight blue suit made of shimmering velvet. His boots were high and black, the heels clacking as he paced around his prisoner. He wore a dramatic crown on his head, a black tower of intricate spikes and blood-coloured rubies. A single, over-sized pearl topped the highest spire of the crown, bright white. It looked out of place, making the whole thing faintly ridiculous. "You are what is important now, Mr Cloak. You disrupted my party, spoiled a perfectly good demonic spell. You have been running around my city terrifying people. Now you have entered my palace without permission and found your way to the only room which is forbidden. What am I to do with you?"

The Cloak stared at the Lordling of Drak. "I *knew* you were a villain!"

"I am the ruler of this city, and you have broken into my palace," said Lord Sinistre. "Are you sure you know which of us is the villain?"

～

After sending Egg away to fetch them some dessert, Clio flipped through the drawings he had given her. Dream Girl saving the day, fighting crime, walking in and out of reality, kissing Invisiblo the Mystery Man... She stared at that picture for quite a while.

"Hey."

Clio looked up and saw Sean McHagrty loping towards her. "I thought you had a date with an amazing redhead," she said.

"I was twenty minutes late and she didn't stick around to wait for me."

"Astonishing," said Clio. What did all those girls see in him anyway? He was vaguely good-looking, but nothing out of the ordinary. He wasn't very tall and his face was kind of narrow, like a weasel. Not that weasels were all that unattractive. They were kind of cute. Not that Sean McHagrty was cute. Okay, his eyes were very blue, but that wasn't anything special...

"Any clues as to what was going on last night?" he asked.

Clio held up the last parchment sketch she had been looking at, the one of Dream Girl and Invisiblo in a passionate clinch.

Sean's eyebrows lifted almost off his face. "Interesting."

She thrust the whole folio into his arms. "You'd better look at these. Apparently we were possessed by Egg's fictional characters last night."

"Okay." Sean leafed through the pages, moving past the Dream Girl pictures to the ones of Invisiblo the Mystery Man. "He kind of looks like me."

"I know. Egg drew most of these months ago, before he met either of us."

"Weird."

"Uh-huh." Clio wasn't sure if she wanted to have a conversation this serious with Sean McHagrty. "Last night wasn't the first time, was it? It happened on the night of the ball, as well. Something took over our bodies."

"That explains a lot," said Sean. "I had two dates that evening, with these sisters? Normally I can swing that kind of thing without a problem, but that night I totally lost track of an hour and they ended up finding out about each other. I couldn't figure out how it happened."

Clio was still shaking her head at him when Egg returned with two large ice cream cones. One was pink and the other was green. He held them both out to Clio. "I didn't get them from the Seaweed Room. The green one's peppermint."

Clio took the pink one. "Thanks. Sean was just leaving."

"Oh, nice," said Sean. "What have you got against me?"

"I believe in romance," she said coldly. "Boys like you make me think I'm wasting my time."

"You think I'm not looking for romance?"

Clio scoffed. "Is that what you call it?"

"Listen," said Sean seriously. "If I found the right girl, I'd stay with her forever. She'd never get rid of me."

"How comforting."

"At least I'm actively looking for love, Miss Cynical. I'm not sitting around waiting for things to turn out like an epic romance, I'm out there examining all the possibilities. Maybe that makes me more of a romantic than you." With that, Sean sauntered away. "Let me know if you find a way to write a happy ending to this superhero thing," he said over his shoulder to Egg.

"Will do," said Egg.

Clio glared at Sean's departing back. "I hate him and I can't figure out why."

"True love?" suggested Egg.

She brandished her ice cream at him. "I don't want to

mash this into your hair, but I will if I have to…"

"Eat up, we've got a Philosophy of Magic lecture in fifteen minutes."

Clio licked her ice cream. "I don't fancy sitting through a lecture. Can't we skip it?"

"Not unless we want Kassa to yell at us. Down side of knowing your teacher."

"We don't even know if she came back from Drak last night. I haven't seen her around today, have you?"

"Worried that she might have caught up with your Uncle Aragon?"

"There's that. Also, I forgot to do the tutorial readings. If she's been locked up for murder, I won't bother."

The Cloak made no response to the taunt. Lord Sinistre prowled around him. "That piece of metal you feel around your throat is a Compelling Collar. A very handy device. As long as you wear it, you belong to me. You must obey my every command. My first command is that you remain exactly where you are. My second command is for you to show me whom you truly are, under that fascinating garment of yours."

The Cloak's hands went reluctantly to his hood. The garment itself was pinned to him by the metal collar, but he was able to brush the hood back. Kassa Daggersharp was revealed.

Lord Sinistre laughed, a truly maniacal laugh. "Oh, Mistress Sharpe. You have outdone yourself. I am glad it's you. I was dreading there would be someone dull under that rag of yours."

"It's on loan," she snapped back. "I'm not the one you're looking for."

"On the contrary," he said. "You are the one that I want. I have some very specific plans for you."

She glared at him. "Oh, that's right. You're the hero and I'm the villain. I suppose you're going to make a public example of me?"

Lord Sinistre smiled. Even now, his smile made part of her feel melty around the knees. Kassa was furious with herself. How dare she be attracted to the man under these circumstances? What kind of woman was she?

"Oh, no," said Lord Sinistre. "You were right all along, Kassa Daggersharp. You're the hero and I'm the villain. That's why I want to marry you."

Most people faced with such an overwhelming enchantment would simply give in to its power. Then again, most people weren't bespelled by their girlfriend on a semi-regular basis. Aragon at least had some experience in dealing with magic compulsions. That, and a fierce determination to beat Kassa Daggersharp at her own game.

He opened his eyes.

The ceiling came into focus. Aragon stared at it for a while, just to make sure it was going to stay there. Then he turned his gaze to the window. Nothing there but Kassa's homemade curtains and scattered belongings.

"No hallucinations this time," he said aloud. "That's what I call progress." At least, that was what he had intended to say, but it came out as a muffled slurry sound. So, no talking for a while. He could cope with not talking. All he had to do was get out of this bed, and find his way back to Drak before Kassa did something that everybody was going to regret.

The spell was still in force, and Aragon's bones felt like they were filled with molten lead. Even his head was too heavy to lift. He gritted his teeth and attempted to roll. Nothing happened. He tensed every muscle in his body, relaxed them all and tried again. His body rocked slightly.

Ten minutes later, Aragon had managed to rotate his body closer to the edge of the mattress. One more roll would do it. He fought another wave of sleepiness and rolled triumphantly out of Kassa's bed.

Crash! His jaw shuddered as his whole body hit the wooden floor hard. Grabbing on to the side of the bed, he dragged himself up, exhausted from the effort as well as the sleeping spell. Now his only problem was finding his boots. And possibly his trousers. Also, figuring out how to stand up and walk.

It was going to be a long haul.

~

Kassa opened her mouth, waiting for a witty comeback to emerge. It didn't. She shut her mouth again. "Um, what? Huh? What?"

"You heard me," said Lord Sinistre.

"I heard you, but apparently my brain didn't believe you. Say it again."

"I want to marry you. Is that so hard to believe?"

She choked a little, which had nothing to do with the metal collar that was clamped around her throat. "I think that's my first marriage proposal from someone who wasn't drunk or insane. No, my mistake. You are *insane*."

"Why?" said Lord Sinistre. "You like me, don't you?"

"No!"

"You are attracted, though? Tell me the truth."

"Far more attracted than I should be," said Kassa. "Did I just say that out loud?"

"Of course," said Lord Sinistre, sounding pleased. "I told

you to tell the truth. The Compelling Collar made you obey me."

"This is your idea of romance?" said Kassa. "What kind of man captures a woman against her will and then asks her to marry him?"

"A man who very much wants the answer to be yes," said Lord Sinistre. "Shall I tell you why?"

Kassa tried to move her feet. "You may as well. Apparently I'm not going anywhere."

"It's the city," said Lord Sinistre. He sounded disconnected, as if he was not necessarily the one choosing what words he was going to speak. "Drak is a hungry place. The draklight feeds on cheerful thoughts and bright impulses, leaving only morbidity and black velvet shadows behind."

Kassa stared at him. "Is that why it's so dark around here?"

"Of course," said Lord Sinistre in that melodious voice of his. "Even the flame from a candle becomes dim as the city feeds. It can't grow big and strong without finding something to feed on. Something more powerful than a candle."

"I don't want this city of yours to grow up big and strong," said Kassa. "If it gets any bigger, Cluft will be swallowed whole, then all of Mocklore."

"Mocklore," said Lord Sinistre, as if the word was a delicious dish on a menu of delicacies. "Such a colourful world out there, sunlight and daisies. Do you have any idea what it is like to have been alone for so long, surrounded by nothing but wasteland, and then suddenly to have a feast surrounding our city as far as the eye can see? We won't swallow Mocklore whole, Mistress Sharpe. We will savour every mouthful, relish every bite."

"That's comforting," said Kassa. "You make me feel much better about the whole thing. What does this have to do with marriage? Nothing so far has encouraged me to make that kind of commitment."

Lord Sinistre smiled. It was a pleasant smile, nothing nasty about it. "You are a hero in your own land, Kassa. Oh, yes, I know who you really are. Kassa Daggersharp, the brave and feisty pirate lass who saved Mocklore from the Glimmer." He sounded regretful. "If only I had been here then. I would have liked to see all those bright colours disappearing under the weight of our shadows. You, Kassa, are the ultimate agent of Chaos and Light. Drak is the ultimate expression of Order and Darkness. By making you my Lady, by feeding your bright and heroic spirit into my city until you are nothing but a sulking creature in black satin, I will make Drak strong for generations. Certainly strong enough to overthrow this energetic little island Empire of yours."

It wasn't often that Kassa was left speechless, even temporarily. "The ultimate agent of Chaos and Light?" she said finally. "Are you sure? I know girls who are much messier than I am. Not to mention nicer. You call me a heroine, but I haven't done much to deserve it."

Lord Sinistre laughed. It was a little less devastatingly sexy than before. *Please, tell me I'm getting over my bad-boy-in-velvet phase,* Kassa thought desperately. *I can't take the embarrassment much longer.*

"I see you more clearly than you see yourself," said Lord Sinistre. "You *are* a heroine and you *will* become the Dark Lady of Drak. Already my city works its will on you. Soon, the heroine will become the villainess and the city will be sated. These things are inevitable."

"Do you actually hear the words you are saying?" demanded Kassa. "Please tell me Egg isn't responsible for these monologues. You sound like something out of a cheap adventure ballad, lacking only the rhyming couplets at the end of each speech."

"Still so brave," said Lord Sinistre. "So rebellious. Where does this strength come from, this unflinching confidence? No one is going to rescue you, Kassa. There will be no last minute reprieve."

For a moment, Kassa was chilled. She hadn't told anyone she was coming here, it was true. Aragon was trapped in her bedroom with the lethargy spell. It might occur to Egg and Clio that she was still in Drak, but they were only kids, what could they do against Lord Sinistre?

Reality kicked in before Kassa could become truly worried. She might not be the person Lord Sinistre thought she was, but she was still Kassa bloody Daggersharp.

He had commanded her by the Compelling Collar to remain exactly where she was and to tell him the truth. He had said nothing about keeping her limbs inert. Kassa kicked, her black-booted leg shooting up in front of her body. She wasn't as limber as she used to be, but she still managed to catch Lord Sinistre under the chin, knocking him to the ground. She glared down at his surprised face.

"Newsflash, creep-fiend. I'm not the girl who gets rescued. I'm the other girl. The one who does the rescuing, and the head-kicking, and the saving the day. Why the hell are you laughing?"

Lord Sinistre lay on his back, nursing his bruised face and chuckling up at her. "You are magnificent. The stronger you are, the more delicious a victory it will be when my city crushes that extraordinary spirit out of you."

"I'm tired of hearing about your vampire city and what it's going to do to me," Kassa said, breathing hard. She was still unable to put one foot in front of the other to escape her current predicament, which was starting to bother her a little. "What are *you* going to do to me?"

Lord Sinistre's eyes gleamed menacingly. "I can't even begin to tell you."

"Try."

Somewhere, there was a sound of breaking glass. Kassa smiled broadly. "Waited too long, Sinistre. Too much poncing around and posturing. You should have just cut my head off or thrown me into your stupid portal, or whatever it was you wanted to do. You see, there is one person who rescues me from time to time. You didn't take him into account."

"A single shout will bring a hundred sword-wielding guards into this room," warned Lord Sinistre.

"It's a small room," said Kassa. "Are you sure they'll all fit?"

Something bashed into the door, a heavy thump that shook the hinges and surrounding walls. Lord Sinistre opened his mouth to shout for help.

"I'll do it for you, if you like," said Kassa. "My friend will still get here first."

There was a second thump, mightier and more threatening than the first.

"What is that?" demanded Lord Sinistre.

"I can't lie to you while I'm wearing this collar," said Kassa. "It's something nasty, and it's not going to be very pleased with you when it gets in here. Speaking of the collar, unfasten it now and we might be convinced to go easy on you, me and my friend."

"I'm not that stupid," Lord Sinistre growled. "You are in my power, Mistress Daggersharp. Let your friend try to rescue you when you can't move a step."

"Fine," said Kassa. "Don't say I didn't warn you." She screamed, a throaty howl.

The door exploded. Woodchips spun out in all directions. A black flying creature burst through the flying splinters, breathing a cloud of flame. Lord Sinistre fell back towards the portal, only preventing himself from falling in by grabbing hold of a chair.

Kassa dropped to her knees. "Collar, collar!"

Singespitter — the demonic Drak version of Singespitter — circled the room twice, flapping his wings and hissing. He swooped down at Kassa, his fangs closing down on the back of her neck.

The Compelling Collar hit the polished floorboards with a tinny little sound.

"Right," said Kassa. She advanced on Lord Sinistre, her eyes flashing like hard, angry pieces of amber. "What was it you were saying about marriage?"

"Well," said Lord Sinistre faintly, backing up against the wall. "I wouldn't want to pressure you into a commitment you don't feel ready for."

"Right," said Kassa. She looked around the room. "I don't see any sign of these guards of yours. Still, it's a big palace. Lots of stairs and corridors, that sort of thing. And it's nearly lunchtime, most of them are probably off having a smoke or a sandwich."

"Possibly," said Lord Sinistre.

"Mind you, I'm sure Singespitter and I will have to fight our way out of here once the cavalry do arrive to save your miserable neck. Not actual cavalry, we hope. Horses would do terrible things to your carpets."

Singespitter smiled. Really, demonic sheep should never smile. It wasn't pretty. A puff of purple smoke emerged from his flared nostrils.

"I needn't tell anyone about all this," said Lord Sinistre, quickly.

"That's what I like to hear," said Kassa. "Who says the pretty ones can't be smart, too?"

Sounds approached — running feet, swishing swords,

shouts along the lines of 'We're coming, my lordship!' and 'Stand together, men, we don't know what we're facing!'

"Ah," said Kassa.

"My guards are very good," said Lord Sinistre. "Your creature might fare well against them, but what about you? You don't even have a sword."

"You're right," said Kassa. Slowly, she lifted the pale grey hood over her hair, becoming the Cloak again. "Luckily for me, I'm really good at taking swords off other people."

9

HOW DRAK WON THE WAR

"I'm worried," said Egg. "Kassa's never this late to class."

"Maybe she found Uncle Aragon last night," said Clio. "Maybe she's busy burying him in a shallow grave."

The two of them sat in the back row of the Second Lecture Hall. The clock on the back wall showed that Mistress Sharpe was eight and a half minutes late. There were perhaps half as many students here as had been at the first lecture, but this was normal for the second week of semester. Egg's last Perspectives of the Profithood seminar had only had three students present of the original thirty. Everyone was slacking off, and the presence of the mysterious Drak had been added to the list of regular excuses, along with the 'I was drinking lots of multi-coloured beers last night and now I can't get out of bed' excuse and the 'My roommate was drinking lots of multi-coloured beers last night and now the carpet is multi-coloured and do you know where the cleaners keep the soap and buckets?' excuse.

The door at the back of the lecture hall opened. The students were busy chattering about how long they should bother to wait before they declared the lecturer an official no-show and made themselves scarce. Egg and Clio were the only ones who heard the door open, and they did not dare to turn around.

A white sheep flew into the lecture hall. It was large, fluffy, and had a pair of broad purple wings. It sailed down the banks of seats, circled twice and then landed very smoothly on the lectern. For once, there was silence as the students stared at the sheep, then turned around to look toward the back of the lecture hall.

Mistress Sharpe made her entrance, limping down the wide steps. She only wore one boot. Her other foot was tightly bandaged with torn white cotton. Her toenails were scarlet. Her bright green skirts were shredded down one side, as were several layers of petticoat, which explained where the makeshift bandage had come from. Blood was spattered here and there on the fabric. The sleeves of her chemise were both ripped. Her leather bodice had several dents in it. Two battered swords hung from her sturdy leather belt, one on each side. They did not look as if they had originally belonged to her, although they certainly did now. A bright grey cloak was also tucked into the belt, draping down to the floor.

Kassa had made no effort to tame her hair into its usual snood, so it stuck out in mad curls all the way down her back. As she reached the lectern and turned to face the students, it was apparent that a large chunk of hair near her left ear had been sliced away. Her lower lip was swollen. She wore an eyepatch over her left eye.

Mistress Sharpe cleared her throat. "Today, we are going to talk about one of the most recent and significant examples of magic gone wrong in Mocklore. Most of you would have been too young to remember much about the First Glimmer, but I expect you heard plenty of tales from your parents. You should all, however, remember where you were when the Second Glimmer tore through this part of the Empire."

The students shifted and giggled amongst themselves. They remembered the Glimmer, all right — and that a certain Kassa Daggersharp had been blamed for setting it off, then later credited with saving the Empire from the fierce magical storm.

"Don't be shy." Mistress Sharpe's fingernails drummed against the side of the lectern. "Let's hear your war stories."

Hands shot up, a few at a time.

"Gammershot?" said Mistress Sharpe.

A tall, thin boy with a very animated skin condition cleared his throat. "We were in Dreadnought at the time, professor. A wet sparkly thing came through the window and changed my sister into a mermaid."

"That must have been very inconvenient," Mistress Sharpe said sympathetically.

"Not really, miss. I got her room when she moved to the Saffron Sea."

Everyone laughed, and a few more hands went up.

Mistress Sharpe nodded at a redheaded girl near Egg. "Cinderbee?"

"The turnip farm next to ours went up in green flames and glitter, Mistress Sharpe. At least, the fields did. All their crops were burnt up, but they eventually made a profit from the glitter. We thought we'd had our near miss, but the next year our crops came out cabbages where we'd planted winterberries and Chiantrian chive-grass."

"A familiar story," agreed Mistress Sharpe. "Whistlestop?"

Nortram Whistlestop, a boy Egg knew quite well from his Introduction to Aristocracy class, kept his hand in the air. It was bright blue from fingertip to wrist, where the ordinary pink skin began. Soft green feathers tufted between his fingers. "Pretty much just this, professor. I opened the shutter for a minute to see if it was all over, and it wasn't."

Mistress Sharpe grinned. "Lucky you didn't put you head outside the window, eh, Nort?"

"That's what my Ma said, professor. After she stopped screaming."

"Right," said Mistress Sharpe. "Everyone knows someone who was affected, even our friends in the more northerly city-states that weren't directly touched by the Glimmer. Most of the crops in the Middens were spared, but we all remember eating pink apricots for two summers, and the sea still washes up man-eating seaweed every three or four moon-cycles. Mocklore is a bit more dangerous than it used to be. Who can tell me what happened here in Cluft when the Glimmer went through?"

A few hands went up, less certainly than before. "Rains of seafood, miss?" suggested Imelda Appleblack.

"Actually, those have always been a feature of this town," said Mistress Sharpe. "It's one of the reasons we can't get rid of those gourmet tourists who keep turning up in coaches. Anyone else?"

Clio put up her hand. "Townhall, professor. The dragon."

"Ah, yes," said Mistress Sharpe. She smiled at the baffled faces before her. "Didn't any of you think that was a funny name for a dragon? Not to mention that all other dragons in Mocklore are barely knee-high to a human, while ours is eight-foot and then some? That's right, Wagstaff-Lamont, our school mascot actually was the Cluft town hall before the Glimmer hit this town. Pallaxer?"

A Zibrian boy in the front row lowered his hand. "That section of Mousefoot Street where all those cobbles are missing, miss, that was the Glimmer, wasn't it?"

"Correct," said Mistress Sharpe. "Particles of the Glimmer known as glints turned that whole section of street into gingerbread. A large number of postgrads promptly held a gingerbread-eating and ale-drinking party, which dealt with the situation. Also, the orange mulberry bush near the highway used to be the post box, and one of our postgraduate students still metamorphoses into a lemon tree or a pile of silver dust whenever he sneezes."

Singespitter, who had been sitting quiet and docile on the lectern for some time now, made a discreet throat-clearing cough.

"Oh, yes," said Kassa. "This is my friend Singespitter. Those of you who make the very brave decision to continue studying the magical arts may eventually have him as a tutor."

The winged sheep smiled modestly.

"He used to be a member of the Hidden Army," Kassa continued. "A human, of course, only a year or two older than you lot when it happened. The Glimmer turned him into a green sheep with purple wings. As you saw on his rather spectacular entrance, he still has the purple wings but his fleece is now a rather more respectable white. A god who owed me a favour did that, and it was the only difference he was able to affect." Kassa's voice became stern. "Magical change is for keeps, children. All those Glimmer stories have one thing in common. No witch or warlock or even the gods could reverse any of the Glimmer's effects. Some magic has a little give and take in it, some wears off eventually and some has loopholes so wide you could drive a coach through, but generally speaking, if you don't want something to last forever, don't apply magic to it. Even if you think the spell is temporary. As your mothers may have told you once upon a time, you never know when the wind will change and you'll be stuck like that. If I worked at it, I could probably turn Singespitter into a duck or a penguin or even a human — not necessarily the same human, but a human nonetheless — but

I cannot undo what the Glimmer did to him. There are no absolutes. It might wear off, or someone might manage to fix it accidentally. But there are no guarantees that he won't be a sheep for the rest of his life."

Professor Sharpe folded her arms and stared expectantly at the students. They stared back at her, solemn. "Magic is irreversible," she said finally. "Except when it isn't. You won't know which it is until it's too late. Write that down somewhere. Remember it. Lesson learned? Class dismissed."

"Short and sweet," Egg muttered to Clio as the students started to empty the hall.

"Maybe her foot hurts," said Clio, watching Singespitter leap off the lectern and flap madly to gain height before soaring up and out of the hall.

"Maybe," said Egg. He found it highly unlikely that Kassa would give into something like a little pain.

As the last of the students piled out of the hall, Kassa shuffled some papers together and glanced up at Egg and Clio. "You two look nervous. Something to tell me?"

Clio and Egg shared an uneasy look. "We — er — found out who the Cloak really was," said Clio.

Kassa smiled. "Ah, yes. That was an exciting surprise. Don't look so worried, Clio. I didn't kill your precious uncle. I barely even wounded him."

"Oh," said Clio. "Good."

Kassa made her way up the stairs, limping painfully. Egg fought the instinct to assist her, as she didn't seem the type to approve of such gallantry. "We have more important things to worry about," said Kassa as she passed them on her way to the door.

Clio hesitated, her eyes taking in the state of Kassa's clothes and hair, not to mention the various cuts, bruises and scrapes. "Did Uncle Aragon do that to you?"

Kassa didn't take offense. "Worrying about what state he

might be in? Don't be. This is from fighting several dozen of Lord Sinistre's guards on my way out of the palace. Who'd have thought they would have any energy left at all after running up all those stairs? Never mind that now. We've got work to do."

"Did you find out anything new about Drak?" asked Clio.

"Not new," said Kassa. "But either Lord Sinistre or his city is barking mad, and Drak — or the draklight, at least — is well on its way to swallowing Mocklore whole. Time to do something about that."

"What sort of something?" asked Egg, fearing the worst.

Kassa grinned at him. "Cheer up, kid. You're going to save the world."

Outside, Clio squinted up at the cloudless blue sky. "Doesn't really look ominous enough, does it?"

"That does," said Kassa, pointing. "I think I just figured out what happened to the half of my class that didn't show up."

Students, many of them clad in the latest Drak-inspired fashions, milled aimlessly around the campus. There was nothing abnormal about this, except that the 'aimless' milling was all headed in the same direction. However casual the students seemed, they were all moving towards the library tower.

"If that isn't suspicious in the second week of semester, I don't know what is," said Kassa.

The three of them overtook most of the slowly-moving students on their way to the library. Kassa's limp didn't slow her down much. "Gods," she gasped as they approached the golden skybridge.

A slow but steady stream of students, staff and even the

occasional dinner lady were making their way up on to the skybridge, heading for Drak. Their clothes shimmered into black velvet and leather boots almost as soon as their feet touched the bridge.

"It's getting closer," said Clio.

Kassa nodded. "They're feeding it. Every time Drak takes one of our people it gets stronger. And what are you going to do about it?"

For one horrible moment, Egg thought she was talking to him, but then he realised that the door to the library tower had opened and Kassa was staring at Mavis, the librarian-goddess of Cluft.

Mavis, tucking the last of several kittens into her handbag, smiled at Kassa. "Not much, I'm afraid, my dear. It's up to you now."

"You're a god," said Kassa. "You're supposed to protect Cluft. You're supposed to protect Mocklore!"

Mavis tugged at her tortoise-shell glasses, and tidied her hair. "Kassa, didn't you ever wonder how a mere Emperor was allowed to Decimalise the gods? Didn't you wonder why we didn't stop the Glimmers before they happened, instead of making an awkward attempt to clean up the mess afterwards? The gods of Mocklore were never much of anything, but right now the cosmos is particularly fragile and we have less power than we ever did. The gods cannot help you banish Drak."

"Are you saying mortals have to fix this?" flared Kassa. "That's crazy. I can't fight magic with magic, that never works." Over her shoulder to Egg and Clio, she added, "That was next week's lecture."

"I can do nothing," said Mavis. "Nothing except to ensure my life force does not assist Drak to be stronger, and the only way to do that is to not be here when the library is taken." She vanished.

"No!" howled Kassa. "This is all wrong!"

Clio tugged at her sleeve. "Kassa, the library's starting to look awfully Drak-ish. I think we should back up."

"Quickly," agreed Egg.

Several girls with velvet hair accessories climbed up on to the skybridge together. The library tower darkened, its bricks glowing black and its roof becoming shiny and sleek, just like the buildings of Drak. Two dozen students, all waiting below the sky-bridge, transformed into velvet-clad Drak people. Several started shoving aggressively at the others, which started a fight of flailing fists.

"The draklight's on the move!" said Clio in alarm.

"Right," said Kassa. "It's up to us." She turned, grabbing on to both Egg and Clio. "Let's go."

They elbowed their way through a steady stream of students and staff members. "Can't we hold them back somehow?" Egg asked pleadingly.

"How?" shot back Kassa. "We have to stop it at the source. Hang on!" She spied Vice-Chancellor Bertie in the crowd and lunged for him, grabbing his arm. "Can't lose you, matey;, we might need a leader at some point. You two go ahead to Egg's room," she added, swinging Bertie around and dragging him behind her. "I'll lock this one in a cupboard."

"What are we going to do?" Egg called after her.

"You're going to write a happy ending!" Kassa yelled as she vanished into the crowd. "Start thinking up a bloody good one!"

"Come on." Clio grabbed Egg's arm and the two of them ran to the square of student residences. "We don't know how long we have before the whole town gets black-velveted."

"Is this all my fault?" Egg couldn't help asking. His feet jarred painfully on the cobbles as they ran.

"I don't know," panted Clio. "If you save everyone, maybe it won't matter. Hey, stop that McHagrty!"

Sean was surrounded by several young women wearing black lipstick. His eyes had a glassy sheen to them. Egg grabbed one of his arms and Clio grabbed the other. "Can I slap him?" she asked.

"Be my guest," said Egg.

Clio's hand cracked over Sean's cheek. He blinked at her. "What did I do now?"

"We're saving you from a major fashion disaster," said Clio. "Back to your room!"

"Okay, but right now I just want to walk towards the library," Sean said amiably.

Clio rolled her eyes. "Like that's a natural urge. Can I slap him again?"

"Better not," said Egg. "You enjoy it too much."

~

Aragon was still battling the lethargy spell. He had fallen unconscious again in Kassa's doorway. Now he had made it to the landing outside her room. He stood unsteadily, gazing down at the spiral staircase. Of course Kassa lived in a tower. A ground floor room would be far too easy. He gazed down at the spiralling stairs, wondering how he could possibly make it down to ground level in one piece.

Was he imagining things, or was every step a different shape and colour? Pink and blue and red and gold and green hexagons, squares, rectangles and triangles swirled in front of Aragon's eyes. He squeezed them shut. There was a banister along one side of the stairwell. Perhaps the best thing would be to simply hang on to that and descend with his eyes closed. A second peek at the stairs with his dazed vision convinced him this was the best idea yet. He clung to the banister, closed his eyes again and took one step, then another.

The urge to sleep continued, but the knowledge that he would probably fall to his death if he did so kept him moving. One step, then another, then another. This was fine. It was working. He could do this.

He was doing really well until his foot reached the step which was a perfect sphere.

∼

"What's going on?" said Sean McHagrty, once they were back in their room. He seemed mostly sane.

"You were trying to join the crowd that's feeding the evil city's power," Clio informed him.

Sean grinned at her. "And you cared enough to save me? I knew you liked me."

Clio snorted. "Egg, what are you going to write?"

Egg sat cross-legged on his bedspread, several pieces of parchment laid out before him. "I don't know," he said, feeling panicky. "I didn't draw half the stuff that's happening now, so I don't know how to fix it."

The door crashed open. "Don't worry," gasped Kassa, breathing hard. "I'll dictate."

"Are you sure that's a good idea?" said Clio. "It's Egg's story."

"Is the Vice-Chancellor okay?" Egg asked.

"I locked him in the cupboard with his Great Reversing Barrel," Kassa said. "I only hope he doesn't fall into the damn thing. Ready to go, Egg?"

Egg unscrewed the lid of one of his inkpots with trembling hands. "I think so. What am I going to draw?"

Kassa sat on Sean's bed. "I haven't the faintest idea," she admitted.

∼

Aragon emerged from the foot of the Mermaid Tower, battered and bruised and shaken but, against the odds, alive. The lethargy spell was still there, but it seemed less important than before. *Drak needs us,* urged the Chamberlain within his mind.

Oh, you're back, are you? I notice you weren't around while I was doing all the work, or the falling down a flight of stairs.

We must return to Drak. Whatever has happened, we need to be at Lord Sinistre's side.

Fine, you do that. I have other priorities, like strangling a certain female pirate we both know.

We must return to Drak.

After I find Kassa.

The sunlight was dazzling. Aragon sighed to himself. The worrying thing was not the two conflicting personalities within his skull. The worrying thing was that there was a third persona inside his head who thought that the building over there looked quite familiar. Neither Aragon nor the Chamberlain had stepped outside Drak since its arrival in Mocklore, and yet the mysterious third part of him remembered climbing that wall recently and peering in through that window at...at Kassa?

Oh, gods. The Cloak that Walks in the Night. She was right, I've been playing the bloody hero on my nights off. Sorry, friend. Drak and his Lordship can wait. I need to find Kassa right this minute.

Are we still planning on strangling her?

Only if we're very good.

~

Egg drew a blank square in the centre of a scraped-clean piece of parchment. "Still waiting."

"Maybe you could draw Drak losing all its power," Kassa suggested.

"How do I draw that?"

"You're the artist."

"You're the bad bad magic expert!"

"This isn't magic," Kassa said crossly. "Not the kind of magic I know anything about."

"Reassuring as ever," said Egg. "Why don't I just draw Drak on its own, with the wasteland back instead of Mocklore?"

"That will make things worse," said Kassa. "That's what the draklight is trying to create. Maybe you should draw Mocklore overwhelming Drak with its nice, colourful everyday chaos."

"Again, difficult thing to draw! I could write it in a speech bubble."

Standing by the window, Clio watched the view outside. The mad, colourful architecture of Cluft was slowly but steadily transforming into the black, uncomfortably elegant architecture of Drak. "Whatever you do, it had better be fast."

Sean joined her at the window. "Scared?"

"Not enough to let you hold my hand."

"Just checking."

Egg was getting panicky. "Whatever we do, it's going to involve Drak, right?"

"Right," said Kassa. "Start with Drak and then we'll figure out what to do next."

"Won't drawing Drak just feed it more power?" Clio asked as Egg dipped his pen into the inkwell and, in quick strokes, sketched the outline of the city of Drak.

Darkness fell.

The building shook as the room was engulfed in shadows. Egg was thrown back against the headboard of his bed. He sprawled on to the floor in a crumpled heap. Clio and Sean both tumbled to the floor. "The room," sputtered Sean, staring around. "What the hell happened to our room?"

The battered, colourless wallpaper and carpet had been replaced by shiny black tiles. The curtains were red velvet, and both beds were draped in black lace and dark blue satin instead of the usual combination of elderly pillows and boy blankets. Kassa rose slowly to her feet, looking around. "I wonder what my room looks like," she said thoughtfully. "What are you staring at, McHagrty?"

"Sorry," said Sean, still staring. "You're a little hard to miss, miss."

Kassa now wore a garnet-red lace frock which hugged all her curves far more closely than was strictly necessary. The neckline was plungingly indecent, the matching red boots were thigh-high and her fingernails were perfectly-mani-cured, glossy black with a red jewel set into each. The Cloak's cloak was still tucked into her belt, although her belt was now a delicate gold hip-chain with no useful pouches or weapons hanging from it. "If I find out you designed this outfit, Egg, I'm going to eat out your heart with a fish fork," she snarled.

Sean turned his attention to Clio. "Look at you."

Like Kassa, Clio's outfit was form-fitting, although it was decidedly un-Draklike — a white catsuit with matching short boots and a long, curly purple wig.

"You look familiar," said Sean, frowning.

Clio stood up. "I look like Dream Girl," she said. "And you look like her partner in crime."

Sean stared down at his own indecently tight blue and white checked suit. "No wonder the guy likes to go invisible," he said. "Who would wear this by choice?"

Kassa made her way over to the fallen Egg, who had not moved. "Everything's unstable. I don't know if Cluft can stand up structurally to this kind of change." She struggled to kneel down in the clingy dress, but rolled Egg over. He wore one of those warlock costumes the draklight liked to impose upon him — a dark blue robe decorated with silver stars, but without a pointy hat or necklaces. The draklight was adapting. Kassa examined him, frowning. "He's breathing, but unconscious. It doesn't look like he hit his head. Why isn't he awake?"

"I can't see daylight," said Clio at the window. "Night, all over Cluft. I think the whole town got — what do I say, drakked? Draklighted?"

"Draklit," said Sean.

"They've won," said Kassa. "The draklight has momentum behind it now. Nothing can stop it."

"So that's it?" Clio demanded. "We just have to get used to wearing these stupid clothes all the time? I can't breathe in this catsuit."

"It's more than just clothes, you stupid girl!" Kassa yelled. "Drak is a state of mind. It is morbid and angry and unpleasant. The longer we stay here, the faster we will lose ourselves. The draklight will swallow up our identities until we're all puppets in the hands of Lord Sinistre."

"The tyrant," Clio agreed calmly. "It is past time we put an end to his evil reign."

Kassa looked at her strangely. "Can't argue with you there. Are you feeling all right?"

"Together we can put a stop to Lord Sinistre's machinations and evil plans," said Sean, holding his hand out to Clio. "Are you with me?"

She gave him a loving look. "Always."

Kassa got to her feet and heard a ripping sound from the tight red lace dress as she did so. "What the glory gods are you two talking about?"

Clio backed away from Sean. "I don't know. What was I saying?"

Sean gave her a funny look. "I don't know."

"Dream Girl," Clio whispered. "We're turning into Egg's heroes."

"Maybe that's a good thing," said Sean, not entirely convinced. "We need some heroes around here, and you and I aren't much use otherwise."

"You just think you have a better chance with Dream Girl than you do with me," Clio spat.

"If she's anything like you I wouldn't touch her with a punting pole," said Sean.

"Tomcat!"

"Ice queen!"

"Shut up, both of you!" said Kassa. "If you don't keep calm and controlled, the draklight will take you over!"

"Why don't you shut up!" Clio yelled back. "You said you could fix this and you made it ten times worse! Egg is hurt because he listened to you, and now we're all turning into evil puppet people from Velvetland. What do you know about anything?"

The building shook again, knocking all three of them to the shiny black floor. The door opened. Aragon Silversword stood in the doorway for a moment before sinking to his knees, gripping the doorframe tightly. "Would anyone mind telling me what is going on around here?"

~

Cluft was not a whirlwind of chaos. If anything, it was a whirlwind of order. The square of student residence had been transformed into an elegant plaza centred around a dark basalt statue of Lord Sinistre at his most dramatic, a flowing cape forming a splashing water feature. Students in dark evening-wear lounged now on intricate gilded love seats, or challenged each other to duels beneath the three clocks which were now set upon identical shiny black pillars.

Various pets (which students and staff were definitely not allowed to keep in their rooms) had been transformed into flying, fire-breathing beasties which circled and spun in the air. It was a beautiful, clear night of stars, the full moon glowing above. It was barely an hour past noon.

At Egg and Sean's window, Kassa stared out at the changes that had been wrought on Cluft. It was the only way she could think of delaying the inevitable conversation with Aragon Silversword.

She was in no immediate danger, as Aragon was far more interested in the young woman who had shyly introduced herself as his niece, pulling off her purple wig in the hope he would recognise her.

"Clio?" he said in astonishment, staggering to his feet. "Aren't you supposed to be about twelve?"

"I was nine last time you came to visit," said Clio sternly. "I'm seventeen now."

"Where does the time go?" said Aragon. A sudden yawn almost sent him back to his knees, and he finally addressed Kassa directly. "Will you take this blasted spell off me, Daggersharp?"

Kassa pushed away from the window and went to him. She placed her palm in the centre of Aragon's chest. Motes of light sprang from his skin and clothes, gathering into a tiny ball of light which she crumpled in her hand and attempted to pop into a pocket. The ridiculous red dress had no pockets, so she trapped the spell in Egg's sock drawer instead.

Clio watched with amazement. "If Egg was awake he'd complain that you told us no spell can be reversed," she pointed out.

"Depends on the spell," said Kassa. Her eyes met Aragon's

for a moment and held, before he deliberately turned back to Clio.

"How's Mother?"

"Annoyed at you," said the girl with a grin. "You should visit her."

"Yes, I suppose I should. I will as soon as we're between catastrophes." Aragon glanced around. "What is the current catastrophe, by the way? I'm out of touch."

"Your city has just invaded our city," said Kassa Dagger-sharp. "Consider yourself a prisoner of war."

10

THE ROOM WITH THE BIG SWIRLY VORTEX

"So," said Aragon Silversword. Kassa now had his full attention. "What happened to your eye?"

"Your Lord and Master's palace guards."

"I see," he said, trying not to smirk. "I must congratulate them; they've never faced anything scarier than a runaway gargoyle before. Why haven't you healed yourself?"

"I'm fine," Kassa snapped.

His hand moved quickly, poking the bruised skin around the leather eyepatch.

"Ow!"

"Sounds painful to me."

"If you go around poking me in the eye, what do you expect?"

Aragon held out a hand.

"All my pouches vanished when the draklight took over," Kassa tried.

Aragon raised an eyebrow, his hand still outstretched.

Grumbling, Kassa rummaged in her hair, extracting a large clip that she handed over. "You know I hate using this stuff on myself."

"I also know that you have no qualms about using it on other people." Aragon snapped the clip open to reveal a compartment filled with a sparkling green powder. "Ah, quick-fix trollgrit. Nothing like the old favourites." He plucked the eyepatch away from Kassa's face, winced at the ugly bruising that had swollen the eye shut, then flung a pinch of the powder straight into her pupil.

Kassa slapped her hand to it. "Gah!" she exclaimed in a pained voice. "Ow-ww!"

Aragon took the opportunity to flick a second pinch of the powder at the ankle that Kassa had obviously been trying to keep her weight off. She screamed, falling to the floor. "Bastard." Her newly-healed foot lashed out and hooked him by the ankle, crashing him to the floor opposite her.

"Uncalled for," said Aragon.

"You can't just strut back in here and play the solicitous boyfriend," Kassa snarled. "We're not even on the same side."

"So you said when you declared war on me two minutes ago. I don't believe a word of it. In case you haven't noticed, Kassa Daggersharp, I am always on your side."

They glared at each other.

"Do you think we should give them some privacy?" Sean asked Clio, who waved him to silence. She had been reading ballads about these two for years, and it was fascinating to see them in action.

"Explain the current situation in words of two syllables or less," Aragon said between gritted teeth.

Kassa counted the syllables out on her fingers. "Drak is eat-ing Mock-lore a-live."

Aragon hesitated. "Are actual teeth involved?"

"The draklight," she huffed. "You know, the dark magic that flows out of that damn city of yours, making everyone think violent thoughts and flirt with each other? The stuff that your pet demons feed on, most likely. It is spreading through Mocklore like a bushfire in the Skullcaps, turning our cities into Drak wannabes and our meadows into deserts of silver sand."

Aragon considered her words. "And is this my fault?"

"I don't know, probably! I plan to blame you until a better-dressed villain comes along."

"And my seventeen-year-old niece is wearing a white leather catsuit because…"

Kassa rolled her eyes. "Because for some reason, Drak wants Clio and Sean and you to run around pretending to be heroes." She untucked the pale grey cloak from her belt and practically threw it at him. "And what Drak wants, Drak gets! You'd better get used to the idea, hero boy."

Is this true? Aragon asked himself silently. *Is the draklight responsible for this part-time heroic mission of ours? Is Drak invading Mocklore?*

How would I know? the Chamberlain responded. *No one tells me anything. How am I expected to administrate a whole new city on top of my duties in Drak, let alone an entire Empire? The paperwork will be crippling.*

Forget I asked.

"Perhaps we could stop blaming me long enough to work out a solution?" Aragon suggested aloud to Kassa.

"Do what you like," she said, getting to her feet and heading for the door. "I'm going to find my sheep."

The door slammed behind Kassa Daggersharp, leaving a temporarily silent room.

"So," said Aragon Silversword after a moment. "What year is it?"

Singespitter had spent the last several hours in the room he shared with Kassa, studying the scroll that he had found in a hidden compartment in Lord Sinistre's private library. He was so fascinated by the contents of the scroll that he had only looked up when the draklight fell over Cluft, and he unexpectedly turned back into a demonic beast. It was true that he was getting used to such transformations by now, but this particular one startled him, causing him to set fire to Kassa's bedspread, and many other things in her room.

He was now learning the hard way about the inherent problems of being a fire-breathing beastie who needed to carry a valuable scroll in his mouth, but so far had only scorched the scroll around the edges.

Flying over the dark and evil new version of Cluft, Singespitter spotted Kassa from the air, marching across the square of student residence in a positively indecent red lace dress. Singespitter swooped down and spat the scroll out at her feet, tapping it with a hoof.

"It's that vortex," she said, by way of greeting. "I knew as soon as I saw it that I'd end up going through the bloody thing. Now's as good a time as any."

Singespitter shook his head madly and breathed a short burst of green flame, with a puff of purple smoke for emphasis.

"I don't know why I think that," said Kassa. "Lord Sinistre said it was forbidden, though. It smells suspicious, and it's the only thing I can think of to do next."

Singespitter picked up the scroll with his mouth again and spat it out a second time. It bounced off Kassa's boot.

"No, I'm not going to marry Lord Sinistre," she snapped. "He's a manipulative little worm in tight trousers. And no, before you say anything, that is not my type!"

Singespitter rolled his eyes. Communication with humans was difficult at the best of times. His most satisfactory results had always been with Kassa, who had an innate talent for listening hard enough to hear what wasn't being said — providing, of course, that she was paying attention.

Kassa leaned down and kissed Singespitter on the top of his head. "You probably shouldn't come with me. Aragon and the others are up in Egg's room. Go help them." She started heading towards Drak. Singespitter sputtered and coughed up what looked like a small ball of lava, which promptly set fire to the scroll again. By the time he had put the flames out and caught up with Kassa, she was halfway across the skybridge.

The green banks of meadow grass were now flat grey stone, dusted with silver sand. The rivers around Cluft ran with thick grey sludge instead of babbling water. The nearby trees had been transformed into shiny basalt statues of trees. "That can't be a good sign," said Kassa.

Singespitter landed on the bridge in front of her. He spat out the scroll, unrolled it and then jumped up and down on it, growling loudly in the hope of gaining her attention.

"What has that got to do with anything?" Kassa said in surprise. For a moment, Singespitter was under the delusion that she had actually noticed the scroll, until she went on to say, "No, I'm not getting back together with Aragon. He's an insane cloak-wearing toadie of darkness and he left me, in case you've forgotten."

Singespitter briefly considered setting Kassa's boots on fire, but she would probably take that as another personal plea for her to patch things up with Aragon bloody Silversword. He settled for a humphing sound and a look of total disgust.

Kassa patted him on the head. "I know you're just trying to delay me because you're worried, but I'll be fine. Fighting big swirly magical disasters is my job. It's a strange job and I don't remember applying for it, but I usually turn out to be pretty good at it. Okay?"

Singespitter tiredly tapped his hoof on the scroll one last time.

Kassa smiled at him. "I know, sweetie. I love you too." She headed off towards the city of Drak, leaving Singespitter behind.

Idiot, he thought furiously after her.

Still, she had given him an idea. Aragon might be willing to listen, or even that Egg boy. Singespitter rerolled the scroll, picked it up in his mouth again and flew towards Cluft.

~

Aragon examined the Cloak's cloak. "You say these Heroes of Justice have been possessing our bodies?"

"That's what we think," said Clio. "We have gaps in our memories from when they took us over."

"You'd think I would be used to that sort of thing by now," Aragon said dryly. "But you're wearing the costumes now and you're yourselves, aren't you?"

"It comes and goes," said Sean McHagrty.

Aragon swirled the cloak experimentally around his shoulders.

I wouldn't do that if I were you, warned the Chamberlain, but it was too late.

~

Egg woke up. The first words he heard were, "His clothes are strange. Is he an agent of the evil tyrant whose Reign of Darkness must be brought to an end?"

"It's only a draft," he muttered before opening his eyes. "I haven't polished all the dialogue yet."

"He looks like a villain," said Clio.

Egg opened his eyes. "What are you talking about?" As the situation swam into focus, he gulped. He had always refused to let his characters gulp obviously when facing something shocking or disturbing. It was one of those gestures that happened in fiction, not real life. Now he knew better. He felt, in fact, as if he had just swallowed half a brick.

The Cloak and Dream Girl leaned over him. Egg had no doubt that it was the Cloak and Dream Girl, not just Aragon Silversword and Clio in the costumes. He could not see Aragon's face — something about the cloak made the face difficult to see — but Clio's expression under the white domino mask was unfamiliar. This was not the Clio he knew.

Egg sat up. The first thing that he noticed was that his bed, formerly covered with ink-spattered grey blankets, was now draped in midnight blue satin and black lace, with (he shuddered to notice) elegant throw cushions. The bed itself was polished blackwood with golden bed knobs instead of the old splintery, creaky, standard-issue bed frame. He had a sudden urge to lie on it and go back to sleep. "Why did we worry about Drak invading us?" he asked, then looked down at himself and remembered.

He was a warlock. This time, it was a robe of dark blue velvet, punctuated with embroidered silver stars. There were no necklaces or sigils around his neck, but the belt he wore had several icons of occult significance upon it. The robe even felt magical — it shivered with possibilities. Egg had a nasty suspicion that Drak wanted him to display magical ability; he was determined that he never would.

The Cloak leaned over, still unpleasantly faceless and still yet able to convey the fact that he was staring directly into Egg's eyes. "Are you one of the tyrant's lackeys?"

"No," said Egg, thinking quickly, "I'm one of your lackeys. Um, I mean I work for you. I'm your warlock. I perform magic to help you in your vital quest to bring about the downfall of the dread tyrant and his Reign of Darkness." He jumped as Invisiblo, who was and was not Sean McHagrty, became suddenly visible.

"I do not remember a warlock," said Invisiblo.

"Neither do I," said the Cloak. "But I appear to have many holes in my memory. Nothing is as clear as once it seemed. You, warlock. How do you help us in our quest?"

"Um," said Egg. "I have a collection of magic bats which spy on Lord Sinistre's every movement."

"Spies?" said Dream Girl. "Spying is neither honourable nor heroic."

"Did I say spy?" said Egg. "I mean — they are sentinels. My magic bats. They keep an eye on the city and tell me when crimes are being committed or when the evil tyrant is being particularly tyrannical."

"And what is the dread tyrant doing now?" the Cloak asked.

"Well," said Egg. "I can't tell you right at this minute, but last time my magic bats got in touch with me they told me he was sitting down to supper, eating peach soufflé and…being very rude to the servant who brought him his food?" It was an educated guess.

"That sounds like the tyrant," said the Cloak with satisfaction. "It is long past time that we brought an end to his Reign of Darkness."

"Yes," said Egg, getting to his feet slowly and carefully. "That's a very good idea. I should go and communicate with my magic bats and ask them when would be a good time for you to do that. You know, catch him by surprise. Next time he's eating peach soufflé, perhaps."

"Excellent," said the Cloak. "Go swiftly, warlock, and gather information from your magical friends. We shall await your word before we begin our battle against the dread tyrant."

"And bring an end to his Reign of Darkness," added Dream Girl, in case they had all forgotten.

"Right," said Egg, edging closer to the door. "Good plan. Back in ten minutes." He opened the door, stepped through, pulled it carefully shut it behind him, then pelted down the corridor as if a horde of evil magical bats were chasing him.

His only thought was to find Kassa. Kassa was sane. She would know exactly what to do.

~

Kassa was lost. Once again she had underestimated how big the palace of Drak was, how many identical corridors it contained, and how much velvet there was everywhere. She was getting quite sick of the sight of the stuff.

Somehow she found herself in the ballroom. This was a surprise, because Kassa was on the fourth floor of the palace at the time. She stepped through a door and fell several feet before landing on the spiral staircase that ran around the six walls of the ballroom. "Ouch!" she exclaimed, staring up at the very inconveniently-placed door. It swung shut, the edge around the door vanishing into the intricate wall-mouldings.

Kassa suspected that she now knew how Lord Sinistre had cut short his entrance on the night of the ball.

She surveyed the damage. The extremely high heels of her red leather boots had not snapped off, but she had managed to rip another long gash in the red lace dress. At this rate she would be wearing nothing but silk underwear and loose threads by the end of the day.

A quick burst of music alerted Kassa, and she looked down into the ballroom below. Lord Sinistre, wearing a suit of black leather and silk, played a sombre tune on a silver flute, whirling around the ballroom in a slow dance of triumph.

"Are we celebrating?" she called down to him as she descended the stairs.

Lord Sinistre smiled as he saw her. "Mistress Sharpe. Of course we're celebrating. My city has swallowed up your city and is now expanding at a steady rate. I have no idea how it happened so quickly, but I'm rather pleased about it."

"It was me," said Kassa, continuing down the winding staircase. "My young cousin Egg has been drawing pictures of Drak, making up stories about it. I think his pictures have been feeding and shaping this city of yours. I ordered him to draw another picture and as soon as he set ink to parchment, darkness fell over Cluft."

Sinistre gazed at her with a mixture of delight and apprehension. "Are you saying you have switched sides, Kassa my love? You wish to marry me after all?"

"Didn't I just say that?" she asked sweetly. "Why a flute, Sinistre? It's not very menacing. Wouldn't some sort of stringed instrument be more appropriately villainous?"

"I tried," he said. "Far too much effort to learn. I don't exactly have much practice time, what with my busy schedule."

"Of course," agreed Kassa. "Long lie in, breakfast, morning tea, important decisions, costume change, lunch, costume change. The day must be packed. And how much harder to do all that without your precious Chamberlain to poach your eggs and wipe your fevered brow and tell you which important decisions you should be making."

"Yes," said Lord Sinistre with a frown. "I do wonder where he's got to. My routine was quite out of kilter this morning."

"Never mind, darling." Kassa crossed the floor, her boots making a satisfying ringing sound as they struck the polished surface. "You don't need any silly old Chamberlain. You have me to help you now."

Sinistre smiled, his eyes seeming to glow with darkness. "You are joining me, then, my Dark Lady?"

"I never left," purred Kassa, meeting him in the middle of the ballroom. "Shall we dance?"

They waltzed perfectly for a few moments, despite the lack of music. "I'm so glad you have come around to my way of thinking," said Lord Sinistre. "With you at my side, Drak will be everywhere."

"What a charming thought," said Kassa, managing to sound as if she meant it. "Will I rule at your side?"

"Of course," said Lord Sinistre. "My city is your city. When shall we have the wedding?"

"As soon as possible," said Kassa. "Can I wear velvet?"

"I wouldn't want it any other way," he assured her.

She gazed at him as they danced. He was awfully good looking, but had misplaced his brain somewhere. Perhaps it was in his other leather suit. Either that, or Egg had never got around to developing the poor man's character beyond a basic 'dark villain' prototype.

Something else struck Kassa about Lord Sinistre's appearance. Every time she saw him, he wore a different dark crown. The little obsidian tiara he had sported at the Ball was quite different to the towering construction he wore when he captured her in the vortex room. Today he wore a wide, spiky coronet with dark red gems glittering on the points. It complemented her own outfit nicely, but that wasn't important. What Kassa had noticed was that, as with the other crowns, this one had a bright white pearl set into it at a slightly odd angle. It didn't match the rest of the outfit, just as it had not matched any of his other outfits. It seemed to be tacked on without thought, an un-Draklike glitch in the otherwise dark and brooding decor. Fascinated, Kassa reached up to touch it.

Lord Sinistre ducked out of the way, releasing his hold on her waist. "Don't do that, my dear."

"Why not?"

"It's a secret, darling." He took hold of her again, whisking her around the room in a dance more sultry and quick-paced than their previous waltz.

Kassa pretended to misunderstand. "But if we're to rule together, Sinny, we can't have secrets. You have to tell me everything."

"Of course," he promised. "After the wedding, my love. What colour roses would you like?"

"Black. Are you sure you don't want to explain it all to me now, sweetie-pie?"

"Perfectly sure, honeybunch. How many bridesmaids would you like?"

"Six. But what about the swirly vortex, cuddlepot?"

"What *about* the vortex, snugglepie?"

"You said it was forbidden. Is it only forbidden to the common folk, or to you and me as well?"

"Only you and I may gaze upon the vortex and admire its presence, dewdrop. But even we are forbidden from going through."

"Oh." Kassa sighed contentedly, resting her forehead on his shoulder as they continued to dance. "Could we admire it now, sugarkins? Together? It's such an impressive sight."

"What a marvellous idea, my little love muppet. We'll trot up there as soon as we finish this dance."

"But, dumpling, there isn't any music. How will we know when the dance is finished?"

Lord Sinistre stopped dancing. "That's a very good point."

"I thought so."

"Shall we head up to the vortex room now?"

"What a good idea. Oh, and Sinny?"

"Yes, Kassy?"

"If you call me your little love muppet again, I'll set fire to you."

"Whatever you say, my pearl."

~

The vortex room was much as Kassa remembered it — which is to say that nothing about the room was particularly memorable except for the swirly vortex of darkness. "Where does it go?" she asked, forgetting to pretend indifference.

"I don't know, jewel of my desire," said Lord Sinistre.

Kassa remembered her innocent act. "But Sinny, shouldn't we know? It might be dangerous. We can't rule this city properly if there's a big wobbly vortex that could go anywhere. We should send a servant through, to discover what's on the other side."

"No, no, kitty cat," said Sinistre, sounding quite worried. "It's *quite* impossible. My father always told me that if anyone ever stepped through the vortex, the world would come to an end."

Kassa looked at him curiously. "Your father? Did he rule Drak before you?"

"Yes," said Sinistre, and then frowned. "At least, I think so. Of course, he must have done. He wouldn't have known about the vortex if he wasn't the Lord of Drak."

Kassa sensed Sinistre's reality starting to unravel. "What was he like, your father?" she asked.

Sinistre looked confused. "I don't — I don't remember," he said. "I know that he told me about the vortex, but I can't — I can't picture him in my head."

Kassa spoke quickly, while he was still muddled. "Your world or my world, Lord Sinistre?"

"What?"

She moved around to face him, a move which placed her

between Sinistre and the swirly vortex. "We come from different worlds, cutiekins. The world that Mocklore belongs to, and the world that Drak belongs to. Which one was going to come to an end if someone stepped through the vortex?"

Lord Sinistre hesitated for a moment, then said, "I suppose it must have been mine."

"Good enough for me." With a flourish, Kassa stepped backwards into the swirly vortex, squeezing her eyes closed for the journey. Everything went cold. A moment later, something tickled her leg.

"Well," remarked Lord Sinistre. "That was an anti-climax."

Kassa opened her eyes. She was still in the vortex room, still in the vortex. Its colourful darkness swirled around her legs, weaving in and out of the red lace dress. The vortex shimmered and shivered around her skin. She had gone exactly nowhere. The vortex, it seemed, was merely a swirly vortex of darkness that didn't do much of anything. "Crap," Kassa muttered.

Lord Sinistre smiled, and extended a gallant hand to Kassa. "If you don't mind, I think this little playacting routine of ours is over. It's time I took you to my dungeon and chained you to a wall. We'll both enjoy that."

"You diabolical creep," said Kassa. "I'm fed up with you and this city and the leather and the velvet — and trust me, I never thought I would get fed up with velvet — and I don't know what the Underworld is going on but I want you to *stop it right now!*"

"So professorial," he said delightedly. "I half expect you to smack me with a ruler at any moment; it's rather delicious."

Kassa was used to threats that begged to be magicked or slashed with a sword or kicked into little tiny pieces. She could deal with chaos and wild magic. It was this orderly, insidious kind of invasion she couldn't cope with. Drak had slid sideways into Cluft and just...taken over. It was dishonest and strange and she couldn't fight it.

All this, plus Aragon Silversword was back in her life.

Anger and frustration and stress reached its maximum peak, and Kassa screamed.

It was not just any scream. Kassa was a songwitch. Magic was in her blood and in her voice. When she sang, people knew about it. When she screamed, people ducked for cover. Shattering glass was nothing to Kassa in mid-scream. Shattered pottery or even concrete was reasonably common. Added to this was the pressure of Drak, the dark, morbid, angry, violent thoughts that had been building up inside Kassa's skull whenever she stepped within the influence of the draklight. Since Cluft had been swallowed whole, Kassa had been struggling to hold herself together and now she could not rein it in any longer.

Her scream was piercing and painful and seemingly endless. The grim paintings fell off the wall. Tiles popped off the empty fireplace and smashed on the glossy hearth. The blood-red furniture crumbled to dust.

Lord Sinistre fainted.

The vortex liked it. It drank Kassa's anger and frustration in greedy gulps. *Just what we want,* it told her.

Kassa attempted to break off the scream, but it had come too far for that. She fell hard and fast into the depths of the swirly vortex. Darkness spun, lights flashed. Gravity seized Kassa by the waist and did peculiar things to her senses. She sank like a stone, flew like a bird, crashed like a waterfall. The vortex swallowed her, sucking every dark emotion and morbid thought out of her soul.

When Kassa woke up, everything had changed.

11

HARMONY

*K*assa felt an overwhelming sensation of peace. There was no other word for it. Her whole body was infused with peace and love and light and a true belief that the world was utterly wonderful. Everything was going to turn out fine. Everything always did. Everything was perfect in a perfectly perfect kind of way.

Something was terribly wrong.

Kassa opened her eyes. She was lying on a bed. The linen of the bed was impossibly white. She had gone through a white lace phase in her teens, and knew from experience that no amount of washing could create that brilliant, blinding hue. "I'm dead," she said immediately. Where but the afterlife could you get whiter than white whites?

The only problem with that theory was that Kassa had been dead before, and she did not remember white as being the signature colour of the Underworld. Mostly, it was dark caves and imps and goth girls. Besides, Kassa knew where she was going when she died. She was heading straight to the section of caves that her parents, troublemakers even in death, had set up as an independent city state after staging a revolution against the higher powers in charge of the Underworld.

The likelihood, therefore, was that she was not dead. Kassa swung her legs over the side of the bed and then stared down at herself.

White. She was wearing an outfit she would have killed for at the age of nine, but which she now felt vaguely embarrassed about. There are very few people in the universe who can carry off a full blown white lace ballgown and Kassa was pretty sure she wasn't one of them.

The little white leather boots were cute, though.

There were important questions to be asked. *Where the hell am I?* would be a good start. *How am I going to get back?* was another fairly important one.

"I think I'll settle for *huh?*" she said finally.

The room was white. Not in a painted walls kind of way, but in a shimmering, mother-of-pearl tiles, marble columns kind of way. The bed stood on a shiny white floor in a perfectly round, perfectly white little room. Kassa was about to start wondering if she had gone snow blind when she noticed a high window, through which she could see a tiny bit of blue sky. She stood up on tiptoe to peek out of the window.

Outside, everything was lush and green. Butterflies danced in a lovely meadowsweet garden. A little water feature was splashing cheerfully. Paradise, only prettier.

"You're awake!"

Kassa skidded on the heels of her cute white boots and grabbed the window ledge to prevent herself from entirely falling over. She stared at the newcomer who had popped his head through the little arched doorway.

It was Lord Sinistre. At least, it would be Lord Sinistre if Lord Sinistre was blond, blue-eyed and had a tendency for wearing floppy white shirts. "What kind of game are we playing here?" she asked.

"I do like games," beamed the intruder, then sighed. "No, that's wrong. Games are frivolous attempts to divert our attention from the true nature of our society."

So in this reality, he was blond and mad. It could be an improvement. "What true nature of our society?"

"The tyranny of peace and love, of course," said the not-Sinistre. He smiled happily. "We're so flattered and humbled that such an important figure as *you* has chosen to join our rebellion."

"Right," said Kassa. "I did that, did I?"

"Of course! Why would such a noble lady appear in the slums of the city if not to join our vital cause?"

Kassa looked around at the shining white walls, the perfect white bed linen and the marble columns on either side of the little arched doorway. "These are the *slums*? What does the rest of your world look like?"

The not-Sinistre looked baffled. "My lady? You seem confused." He brightened instantly. "But of course, where are my manners? You don't know who I am! You were unconscious when we found you. We assumed you had fainted from the shock of seeing the foul conditions in which we of the outer city live."

"Um, yes," said Kassa, figuring it was probably best to play along. She lifted a hand to her forehead. "Ah, me. All this white marble. How you poor peasants are suffering!"

"My name is Ortsino," said the not-Sinistre. "Would you like to meet the others?"

"I would love to do that," said Kassa. "And perhaps you could remind me of some of the details of your rebellion as we go?"

"I would be honoured, my lady," said Ortsino, with a gallant bow. "Please follow me, and try not to be too badly affected by what you see of our horrendous living conditions. Your presence here is a grand gesture towards changing our society once and for all."

"Can't wait," said Kassa Daggersharp.

Ortsino led the way down many shiny white staircases and through many shiny white corridors. Everywhere she looked, Kassa saw people dressed in floppy white clothes, smiling at each other. She was beginning to see what Ortsino meant by the horrendous living conditions. Everyone she passed greeted her in soft, happy voices.

"Peace and light to you, mistress."

"Happy morning."

"Serenity for all."

"Love and light, light and love."

Kassa felt a little queasy. "Is everyone this happy?" she asked Ortsino.

"They do not know any better, my lady," he whispered discreetly. "That is what our rebellion is fighting against."

"Are they on drugs?"

"Alas, no. That we could do something about. Tragically, their peace and contentment comes from within."

"And do many poor people work behind the scenes to fund this lifestyle?" she asked.

Ortsino gave her a peculiar look. "These are the poor people, my lady."

Every now and then they passed a window through which Kassa saw the same lush green garden, the same water feature, the same butterflies. "Do all the gardens look the same around here?" she whispered to Ortsino.

"There is only one garden, lady," he whispered back. "I have heard that in the Inner City, you have the luxury of several different window views. That must indeed be wondrous to behold. Alas, here in the Outer City we have the same one, which was voted as the most pleasing image. Every year we have a new vote, but the result is always the same, since we are never shown the alternative. Ah, here we are."

He hovered outside a door and, with the exaggerated movements of an amateur criminal drawing attention to the fact that he was desperate not to be noticed, knocked three times.

"Password?" hissed a voice.

Ortsino took a deep breath, blushing with the effort. "Unpleasant but necessary action," he blurted out in a hoarse whisper.

The door opened quickly. Ortsino ushered Kassa in, and looked both ways up and down the corridor before ducking in himself and closing the door behind him. "Welcome to the rebellion, Ladybird," he declared.

Kassa bit her lip to not correct him about her name. If he thought she was this Ladybird person, she had better go along with it. This was a hardened gang of desperado rebels. Or as hardened a gang as one could gather in such a bright white city of peace and light.

Including Ortsino, there were four of them, staring at Kassa with something like awe. Ortsino pulled off his floppy white shirt, sticking his chest out proudly. Underneath, he wore a short-sleeved tunic which was — Kassa realised after a long moment — slightly less pure white than everything else in the 'slums' of this city. The garment was greyish, and letters had been embroidered across the front in pale green thread to spell the words 'Too Much Peace in Harmony!' It sounded nonsensical to Kassa, so she turned her attention to the other rebels.

The others also wore greyish tunics with slogans, rebelling against the local style police. A tall young man, whose tunic read 'Happiness is Tyranny', wore lilac trousers. An older fellow with a straggly beard, whose tunic read, 'Turn Down the Light', had a blue ink tattoo drawn on his left forearm, a circle indicating a face, two dots indicating eyes and a curved line indicating a downturned, frowning mouth. The effect was slightly spoiled by the scribbled-over practice efforts that were visible on his right forearm, all three of which wore smiley mouths.

The only woman of the group, whose tunic read 'The Light Lords Of Harmony City Have Been Unfairly Forcing Our Society To Be Happy And Peaceful By Peculiar and Arcane Means For Far Too Long Now, And We Are Tired of Being Surrounded By Light And Love Constantly And Couldn't We Just Be Unhappy Occasionally If We Really Want To???' in far superior embroidery to the others, had used makeup to draw dark frown lines into her face, worry lines into her forehead and mournful grey bags under her eyes. The effect was totally spoiled by her bright and sunny smile. She was holding a quill and inkwell, and was trying to use them to black up her white-blonde hair.

"This is Iason, Deevis and Strella," said Ortsino.

"Right," said Kassa, halfway through reading Strella's remarkably informative tunic. "So you are the rebellion that plans to overthrow Harmony City and get rid of the...Light Lords, who are responsible for making everyone so happy. Am I right?"

"The other three Light Lords, of course," said Ortsino, with a chuckle. "We don't want to overthrow you or Quill-smith, now do we?"

The others all giggled.

"Of course not," said Kassa, laughing along. "Because I'm a Light Lord, aren't I? Ha ha."

"Quillsmith told us that one of the other Light Lords might be persuaded to aid our cause," said Ortsino. "But we never guessed he meant you! I mean, we always thought that you were, well..."

"The most tyrannical bitch of them all," volunteered

Strella. She blushed. "Sorry. I'm just practising the use of confrontational language."

"You're very good at it," Kassa assured her. "So, where's Quillsmith? I take it he's the instigator of this little gang?"

The rebels looked at each other, worried. "Don't you know?" said Ortsino. "We thought that was why you had finally revealed yourself to us."

"Um," said Kassa. "You know, I'm not sure I've recovered from that fainting spell I had earlier. The shock of seeing all that...white marble. I may have hit my head."

"They captured Quillsmith," said Strella. "That's why we're so happy — I mean, that's why our rebellion of anti-happiness has been given new hope of eventual occasional unhappiness. You're here to help us rescue him, aren't you?"

"Of course I am!" said Kassa. "Rescuing Quillsmith. Brilliant plan. Let's get started, shall we?"

~

The four intrepid rebels, accompanied by the interloper from another world, crept and scuttled and generally made a spectacle of themselves in their efforts to travel discreetly from their hideout to the prison block. Each of them wore ordinary Harmony clothes, floppy and bright white. Strella had braided her hair back to disguise the inky black clumps. They looked like five very ordinary citizens of Harmony, except that four of them were acting like guilty criminals.

Kassa attempted to walk like a normal person, but eventually had to resort to the same hunched gait as the others in order to be able to speak to Ortsino. "Awfully brave, Quillsmith, wasn't he?" she said, in the hope of a more detailed explanation than that provided by the embroidery on Strella's tunic. "I mean, contacting you rebels, endangering his own position of authority..."

"No more brave than yourself for doing the same, Ladybird," Ortsino assured her.

"But he did it first," said Kassa. "Or you would never have known what was going on..." *Please please please tell me what's going on.*

"You are right," Ortsino agreed. "We would never have known the truth about our unnaturally peaceful and happy city."

Kassa waited, but he was not forthcoming with any more details. "Flying blind as usual," she sighed.

"I beg your pardon?"

"Don't mind me. What's happening over there?"

They were near what looked like a small cafeteria. A crowd of aristocratic-looking people in well-tailored floppy white clothes sat at tables, eating salad from large white plates and staring at a large window which took up the whole back wall.

Through the window, you could see Drak.

Here in Harmony, the image of the dark, brooding city with its high buildings and black shadows was particularly dramatic. Ortsino and the rebels stared with wide eyes as the window displayed a series of images — Lord Sinistre walking down a staircase with his face like thunder, a miserable-looking gardener tending the moonflowers in a park full of basalt sculptures, a woman in a long black dress looking scared as she hurried through a dark alleyway.

As if by magic, words scrolled across the window. *Drak — Aren't you glad you don't live there?*

"Sort of reverse tourism," Kassa observed.

"I never imagined such a place existed," Ortsino gasped. Without taking their eyes off the window, he and the rebels found an empty table and sat down.

Five people in bright costumes ran along a typical Drak street. Kassa recognised the Cloak, Dream Girl and Invisiblo.

The other two were dressed just as luridly. Kassa didn't recognise the man in the gold cloak, but the woman looked uncomfortably like Kassa herself, in a pink and white candy-striped version of her usual pirate garb, with bright pink hair and albino eyes.

"We are the Heroes of Justice!" the pink and white Kassa announced in a sugary voice.

"Our job is to make Drak a safer, happier place," simpered Dream Girl.

"If only Drak was as peaceful and orderly as Harmony," said the Cloak.

"Perhaps, one day, it will be!" said Invisiblo with a cheesy grin.

Kassa had seen enough. "Which way to this prison?" she asked Ortsino in an undertone.

He gestured behind them, his gaze still fixed to the images in the window. "Along the corridor, pretty little plaza. Can't miss it."

"Right," said Kassa. "Wish me luck, hardened rebels."

"Bye," said Strella.

The Heroes of Justice rescued a small child who was stuck at the top of an obsidian statue. As they worked, they smiled broadly and continued to declaim inspirational phrases. The rebels gazed wonderingly at the images through the window, oohing and ahhing with the rest of the crowd. Kassa left them to it.

She walked along the corridor until it opened out into a bright white courtyard. Through several archways you could glimpse the same image of that meadowsweet garden and butterflies, over and over. Two men in long white robes stood in front of the last archway, their posture suggesting that they were sentries of some kind.

A sign above the archway spelled out the words 'Harmony High-Security Prison' in bright gold letters. Ortsino was right, you couldn't miss it.

It did not look like any prison she had ever heard about.

Kassa shrugged to herself. When in doubt, get captured and hope someone starts explaining things to you. She squared her shoulders and marched up to the sentries. "Hi, my name is…" The words '…Kassa and I'm from out of town, could you direct me to the nearest dungeon' froze on her lips as the two sentries immediately bowed.

"At your service, Lord Ladybird," they said in high, sing-song voices.

"Right," said Kassa. She couldn't think of anything convincing to say, and she didn't have Ortsino to advise her on local protocol. "I'd like to visit the prisoner Quillsmith," she tried.

"Of course, my lady." The sentries stepped aside, and a door slid open to let her through the archway.

Kassa stepped inside the Harmony prison.

~

Inside, it was even less like a prison than Kassa expected. For a start, it was green and it was big. There was grass underfoot. There were butterflies, huge colourful creatures flopping around in the air. The white ceiling above made it quite clear that Kassa was not outside, but apart from the lack of sky it seemed as if she had stepped straight into the garden that was visible from every window in the Outer City of Harmony.

The water feature was splashing away, which reminded Kassa that she was thirsty. She had little hope that the water feature would contain actual water, as a butterfly had just flapped its way through her arm and out the other side, suggesting that this environment was not entirely real. She made for the small hill, hoping to be able to see something interesting from the top of it.

The prisoner sat on the other side of the grassy slope, busying himself with a tea tray, pouring hot water into little china cups. He wasn't chained to anything.

It was Egg.

Kassa took a deep breath. This was not the Egg she had met in recent weeks, an unsure boy on the verge of being an adult. This was Egg as he might be in ten or more years, a solid man with a reliable set to his shoulders. He also, she realised with a familiar sinking feeling, looked a lot like that fifth Hero of Justice, the one who wasn't Aragon or Clio or Sean or herself. *That makes a horrible kind of sense.* "Hello, little cousin," she said quietly.

He jumped. Literally jumped nearly a foot in the air, from a curled up sitting position to land smack on his feet. "Lady-bird," he gasped, his whole body tense at the sight of her. "What are you going to do to me?"

"That depends," said Kassa Daggersharp. "I was going to grab you by the ankles and shake you upside down until you had explained every detail of this world to me, but I'm not sure that's going to be necessary now. I know exactly what's going on around here."

Quillsmith looked at her curiously. "Do you think you could explain it to me?"

~

Egg searched for Kassa. He had tried the Mermaid Tower, but he didn't know which room was hers. Thanks to the invasion of Drak, the grey concrete walls of the Seaweed Room were now black and shiny, draped with gold taffeta. Mistress Brim's hair (previously as flat and grey as the walls) was a towering beehive of silver, her matronly figure squeezed into a floor-length ballgown. The food troughs were piled high with tiny delicacies like poached lobster eggs, trout mousse niblets and iceberry jelly-puffs. Mistress Brim still served everything with a giant steel scooping spoon. It was nice to see that some things hadn't changed.

No one had seen Kassa. Most of the students he asked barely remembered who Egg was, let alone a professor called Mistress Sharpe. The effect of the draklight was getting stronger, stranger. Egg barely managed to avoid being dragged into three separate duels and several seductions between the square of student residence and the library tower.

A black, winged monster emerged from behind the library tower, screaming in a hoarse, horrible voice as it dove straight at Egg. "Yaaarg!" he yelled, before realising it was Singespitter. "Oh, it's you." He took a deep breath to calm himself. "Where is she?"

Singespitter landed on the edge of the golden skybridge. He spat out the large scroll he had been holding in his mouth and baaed meaningfully. The sound came out as a cross between a shipping siren and the death rattle of a giant cow. Smoke billowed out of his nostrils.

"She's not over there having an intimate supper with the enemy again, is she?" asked Egg.

Singespitter gave him a dirty look and rolled his eyes.

"Well, it's not unheard of!"

"Ooh, look who it is," cooed a very female voice, echoed by the giggles of two others. Egg turned around slowly to see Imani Almondstone, Brittany Yarrowstalk and Rosehip Moonweaver bearing down on him. All three had followed the 'Drak fashion' before it became compulsory, wearing black lace in their hair, squeezing into velvet tops and tottering around in leather boots with heels higher than the rest of their shoes put together.

Now they were well and truly Drakked, their hair dark and glossy, gold baubles hanging from velvet chokers around their necks and long, midnight-coloured ballgowns sweeping the black and shiny paving stones around the library tower.

"Is he a real warlock, do you think?" Almondstone giggled, reaching out to tug the collar of the robe that Egg had momentarily forgotten he was wearing. Her touch sent a sudden spark across his skin, but he gritted his teeth and ignored it. He had spent the last seventeen years not doing magic. He wasn't going to start now, no matter how strongly the garment he wore seemed to want him to.

"Turn me into a frog," said Yarrowstalk, also giggling.

Egg manfully resisted the temptation to do so.

Moonweaver pouted, leaning forward a little to display her cleavage. "I don't think he's a real warlock. I think he's pretending."

"Let's play with him anyway," said Almondstone.

Egg backed away. Finding Kassa was a definite priority. These girls had been silly to start with, who could tell what they would do if the influence of Drak continued much longer? "Can't right now. Have to see a sheep about a lady."

"Will you come back?" asked Yarrowstalk. The three of them closed in around him.

"Maybe?" said Egg, reaching up to grasp the edge of the skybridge. All three of them sighed at once, their bosoms rising and falling beneath the clingy bodices of the ballgowns. Egg was finding it quite hard to tear his eyes away. "Um, bye?"

Singespitter bit his hand, gently but firmly. "Yah!" Egg yelled, but he got the point. He pulled himself up to the skybridge and kept walking even as the three girls giggled and called out to him. "Don't give me that look," he muttered to the sheep. "You would have been distracted if they were ewes."

~

"Okay," said Kassa two minutes later, sitting cross-legged on the fake grass with her white lace skirt spread out in all directions and a small china cup of tea balanced on her right knee. "The first thing you need to know is that I'm not Ladybird, or Lord Ladybird, or any other kind of lady. My name is Kassa Daggersharp and I live in a place called Mocklore. I don't know if it's on another continent or another world or even in another cosmos, but it's a long way from Harmony. Got it?"

"I see," said Quillsmith, sounding a little suspicious. "And you wouldn't just be Ladybird setting a trap for me, would you?"

"I don't know much about this Ladybird character," said Kassa. "Is she the kind of person who would come up with something so subtle and devious?"

"Devious, yes. Subtle, no. All right, I'll believe you." He shook his head slowly. "So you're from the outsider world."

"It's outside is it?" said Kassa. "Nice to have a point of reference. I was beginning to think no one would be able to direct me home."

"I don't know how you got here," said Quillsmith. "I have no idea how to get you back."

"I can worry about that later," said Kassa, trying to ignore the little voice that immediately piped up in the back of her mind. *Yes, what about that? He makes an interesting point, Daggersharp. Which way is home?* "In the mean time, I need to find out exactly who you are, what this place is and what the hell's going on. Drak is eating my world alive."

"I know," Quillsmith said sadly. "It started out as a story," he added. "It wasn't supposed to go this far."

Kassa looked at him. "That sounds familiar. Go on, then. Tell me your tale."

"I thought you knew what was going on."

"I know a lot," said Kassa. "I saw your little propaganda show out there, and then I saw you. Drak is the dark half and Harmony is the light half. Which is real?"

Quillsmith sighed. "I'm not sure I know anymore." He took a deep breath. "It was Ladybird who worked out that magic could be separated. We — the Light Lords could funnel the darkness away from our city, leaving only the light. It wasn't long before we discovered how to do it with people, too. The only trouble was finding a safe way to contain the dark energy so that it would never contaminate our perfect society. I was visited by, well, a muse I suppose. She inspired me to write about a city, equal and opposite to Harmony, a place that would feed on the darkness and enjoy it just as we enjoyed the light. The other Light Lords took my story and built the dark city — Drak — for real, constructing it out of magic and placing it on the far side of our world. It wasn't long before it became too powerful for us to control."

"So why isn't Drak currently destroying *your* city?" Kassa asked.

"Half a year ago, a stranger appeared in Drak. The Chamberlain."

Kassa frowned. "Aragon Silversword?"

Quillsmith nodded. "Drak was becoming dangerously powerful. And then suddenly we had evidence that another world existed, beyond our own. The Chamberlain's world. Somewhere we could safely send Drak, far from us."

"A convenient dumping ground," Kassa said acidly.

"I spoke out," Quillsmith insisted. "I refused to be a part of their sinister scheme any longer."

"After the damage was done."

"Well, yes."

"Very noble of you, I'm sure."

"I broke away from the Light Lords and began encouraging rebellion in the Outer City. It occurred to me that if we incorporated darkness back into Harmony, the danger of Drak might be neutralised. I lost my head, though, and said something in public that embarrassed the other Light Lords. They declared me a traitor and sent me here."

"But how did Aragon get here in the first place?"

"I don't know. If he had not, we would never have discovered the outsider world."

"Now we're getting to the interesting meat," said Kassa. "What power does your world have over ours?"

"You are Lord Ladybird," Quillsmith explained. "You may seem like different people, but your essential substance is the same. Just as every citizen of Drak has a counterpart in Harmony, so every citizen of Harmony has a counterpart in the place you call Mocklore."

"But you made Drak that way," argued Kassa. "You didn't make Mocklore. Why do the same people exist in different worlds?"

Quillsmith shrugged. "Perhaps every world in the cosmos contains the same people, living different lives."

"That's a depressing thought. Let's go back a few steps. The Light Lords of Harmony became the Heroes of Justice in Drak. Why?"

"We thought they might have a...calming effect on the dark powers of Drak. That was when we started broadcasting the adventures of the Heroes of Justice into the Inner City, to remind our citizens of how lucky they were."

"Yes, I saw your little PR exercise. When did Aragon become the Cloak?"

"It was a mistake," admitted Quillsmith. "Lord Kloakor briefly took control of his Drak counterpart, the Cloak, in order to get close to this Aragon and alter his memories so that he thought he had been the Chamberlain all his life. Because all three of them were matching counterparts, they merged together. The Chamberlain and the Cloak became the same person, and Lord Kloakor was able to control them with a thought whenever he wished to." He smiled suddenly, looking much younger. "Our viewers were very excited by the secret identity twist when it was revealed."

"Really trying not to be judgmental," Kassa warned. "You're not making it easy."

"Sorry. Anyway, this is how we discovered that we had an influence over our counterparts in the outsider world as well as in Drak. I found the boy Egg and implanted images of Drak in his mind. I was able to reach back through time, implanting the stories in his head as far back as his childhood."

Kassa nodded. She had expected something like this. "So you used Egg. When he drew those images and stories, he gave Drak an existence in our world. You Light Lords used that to focus your magic, transporting the whole city from your world to ours. Didn't it occur to you that such a huge feat of magic might have dangerous repercussions?" She realised she was sounding shrill, and tried to rein her emotions in for a moment. She swallowed some tea, and then some more. It was quite nice, if a little on the cold side.

"You have to understand," said Quillsmith. "Our whole city runs on magic. We have no fertile soil as you do, no plentiful water supply, no animals or...what are those things with feathery skin?"

"Birds."

"They are very peculiar. We have none of those things, except for the gargoyles and demonic creatures we created for Drak. Everything we eat, drink, wear and breathe comes from magic. Harmony is the only city in our world, and it is the duty of the Light Lords to keep the Harmonians protected and happy for the rest of their lives."

Kassa interrupted. "But all this peace and love stuff isn't

natural, is it? You drained all that negative energy out of your city to make the people *think* they are happy."

Quillsmith didn't seem to think that was a problem. "What's the difference between being happy and only thinking you are happy?"

Kassa stared at him incredulously. "Using magic to control the emotions of your populace? No wonder you ended up in this mess."

"I thought you were trying not to be judgmental."

"Trying, not succeeding. You people are nuts."

"Believe me," said Quillsmith. "We didn't know that Drak would feed upon your world as it has done. The transportation must have affected the dark energy reserves within Drak, allowing its essence to convert the chaotic energy of Mocklore into fuel. I objected to what had happened — that's why I'm here."

Kassa regarded him skeptically. "You ended up in prison because you tried to save my world?"

"It was too late. We drained our power reserves when we transported Drak. Our magic will return, slowly, but we need what little we have to maintain the wellbeing of Harmony, to purify the air and to continue providing food and water. By the time we have any magic to spare, it will be too late for Mocklore."

Kassa set down her cup and saucer, trying to remain calm. "Nothing but good news today."

A melodious female voice called out from the far side of the hill. "Quillsmith, sweetie, where are you?"

In one shocked instant, Kassa recognised the voice. It was her own.

"Hide," said Quillsmith, gesturing towards a clump of pretty flowering shrubs.

Kassa rolled until she was certain that the shrubs concealed her from view. When she could no longer resist the temptation (about six and a half seconds later), she peeked out to get a quick look at the newcomer.

It was Kassa, a slightly taller, slimmer version of Kassa with pink hair, white skin and horribly bright white eyes, but unmistakably Kassa.

"Can you believe those idiot guards thought I was already in here?" drawled Lord Ladybird. She eyed the two used china cups. "Have you been entertaining guests?"

"I drink a lot of tea," said Quillsmith. "There's nothing else to do in here."

"You should be grateful, darling. Think what passes for a prison in Drak, all those dungeony shadows and clanking chains, ugh." Ladybird gazed around the pretty garden of illusion. A large butterfly perched for a moment on her hair before flying off again. "Charming," she said. "This must be the nicest place in Harmony."

"I can see why you think so," said Quillsmith. "You can leave whenever you like. What do you want, Ladybird?"

"Oh, not much. I just came to tell you that we've done it. We've made contact! Well, I haven't, my target is proving a little resilient, but the others have."

"Contact?" said Quillsmith, frowning. "What contact? With whom?"

"With our counterparts in the outsider world, silly. Dreamer and Kloakor and Invisiblus have managed to make their outsider counterparts believe they are the Heroes of Justice. Since Drak has got so much more powerful, it seems to have stuck. Isn't that lovely news?"

"I don't understand. Why are you doing this?"

"We don't all have the ability to put picture stories into people's heads, Quillie. We have to try other methods if we're going to transport ourselves out there."

"You're planning to invade?"

"Colonise, sweetie. What's the point of letting Drak take

over that nice fertile world when we could do it ourselves? We'll do a straight swap, pop stinky old Drak back here out of harm's way and move Harmony into a fresh new world."

"It's called Mocklore."

"Whatever."

"It's fully populated."

"So? They can move. Or, I know, we could zap them all back here. Make a fresh start over there with no pesky little local people to bother us."

Quillsmith stared at her. "How much magic will this take?"

"Lots, I expect. Doesn't matter, we can always get more."

"From where? We were all drained by the transportation of Drak."

"Some of us kept a little back, Quillie. Besides, have you had a look at this Mocklore place? It's just bursting with magic. What do they need all those colours for, anyway? We'll borrow all the power we need from them. Isn't it a gorgeous plan?"

"She was right," Quillsmith said bitterly. "We are nuts. Did you stop to think that this might be why our world became a wasteland of silver sand in the first place?"

Ladybird looked at him sharply. "She? Who, your little teacup friend? Have you been receiving visitors without permission, you naughty boy?"

Kassa stood up, stepping through the flowering shrubs to confront Ladybird. "I'm Kassa Daggersharp," she said. "It's so nice to meet me."

Ladybird looked her double up and down. "Well," she said. "Aren't you a clever little mirror-creature?"

"Do you always talk like a six-year old duchess?" asked Kassa. "It's really annoying."

Ladybird's white eyes gleamed. "I'd be interested to know how you got here, cutie."

"So you can use my shortcut yourself?" said Kassa. "Sorry, you'll have to do it the long way around. I can't help you."

"Oh, I think you can," said Ladybird, stretching out a hand to touch Kassa's face. "Let's just see what secrets are locked up in your darling little brain, shall we?"

~

"She could be anywhere," Egg complained to Singespitter.

The palace butler was surprisingly helpful, telling them that yes, Mistress Sharpe had arrived a little while ago, although no, he was terribly sorry that he didn't know which of the seven hundred rooms of the palace she was currently located in.

Come to think of it, he hadn't been all that helpful.

Egg promptly got himself and Singespitter lost. They stumbled into the Hall of Wardrobe, a seemingly endless room packed solid with racks and racks of Lord Sinistre's costumes, mostly an assortment of black leather, silk and velvet formal wear, casual wear, sleepwear and fancy dress costumes.

Singespitter spat out the scroll that he held in his mouth, and stamped his hoof meaningfully on it.

"You want me to read that scroll?" said Egg.

Singespitter almost fainted with relief. He did a little sheep dance of joy while Egg unrolled the scroll and looked at it.

"Ah," said Egg after a moment. "Blimey. That's me, all grown up. And two Kassas."

Singespitter nodded. He had found the scroll in the library of Drak, in the darkest corner of the least-used scroll bucket. Instead of words or pictures, it contained moving images of another world.

"It's all white and cheerful," said Egg. "Is this the light version of Drak?"

Singespitter shrugged. It was as good a theory as any.

"So one of those Kassas must be ours?"

The boy was bright. Who'd have guessed it?

"Hey!" yelled Egg. "Kassa just vanished. The other Kassa touched her, and she disappeared."

Singespitter stared worriedly at the scroll. *The vortex*, he thought clearly.

"How do we find the vortex?" Egg asked obediently.

Contact has been made! Singespitter was always chuffed when a new human learned to hear his unspoken sentences. He baaed happily.

Kassa stood in a small room with dark red walls. She blinked and touched her cheek, where she could still feel the cool imprint of Ladybird's touch. This was a familiar place. The furniture was gone, but the paintings still lay scattered over the broken floor-tiles. It was the vortex room in Drak. She was, in fact, standing where the vortex had been.

There was no swirling light or swirling darkness. Kassa walked slowly across the room and stared at the place where the vortex had been. There was nothing there. The portal to Harmony was closed — or, more likely, broken.

"Very, very strange," she said aloud, staring down at herself to check that she was still in one piece. The ridiculous red lace gown was back, and the knee-high scarlet boots. It was faintly reassuring. At least there was colour in this world, even if it was so very dark and shadowy after the bright whiteness of Harmony. Of course, Drak had always been dark and shadowy, but Kassa had a feeling that she would even find the sunlight of Cluft quite dull right now.

Except, of course, there would not be any sunlight in Cluft. Drak had invaded. Darkness ruled. "Back to work," sighed Kassa. "With a slightly better idea of what is going on behind the scenes, but no great world-saving plans coming immediately to mind."

No plans at all, in fact. She didn't have the faintest idea what to do next. Lord Sinistre was nowhere in sight, so finding him might be a good start. Also, lunch. Kassa was starving. When had she last eaten? All she had consumed in Harmony was a cup of tea, and she wasn't even sure if that had been real. She wondered what time of day it was — she could usually rely on her own body clock to inform her whether it was lunch time, supper time or breakfast time, but the combination of her trip to Harmony and the ever-present evening of Drak had knocked her out of balance.

"I'll ask the kitchens," she decided in a brief flash of brilliance. "Right. Getting a plan together. On the right track. Kitchens first, find out what time it is, eat something nutritious, find Lord Sinistre, save the world. Okay."

She strode confidently out of the vortex room and along the corridor, maintaining her confidence right up to the point where she realised she didn't know where the kitchens were.

12

INTO THE LIGHT

*I*n downtown Drak, the Heroes of Justice stared at each other.

"What are we doing?" asked Invisiblo the Mystery Man.

"We were in that room, waiting for the warlock to return," said Dream Girl. "Then suddenly we were here, rescuing a small boy from the top of that statue." She stared up at the ten foot obsidian statue of a gargoyle, its wings outstretched. "What was a small boy doing up there in the first place?"

"We were talking," the Cloak said intently. "We were talking about ourselves in very loud voices." *If only Drak was as peaceful and orderly as Harmony.* "And we were staring straight at this wall, as if…"

"As if we had an audience," Invisiblo completed.

"What do we do now?" said Dream Girl. "Should we go back and wait for that warlock?"

"Spies and warlocks," said the Cloak. "That is not the way we do things."

"If only we could remember the way we do things," said Dream Girl.

"We must bring an end to the tyrant's reign of darkness," said Invisiblo the Mystery Man.

"Let's do that," said the Cloak.

~

In Harmony, the three Light Lords known as Lord Kloakor, Lord Dreamer and Lord Invisiblus stood around the wide window which displayed an image of Drak.

"They keep getting confused," said Lord Kloakor. "Do we have to do everything ourselves?"

"Why don't we let them go after that silly tyrant if that's what they want to do," said Lord Dreamer. "Surely that will give them more reality. Overthrowing the reign of darkness is their quest, after all."

"Their quest, not ours," said Lord Kloakor. "We need them to take on our identities, not get caught up in this silly superhero behavior."

"What are they doing now?" said Lord Invisiblus. "I can't see anything."

"That's because you're invisible," Lord Kloakor said patiently. "Your retinas don't have anything to reflect off."

"Oh, right." Lord Invisiblus gradually faded into view. "That's better."

They watched the Heroes of Justice head towards the palace of Drak.

"Where's Ladybird?" complained Lord Dreamer. "Her counterpart should be with them."

"She hasn't had much luck making her counterpart do anything," said Invisiblus.

"I haven't seen Ladybird's counterpart lately," said Lord Kloakor thoughtfully. "I wonder what she's up to."

"I'll tell you exactly what she has been up to," thundered Lord Ladybird, bursting through the doorway, a blinding vision in pink and white stripes. She dragged Quillsmith behind her, almost pulling his arm out of the socket. "She has been trotting through Harmony as if she owned the place, with this traitor helping her every step of the way!"

"Quillsmith," said Lord Kloakor. "About time you stopped messing around in that prison and got back to work. We've got something you can help us with."

"Help us?" Ladybird screeched. "Didn't you hear what I just said? He's a traitor!"

"Yes, dear," said Kloakor. "We know he's a traitor. It's one of the reasons we put him in prison. But we need him now, so could we have a bit of shush from you?"

"Shush?" she repeated piercingly.

Quillsmith pulled his arm away from Ladybird. "Sorry, Kloakor. I won't help you invade that little country. We've done enough to it already."

Lord Kloakor raised an eyebrow. "You'd prefer to see Drak turn it into a velvet-clad wasteland, would you? Wouldn't have thought you were the cruel type."

Quillsmith hesitated. "*She* was talking about the native inhabitants like they were furniture that could be moved out at our convenience."

"And why not?" Ladybird demanded.

"We should bring Drak here and face our responsibility," said Quillsmith.

"We should use that stupid little Mogglore place to fuel our magic and become more powerful than we have ever been," spat Ladybird.

Lord Kloakor looked from one to the other, amused. "Are you challenging Ladybird for the leadership, Quillers?"

"He wouldn't dare," said Ladybird. She glared at Lord Dreamer and then at Lord Invisiblus (who promptly vanished so he wouldn't have to see the scary expression in her bright white eyes) and finally at Lord Kloakor. "You wouldn't let him!"

"I wouldn't have any choice," said Kloakor. "You know the rules, Ladybird. If there's a challenge to the leadership, the rest of us have to remain impartial."

"I know I am," said Dreamer sweetly. She had always hated Ladybird.

"I challenge the leadership," Quillsmith said, getting the hint.

"You little toad!" Ladybird screamed.

"I have an idea," said Kloakor as if it had just occurred to him. "Quillers, you might not know, but we're planning to invade the outsider world. Dreamer and Invisiblus and I have managed to make contact with our counterparts in the outsider world, making them take on the identities of the Heroes of Justice. The next step is to take them over with our own personalities. What do you think?"

"Should be feasible," said Quillsmith.

Ladybird turned on him, furious. "You hate the idea."

"No, no, it has possibilities," Quillsmith said, infuriatingly calm.

"It should be a fair test," said Kloakor. "Whichever of you can fully make contact with your counterpart — and sustain it the longest, in the event of a tie — should be our leader."

"Sounds fair!" said the empty patch of space which was Invisiblus.

"Very fair," said Dreamer.

Ladybird looked stunned. "But you know I haven't been able to do it. That Kassa person is completely immune to my influence. She's unnatural."

"Actually, you have the advantage," Quillsmith pointed out. "You've practiced this. I haven't. Still, I don't mind."

"She's not there anyway," said Ladybird. "She was here,

and she exploded into dust when I touched her, didn't she?" She turned to Quillsmith to support her argument.

"It did look as if she exploded into dust," he agreed. "She could be anywhere."

"Here she is," said Lord Dreamer, who had been fiddling with the Drak-viewing window. "She got safely home."

They all stared at the image of Kassa sitting in the kitchens of Drak, eating from a wide silver platter of elegant hors d'oeuvres and chatting to the head cook.

"Well, that's all right, then," said Quillsmith. "Ladies first."

"What was that?" Egg said in alarm. He and Singespitter were still in the Hall of Wardrobe, surrounded by the maze of costume racks. They were both jumpy, and Singespitter had been forced to give Egg the important scroll to tuck into his belt after accidentally setting fire to it three more times out of sheer nervousness.

As they reached the crossroads between the velvet trouser collection, the long leather coat collection, the naughty underwear collection and the collection of gilded costume accessories, a grey figure stepped out from behind a rack of leather coats. "What are you doing, warlock?" boomed the Cloak.

"Gahh!" said Egg in shock. "I mean, um, I'm doing what I told you I was going to do." Nervously, he racked his brain to remember what that was.

"We do not believe you," Dream Girl hissed in his ear, coming up behind him.

"Where are your clockwork bats, warlock?" taunted Invisiblo, an unseen presence.

"Consorting with a demonic beast," said the Cloak, eyeing Singespitter with distaste. "Creeping around this accursed city, claiming to be our spy? We do not trust you, warlock. We think you are working for the dread tyrant. We think you are a supporter of the Reign of Darkness."

"A villain," said Dream Girl. "We think you are a villain. There is only one way to deal with villains."

Egg thought fast. Short of hiding under Singespitter, he couldn't see a way out of this. He groped a hand blindly into the nearest display of glittering belts, hats and ornate jewellery, hoping to find something that he could use as a weapon, or a shield. His hand brushed something hard and he gripped it. It felt too light to be of any use, thin and curved.

It was a mask.

"She's been doing this for ages," complained Lord Invisiblus. The Light Lords gathered around Ladybird as she struggled to impose her will on the impenetrable mind of Kassa Daggersharp.

"It's — not — working," panted Ladybird, breathing hard. "I tell you, there's something wrong with that woman. She is too strong-minded to allow anyone to take her over."

"More strong-minded than you?" said Lord Kloakor in pretended surprise. "How could that be, Ladybird? Are you not essentially the same person?"

"And if you are not as strong-minded as your counter-part," said Lord Dreamer, "Perhaps Lord Quillsmith is right to challenge your leadership."

Ladybird's white eyes flared. "This is unworthy of you all."

"On the contrary, Ladybird," said Kloakor. "It would seem the task is unworthy of you. Quillsmith, fancy a shot at it?"

"I'll have a go," said Quillsmith.

Dreamer did something to the viewing window, and the image changed. Now they saw Egg and the Heroes of Justice, surrounded by racks of black velvet garments. Dream Girl held a struggling Egg, while the Cloak came under attack from a black winged monster. Invisiblo the Mystery Man became visible just long enough to see what was happening, and flung himself at the monster that was attacking the Cloak.

Quillsmith glanced over his shoulder at the fuming Lady-bird. "This should be easy," he remarked.

~

Egg stood up straight. His power crackled like an electric storm, forcing Dream Girl back from him. He turned to face her, placing Lord Sinistre's gold party mask over his own features. "Do you not know me, Dream Girl?"

He was taller than before, his shoulders broader. His voice sounded older. His robe was white, with gold embroidery displaying the complex alphabet of Harmony in bright sigils. His long gold cape fluttered, although there was no breeze here in the Hall of Wardrobe.

"The Penman," Dream Girl breathed.

Invisiblo grabbed hold of Singespitter, and hurled the sheep-monster into a rack of slippery taffeta undergarments. Singespitter hit the floor with a nasty crash and thump which rendered him unconscious.

Egg — the Penman — tilted his gold mask in Invisiblo's direction. "Was that necessary?"

"It's a monster," said Invisiblo. "Monsters are in league with villains and must be slain or rendered unconscious by heroes. Shall I slay it?"

The Penman approved of Invisiblo's zeal. "Leave it for

now. We have more important things to do. Do we not, Cloak?"

"Indeed, Penman," said the Cloak. "We must bring about the downfall of the dread tyrant."

"We must bring light to Drak," said Invisiblo, helping Dream Girl to her feet.

Dream Girl ignored his attentions, gazing at the Penman. "We must End the Reign of Darkness," she said.

"Let us away!" declared the Penman, sweeping his golden cape around in a dramatic flourish. "Heroes of Justice, follow me!"

~

Lord Sinistre was unhappy. There was no sign of the Chamberlain, which meant that Lord Sinistre had been forced to eat his supper — a sliver of smoked duck omelette followed by almond soup, then steamed lettuce salad and finally a compote of frozen rosebuds in raspberry custard adorned by a single grape carved into an amusing caricature of his own head — without hearing the three most interesting items of the day's news, graded carefully so that he was told the most interesting bit last.

Lord Sinistre had been feeling especially grumpy since Kassa had vanished into the vortex — and, more importantly, spurned his proposal of marriage. Such a shame. She had a great deal of potential to be a Dark Queen. He had tried to cheer himself up by watching the goings-on in Cluft (now a suburb of Drak) through his spyglass all afternoon. It was amusing, watching the staff and students of that prissy little town glide about like proper citizens of Drak. Lord Sinistre would have liked to gloat, but it didn't feel right to do so until the Chamberlain officially told him about the conquest of Cluft. It wasn't real news otherwise.

After the novelty of Cluft-watching wore off, he had been left with nothing to do but change his clothes for supper, and by that stage was so depressed that he only spent fifteen minutes selecting which outfit was most suitable to match duck omelette and almond soup. His heart wasn't in it.

The door opened. Sinistre looked up, expecting to see a serving maid with his hibiscus and peppermint tea. Perhaps he could get her to tell him about the invasion of Cluft. She wouldn't do it as well as the Chamberlain, but it would be better than nothing.

It was not the serving maid. "Oh," Lord Sinistre sighed. "It's you lot. What do you want?"

Kassa finally managed to tear herself away from the kitchens. The kitchen staff were startled when his Lordship's new paramour appeared among them, but they relaxed as soon as she mentioned that she was a friend of the Chamberlain. The Head Cook had practically force-fed Kassa all the nicest things she could find, all the while chattering about what a lovely man the Chamberlain was, how good he was at his job, how well he handled Lord Sinistre when their employer was in his 'funny moods'. They all seemed to adore him.

It didn't sound much like Aragon Silversword. Had he changed so much in three years?

Kassa was now fed, watered, rested and ready for the next stage in her plan — saving Cluft from the dread influence of Drak. That was as detailed as the plan got. Kassa had never been much for details. She was an ideas woman, but usually left the practical bits up to her crew.

Being a pirate queen wasn't any fun without a crew.

As Kassa emerged from the kitchens into the front hall of the palace, she saw Singespitter dragging himself down the final steps of the Great Staircase. His monstrous face was puffy and bruised. He limped heavily, the tendon above one of his cloven hoofs damaged. His wings were bedraggled, one of them torn and weeping blood. He looked exhausted.

Kassa ran to him. "What happened to you?"

He looked at her with his big eyes, and puffed a little green smoke from his nostrils.

She hugged him hard, trying not to touch any of his wounded bits as she did so. "You're not supposed to take lumps like this unless you're protecting me."

He made a little growling sound which Kassa, her full attention focused on him for once, understood perfectly. "You were protecting Egg? What happened to him?"

Singespitter rolled his eyes and stuck his tongue out, communicating the concept that Egg was now, for no apparent reason, completely batshit insane.

"We've lost him too," moaned Kassa. "Damn. I was hoping to pick his brains. He looked like a details kind of boy."

Singespitter nodded sadly.

"I need him back," Kassa decided. "Aragon too, so he can explain how the hell he got to Drak in the first place. Singespitter, I need a *crew*."

"Baa?" Singespitter said hopefully.

"Not that crew," she said, thinking of the old days. "Daggar's far too busy in his new career, Sparrow refused point blank to ever take any orders from me, Tippett is making a name for himself writing grim poetry, Vervain and the Dark One are running that dress shop in Zibria. They've all moved on with their lives. The last thing they need is me crashing in on them."

Singespitter said "Baa," again, in a questioning tone.

Kassa kissed him on the forehead. "Of course we're keeping Aragon. He's ours. The kids will come in handy, too. A new crew. We just have to figure out how to get rid of this

Heroes of Justice nonsense." A thought struck her. "I don't suppose…no, it would never work."

Singespitter waited patiently.

Kassa grinned at him. "I think I have a plan. It even has a detail or two. I don't know if it's going to achieve anything, but we might as well try." She stood up, awkward in the tight red lace dress. "The first thing I need is a costume change. Turn the other way, I'm going to use an unnecessary amount of magic and I don't want you to witness how far I've sunk."

Singespitter breathed a small amount of flame at her, affectionately. Things were always rosier when Kassa took charge.

~

"It seems obvious who has won this little challenge," said Lord Kloakor with satisfaction.

The Light Lords watched the scene unfolding in the viewing-window. *The Heroes of Justice, led by the Penman, had captured Lord Sinistre, tied him to a chair and dragged him into the ballroom, declaring that they were about to bring about the tyrant's downfall, and End the Reign of Darkness he had inflicted on Drak for so long.*

The Heroes were unsure what to do next. Their mission had, to all intents and purposes, been successfully completed.

"What do we do now?" asked Dream Girl.

"I do not remember," said the Cloak.

They all looked at the Penman, who shrugged and tossed back his glittering gold cloak. "Perhaps we should let him go and then capture him again?"

In Harmony, Kloakor and Quillsmith exchanged satisfied glances. "Their characters have reached a limit," Quillsmith explained. "They are questioning their own reality. This is the perfect time to attempt the next stage, imposing our personalities upon our counterparts."

"I don't agree," said Ladybird.

"Are you still here, sweetie?" said Dreamer. "I thought you would have run off to hide your head in embarrassment by now."

"It's not over yet," Ladybird said between clenched teeth.

The largest doors in the ballroom of Drak swung open, and a figure made her impressive entrance. It was Kassa Daggersharp, only...well, she looked different. Her hair was striped white and candy pink. She wore a tight leather bodice and wide sweeping skirts in the same colour combination, including bright pink boots. A pair of buzzing silver insect wings spread out from the centre of her back. She strode across the ballroom floor, regarding the Heroes of Justice with an icy stare. "Don't tell me you started without me, darlings."

The Light Lords stared at Ladybird.

"Did you do that?" Quillsmith said finally.

Ladybird lifted her chin haughtily. "What do you think, pen-boy?"

"Queenbeetle," gasped the Penman, bowing low. The other Heroes of Justice all followed suit. "Finally, we are all united."

"That's right, my friends," said the radically altered Kassa Daggersharp. "With my leadership, we will bring about the downfall of the dread tyrant and bring an end to the Reign of Darkness."

"We've done that," Dream Girl said. "We don't know what to do next."

"Simple," said Queenbeetle. "We must take the tyrant out of this evil city, beyond the black borders and into the light. His powers will be destroyed and the Reign of Darkness will be Ended."

"A masterful plan, Queenbeetle!" agreed the Penman.

The others nodded. It made perfect sense. Dream Girl and Invisiblo lifted up Lord Sinistre, still tied to his chair, and they all marched out of the ballroom together.

"Interesting," said Kloakor. "Why did you do that, Ladybird?"

"If they move outside the influence of Drak, they will revert to their natural personalities," Quillsmith agreed.

"Nonsense," said Ladybird, smiling fixedly. "The Cloak travelled to Cluft without incident, before the Drak borders spread that far."

"Only for a short while," said Lord Kloakor, staring at her. "I felt his control slipping after only ten minutes outside of Drak, and that was only because the cloak itself gave him some protection."

"It's all part of my plan," she blustered.

"No, it isn't," said Quillsmith, gazing thoughtfully at the viewing-window. "You are not controlling Kassa at all. Kassa is deceiving the Hero personalities into believing she is their leader."

"We have to do something," said Lord Invisiblus.

"Way ahead of you," said Quillsmith.

∾

The Cloak assisted Invisiblo and Dream Girl to carry Lord Sinistre across the skybridge. The Penman hung back, walking alongside Queenbeetle. Quietly, so as not to draw attention to them, he took hold of her sleeve. "I know what you're doing, Kassa Daggersharp," he said in a low voice.

She glanced at him, her golden eyes calm. "Hello, Quillsmith. Decided to join your friends in their takeover bid, did you?"

He shrugged, unable to explain his true motives with the other Light Lords listening to every word. "They're my people, you're not. If I don't lead them, Ladybird will, and I hate to think what might happen. It's about survival."

"Funny," said Kassa. "I thought it was about invasion."

He eyed the other Heroes of Justice as they manhandled the bound and chaired Lord Sinistre down the slippery far side of the skybridge. "I manipulate these characters on a daily basis. I invented these characters. Do you think I can't convince them that you are a villain?"

"I'm sure you could," agreed Kassa, placing her other hand over his.

Light flashed behind Quillsmith's eyeballs. Slowly, he keeled over and fell flat on the bridge, unconscious.

"Oh, Cloak, sweetie!" Kassa called out. "The Penman seems to have fainted. Could you help me carry him into the light?"

The draklight covered all of Cluft and quite a bit of the surrounding land. Silver sand was underfoot. The grass was gone, and whole trees had disappeared or been transformed into statues of trees. Since Cluft spread out on both sides of the Great Mocklore Highway, part of the road was also affected by the draklight, although this made little difference since roads are usually black and shiny anyway.

The Heroes of Justice stood on the highway, looking at the road as it stretched out to the west. Up ahead, there was a glimmer of daylight.

"Into the light," announced Kassa/Queenbeetle, pointing imperiously, and dropping one of the Penman's legs as she did so (the Cloak was holding the Penman's arms).

"Into the light!" the others chorused joyfully.

The road was far from empty as they marched along it, Dream Girl and Invisiblo carrying the tyrant on his chair. Various citizens from Dreadnought, the nearest city, wandered purposefully towards the draklight, which transformed them into good little citizens of Drak as soon as they stepped across the border. Drak must be summoning them, Kassa guessed, luring them into its web as it had the people of Cluft. She turned to look behind her, and saw several shepherds from the Teatime Mountain and many bearded, braided Axgaardians approaching Cluft from the other direction.

If the lure of Drak had reached as far as Axgaard, they were in real trouble. The draklight would keep spreading. Nowhere was safe. "Let's hurry it up, sweeties," Kassa said in her Ladybird voice.

Finally, they reached the edge of the draklight. The Heroes of Justice exchanged gleeful looks, certain that their quest was complete, that the Reign of Darkness would be Ended and the tyrant's downfall brought about.

Lord Sinistre, the tyrant in question, managed to look an extra bit anxious.

Kassa had never been so pleased by the sight of sunlight. It wasn't that bright, since it should be nearly the end of the day. That didn't matter. It was light enough for her purposes. She was looking forward to giving her brain a rest from the relentless draklight — not to mention shedding the candy-striped costume. She sped up a bit, and the Cloak moved faster to keep up with her. The limp body of the Penman swung between them.

Dream Girl and Invisiblo increased their pace as well, despite the heavy load of Lord Sinistre and his chair.

All six of them stepped out of the unreal darkness and into the fading sunlight of the afternoon.

DRAK SIDE OF THE LIGHT

*K*assa kept moving for as many steps as she could manage, out in the normal daylight. She was worried that the draklight would expand in another leap and swallow them before they had a chance to shake off its effects. Finally she collapsed by the side of the road, dropping Egg (no longer the Penman or Quillsmith) on a grassy bank.

The Cloak pulled off his cloak, casting it aside as if he never wanted to see it again.

"Not ready to talk to you yet," said Kassa, enjoying the feel of the last of the afternoon's sun on her face.

"Fair enough," said Aragon Silversword, sitting on the other side of Egg's unconscious body.

They were quite a way out of Cluft now, in a relatively normal part of the countryside. To their left were Drak and Cluft, both cities shrouded beneath a dome of dark, menacing draklight. The green and swampy Middens lay behind them, the brightly coloured Skullcap Mountains loomed to their right and they could see a hint of the ocean straight ahead, peeping through the distant trees.

All this will be gone too, if Drak has its way.

Kassa raised herself up on her elbows, looking across at Lord Sinistre. "Still here, then? I was half-expecting you to vanish. You are a fictional character, after all."

Still bound to his chair and gagged, lying sideways in the road where Clio and Sean had dumped him, Lord Sinistre looked much the same as he had within Drak; still garbed in a fancy black costume with another of those towering dark coronets pinned precariously to his head. Outside Drak, the outfit looked just a bit silly.

Sean and Clio had changed. Their Dream Girl and Invisiblo costumes vanished as soon as they crossed over (as had Egg's, apart from the gold mask), leaving them dressed normally but with a sudden, horrible gap in their memories.

"Have I been kissing you again?" Clio asked in distaste.

"I'm sure I'd have the teeth marks," Sean shot back.

They both sat down near Kassa on the bank, managing to do so without sitting anywhere near each other.

Egg woke up in a sudden rush. "Yah!" he exclaimed, staring around.

Kassa leaned over and plucked the gold mask from his face. "How are you doing, kiddo?"

"My mouth hurts," he said, staring at the sky. "Is that daylight?"

"Yep," said Kassa.

"Is it all over? You fixed it? Everything's okay?"

"Nope," said Kassa, drawing his attention to the seething dark dome which covered Drak, Cluft and quite a bit of the space between both of them.

"Oh," said Egg. "Why does my mouth hurt?"

"I had to stun you," said Kassa. "The chap who possessed your body was getting a bit too good at it. I might have overdone the zap a bit, sorry. It's not something I do very often."

"Right." Egg looked at the gold mask she was holding

between her fingers. His shoulders sagged slowly. "I wasn't the Penman, was I?"

"You were."

Egg was appalled. "He wasn't even a serious character! I never finished drawing him because I couldn't figure out if he was a hero or a villain."

"He decided for you," said Kassa. "What was Queenbeetle, hero or villain?"

"Oh, a villain," said Egg. "The stories seemed to try and make her one of the heroes, but I wasn't fooled. She was one of those nasty types."

Kassa smiled faintly. "That she was."

Egg glanced over at Clio. "Are you all right?"

"Mostly," she muttered.

"Good." He looked back at Kassa. "What about Singe-spitter?"

"He was supposed to come on ahead," she said. "I'm not sure where he is."

"May I ask a question?" asked Aragon.

Kassa sighed, wishing it didn't feel so right to hear his familiar, dry voice interjecting. "If you must."

"What *are* you wearing?"

She looked down at herself, to see that the pink candy-striped dress and hair were still firmly in place. "Oh, that's horrible!"

"That's what I thought," agreed Aragon.

Kassa sang a single note, running her hands over the dress. The pink and white illusion vanished, leaving her in the dark red lace gown she had worn in Drak. She frowned. "That's not right. That one should have vanished as soon as we left." She tried again with a different note and different hand-gestures, and ended up in a wide-skirted denim dress with white petticoats and black boots. She couldn't make any jewellery appear no matter how loudly she sang, so she gave up on it. Her belt was there at least, a reassuring strap of leather with useful pouches, knives and other trinkets hanging from it.

"Your hair's still pink," said Aragon.

"Shut up." Kassa transformed her hair with another note. "Don't look at me like that," she added to Egg, who had been watching her various transformations with narrow eyes. "Some situations are emergencies because they are." She looked down at her new clothes. "This will have to do."

A shape flew over them. It was Singespitter, his white fluffy sheep body and bright green wings fully restored. He gave Egg an affectionate head-butt on the forehead, then jumped straight into Kassa's arms.

She hugged him hard. "At least your wings weren't damaged." She felt for the familiar pouches which hung from her belt again, as it should be. "Shall I fix you up?"

Singespitter, whose face was badly bruised from his fight with the Heroes of Justice, nodded.

Kassa rummaged in various pouches, pulling out powders and potions which she tossed in Singespitter's face and rubbed on his legs. Within a few minutes, he looked quite normal.

"Should we untie the Lordling?" Clio asked. The various Mocklore citizens who were still being lured into the drak-light were having to step over or around Lord Sinistre in order to reach their destination.

"Shouldn't we stop them?" Sean countered, pointing at the citizens. "They'll give Drak even more power."

"Don't ask me these things," said Kassa. "I need a nap."

Aragon stood up and went over to the fallen Lordling. In one swift movement, he lifted Lord Sinistre up and sat him upright on his chair, then ripped the gag from around his mouth. He then headed back to the grassy bank and sat down, leaving Lord Sinistre still stranded in the middle of the road.

"Chamberlain," Lord Sinistre commanded. "Untie me at once!"

"I don't think so," said Aragon. "Not until we know which side you're on."

"Which side are we on?" asked Egg.

"Also something we should establish," Aragon said calmly.

"We have to stop Harmony," said Kassa. "They're responsible for all this. That Ladybird bitch most of all. If we can shut down their operation we might have half a chance of squeezing Drak out of our dimension and back where it belongs."

They all stared at her. "Who are Harmony?" Clio asked in a small voice.

"Who's Ladybird?" asked Egg.

"Where does Drak come from?" asked a subdued Lord Sinistre.

Kassa sighed. "I suppose I had better explain a few things."

$\sim$

"I refuse to believe you," said Lord Sinistre, as Kassa's tale about her adventures in the bright white city of Harmony came to an end. "Drak is a real city, not some storybook construct. We have a history going back a hundred years!"

"He does," Aragon confirmed. "I looked it up in the library one afternoon."

"Exactly a hundred years?" said Kassa. "That's suspicious for a start."

"My father ruled the city before me, and his father before him," Sinistre insisted.

"I've seen the portraits," said Aragon.

"So have I," scoffed Kassa. "They both look like him with different beards stuck on."

"Also, the Chamberlain's father was Chamberlain before him, and his before him," Lord Sinistre continued.

"Ah," said Aragon. "I'm afraid that's where our versions of reality differ, my lord. My father was a knight errant named Howard Blackblade, and his father was a dragon farmer called Pludd. I'm a citizen of Mocklore, not Drak."

"Which raises an interesting question," said Kassa. "How exactly did you get to Drak in the first place, Silversword?"

He looked directly at her, his grey eyes calm. "I was hoping you'd tell me that, Daggersharp. Sooner or later."

"Uh oh," murmured Egg. He extricated himself from between the two of them and began to back slowly away. Clio, Sean and Singespitter all had a similar idea, moving along the bank. Even Lord Sinistre was attempting to sidle away, although his tied-to-chair predicament made this difficult.

"Are you implying," said Kassa, "that I had something to do with your little inter-dimensional jaunt?"

"Are you suggesting you are incapable of such a feat?" replied Aragon.

"Are you trying to weasel out of the undisputed fact that *you left me?*"

"Are you saying that you have never used your magic on me before, in revenge for whatever little thing happened to annoy you at the time?"

"Do you really think I would do this to you?" Kassa yelled.

"Am I supposed to believe that you didn't?" Aragon yelled back. "I've been trapped in that damned city for months, Kassa. Who but you would do that to me?"

"Years," she said quietly.

"What?"

"I woke up on Midsummer's Day in the Year of the

Mystical Lake and you were gone, Aragon. That was three years ago."

"Clio," he said abruptly, turning away. "How old did you say you were?"

"Seventeen, uncle."

"No wonder that didn't make sense," he muttered.

A carriage rattled along the highway, packed with more wannabe immigrants for Drak. The horses swerved around Lord Sinistre and kept going until they plunged their passengers into the dark, seething mass of shadows.

The dome of draklight expanded just a little bit further.

Lord Sinistre was attempting to edge his chair in hopeful bumps and jumps towards the draklight.

"We need to stop people doing that," said Kassa.

Aragon nodded. "Do you think there's a way to cut Harmony entirely off from Drak? At least they then can't interfere with what we do."

"I don't see how we can touch them," said Kassa. "I don't know where Harmony is, and the only route there has been cut off since I did whatever I did to the spiralling vortex."

"You said they kept referring to us as the outsider world," said Aragon. "I wonder what that means."

"There must be something of Harmony in Drak," Kassa agreed. "Some little trace, something we can hold on to."

"Or do something nasty to," he said with a twisted grin.

They looked at each other, surprised and slightly pleased, but trying not to show it.

"They're good at this," Clio whispered.

"Years of practice," Egg whispered back.

"Does that mean they're not going to kill each other now?" whispered Sean.

"Who can say?" Clio had her 'isn't it romantic?' expression on, which meant Egg and Sean just had to exchange a 'what is she on about?' expression for the sake of male solidarity.

"What are you looking at?" demanded Lord Sinistre. Outside the influence of Drak, his voice had become rather high-pitched and whiny. "What do you think you are doing?"

Kassa and Aragon circled around him, examining him with interest. Of particular interest was the towering — now slightly lopsided — coronet that he wore. It was black and layered, with spiky bits around the lower layer, large blood-coloured jewels around the middle layer and a motif of engraved bats around the top layer. At the very top was the small, bright white jewel which appeared on all of his crowns and coronets, and was entirely un-Draklike.

"A piece of home?" Aragon suggested.

"I always thought that looked wrong," Kassa agreed. She pulled a nasty pair of tweezers out of one of her medicinal pouches. "Now, Sinnie my love, be calm. This won't hurt a bit."

"You can't do this!" said Lord Sinistre, outraged. "I'm the one who ties people to chairs! It's my job! Just look at me! Would I be wearing this much tight-fitting black leather if I wasn't a villain? I don't think so! I have pockets full of unnameable torture devices and other villainous props. I am not going to take this lying down!"

It is an unfortunate fact of life that anyone who is naïve enough to use the phrase 'I am not going to take this lying down' will inevitably find themselves flat on their back within a moment. Lord Sinistre's chair bounced back and forth as he attempted to back away from Kassa and the tweezers. Gravity entered the equation and the chair toppled backwards, crashing Lord Sinistre to the ground. His leather-clad legs kicked feebly.

Kassa took hold of the small, bright white sphere with the business end of her tweezers and plucked. The little gem came free. She balanced it on the palm of her hand, gazing at it. "I thought it was a pearl, but it's not."

Aragon came closer, looking it over. "It is a piece of Harmony, though?"

"Oh, yes. It has to be." Aragon was close enough to touch, something Kassa was determined would not happen. She closed her hand over the white gem. "So what do we do with it?"

"Shouldn't we find out before we do anything?" Aragon said sharply.

"Oh, I think that would make things needlessly complicated."

~

In Harmony, the Light Lords all pulled back from their viewing mirror, regarding each other with some concern.

"Who let a piece of Harmony into the outsider world?" demanded Ladybird.

"It has always been there," said Lord Kloakor. "It was how we discovered the outsider world in the first place."

"Doesn't she know?" said Lord Dreamer scornfully. "Is she so busy listening to herself talk at our council meetings that she hasn't the faintest idea what is going on?"

Quillsmith sighed. "Listen carefully, Ladybird. The reason they are the outsider world is because we are the insider world. We are inside, they are outside. That little bauble your counterpart has picked up isn't a piece of our world. It *is* our world."

~

Kassa closed her hand around the bright white gem.

"So," said Aragon Silversword. "How can we get most use out of this fragment of nice evil city? Suggestions, anyone?"

"I have a few," said Kassa. "Mostly involving the digestive system of a flying sheep."

Egg half-raised his hand. "I have an idea. It might be a bit chaotic, though."

"Couldn't be more chaotic than the day I've had so far," said Kassa. "Hit me."

"Bertie," said Egg.

Kassa looked at him with an amazed grin. "I just *knew* you'd be good at coming up with plans. I'm ashamed I didn't think of that myself."

"Who is Bertie?" asked Aragon.

"Vice-Chancellor Bertie Peacock," said Kassa gleefully. "Inventor of the postgraduate thesis and the Great Reversing Barrel and various other oddities in between. He's the Lordling of Cluft and the most absent-minded old coot you'll ever meet, but he also happens to be the greatest authority in Mocklore on magical catastrophes."

Aragon blinked. "I thought *you* were the greatest authority in Mocklore when it came to magical catastrophes."

"Are you kidding? I'm strictly amateur. Bertie's got forty years on me. He was around for the Aardvaalk Massacre and the Giant Man-Eating Sea-Succubus and the Blue Death, not to mention the Great Badger Flood and the Vampyre Aelves and all the sparkly magic bits of the Fifty-Seven Year War. There's priceless wisdom locked up in that head of his. We just have to drag it out of him." She tucked the little piece of Harmony into one of her many belt pouches. "And to do that I have to drag him out of the draklight. Won't be long."

"Hold on," said Aragon. "You're going back into Cluft? It's dangerous in there."

"Dangerous for you, hero boy," Kassa said lightly. "Luckily, one of this group is immune to the influence of the drak-light, and it just happens to be me."

"Entirely immune?" said Aragon. It was a fair question, considering that a half-feral Kassa had plunged a knife between his ribs not so long ago.

"So I get a little hot and bothered," said Kassa. "Nothing I can't control. At least I don't turn into an entirely different person. None of the rest of you can be trusted in there, you'd revert to costumed idiots."

"You don't know how long your so-called immunity will last," Aragon insisted. "What if this Ladybird figures out how to control you like the others controlled us?"

"She's an incompetent little psychopath who has sniffed her own hair dye one too many times. I'm not unreasonable, Silversword. We don't have an alternative plan. I don't know if we're ever going to get Cluft back and I am *not* going to lose any more territory. If Bertie can be of use to us, I'm fetching him. I know exactly where he is; I locked him in a cupboard when all this started happening. It will take me fifteen minutes, tops."

"You always do this, Kassa. You haven't got the faintest idea of how to solve the problem, so you throw yourself into jeopardy in the hope that the resulting chaos will work in your favour."

"Chaos has been good to me over the years," she shot back. "If I knew what I was doing, we'd be in real trouble."

"I am not going to let you go in there alone."

Kassa rolled her eyes at him. "You want to come with me? Noble *and* stupid. You'll turn into the Cloak the second you step back into the draklight, and I'll just have to knock you unconscious. Why put me to the trouble?"

"Because for once in our lives I'd like you to think things over for five minutes before rushing into an impossibly dangerous situation!"

"If I thought about it for five minutes I wouldn't go, and then where would we be?" Kassa marched over to Lord Sinistre and righted his chair, then started rummaging through the pockets of his long leather coat. "Right, mister evil genius. Tell me about these villainous props you have in your pockets."

Lord Sinistre eyed her. "There's the Compelling Collar, and my spyglass, and several unnameable torture devices…"

"Any swords?" she asked briskly.

"Under here," said Sinistre, wiggling around and patting his right hip. Kassa felt under the coat. "I'm afraid you won't be able to get it out without untying me," he added.

"Watch me," said Kassa Daggersharp.

Aragon approached as Kassa dug under the tightly bound rope with her fingers. "Kassa, why do you feel that you need a sword?"

"Because I'm going into a dark, shadowy wasteland filled with students who were never that civilised to begin with," said Kassa. She lay flat on her back and slid under the chair, still tugging at the sword that was apparently attached to Lord Sinistre, wedged under his coat by the rope. "They were challenging each other to duels when we left, it's probably gang warfare by now. You wouldn't want to me to travel unprotected, would you?"

The sword flew free from under Lord Sinistre's coat and bounced twice on the road, making a loud clanking noise.

Lord Sinistre winced. "I say, that is an heirloom, you know."

"Your city only came into existence a few months ago," said Kassa. "It can't be that much of an heirloom."

"It happens to be the doomed blade of Dathazarrr," said Lord Sinistre. "It was wielded by the first Lord of Drak two hundred years ago."

"Interesting," said Kassa. "I thought you told me Drak had only been around for one hundred years."

That shut up Lord Sinistre long enough for Kassa to examine the doomed blade of Dathazarrr. It was long and very thin, light enough for a child to carry if it was a very tall child and you were the sort of person who let your child play with edged weapons. The metal was dark, with a silvery pattern picked out across the blade. The hilt was ornate, with black jewels set into loops and braids of dark, twisted steel. It would do.

Kassa extended her arm so that the tip of the blade was pointing directly at Aragon Silversword. "Tell me again where you've been for the last three years?"

"Kassa, this isn't funny."

"No," she said, one eye on the dome of draklight that had enshrouded both cities, Drak and Cluft. "That's what isn't funny. I need to do something about it. Now, right away. It's what I do."

"Fair enough," he said. "I'm not stopping you."

She was instantly suspicious. "You're not?"

"You're so keen on getting yourself killed, why should I bother to talk you out of it?"

"Don't you care?" she said in a small voice.

"You're the one holding the sword, Kassa. You can do whatever you like. Of course, you're holding it wrong."

Kassa lowered the sword and stared at the way that her hand gripped the hilt. "This isn't right?"

Aragon moved in beside her, altering the spread of her fingers and the angle of her wrist. "There, like that."

"That does feel better," she agreed.

"Of course, if you were taller I'd suggest this grip, it enables better control." He took the sword off her to demonstrate, then smoothly held it at arm's length away from her. "Ready to discuss alternative plans yet?"

Kassa glared at him. "That's not fair."

"How does this immunity of yours work?" Aragon asked in a low voice. "How do you know it won't suddenly run out? Please think this through."

"I have thought this through!" said Kassa. Since she didn't have a sword any more, she drew a dagger from her belt. "The draklight is getting more powerful by the second and we have done exactly nothing to slow it down. Cluft is my home now. These are my people, and Drak has swallowed them whole. I'm doing everything I can to restrain myself from using magic, because the side effects from that could be catastrophic. Finding Bertie is the only constructive thing I can think of doing which will not automatically make things ten times worse, and *why the hell are you looking at me like that?*"

Aragon was staring at her. "You almost sound as if you know what you're doing."

Kassa stabbed him in the thigh.

Aragon fell backward, swearing profusely. On his way down, he let go of the doomed blade of Dathazarrr.

Kassa scooped up the sword and rummaged in one pouch, pulling out a small twist of paper which she tossed to Egg. "Scatter this over him and don't let him follow me," she said, then turned and ran full-tilt down the road until the seething mass of draklight swallowed her up.

Singespitter trotted after her at great speed, his wings lifting him as he passed into the draklight. He shot a scornful look over his shoulder which clearly said: *As if I'd ever let her go into danger alone.*

~

The three students stared at each other, and then at the bleeding, swearing Aragon Silversword.

"What does she do when you hand in an essay late?" asked Sean.

"You don't want to know," said Clio.

"Spell, now," ordered Aragon through gritted teeth.

Egg opened the little twist of paper and scattered its contents. They were tiny crystalline granules, sparkling pink in the sunlight. To his horror, Egg suddenly felt a surge of power leaving his own body and boosting the spell. The dagger flew out at great speed, almost slicing off Lord Sinistre's ear before it embedded itself in the grass on the far side of the Great Mocklore Road. The wound vanished, as did the blood, which presumably had been put back into Aragon's veins where it belonged.

Aragon Silversword had not only been un-stabbed, but glowed with health. "Good spell," he said, sitting up.

Egg managed to control himself, forcing the power back under his ribcage where it belonged. At least, he thought it was in his ribcage. Some of it was probably near his stomach, judging by how sick he felt.

The first thing that happened when Kassa crossed into the draklight was yet another costume change. This time it was another tight-fitting lace number with high boots, all in black. Kassa quickly used the doomed blade of Dathazarrr to slice the lower seams of the tight dress open, then slit the lacings of the boots so that she could shake them off and stride along in her stockinged feet. She didn't have time to play the hobbling fashion victim.

The Great Mocklore Road had been laid down sixty years earlier, its meandering path specifically designed to avoid all the major battle sites, since the Fifty-Seven Year War had been in full swing at that time. The planned route of the

Road had run straight through the most popular tavern in all Mocklore, The Boar's Revenge, owned by one Wilbermore Tapster. Before the Emperor's roadsmiths could demolish the tavern, Tapster got in first, cutting the building in half and dragging the two halves wide enough apart that the Road could run through the middle. It was a success, overall. He lost more than the average number of barmaids to carriage accidents, but travellers in a hurry enjoyed the opportunity to grab a beer and a ploughman's lunch without stopping.

When Wilbermore's grandson Cluft inherited the tavern (retitled The Split Boar) he made use of its prime location to sell education, and the Polyhedrotechnical College was born. The Split Boar was still an active tavern in these modern times, one of many that catered to the student population. As the Split Boar contained the entrances to many secret passages, it was also quite popular with staff who liked being able to escape in a hurry if earnest students came along to dispute an essay mark.

Kassa was relying on the secret tunnels to get her to Vice-Chancellor Bertie and remove him from the draklight before she was forced to use her new sword on people.

Some hope. There were people everywhere. They must be flooding in from overland as well as the roads. There were quite a few Axgaardians, and even a Zibrian or two. The siren song of the draklight had extended even further than Kassa feared. This was a serious situation, but she couldn't help finding it amusing to see so many rough, tough Axgaard warriors (whose idea of formal attire was to bury their fur and leather garments in the ground overnight to get rid of the worst of the smell) forced into elegant velvet doublets and jewelled hose, trying to kill each other with spindly little rapiers and daggers instead of their usual meaty chopping and hacking weapons.

Still, they *were* trying to kill each other. Axgaardians were already aggressive, and the influence of the draklight was making it worse. Needle-thin blades flew back and forth, slicing through puffed sleeves and padded collars. The air was filled with flying swatches of mulberry silk and midnight satin.

Kassa elbowed her way through the dangerous crowd. She could feel the draklight working away at her mind, trying to find a way in. *Morbid thoughts, violent urges, seductive impulses...* "Stop it, don't have time," she said aloud, ducking as a large, bearded warrior whirled his beaded cummerbund over his head.

Singespitter landed on the bar, snarling. He was a nastier monster this time, with rows of spikes down the spines of his wings and claws. His several large red eyes glared at Kassa. A long drip of dribble slid out of his slavering mouth, plopping on to the wooden floorboards and burning a hole straight through them.

"Nice," said Kassa, unable to help a shudder. "Hope you're still on my side."

Singespitter leaped down on the far side of the bar. Kassa followed him, sliding over the surface of the bar. She tapped one of the knots in the wooden floor and stood back as a trapdoor slid slowly open. "Demonic creatures first," she said politely.

Singespitter gave her a dirty look and plunged down the creaky staircase. Kassa went after him, pulling the trapdoor closed behind her.

Now she just had to get to the administration cottage near the square of student residence, and the cupboard in which she had locked Vice-Chancellor Bertie for his own safety. That was the same cupboard in which the Great Reversing Barrel was stored, as well as all the most secret student files (or at least the most entertaining ones for reading out at conferences) and the petty cash box. The cupboard had been constructed from fourth generation steel-oak, one of the hardiest woods known to Mocklore. It was utterly secure, so Kassa was pretty certain that Bertie would still be there.

She had last seen the key several costume changes ago, but there would be time enough to worry about that.

14

THE GREAT REVERSING BARREL

*A*ragon was using Lord Sinistre's spyglass to scan the dome of draklight, in the hope of spotting Kassa. Clio and Sean had got it into their heads to try to stop the various passers-by who were being lured towards Drak. They were having very little success, as they could only physically restrain one or two people at a time — as soon as they let go, the people in question would run straight for the dome of draklight.

Egg didn't have the heart to assist in this fruitless quest. His head and belly ached from the spell he had amplified. He had performed magic. An actual spell. No wonder Kassa was so negative about the whole process. It felt horrible.

A bright orange raven flew overhead, circling around the dome of draklight. A lavender parrot followed, then a bright yellow kestrel. Next came the bats, in at least twelve different shades of pink and blue. There were insects, too, in so many different colours that they formed a flying mass of plaid. A low, urgent buzzing filled the air.

The birds, bats and insects did not seem as tempted to cross into the dome of draklight as the citizens of Mocklore were. Instead, they hovered around the dome, keeping their distance.

"Very sensible," Egg muttered to himself. "Wouldn't have thought they'd have it in them."

Aragon trained the spyglass on the mass of winged things that were still coming, creating a wide circle of colours around the huge dome of draklight. "I've never seen birds act like that before."

"Not birds," said Egg. "Or bats, or flies. Those are warlocks."

After getting turned around twice in the tunnels, Kassa and Singespitter found their way into the administration cottage. Like many of the cottages of Cluft, it had been built upside down thanks to the whims of a mad Emperor. Several of the windows had been broken, and scorch marks ran along the sloped and thatched floors.

The draklight was having a sinister influence over the highly susceptible students and staff of Cluft. Elegance had descended into anarchy. Kassa could hear shouts and screams from outside.

Time to work fast.

She located the sturdy wooden door of the cupboard and set Singespitter on it. The monstrous creature that Singespitter had become spat acid at the lock, then breathed a hot jet of flame on to it. Finally, Kassa hit the lock several times with the doomed blade of Dathazarrr, and the lock completely fell out of it.

It was dark inside the cupboard, darker than anywhere else in this draklight version of Cluft. Kassa took two steps into the blackness, and scraped her shin on something large which just had to be the Great Reversing Barrel. "If only I could fit a whole city inside you," she murmured to herself. "My problems would be solved. Then again, you'd probably just reverse Drak from being a deadly threat into being an impossibly huge deadly threat." She remembered the fate of the ham sandwiches and shuddered. "Or turn a city full of live people into a city full of dead people."

Kassa peered into the blackness, trying to remember how far back the cupboard actually went. He should have heard her if he was in here, surely. "Vice-Chancellor? Where are you?"

Singespitter squeaked. It was not a roar or a growl or a monstrous howl. It was a squeak of terror, which was totally out of character. His several red eyes glowing in the darkness of the cupboard, looking upwards.

Bracing herself for something truly horrible, Kassa followed his gaze, looking up above her head.

It was truly horrible.

~

A rose-coloured bat detached itself from the swarm of flying creatures and flapped slowly down towards Egg. As it neared him, it transformed into human shape. He was utterly unsurprised to see that it was the apricot-bearded representative of the Harvestmoon Order of Warlocks who had attempted to recruit him a few days ago.

Was it really only a few days ago?

"Ah, Egfried," the young warlock said pompously. "Our High Poppinpoose, Master Tribalchio, bids you greetings."

"You'd better get your High Poppinpoose down here," said Egg.

"That would be most irregular," said the warlock. "Anything you wish to say to the High Poppinpoose can be related through me…"

"Do it," Egg demanded in a loud voice. "And while you're at it, bring down the Masters of any other Orders, too. I know there's not just one of you up there."

The apricot-bearded warlock stared at him in utter astonishment. Clio, Sean and Aragon stared at him, too.

"Did I say you should take your time about it?" Egg asked.

The apricot-bearded warlock transformed back into the rose-coloured bat and flapped up to the circling birds, bats and insects. Whatever he said to them caused quite a commotion. There was a lot of squawking and ruffling of feathers.

Clio left the others and came over to Egg. "When did you get so confident?"

He grinned weakly at her. "It's easy, really. I just pretend I'm Kassa and I can handle anything."

~

Vice-Chancellor Bertie hung upside down from clawed feet, his skin sallow and ghoulish beneath a pointy black beard. His body was shrouded by a tattered cape of dark gold tweed. His arms were folded peacefully over his chest. He looked dead. Just as that thought flitted across Kassa's mind, Bertie's eyes snapped open. The lids slid aside to reveal pupils that glowed with an intense silver light. Bertie's lips parted slightly, revealing a set of pointed, brilliantly white teeth.

"This can't be good," Kassa decided. She meant to get herself out of the confined space of the cupboard as quickly as possible, but Vice-Chancellor Bertie moved first and he moved fast.

Kassa had never seen him move so speedily before, not even when he was trying to avoid Parent Discussion Night. She did not, in fact, see him move at all. One minute he was hanging upside down, his eyes glowing silver, and the next he was standing in the doorway of the cupboard, blocking the exit.

Singespitter hissed. Vice-Chancellor Bertie made a nasty whining sound in the back of his throat.

Kassa tried to back away, but her calves rubbed up against the Great Reversing Barrel. "Why am I the only one who doesn't get transformed into a dark and evil creature?" she complained. "I could do with a pair of fangs right about now."

Bertie and Singespitter eyed each other off, both ready to pounce.

Nervous for herself as well as them, Kassa rummaged in her pouches in the hope of finding something useful. She had left her best knife in Aragon's upper leg, but she still had a few blades somewhere...including a sword, now she came to think of it, although she had no idea where the doomed blade of Dathazarrr had got to. She must have dropped it somewhere.

Resisting the urge to bring something magical out of her pouches, Kassa's fingers closed instead around the bright white pearl that she had extracted from Lord Sinistre's crown. She held it up desperately, hoping to distract Bertie. "Shiny thing?"

He looked at her and the dangerous expression vanished, becoming earnest and familiar in an entirely wrong way. "Kassa, be careful with that."

It was not Bertie, though it was his voice. The intonation was all wrong. The expression on his face was wrong, too. It belonged to another face. "Quillsmith?" she said. "How are you doing that?"

"With great difficulty," Egg's other half said through Vice-Chancellor Bertie's mouth. "I can't speak for long, the others are busy gawping at Aragon and the warlocks, but they might decide to check on you soon."

"I thought you had gone over to their side?"

"I need them to think so. They want me to take the leadership from Ladybird. For the time being, I have to go along with this invasion plan and prove I'm more competent at it than she is."

"I suppose that makes sense. As long as you don't actually go through with the invasion."

"I hope that won't be necessary."

"You hope?"

His eyes — Vice-Chancellor Bertie's eyes, under Quill-smith's control — kept following the bright white pearl. "Kassa, be careful with that."

She frowned, flicking it back and forth between her fingers. "You said that before. What's so special about it?"

"Don't you know what it is?'

"A piece of Harmony, I assumed."

"Not a piece, Kassa. That is Harmony."

She stopped, staring at the brilliant white gem. "What?"

"Our entire world is contained within that ball."

"I thought you were...well, I didn't think *where* you were. Another dimension, or a world far away. I didn't think you were just very small."

"We prefer to think of you being unnaturally big."

"I bet you do. So that's why you called us the outsider world. Why are you telling me this? What makes you think I won't just grind this bauble under my heel and put paid to this little invasion of yours forever? Baubles and I do not have a fantastic history together."

"Light Lords aren't the only ones who live in Harmony," said Quillsmith. "There are thousands of innocents living here. You met some of them. I know you would protect their lives as fervently as you protect those of your own people."

Kassa sighed. "You know me too well. "

"Give me time, if you can. Once my leadership is established, we can make some kind of accord."

"As long as the other Light Lords don't insist that you invade Mocklore first."

Quillsmith smiled and left. She could see his expression fading from Vice-Chancellor Bertie's face.

"Wait a minute," Kassa said suddenly. "What the hell do you mean, Aragon and the warlocks? What is Aragon doing with warlocks?" There was no answer. Kassa held the little pearl that was Harmony between thumb and forefinger, leaning over to stare into the depths of the Great Reversing Barrel. "So tempting," she sighed. "Why do I have to be such a trustworthy person? Even the villains trust me."

There was a snarl from Vice-Chancellor Bertie, or possibly from Singespitter. The two leaped at each other, hissing and spitting. Kassa half-turned towards them, just as Bertie flung Singespitter bodily at her.

He was quite a heavy sheep, especially with the extra weight of the wings and giant claws. He slammed into Kassa's side, throwing her over the Great Reversing Barrel. They both landed on top of it with a crash.

Vice-Chancellor Bertie had built the Great Reversing Barrel with magical properties in mind, not sturdiness. The wood cracked under the combined weight of Kassa and the projectile Singespitter. They both landed flat on the floor, surrounded by split panels of wood. The tiny pearl which was the city of Harmony was still clutched tightly in Kassa's hand as she burst through the Great Reversing Barrel.

Several things happened all at once.

～

Singespitter sat up. He brushed splinters from his arms and legs and checked to see how Kassa was. She was unconscious. She was dressed all in white, her hair a soft pink colour, and the cupboard around them was also blindingly bright. There were no shadows, no hints of darkness at all, certainly no draklight. *Harmony*, he thought, recognising the similarity between this new brightness and the images he had watched in the scroll. *Have we gone to it or has it come to us?*

He picked a few splinters from Kassa's hair and prodded her neck to make sure it was not broken. Slowly, he gazed at his hands. They were pink, and more creased than he remembered. They were actual human hands. He was human again.

"Bloody hell," he said aloud, the first words he had physically spoken in four and a half years.

Later study by a postgraduate class led by Vice-Chancellor Bertie sorted through the various theories and decided that three vital events had occurred a split second after the accident involving the Great Reversing Barrel:

1) The magical influence which had, four and a half years earlier, transformed Singespitter into a sheep, had now been Greatly Reversed so that he was again a human (although the four and a half years as a sheep had aged him approximately twenty-five human years). This was the most undeniable of the outcomes, and caused little in the way of debate.

2) The Draklight Condition (sometimes referred to by scholars as the Draklight Plague or the Spreading Draklight) was Greatly Reversed, turning it into a Harmonylight Condition, which had much the same effect and formed a dome which covered a similar area, only now all the people within the dome were swamped with peace, love and light instead of darkness, violence, morbidity and velvet. The only real

debate concerning this issue were the various different names for the conditions, every student coming up with a new way of describing exactly what had happened, using more and more words until the introductory essay of the Philosophy of Magic II (advanced) course metamorphosed into a six-page definition of what the draklight had done, and how it had been transformed when the harmonylight took its place. All lyric poets and people with a tendency towards metaphor were forcibly banned from taking that particular course.

3) Kassa's apparent genetic immunity to mind control of any kind was Greatly Reversed, rendering her entirely under the control of the wave of peace, love and light that had flooded the white dome of harmonylight. This was the most controversial issue, hotly debated by scholars. Even an article by Kassa herself, written only a few months after the event, failed to solve the issue. It was unbelievable that the ultimate agent for chaos had, however briefly, been an agent of Harmony.

∼

As Singespitter leaned over to pick further splinters from Kassa's face and hair, she opened her eyes and stared at him with a soft, dazed expression. "You're human again," she said with a smile. "How does it feel?"

He shrugged, not comfortable with speech yet. How was she? That was the important question.

Kassa's shoulders relaxed as she lay among the broken remains of the Great Reversing Barrel. "Isn't the world wonderful?" she breathed.

Singespitter let his head fall into his hands. Something was wrong, with the world and with Kassa. He didn't have the faintest idea what to do about it.

All this, and he was wearing a sheepskin coat. Whatever strange force was at work here had a warped sense of humour. "Bastards," Singespitter said aloud.

～

Four master warlocks gathered around Egg. They were the High Poppinpoose of the Harvestmoon Order, the Grand Duchydor of the Silversigil Order, the Sublime Goanna of the Lizardblood Order and the Fat False Idol of the Bronzfetish Order. All four of them were talking very loudly, and not listening to each other.

Egg had attempted to update them on what had happened in the hope that they might put the information to some practical use, but they were not listening to him either. The rest of the warlocks, including the apricot-bearded one, were huddled some way away, trying not to get involved. After several minutes of all this, Aragon joined the group of master warlocks, adding his angry voice to Egg's. Nothing was anywhere near being resolved.

Clio and Sean sat on the grassy bank, left out of things. It was getting dark and cold, which was quite creepy because this made it harder to see where the edge of the dome of draklight began.

"We can't go to sleep," Clio said quietly. "We just can't. The dome might expand again and swallow us up."

"We could move further away," Sean suggested.

"It might swallow us up anyway," she said. "I'm so tired. I just want to be back in my own little bed, arguing with Lemissa about whether the window should be open or shut. I'm sick of all this." She stared at the dome of draklight, shivering. "I wonder where Lemissa is now."

"I wonder where Kassa is," said Egg, joining them. He had given up on the warlocks, who were being constructively unhelpful. Aragon was still trying to explain to them that the draklight phenomenon was not a mass hallucination caused by sea slugs, the most popular theory among the Lizard-bloods and Silversigils.

The lesser warlocks were being oddly practical, and had lit some campfires on the far side of the Highway. One apprentice came over to ask shyly if Egg, Sean and Clio would like something to eat.

Lord Sinistre, still strapped to his chair, had already been carried over to the campfire and was being fed, although he had plaintively requested that his baked potato be cut into small flower shapes, and were they sure they didn't have any poached caviar?

Egg, Clio and Sean were just heading across to the campfires when the dome of draklight exploded, turned inside out and started glowing a brilliant white.

Egg staggered as something within him burned cold and dark and powerful. His head ached furiously. Everyone else stared at the newly white dome.

"Oh gods," said Aragon Silversword in a strangled voice. "What has she done now?"

Drak was still there, and Cluft, but both cities were now unrecognisable. Everything within the dome was whiter than white. It stood out brilliantly against the dusk that had fallen around ordinary Mocklore. When a few straggling travellers crossed the border, their shabby, colourful clothes trans-formed into pale silk and gleaming samite instead of black velvet and satin.

"One plague replaced with another," said Aragon. His voice was heavy with having seen this sort of thing happen before.

The master warlocks started arguing again, their theories becoming even more outlandish.

Clio stared at the dome of harmonylight for exactly half a

minute, then turned towards the campfires of the warlocks. "I'm hungry."

Sean shrugged, and followed her. Egg remained for a few moments, wondering why the transference of the dome from draklight to harmonylight had affected him so closely. He pushed that thought aside as one of many things to ask Kassa about when she returned, then went to join Clio and Sean. All three of them were handed bowls full of sausages and boiled peas, which were surprisingly tasty.

After a while, Aragon joined them. "Warlocks aren't what they used to be," he said in a sour voice.

"Should we be worrying about Kassa?" Clio asked with her mouth full.

Aragon smiled thinly, accepting a bowl from one of the younger warlocks. "I suppose you think I should be dashing in there to save her, like one of those ballads of epic romance. Trust me, that never works out well. Unless she actually gets herself killed, she's better off with the rest of us out from under her feet." He glared over his shoulder at the squabbling master warlocks. "Doesn't look like the problem will be solved from the outside. Maybe Kassa can make a difference from in there."

"But you *tried* to stop her," said Egg.

Aragon chewed a particularly knotty piece of sausage, and swallowed. "Of course I did. It would have hurt her feelings if I hadn't made the effort."

Egg was thinking. "If the harmonylight is here and Drak is still here, where did the draklight go? Did it swap places with the harmonylight?"

"How would we know?" said Aragon.

Egg slapped himself on the forehead. "Ow." He reached down to his belt and pulled out the harmony scroll that Singespitter had given him for safekeeping. "I'm an idiot. We can just look."

He unrolled the scroll, and stared at what it showed him.

Harmony was still technically in one piece: bright marble, garden views, people in white floppy clothes. Wherever the draklight had gone, it was not there. This had proved to be something of a problem for a city which ran entirely on magic.

Without the harmonylight, the essential magic of the city, Harmony was dead. There was no movement there, no life. The white-clothed people of Harmony had ceased to move. They looked like statues, frozen in place. Some of them had familiar faces, which made it worse somehow.

Egg rolled the scroll up and laid it to one side. His hand was shaking. "No one's doing this, are they? There aren't any villains to fight. It's just a colossal natural disaster." He tried to laugh, and couldn't. "The harmonylight is a threat to our world, but the lack of it killed theirs. It's so random."

"Villains are easier," Aragon agreed. "People are predictable. They have needs and weaknesses. A catastrophe is just a catastrophe. The best thing you can do is stay out of its way and try to repair the damage afterwards."

"It's not good enough," Egg said fiercely. "People are dead and more are going to die. I wish I had the power to fix it, to stop bad things happening."

Aragon looked amused. "You sound like Kassa."

"Kassa doesn't think power should be used," Egg said, trying not to sound as disgusted as he felt.

"I know. You sound like Kassa did before she knew what she was talking about. Sometimes the cure is more dangerous than the disease." Aragon motioned towards the bickering master warlocks. "Look at that lot. As long as they argue, they're harmless. Can you imagine what might happen if they actually tried to use magic? Would you trust them to save the world?"

"There should be a better way of doing things," Egg said stubbornly.

"Won't argue with you there," said Aragon. "If I was in charge of the universe, things would be much better organised."

The master warlocks argued into the night. The High Poppinpoose of the Harvestmoons (puce and chartreuse polka-dotted beard) was of the opinion that none of this was happening, that it was a mass hallucination of all the wild mice in the area and that the problem would be solved by strangling all the mice.

The Grand Duchydor of the Silversigils (blue and silver speckled moustache) was of a similar opinion, only he thought it was the field goblins who were having the mass hallucination, and that they should be shot, not strangled.

Both agreed fervently that while they no longer believed that sea slugs were responsible for the mass hallucination, they should probably also be killed to be on the safe side, possibly by scattering a lot of poisoned salt around the general area.

The Sublime Goanna of the Lizardbloods (clean-shaven with various green-jewelled piercings in his left eyebrow, lip and chin) was the only one who had at least half-listened to Egg and Aragon's explanations about what was happening, and fervently believed that they were being invaded by creatures from another world. Unfortunately, he was also under the impression that these creatures from another world would all be seven-foot temptresses with platinum hair and easily-removable space suits. If said creatures were looking for suitable mates, he, for one, was quite enthusiastic to volunteer.

The Fat False Idol of the Bronzfetishes (plaid goatee, with sideburns) believed that the end of the world was nigh, and there was absolutely nothing any of them could do to stop it, or anything which wouldn't make everything ten times worse, unless anyone else felt like blowing a few things up? He had a lot of explosive charms that had yet to be tested.

The young apprentice warlocks, who obviously tried to ignore their masters most of the time, again proved handy when it came to tying knots and making camp and all manner of other useful things. They produced blankets and padded bedrolls, then organised a rotational watch to keep an eye on any movement of the dome of harmonylight, so they could warn the sleepers if it started expanding again.

Aragon, despite his spoken confidence in Kassa's ability to handle anything, got more restless as the evening went on, pacing back and forth around the edge of the white dome, and trying to peer into Cluft with Lord Sinistre's spyglass.

Egg, Clio and Sean accepted bedrolls and blankets from the apprentices and bedded down on the grassy bank, all three of them exhausted.

Egg was kicked awake once by a passing apprentice, in the middle of the night. The dome of harmonylight had expanded again. Several of the less-vigilant apprentices had been swallowed up by it, but since they were all roped to each other's legs, they had been hauled back quickly.

"Wake up, Clio," Egg muttered, shaking her. "We're too close. Got to move over."

Clio made a face and buried herself further in the damp grass.

Egg woke up Sean instead. The two of them rolled her, blankets and all, over and over until she was a reasonable distance from the new border. They settled down on either side of her, taking turns to stay awake and keep an eye on what was going on.

Nothing else happened until morning.

INK BLACK MAGIC

Kassa had never felt so completely happy in her life. She sat at a cafe table outside the Majestic dining hall, discussing the pleasant nature of peace, love and light with several of her students.

Brittany Yarrowstalk, Imani Almondstone and Rosehip Moonweaver had all made the transition quite smoothly from Drak vamps to modest, almost nun-like, Harmony citizens. They wore flowing white gowns and braided flowers. They were still quite silly, but manageably so. When a scruffy mercenary called Singespitter joined them at the table, not one of the girls giggled or flirted. They just smiled serenely and included him in the conversation.

They were all drinking mint tea.

Kassa stretched out her legs, breathing in the contentment. Everything looked so nice and clean and white. A placidly happy couple strolled by, arm in arm, and she recognised them as Errol Fitzdeath and Penelopa Profitscoundrel, who had been at odds with each other since both started at the college the previous year. Vice-Chancellor Bertie, clad in snowy white robes, was snoozing on a nearby bench, his face even more peaceful than it usually looked on the first day of the summer holidays.

She sipped her tea and thought of Aragon. Perhaps she should let him know that she was all right? But that was silly. How could she be otherwise, in this marvellous place? If she stayed here long enough, he might come and join her. That would be much better. Everyone needed to relax.

Kassa wriggled her stockinged toes in the fine silver sand that covered the ground.

∽

"What the hell is going on?" snarled Ladybird.

Quillsmith said nothing. Admitting that he didn't know

would be admitting failure, and he was so close to winning the leadership once and for all. *See how you like Harmony's prison after a few weeks within its walls, Ladybird.*

"Where are we?" asked Lord Dreamer. It was a valid question. This looked like Harmony, bright and white and dazzlingly peaceful. They were in a huge ballroom which resembled a room they had at home. It was not theirs, however. Not quite familiar...

"This is Drak," said Lord Kloakor in sudden recognition.

"But it's not dark," said Invisiblus, always the last to catch on.

"This is how Drak would look if Drak was Harmony," said Dreamer softly.

Quillsmith levitated himself to the high windows of the ballroom and stared out. Those were the shambling, thatched buildings of Cluft, recognisable even as they glowed gloriously white and bright. Beyond them were verdant fields of Mocklore that he had seen every night in his dreams. "We are in the outsider world," he said, trying to sound as if this came as no surprise to him. *Kassa, what have you done? They will eat your world whole and I will not be able to stop them.* "The magic of Harmony has been brought to Drak, and we came with it. Look outside, Light Lords. Our invasion has begun."

The others, all except the sulking Ladybird, floated up to join him. They gazed out at the white brightness of Cluft, and the pale skybridge which arced between it and themselves. Beyond that, there was colour and a different kind of light. It was nearly morning.

"Our new home," breathed Dreamer.

"Did you do this?" Lord Kloakor asked Quillsmith, who smiled modestly and said nothing.

"What is happening to my feet?" demanded Ladybird.

The four of them turned in mid-air and stared down at her. Her feet were, indeed, missing. The floor was now black and shiny, a stark contrast to the bright whiteness of the walls. Soon the hem of Ladybird's candy-striped skirts had vanished, and a dark stripe ran around the lowest part of the ballroom's six large walls.

"It's unstable," Dreamer said in alarm.

"Not that," said Quillsmith, looking outside. The dome of harmonylight was rising slowly in the air, leaving behind the remnants of Drak and Cluft. "Someone is doing this, extracting the harmonylight by magic."

"Then we are doomed," said Lord Kloakor.

"You're doomed?" shrieked Ladybird, who now only existed from the waist up. "But what about *me*?"

Amongst the pleasant haze, something made Kassa glance at her feet. Her pearly white stockings now ended at the ankle, replaced from there down with thick, green and white striped socks. "How strange," she murmured.

The socks were winning. Slowly, the green and white stripes rose up her legs, until they vanished under the brilliant white lace hem of her full, flouncy skirts. Then the hem changed, darkening and becoming rougher. Blue denim?

Singespitter was changing, his floppy white trews and tunic becoming rough, falling-apart garments. His ankle-length sheepskin coat was the only thing not to change. The girls were transforming too, their white gowns changing into their original clothes, the mock-Drak garments they had been wearing before everything had happened.

Kassa saw green grass sticking through the uneven cobbles of Cluft, and it made her unreasonably happy. She shivered wildly as the last of the harmonylight was dragged from her, and she became entirely herself again. "Gods," she gasped.

"Gods are behind this?" said Singespitter, alert.

"No," Kassa said, gazing up at the huge dome of Harmonylight which continued to rise steadily into the air, leaving the original buildings of Cluft behind. "It's worse than that. It's warlocks."

15

BRIGHT RAIN

*E*gg woke up as daylight struck him in the face, a brilliant burst of sunshine. It was early, not quite dawn, and it was not sunshine that was shining so brightly in his face. It was Harmony.

The dome of harmonylight had been peeled from both Cluft and Drak, leaving the buildings, grounds (and, apparently, the people) intact. The harmonylight now hovered in the sky above them all, shaped into a massive, blindingly bright sphere. The master warlocks, having done this, were now squabbling about what they should do with the sphere, while the apprentices supported the brunt of the magic necessary to keep the giant sphere in place.

Egg stared in a numb kind of horror. With one hand, he shook Clio awake. She sat up so quickly that Sean, on the other side of her, awoke too. "What's going on?" Sean mumbled.

Clio gazed at the sphere. "You wanted them to do something," she said to Egg.

"I know," he said. "But if they can't agree on what caused the problem, can we trust them to find a solution?"

They went over to where Aragon stood a little way from the warlocks, watching the magical activity. Lord Sinistre, unusually silent, stood beside him.

"You untied him?" Clio asked.

"Drak is his city," said Aragon. "He might as well watch what these idiots are going to do to it."

"It doesn't look so bad," said Sean hopefully. "Maybe they know what they're doing."

Aragon closed his eyes briefly, as if trying to block out what Sean had just said. "Fifteen minutes," he said. "I went to sleep for fifteen minutes and they did this."

"Kassa's going to kill us," Egg added.

Aragon almost smiled. "With that in the sky," he said, jabbing a finger at the menacing sphere, "we have so many different ways to die today."

~

The Light Lords swam within a bright, marshmallowy gooeyness. It felt right. It felt like home. It felt entirely unfamiliar.

"Where are we now?" whisper/screamed Dreamer.

"Harmony, of course," said Invisiblus. "Can't you taste it?"

"The magic of Harmony," scream/whispered Quillsmith. "Not the city itself. We exist only in the magic. What is happening to our people at home without the magic to sustain them?" *Is this your fault, Kassa, or is it mine?*

"What does that matter?" said Ladybird. "We're in this world now. What does it matter what happened to the old one?"

"Ladybird is right," agreed Kloakor. "We must look to our own survival."

"I want to see," said Quillsmith. "You have a skill for looking into other worlds, Ladybird. It was you who first saw beyond Harmony and discovered the outsider world. Please, look back into our world and show me that something is still alive there."

"You care too much," said Kloakor.

"Is that bad?" said Dreamer. "I wish I cared more."

"Very well," said Ladybird. Within the swirling goo of bright magic, they felt her begin to concentrate.

Suddenly the vision flew from Ladybird's mind into theirs, a terrible image of frozen figures and a world without magic. There was no silver sand, no movement, no life.

The vision of their carelessly destroyed world shocked the Light Lords, wounded them deeply, even those who had claimed to be indifferent.

It broke Quillsmith.

~

Egg could feel the power of the harmonylight sphere, and the power of the warlocks who held it in place. It was so strong. They were stronger. Every warlock in that mob was confident in their ability to keep the sphere aloft, and safe. Each of them only had to contribute a little to the whole. Egg could feel how easy it was for them to control the sphere and, eventually, dispose of it safely.

It was the most vulnerable thing he had ever seen in his life.

Aragon raised the spyglass. "How are you three at running?"

"You think we can outrun that thing?" said Clio, gesturing at the huge Harmony sphere.

"I'm not talking about that," said Aragon, handing the spyglass back to Lord Sinistre. "I'm talking about her."

Kassa came barreling out of Cluft, her dark red curls streaming behind her. Aragon moved, not away as Egg had half-expected, but running straight at Kassa. As she reached the warlocks, she opened her mouth in shock, and no sound came out. For once in her life, Kassa Daggersharp had absolutely nothing to say.

Aragon reached her side and hooked one arm around her waist. He pulled her slowly past the warlocks and towards Egg and the others, speaking quietly to her the whole time.

Egg heard a little of it as they neared. "...know you want to shriek every abusive word under the sun at them, but all you would do at this point is distract the nice men who are trying to keep that damn thing under control and if, by some fluke, something doesn't actually go horribly wrong here today, or even if it does, you screeching loudly at them will only make things worse and you *know* that, Daggersharp..."

"Numbskulls," Kassa gasped, hardly managing to walk.

"I know," said Aragon, still guiding her along. "They can't help it. Move on. We can't do anything right now except get out of the danger zone."

"Danger zone?" she demanded, gesturing at the massive sphere which hung ominously over their heads. "Do you know a quick and convenient method of leaving the island?"

Egg tried to think what to say as Kassa reached him. He hadn't agreed with her 'no magic' policy, but he was now pretty sure that he saw her point. "Sorry," he managed. "They wouldn't listen to anything we said." *And I wanted them to do something*, he thought guiltily.

Kassa managed to smile faintly. "Not your fault, kiddo. Warlocks never listen to anyone. They spend nine-tenths of their time wallowing in inaction and when they finally decide to do something it's almost always catastrophically bad." She glanced back at the master warlocks, who continued to argue about what they were doing with the sphere. "You can let go of me now," she said to Aragon. "I accept that I can't do anything." She sighed. "I can't even shout at them. I would feel *so* much better after a good yell."

"Afterwards," said Aragon, not moving his arm from around her waist. "When all this is over, if any of them are left alive, I'll round them all up and you can yell at them to your heart's content."

"Promise?"

"I promise, Kassa."

Singespitter arrived, wheezing hard as he reached Kassa's side. On his woefully unpracticed human legs, it was amazing he had caught up at all. Aragon gave him a strange, sideways look and then extended the arm which was not holding Kassa. "Singespitter. Good to see you again."

Singespitter grasped the arm briefly, then grinned at the surprised Egg, Clio and Sean. "Didn't recognise me without the fleece?"

"You've still got the fleece," said Clio, tugging a sleeve of the sheepskin coat.

Singespitter had hoped the damned thing would change when Harmony was extracted from Cluft, but no such luck. He would have thrown it on a handy rubbish heap by now, but it was a cool morning and he was, after all, used to having a layer of fleece to keep him warm.

"Skullcaps or Middens?" Kassa said thoughtfully.

"Middens are closer," said Aragon. "Not much protection, though."

"Oh, I don't know. Mud, trees, ditches. I could lie in a ditch right now."

It began to rain, a few speckles at first, then a steady patter. One of the many young warlocks who were holding the sphere steady sneezed, then wiped his nose to counteract further sniffles.

"Middens," Aragon agreed.

The bright white sphere shimmered in the sky, becoming a little unsteady.

"Run!" Kassa urged the others. She wriggled away from Aragon and grabbed Singespitter's hand, and Clio's. She started running for the grassy bank.

Egg and Sean scrambled after them, their hands and feet made slippery by the rain as they negotiated the steep bit of bank. Aragon caught up easily, glancing behind to see if Lord Sinistre was following. The Lordling of Drak hurried along, the heels of his shiny black boots sinking deeply into the soft, grassy ground.

Several more warlocks sneezed. The rain grew heavier. The master warlocks stopped arguing. They stared up at the large sphere in an uneasy silence, then threw their own extra layers of magic to keep the harmonylight contained.

The bright white sphere exploded with a painful scream, staining the sky with a spearing mass of whiteness that flung itself from horizon to horizon. The noise was so piercing that Kassa and her fleeing band all fell to the grass, momentarily stunned. The gathering rain clouds filled with expanding, mad magic from edge to edge.

With a deafening rumble, a darker and deeper sound than ever before, the storm began. The white magic filled the sky with a crackle and a screech. The rain came thicker and faster now, bringing with it a shower of jagged whiteness.

"Up, up, up!" screamed Kassa, trying to drag everyone to their feet at once. Frozen fire, silver wind, white dust and burning water rained around them.

Aragon caught hold of Kassa's arm. "We should head for Drak," he yelled, trying to be heard over the screaming storm.

Kassa nodded in agreement and half-turned towards Drak, just in time to see the highest dark tower incinerated by a bolt of bright whiteness which might have been lightning. Black dust rained over Drak. "Any shelter is better than none..."

"Tents," said Egg, staring through the bright rain towards the north.

"Tents?" Kassa demanded. "*Tents* are going to protect us?"

Aragon saw them too. Across the field, several large, shambling brown tents had been stretched over huge poles of wood. The bright rain and all the other nasty, stabbing things that were falling from the sky did not touch the tents at all. Some strange force was protecting them from harm.

"Isn't that interesting?" Aragon said aloud.

"Good plan," Kassa agreed, motioning them all in that direction. Their ragged little group staggered through the powerful wind and burning, icy rain.

Clio's hair was set alight by a burning piece of debris. Egg and Sean both leaped to her rescue. Since they both used handfuls of mud to douse the flames, she was less than grateful.

An impossibly thin shard of ice struck Egg in the shoulder as he ran, sending a needle-sharp burst of pain through his body. It took all his strength to keep himself upright and moving.

A much larger shard of ice would have carved Kassa in two, but Singespitter saw it coming and shoved her roughly aside.

A fiery breeze ripped the sleeves and collar of Lord Sinistre's leather coat, robbing him of the last vestiges of his dignity.

They made it to the nearest of the tents without losing any actual limbs or companions. They all crowded inside, half-collapsing on the fur-strewn floor. "Egg, Clio," Kassa gasped, leaning on Singespitter for support. "I'm going to require an essay about this one. A really long essay."

"And what have we here?" boomed a solid, female voice.

~

Aragon had not given any thought to who — or what — might reside within the tents which were so strangely impervious to the ice shards, flaming missiles and occasional boulders that poured down upon Mocklore.

There was a surfeit of leather within this tent, in varying shades of natural brown. Even the tent itself was constructed from scraped animal hides, neatly sewn together. This was not what immediately captured the attention of the refugees. It was hard for anything else to capture your attention with such an astounding female presence in the room.

She was very tall and very wide. She wore leather in layers, sculpted to her buxom body. A large axe hung around her neck, and several more were woven into her floor-length braids. She wore a wooden helmet with several horns attached to it, including one rather large horn in the centre from which a pale piece of gauze fluttered prettily. In one hand, she held a glaive, a sharp blade set on a pole taller than anyone in the room.

Beside her stood a handsome, well-muscled man built from polished, golden metal. His chest was draped in fur, and the whirring sound of clockwork could be heard whenever he moved any of his limbs.

Fur hung from everywhere in the tent that was not covered in leather, and these were not the elegant, preened furs that aristocratic ladies wore around their shoulders but stiff, mangy hunting furs, occasionally with a few bits of dead animal (paws, teeth, bone) still attached.

The leather-clad lady and her clockwork companion were surrounded on all sides by several similarly leather and fur-clad men, but there was no doubt that she was in charge. For a start, her boots were blocked up so that she was taller than any of them.

Aragon reacted first, his diplomatic Chamberlain skills coming to the fore. "You must be our host. Jarl Svenhilda of Axgaard, I presume?"

"Baron Svenhilda," corrected the impressive female in a hard, but equally polite, voice. "I am trying to bring the people of Axgaard into the modern world, and accepting generic Mocklore titles is part of this."

Several of the leather-clad Axgaardian men growled threateningly at this speech, but Baron Svenhilda's metal consort cleared his throat politely, and they all fell silent.

Aragon bowed low in true courtier style. "Baron Svenhilda, I am Aragon Silversword, twice former Champion of the Empire and current Chamberlain of Drak. May I introduce my companions?"

"You may, ex-Sir Silversword," said the Lordling of Axgaard, sounding amused.

Aragon grabbed Lord Sinistre and pushed him to the front of the party. With any luck, the two Lordlings would keep each other occupied while the rest of them just got on with things. "I present Lord Sinistre, ruling Lord of the new city of Drak."

Svenhilda inclined her head, still keeping a firm hold on her glaive. "So nice to meet you."

"And you, most gracious lady of Axgaard," said Sinistre, recovering a little of his aristocratic poise. "I am honoured to meet a fellow ruling Lord." By the end of that small speech, he had managed to recapture his trademark seductive purr of a voice. Aragon did not feel this was an improvement.

"May I also present Mistress Kassa Daggersharp, Professor of Cluft," Aragon continued smoothly. "And Master Singespitter, the, er..." The word 'mercenary' was on the tip of his tongue, since this human version of Singespitter had belonged to the Hidden Army of Mercenaries when their paths had first crossed. Since mercenaries were just about the only banned profession in the Empire, it would be less than tactful to refer to that.

"Tutor," Singespitter said in an undertone.

"Of course," said Aragon with some relief. "Master Singespitter the tutor, also of Cluft. And some of Mistress Daggersharp's students, Clio Wagstaff-Lamont…"

"Egfried Friefriedsson and Seanicus McHagrty," Kassa said briskly. She stepped forward and held a hand out to Baron Svenhilda. "Nice to meet your Ladyship."

Svenhilda returned the gesture, grasping Kassa's hand like a comrade. "Nice to meet you too, Mistress Daggersharp. Always interesting to meet a legend."

"Must be more fun than being one," said Kassa. "We need to talk."

"Hospitality first," said Svenhilda, handing her glaive to her metal companion and stepping off her blocked-up shoes to take Kassa's arm. They were now about the same height. "Have any of you had breakfast?"

"No, your ladyship," said the Chamberlain of Drak. "None of us have breakfasted."

And why is that relevant? demanded the inner Aragon.

It is our job to ensure everyone is taken care of, sniffed the Chamberlain. *We take pride in our job.*

Your job, not mine. Damn, you're insidious.

The Axgaard tents, each constructed from the same sturdy leather, were connected together by a series of equally sturdy and leathery corridors. The dining tent was huge, furnished with giant tables and benches which had been hewn from whole trees. "This is a temporary camp?" Kassa said in astonishment.

"We like to be comfortable," said Svenhilda.

While everyone else sat at the tables to be served with large bowls of meaty stew — the traditional Axgaardian breakfast, apparently — Egg concealed himself in a corner. His shoulder was still killing him, and he had an idea of how to stop it.

Concentrating, he summoned up the magic that he had only recently discovered inside himself. Carefully, he formed a tiny ball of the magic near his shoulder and nudged at the splinter of ice which had lodged there during their flight from the storm.

Pain burned his whole arm for a moment. Egg gritted his teeth, and pressed the ball of magic more firmly against the splinter, bringing it upwards. The splinter flew out of his shoulder at great speed, lodging in the saggy leather ceiling. The sharp pain vanished. Egg relaxed, quite pleased with himself.

A moment later, he felt a different pain because Kassa — who had seen exactly what he was doing from her seat at the dining table — had come over to smack him on the back of the head. "Since when have you been able to do that sort of thing?" she demanded.

Egg rubbed the back of his head. "Are you allowed to hit students?"

"You're family, sweetie, I can smack you as much as I like. How long?"

"I accidentally boosted the anti-stabbing spell you gave us for Aragon," he admitted. "That's when I found out I had more power than before. I think Drak started it, though. The last set of warlock robes it gave me made me feel all tingly and…well, magical."

Kassa dropped to the floor beside him, rocking on her heels. "And you thought the best way to test this newfound power of yours was to heal a hurt inflicted on you by a magical storm? A storm which, incidentally, was created by warlocks trying to fight magic with magic?"

"I removed the splinter," Egg protested. "I didn't heal anything."

"That would explain why you're bleeding."

Egg stared at his shoulder. Warm, sticky blood oozed quite steadily from the tiny wound. "How do I fix it?"

Kassa slapped a handful of gauzy cotton into his hand. "With a bandage, dingbat."

~

After the meal, Baron Svenhilda beckoned for Egg to join her. He came to the table shyly, squeezing in between Clio and the Lordling of Axgaard. Clio was having her hair combed and braided by two of Svenhilda's buxom ladies-in-waiting, who squabbled about whether she should have daggers or spiked leather as accessories.

"Egfried Friefriedsson," said Svenhilda, making it almost sound like a question.

Egg's shoulder had begun hurting again, a dull throb this time, which he was certain was caused by the tightness of the bandage Kassa had wrapped around his wound. "Hi, Aunty," he said dismally.

Svenhilda grinned. "I noticed your father didn't come to my coronation ceremony — or have the manners to bring my nephew to visit me?"

"I think he was a bit worried that the people of Axgaard might want him to be Jarl," said Egg. "He was the eldest son before...you know, all the scandal and stuff."

"My people are not what he needed to worry about," Svenhilda said grimly. "I would have put him on the damn throne myself. Egfried, dear, I'd like you to meet my husband, Doc. I suppose he would be your uncle."

The clockwork man inclined his head politely towards Egg. "Nice to meet you, young Egfried," he said conversationally. "And how is school?"

"Um," said Egg. "It's under attack by a vicious elemental storm at the moment. But I got an A in my first Social Studies of Heroes and Villains test. So that's good."

"You know," said Svenhilda. "Having a husband who is made out of clockwork makes it quite difficult for me to provide an heir for Axgaard. I suppose I will have to look elsewhere in the family." She smiled sweetly at Egg. "I hope you're taking plenty of Ruling Aristocracy classes."

He gazed at her in panic.

"Perhaps now would be a good moment to have that meeting, your ladyship?" said Kassa, coming to Egg's rescue. "The one about Mocklore's impending doom?"

"Of course," said Svenhilda. "Other matters can be discussed later." She gave Egg a meaningful look.

A bearded and braided Axgaard warrior entered the dining hall, shaking his axe above his head in what seemed to be a form of salute. "More visitors, Jarl!"

"Baron," Svenhilda corrected coldly.

"More visitors, Baron," said the warrior. "From Cluft, requesting shelter from the storm. Can we set fire to them?"

"No," said Svenhilda, getting to her feet. "I've told you before, Harridanfried. Setting fire to people is now restricted to special feast days. No exceptions. Mistress Daggersharp, would you like to join me to greet your fellow Cluftians?"

Kassa, already at the mouth of the leather corridor, hung back reluctantly to wait for the Baron. "Thank you, your ladyship," she said, tapping her foot impatiently. "I would be glad to."

The dining table was momentarily silenced after they had left.

"So," Clio said brightly to Egg. "A warlock and heir to the Jarl of Axgaard? You're turning out to be quite a catch."

"I have a headache," he muttered.

~

"Interesting set up you have here," Kassa said as she and Baron Svenhilda walked along one of the leather corridors. It was killing Kassa to walk slowly, but for the sake of politeness she kept pace with the Lordling of Axgaard, who was in no hurry.

Svenhilda tapped the leather walls with some pride. "Chandelak hide," she said cheerfully. "Have you ever seen a Chandelak?"

Kassa, who had seen just about every horrible hairy (or slimy, or scaled) monster that Mocklore had to offer, shook her head.

"They live underground, in caves beneath the Skullcap mountains. They have become quite resilient to magic over the years." Svenhilda frowned at a drip that was forming in the corner of one of the corridor's seams. "It lets the rain in, but no magic can penetrate these walls."

Something heavy and boulder-shaped made a thumping dent in the ceiling. Kassa winced, but Svenhilda shrugged and kept walking. "As soon as some of my best warriors started wandering away from Axgaard and muttering about the lure of the velvety darkness, or possibly the dark velvetiness, I sensed something was wrong. Thought I'd come and see if I could do anything to get my people back. Good hunter-gatherers are hard to find, you know."

They came to the tent which served as Svenhilda's entrance hall. Two cloaked figures and several dripping Axgaard warriors waited there. The warriors looked quite shamefaced as Svenhilda approached and glared at them.

"Not interested in velvet any more?" she said sarcastically. "Lost the taste for black satin trousers and strangely seductive demon-cities? Go, get something to eat. I'll deal with you later."

The warriors shuffled their feet and started heading for the dining tent.

"It's not their fault the city brainwashed them," Kassa couldn't help saying. "The draklight was incredibly powerful."

"Brainwashed," Svenhilda said, her tone heavy with disgust. "They're warriors, their brains shouldn't come into it."

"An interesting topic, hmm?" said a voice. "Is it more embarrassing to have your mind enslaved if you are an intelligent, educated person?"

Kassa grinned. "Bertie!"

Vice-Chancellor Bertie was unwrapping himself from a huge, wet cloak with many pockets in it. "Bit of a storm out there, what?" he said cheerfully. "How are you doing, Mistress Sharpe?"

"Managing quite well, under the circumstances. It is good to see you."

"I should think so, too. And look here!" He produced several cracked pieces of wood from his many pockets. "I saved the Great Reversing Barrel! Just a few nails and it will be as right as rain."

Kassa felt the smile fade from her face. "You think it will be useful, do you?"

"Oh, yes," said Bertie. "And look who else I found!"

The second cloak shimmered and fell away, revealing the mousy figure of Mavis, the goddess of Cluft.

"You?" said Kassa. "I thought you abandoned us to our fate. I thought the cosmos was too fragile for you gods to be able to make a difference. I thought the most constructive thing you were willing to do was disappear?"

"Things have changed," said Mavis.

Kassa eyed the tent flap, through which she could see the chaotic storm of wild magic and bright, burning rain. "You could say that."

"We need to talk," said the goddess.

"Are you helping us now?"

"Not exactly." Mavis smiled, peering over her spectacles at Kassa. "But I may be able to point you in the direction of the right god."

~

Kassa and Svenhilda swept into the dining hall like two stately galleons. Vice-Chancellor Bertie and Mavis the goddess followed behind them. "Time for a conference!" Kassa announced. "Where is everybody?"

The warriors who had recently escaped the lure of Drak did not even look up from their stew bowls.

Egg and Doc were playing an Axgaard board game in which your pieces not only captured your opponent's pieces when you jumped over them, but smashed them into little pieces and then ate them, singing about the glories of battle. Singespitter was snoozing in a corner of the tent, his sheepskin coat tucked around his curled-up body. Sean McHagrty was attempting to chat up several of Svenhilda's ladies-in-waiting, who were alternately fluttering their eyelashes at this charming stranger and threatening him with their hair-axes.

Aragon Silversword, Lord Sinistre and Clio were nowhere to be seen.

"Right," said Kassa. "Egg, find Aragon and get him here now. Sean, find the Lordling. We'll need his input. If either of you see Clio, grab her too. We don't want people wandering around and getting lost."

Doc produced an umbrella made of the same leather as the tents. He smiled at Egg. "I believe ex-Sir Silversword went for a walk outside."

"Brilliant," Egg grumbled.

Sean grinned at him, pleased to be getting the better end of the bargain, and headed down one of the other leather corridors in search of Lord Sinistre.

~

The storm was getting worse. The wind howled painfully around the tent-tops. The rain was colder than before, and wetter if that were possible. The rain still had that eerie brightness about it that suggested it was not natural... although such terms were difficult to define in Mocklore. Nothing large and pointy had fallen out of the sky in a while, which had to be a good thing. Egg huddled under the large leather umbrella, and set out in search of Aragon Silversword.

Who in their right mind would go for a random walk in the middle of a chaotic magical weather disaster?

A large icicle embedded itself in the mud at Egg's feet, making him swear and jump. It was hard to see in any direction. For one horrible moment he wondered what was happening to Cluft, to all the people he knew there. The storm had obliterated at least one of Drak's towers quite effortlessly. How would Cluft be holding up under such conditions?

Having taken his mind off the search for Aragon, Egg immediately found him. The Chamberlain of Drak and ex-Champion of two Emperors of Mocklore was sitting on a large white boulder, which may or may not recently have fallen from the sky as part of the elemental storm. He was not even wearing a coat. His shirt was wet to the skin. He stared ahead at a fixed point in space.

White flame zigzagged from the bright sky, almost incinerating Aragon's left foot. He did not move.

Egg hurried forward, and finally saw what strange vision had Aragon Silversword so mesmerised that he didn't notice the danger or the mad, magical chaos that surrounded him.

It was Dahla. So much had happened since Egg last saw the ghostly girl, he had almost forgotten about her. The bright rain poured through her translucent body and pale coppery hair, lighting her up from within. Her eyes were red-rimmed, but she seemed happier. Egg gave her a little wave, and Dahla responded with a very sweet smile before vanishing.

Another small fireball crashed nearby. Egg held the leather umbrella so that it covered Aragon as well as himself. "You've met my ghost, then."

Aragon looked around in surprise. "Ghost?"

"She used to visit our room," said Egg. "I thought maybe she was a former student."

"Not exactly," said Aragon.

"Did she tell you what she was looking for? She would never tell me."

"She doesn't know," said Aragon. "It doesn't matter. She's very close to finding it. Kassa wants me, I suppose."

"Doesn't she always?" said Egg. Then, blushing, he added, "I mean…"

"Don't worry about it," said Aragon Silversword, ignoring the umbrella and striding back towards the Axgaard encampment. "I know what you meant."

16

THE ESSENCE OF ROMANCE

*C*lio was lost. She had only wanted to get away from everyone for a few minutes to clear her head, but now she had forgotten which corridor was which. She was stranded in a maze of leather and had lost all sense of direction. It was with some relief that she heard someone coming, although it turned out to be Lord Sinistre.

"Are you all right?" Clio couldn't help asking.

Lord Sinistre stared at her. His beautiful face was pale and hollow-looking, with dark shadows around each eye. "How do you stand it?" he asked.

"Stand what?"

"This dreadful normality. You were in my beloved Drak; you felt the exquisite power of the draklight."

"I didn't like it much," Clio admitted.

"You don't know what you were missing." His skin was clammy, glistening in the dim light of the corridor. "And now what am I? Without my city, without my draklight? I'm not a Lord. No one is even treating me like a villain any more. I'm not important enough to be considered a threat."

He was too close to her. "I'm not overly comfortable

around you right now, if that makes you feel better," said Clio. What she wanted to do was back away from him and flee down the corridor.

"Really?" said Lord Sinistre. He rummaged through his pockets. "I don't have the doomed blade of Dathazarrr any more, but I have my spyglass and my Compelling Collar and my various unnameable torture instruments..." He stared at a nasty-looking narrow blade. "Actually, I think this is a cuticle-slice."

He really was quite pathetic. "Do you want us to tie to you a chair again?" Clio sighed. "Would that make you happy?"

"Ah," Lord Sinistre said. "At least then I would know which side I was on."

"Can't you just be on our side?"

Sinistre moved in an instant, pinning Clio to the wall with one arm. He held the cuticle-slice to her throat. "Are you suggesting that I become a..." he choked on the word, "...hero?"

"I don't think we're heroes really," said Clio, trying not to think about the proximity of the blade. "We're defending the place where we live, trying to survive. You live here too, now. With the draklight gone, you're just like us. Why shouldn't you help us save Mocklore?"

"I don't know," breathed Lord Sinistre, his eyes gleaming. "Who would be the villain?"

"There aren't any," said Clio. "I mean, maybe the Light Lords, but we haven't seen them for ages. They probably died when their world did. The main threat is the storm and I don't think it can tell the difference between heroes or villains."

"And which am I again?"

Clio winced as the wicked blade of the cuticle-slice pressed harder against her throat. "Not sure," she whispered. "What do you think?"

"Let her go!" shouted an outraged voice. It was Sean McHagrty. So that was going to be helpful.

"It's okay," Clio insisted, not wanting him to scare Lord Sinistre.

Sean stopped a few feet from them, taking in the sharp instrument that Lord Sinistre was holding to her throat. "How is this okay?"

Clio thought about it. "Good point. Get off me!"

Lord Sinistre backed away, lowering the cuticle-slice. "You think I'm a villain."

"Not a very good one," admitted Clio, rubbing her throat.

"At this stage, I'll take what I can get." Lord Sinistre paused, as if about to laugh maniacally, then seemed to think better of it. He ran off down the corridor.

Clio breathed out, shivering. "Yikes." That had been close, and yet she had never felt entirely in danger. He was such a bad villain.

"You all right?" Sean asked.

"You don't have to play the hero, you know. It doesn't impress me."

"Why do you always assume I'm trying to impress you?"

"Because I'm female and I have a pulse."

"Oh, very nice. I'm not this sex-mad caricature you seem to think I am."

Clio started counting off on her fingers. "Lemissa, Nannandra, Beanka, Chantelle, Meridia, Sallix…"

"You're keeping score?"

"Those are just the girls in my immediate acquaintance whose hearts you happen to have broken. Recently."

"It's not my fault they got their hearts involved. I never asked them to." Sean gave her a sidelong look. "So you don't want to give me a chance to do the same to you?"

Clio shot a scornful look at him. "I don't like you enough

to give you that chance. This isn't banter, in case you were wondering. It's disdain."

"Charming. Do you give Egg this much of a hard time?"

"He doesn't deserve it as much as you do. Anyway, Egg and I are friends."

"Who says that's not what I want?"

Clio laughed. "You want to be friends with me?"

"Why not?"

"Why?"

"I'm jealous."

"Of me and Egg?"

"You two are so easy with each other, you have fun. I've never had a friend like that."

"Never?"

Sean shrugged again, looking more uncomfortable. "I'm not good at making friends. I'm good at chatting up girls."

"That sounds like a chat up line in itself."

"I know. Can't help it. I was born to flirt."

"If we're going to be friends and you accept that we won't be anything else, that means no more flirting."

Sean sounded baffled. "Never?"

"Never ever."

"But you flirt with Egg all the time."

Good point, Clio. Work that one out. "That's different."

"How?"

"It just is. Can you do it, McHagrty?"

"I don't know. I've never tried not to flirt with someone."

"Try now." She gestured down the corridor. "Is this the way back to the others?"

"Yep. It's a bit of a walk."

"Fine."

They walked along the corridor in silence for a minute or two. Sean broke first. "Look, I can't do this. I have to tell you how cute you look in those braids."

Clio tore the spiked leather thong out of one of her braids and unplaited it violently.

"Hey, don't do that. The Axgaard ladies will get cranky." He picked up the spiked leather thong and leaned in, quickly rebraiding it.

Clio waited for him to make a move, to try to smooch her or flirt, but instead he seemed genuinely interested in repairing the braid. "What are you doing?"

"Fixing the mess you just made."

"You know how to braid hair?"

"Hey, I have a sister. And lots of girlfriends." He worked in silence for a few moments, then tied off the braid with the spiky leather. "It doesn't quite match the other one."

"It'll do," she said.

"Are we friends yet?"

"You're not planning to kiss me, are you?"

"Not unless we get possessed by superhero demon creatures from another world again. Been there, done that, bought the limited edition souvenir tunic."

"I think we can be friends, then."

"Excellent."

"Most of our people are sheltering in the cellars under Cluft," Vice-Chancellor Bertie told Kassa when Egg and a dripping-wet Aragon returned to the dining tent, which had been turned into a conference room. "We lost the Third Lecture Theatre and a large chunk of the square of student residence, but luckily there doesn't seem to have been anyone inside at the time."

"Is the library all right?" Singespitter asked.

Mavis smiled approvingly at him, a student with the right priorities. "All the scrolls are safe."

"Does Drak have cellars?" Svenhilda asked.

"Dungeons," said Kassa.

"And an underground zoo," contributed Aragon, joining the table. "Plenty of places to shelter."

"Clio said that Lord Sinistre is reacting badly to the loss of the draklight," Kassa told him. "He attacked her in the corridor."

Aragon glanced over to the far side of the tent, where Clio and Sean sat at one of the other tables in quiet conversation. "He didn't hurt her?"

"She says not. But will all the people of Drak have a similar reaction?"

"I don't know." He sat on the bench opposite her. "Some of the courtiers, maybe. The so-called nobles. I imagine the servants will just get on with things. They usually do." A brief look of worry crossed over his face. "I hope they're all right."

"Worrying about your staff?" she asked, teasing a little.

He gave her a rueful look. "I feel responsible for them."

"I know the feeling."

Their eyes met, briefly. Kassa looked away first. "Mavis, don't you think it's time you told us what you know about all this?"

~

From where Egg stood, Clio and Sean were talking quite intently about something. He hesitated to interrupt them until Clio caught his eye and waved him over.

"Well," Sean was saying. "*My* uncle is the great inventor Imago Void who lives in a giant castle in the ruins of the ancient witch-city of Shadowe. He designed the Clockwork Comet which still appears in the sky every thirteen and a half years."

Clio smiled sadly. "Well…"

"You shouldn't play this game with her," Egg told Sean.

"My father was convicted of High Treason against Emperor Timregis and was executed by the Imperial Champion, his own brother," said Clio, before Egg could stop her.

Sean didn't look fazed in the least. "My dad was the Captain of the Dreadnought Blackguards when old Emperor Timregis died. After a few replacement Emperors kicked the bucket, the leaders of Dreadnought forced my dad to take the throne. He lasted two months before being assassinated. My mother was left with six kids and no husband. Then, several Emperors later, the leaders of Dreadnought grabbed my eldest brother Tam, and forced him to take the throne. He was only twenty-two. He survived for three weeks. Then our dog died." He took a sip of foamy beer from a tankard.

Clio stared at him, tears welling up in her wide blue eyes. "My mother died in a house fire when I was a baby. I don't even know what she looked like."

Egg let his head hit the table. "Clio, you have to stop playing this game. It is the opposite of fun."

"I know," she said, wiping her eyes. "Sorry. Shall we talk about something else?"

~

Vice-Chancellor Bertie had taken over half of the conference table with various tools and bits of broken wood, as he attempted to repair the Great Reversing Barrel.

Everyone else was looking at Mavis.

"Is this the end of it?" Kassa asked first. "Are we safe once the storm has ended?"

Mavis pulled some crumpled knitting out of her handbag and started to click her needles. "When is anyone ever safe in Mocklore? I don't see why the storm shouldn't be the last of it, assuming it ever ends."

"There will be a lot of damage to clean up," said Svenhilda grimly.

"That's nothing new," said Kassa. "I'm hoping we don't have any more surprises coming to us." She looked sideways at Mavis. "You said one of our gods might know something?"

"Oh, yes," said Mavis. "The cause of this whole disaster is much closer to home than you might imagine."

"But the Light Lords of Harmony created Drak, caused all the trouble. What have our gods got to do with anything?"

"Did you never stop to wonder who created Harmony?"

"Oh," said Kassa. "It seemed like a real place. Creepy, but real. It had a history."

"Anyone can write history," said Mavis. "I imagine the people of Drak thought they had a history."

"Not a very good one," said Aragon. It was the first thing he had said for a while. "Lord Sinistre never could remember what his father looked like."

"I had better start at the beginning," said Mavis. "Some time ago, Raglah the Golden and myself had a debate about human needs. He insisted that a mortal society could run on magic, that if there was enough magic then such things as agriculture, industry and even biological reproduction were unnecessary." She looked a little embarrassed. "That was when Amorata got involved."

"I imagine she took it quite personally, the idea that humans didn't need to mate," agreed Kassa.

"It was an argument, nothing more," Mavis said crossly. "But that silly little lust-goddess created Harmony to prove Raglah wrong."

"Did it prove him wrong?" asked Baron Svenhilda.

"He claimed not," said Mavis. "Everyone else took one look at the society of Harmony and shuddered, but Raglah thought it was perfectly functional. The debate went on…"

"And so did Harmony," said Kassa.

"They were sentient," said Mavis. "We couldn't just obliterate them. Well, Lady Luck wanted to, but she was out-
voted. We chose the most impartial of us to guard the
Harmony gem and make sure it was permanently contained."

"But then Aragon Silversword mysteriously appeared
inside Harmony's own little fake city and inadvertently
showed them that there was a way out," said Kassa. "We still
don't know how that happened, assuming everyone is being
truthful about it."

"Yes," said Aragon, giving her a hard look. "Assuming
that."

"Who was supposed to be looking after the gem?" asked
Kassa. "No, don't tell me. I think I can guess which of the
gods is considered an impartial judge. Your ladyship, I don't
suppose there's any seawater around here?"

Svenhilda blinked at the unusual request. "There might be
some sea salt in the kitchen tents."

"That'll do," said Kassa, sweeping away from the table.

"Hmmph?" said Vice-Chancellor Bertie. "Where's she
gone, then?"

"To visit her godfather," Aragon said in unison with
Singespitter, in the same weary tone. They stared at each
other in surprise.

The sea salt was the good stuff, white and crusty. Kassa stood
in a small ante-tent, crumbling it between her fingers. Slowly
she walked in a circle, scattering the salt to trace the shape on
the leather floor. When it was completed to her satisfaction,
she sat in the centre to wait.

Skeylles the Fishy Judge, Lord of the Underwater, one of
the ten remaining deities of Mocklore, had been named
Kassa's godfather when she was eight days old. She didn't

have the faintest idea why. Neither of her parents had bothered to enlighten her either before or after their deaths, and Skeylles himself had been silent on the matter. Of course he was the god of the ocean and Kassa's parents had both been pirates who sailed the seventeen seas, but that seemed a fairly tenuous connection. There was a story there, and if ever Kassa had a spare five minutes in her life she planned to track it down.

Meanwhile, a godfather who was an actual god came in quite handy at times, particularly when Kassa was in danger of drowning. He sent great birthday presents, too. The live kraken she had received for her sixth birthday was the best. She called it Fido, and kept it as a pet for years, even after it completely outgrew the bathtub and had to be dragged behind her father's ship on a leash.

Skeylles had also provided damage control after the catastrophic Second Glimmer rampaged across Mocklore, and he had taken a direct interest when the very dangerous goddess Lady Luck developed a serious grudge against his god-daughter. Still, he wasn't the kind of deity who tolerated being summoned very often. All Kassa could do was hope that he was in a good mood.

There were soft footsteps on the leather floor of the corridor outside. Aragon Silversword stood at the door flap, looking in at her. "Any luck?"

"Not yet."

"You should be careful, you know. Lord Sinistre is still running around the tents threatening people."

Kassa tapped her belt, where a few small herb-daggers hung. "I can look after myself."

"I'm sure you can," said Aragon. He opened his hand, revealing a wicked blade. "I thought you might like this one back."

"I can't break the circle," she said.

"I can wait." Aragon dropped to the floor outside the circle of salt, resting the knife easily on his knee.

"Strange to think of you playing Chamberlain," she said after a moment. "How long were you in Drak?"

"Hard to say," said Aragon. "It's difficult to count the moon-cycles when the moon is always full, but a friend of mine reckoned it at about half a year. I fell into the routine easily enough. Being a Lordling's Chamberlain isn't that different to being an Emperor's Champion. Or a pirate queen's lieutenant, come to that. I seem to suit being second-in-command."

"So," said Kassa. "Where were you the rest of the time?" She met his gaze this time. Golden eyes looked into grey.

"I was in Drak."

"For a half a year. You've been gone three."

"I can't explain how that happened." He looked at her. "Do you actually think that I left you? That I woke up one morning and walked out?"

"Are you saying you didn't?"

His eyes were disturbingly calm. "I suppose I am."

Kassa could feel the anger boiling up inside her. "And am I supposed to believe you, to take your word for it?"

"I don't see why not. I certainly can't prove it."

She gave a strangled little laugh. "They love you, you know. The servants and staff of Drak. They think you're good at your job. They respect you."

"And you thought I was such a villain."

This time, Kassa's laugh turned into a strangled sob.

Aragon carefully wiped some of the salt aside and crawled into the circle.

"I'll have to do that again," said Kassa.

"Later. It doesn't matter now."

"But if I can stop the storm..."

"Even the gods can't do that without setting off some

other stupid side-effect. Better to let it blow itself out." Aragon placed the knife to one side of them both, then pulled Kassa to him. They were close enough for him to taste her tears. "I did not leave you by choice."

"If you say so." But she didn't pull out of his arms.

"What happened to the ship?" he asked after a moment.

For a moment Kassa couldn't quite think what he was talking about. "The *Splashdance*? I tried to give her to Daggar, but he didn't have the heart to captain her without the rest of us." She pulled at the long silver chain that hung around her neck, the end of it vanishing into her cleavage. "It's jewellery now. The crew went their separate ways."

"And you became a professor of magic?"

"I like teaching. Turns out I'm good at it. I've never been really good at anything before." Kassa laughed suddenly. "I made such a bad pirate."

"I wouldn't say that. You had the right costumes, the right vocabulary, the training. Of course you never did much in the way of actual piracy…"

"I was a terrible witch, too."

"I won't argue with that."

"Mind you, you weren't a very good Champion," she said.

"I was an excellent Champion. Don't let a few betrayals here and there fool you."

"You do realise that Lord Sinistre is the only employer you've ever had whom you haven't betrayed?"

Aragon grinned bitingly. "There's still time."

"Look at us," said Kassa. "We both grew up and found real jobs."

"I suppose we did. So much for the outlaw and the traitor." He tucked a stray red curl of her hair behind one ear.

The tent walls rattled wildly.

"I think it's quieting down," said Aragon, making light of the storm.

Kassa couldn't joke about it. "How many people do you think died in that mess?"

"Hopefully most of those damned master warlocks. Don't do this to yourself, Kassa. You are not responsible for every magical catastrophe in Mocklore. I'm not even entirely sure that you had much to do with the Second Glimmer, for all you keep taking the blame for it."

"Don't say that," she protested, starting to laugh. "You'll ruin my reputation."

He touched her cheek with his fingers. "I did not leave you by choice."

"You already said that."

"I thought it was worth repeating."

She kissed him, fiercely. He kissed her back. They had so much time to make up for.

What with one thing and another, they made a bit of a mess of the salt circle.

~

Some time later, Kassa opened her eyes and found herself standing in the bone-tiled hall of Skeylles the Fishy Judge, Lord of the Underwater. Shimmery lights danced around the room, reminding her that this place was a long way underwater.

"You Summoned Me?" boomed the huge voice of her godfather. The echoes went on for some time, bouncing from every tile on every wall. There was still no sight of the god himself.

"Well, I was going to," said Kassa. "Then I got distracted." Self-consciously, she brushed sea salt from the folds of her skirt. "Still, no point in wasting a good manifestation. What's going on?"

Skeylles stepped out from behind a six-foot abalone-plated statue of a whelk. He was thinner than ever, gaunt around the eyes and cheekbones. He seemed to be overly weighed down by the chain of fish skulls that he wore around his neck. "Generally, or specifically?" he asked.

Kassa stared at him. "What happened to your voice?"

"Oh, Sorry. Generally Or Specifically?"

"Don't mess about. Drak, Harmony, the draklight, the Light Lords, the elemental storm, fire and ice falling from the sky. Do I have to continue?"

"Please Don't," Skeylles boomed quietly. He found a large rock with half of a shipwreck embedded in the side of it, and sat down upon it.

Kassa sighed. "Was Harmony built by the Mocklore gods to settle some kind of bet?"

"Yes," said Skeylles.

"And as the Fishy Judge you were considered impartial enough to look after it, make sure nothing bad happened to the inhabitants but also make sure that no one from Mocklore could interfere."

"Yes," said Skeylles.

"So," said Kassa. "What the hell happened, if you don't mind me asking?"

Skeylles lifted a bone-thin arm and pointed towards a large pile of discarded scallop shells. An equally pitiful figure emerged from behind the shells.

It took Kassa a few moments to realise that it was Amorata, brunette goddess of love beads and naughty night-wear. Kassa had seen this goddess before — she was usually a flirtatious glamour queen with a curvaceous body generously crammed into something like a string bikini or a tiny pair of gold hotpants. Her chestnut hair was usually as bouncy as the rest of her, and she was never seen without a pair of stiletto sandals, her toenails prettily painted and bejewelled.

This new version of Amorata had lank, colourless hair

that fell in knots and tangles to her waist. She wore a grimy bathrobe made from towelling fabric that had once been blue but was now a faded and grubby bluish grey. Her shuffling feet were shoved into falling-apart sheepskin boots. She was not so much weeping as snivelling. She pulled a wad of tissue from a pocket in order to blow her nose and blot her face.

"What happened to you?" Kassa asked.

Amorata flopped on the bone-tiled floor and burst into noisy sobs.

Kassa edged away from her, turning to Skeylles instead. "What happened to her?"

"Drak," said Skeylles. "Harmony. And the rest. She's in it up to her pretty eyeballs."

"They're not that pretty right now," said Kassa. "What with being all bloodshot."

"Do you want to hear this or not?"

"Your voice has gone normal again."

"I know. It's part of what I'm going to tell you about."

"I'm all ears."

"Amorata came here every day to watch what was happening in Harmony," Skeylles began. "I didn't see any harm in it. She was fascinated by a world without love and sex and procreation. The people of Harmony didn't bother about all that."

"They have no idea what they're missing," said Kassa. It was strange, hearing Skeylles talk like a normal person. Almost as if he was a real godfather, not a god at all. Staring at his thin face, Kassa resolved to bring him a nice big pot of oyster stew. Or she would, if she knew how to cook oyster stew. Maybe she should just bring him the oysters. On the other hand, he was the Lord of the Underwater. He had an unlimited supply of oysters. So much for that plan.

"Indeed. The false happiness provided by the Light Lords kept the Harmonyites content without the need to form romantic relationships. Eventually, Amorata — while I was not paying attention, I might add — stepped inside and introduced herself to one of the residents."

"Quillsmith," sniffed the snivelling wreck of a lust goddess. "Such a sweet boy."

"She described exactly what they were missing," said Skeylles. "She talked about attraction and seduction, dressing to impress, dancing the night away with someone you adore, fighting duels to defend your lady's honour…"

"Oh crap," said Kassa. She could see where this was going.

"I may have emphasised the dressing up part a little too much," sniffed Amorata.

"You're responsible for all that velvet?" said Kassa.

"I like velvet," said Amorata. "Anyway, he misinterpreted a lot of what I said. I don't think he really understood."

"I'm hardly surprised," said Kassa.

"He added all the demon bits himself," Amorata said quite viciously. "He turned my discussion about the essence of romance into a demon city of horribleness."

"He and the Light Lords built Drak to be a conduit for dark magic," said Kassa. "Demons were probably inevitable."

"I didn't know that at the time!"

"This is what you get for encouraging those creative types. They take perfectly rational things you may have said to them and put them down in fiction. Back when I had a poet in my crew I was always finding myself quoted in lyric metre." Kassa looked from Skeylles to Amorata. "Tell me about Aragon, then. How did he end up there?"

Amorata hid her guilty face behind straggly hair.

"It's an interesting story," Skeylles began.

"Don't you protect her," Kassa growled. "I want to hear it from her own ruby red lips."

"I meant well," said Amorata in a small voice.

"Amazing how many disasters start out that way."

"We gods can see into the future," explained the goddess, biting her lip. "Not perfectly, just the occasional glimpse of a likely possibility. Half a year ago, I had a vision of a future where Quillsmith's strange demon city had invaded Mocklore, and you were fighting against it."

"So instead of telling the rest of us about the invasion so that we could do something before the possibility became a reality," Skeylles contributed, "she used the opportunity to do a little matchmaking."

"Well, it was so sad when Aragon disappeared!" Amorata burst out. "I loved your whole little star-crossed romance, with the bickering and the hating each other and the finally realising you were meant to be together. I almost bit my favourite temple in half when he vanished without warning. The ballads after that just weren't the same."

"I wasn't too happy about it myself," Kassa growled.

"I thought that if he was on one side of the battle with Drak and you were on the other," the goddess said sadly, "you could start again with the bickering and the conflict and the falling in love all over again…"

"How did you find him?" asked Kassa. This was the interesting bit, the question which had been most closely on her mind. "Where was he?"

"I'm a god, not a surgeon," Amorata snapped. "I don't usually need to know what I'm doing in order to do something. I just waved my hand to make him appear in Drak."

"It was the first sign," said Skeylles. "Amorata's little love miracle went wrong, my voice started losing its boom, Raglah the Golden lost interest in women, Binx the drunkard became a health-food nut overnight."

"I even heard that Dame Kind the Fairy Spritemother has started wearing leather and hanging out with a gang," Amorata said tearfully.

"First sign of what?" asked Kassa. "What is going on? Mavis said something about the cosmos being fragile."

"She's the one who worked it out for us," said Skeylles. "It helps, having a librarian in the family. Turns out that we have reached the exact centre of all time and space allotted to our particular cosmos."

Kassa frowned. "I don't understand."

Amorata blew her nose noisily. "We're at the halfway point between all the history that ever was and all the history yet to come. Apparently every god in the cosmos is experiencing a kind of mid-existence crisis."

"We're lucky, really," said Skeylles. "There are only ten of us in Mocklore. We can keep an eye on each other. If we still had the hundreds of deities that were running around before the Decimalisation, there's no telling what could have happened."

"So you can't help," said Kassa. "That's why Mavis said there was no point asking any gods to do something. Your powers are unreliable right now." Typical.

"For now," Skeylles agreed. "We believe we will start regaining our control some time during the next few years. I'm afraid that will probably be a little late to help with this particular situation, although with any luck the elemental storm will be the last of the damage caused to Mocklore."

"We haven't had a whole lot of luck lately," Kassa said grimly. She glared at Amorata. "Aragon appeared in Drak like you planned. So what went wrong?"

Amorata gave a big sniff. "It was the timing that was out of whack," she said. "The reason he vanished so unexpectedly three years ago is because I sent him into Drak six months ago. I accidentally moved him forward in time."

"Oh," said Kassa. She thought of the misery she had gone through three years ago when she thought he left without a word, without even an argument. Despite all that, she couldn't stop herself smiling.

"I feel really bad about it," Amorata assured her, bottom lip trembling.

"So you should," said Kassa. *I did not leave you by choice*, he had insisted. Trust was all very well, but it was nice to have confirmation. "Couldn't be helped. Blame the cosmos." She was still smiling.

"Oh," blubbered the goddess of elegant bubbled drinks and long walks on the beach. "You're being so nice!"

"That's me," said Kassa. "Nice as pie."

Amorata jumped to her feet, stretching out her hand. "I want to do something for you. To make up for it." She smiled wanly. "It's the only power I have left that still works…"

Kassa jumped hastily out of the way. "Oh, really, there's no need. I'd be happy with a box of chocolates. No need to do anything strenuous!"

"Trust me," said Amorata, touching Kassa's face with soft fingers.

~

Everything lurched to the left. Kassa squeezed her eyes tightly shut and then opened them slowly.

It was a study, of sorts. Scroll buckets lined the walls. The view through the big glass windows was a bright green valley, with trees on all sides. Kassa half-recognised the area as being a little north of the Middens. It was a beautiful, calm day.

Aragon entered the study. He flicked through some papers, then sat in the large leather chair and started writing a letter. His hair was grey. His face was creased. He was perhaps twenty years older than her Aragon. He glanced up and through the window, not seeing Kassa, though she stood between him and the glass.

It felt like being a ghost.

A girl burst in through the doorway, golden hair flying. Kassa thought at first that it was Clio, but the curve of her face was different and her hair far wilder than Aragon's niece. Plus, if this was a vision of twenty years in the future, Clio would be in her late thirties.

"Dad, where is she?" The girl sounded panicky, worried.

Aragon laid down his pen and looked curiously at her. "Sorry, love. She took Kit to visit your grandparents."

His daughter shook her hair back impatiently. "But we don't have any...wait, do you mean our *dead* grandparents?"

"I've been trying not to think about it," he said. "Can I help?"

"I really hope so," said Aragon's daughter.

Kassa reeled back, staring at the girl's face. Her eyes were as golden as her hair.

THE CALM BETWEEN
CATASTROPHES

S *nap!* Kassa was back in the bone-tiled hall of Skeylles the Fishy Judge, Lord of the Underwater. She blinked rapidly, accustoming herself to the change. There had been far too much mysterious transportation lately. She was dizzy. "What the hell was that?"

"A possibility," said Amorata, her eyes welling up with sentiment.

"Right," said Kassa, trying to recover her equilibrium. She looked at Amorata and then at Skeylles. "So this time the gods have caused the catastrophe and the mortals have to clean up the mess."

"Makes A Change," he said, making an extra effort to restore the boom to his voice. It was still diminished.

"Charming as ever," said Kassa. "Can you zap me back to the Axgaard tents, or is the mid-cosmos crisis likely to balls that up too?"

"It is easy to return you," said Skeylles. "You Were Never Really Here."

~

Kassa opened her eyes. She sat up, finding herself back in the little leather ante-tent. She brushed salt from her bodice and realised that it was half-unlaced. She stood up, tidying herself up a little, relacing her bodice and checking that the rest of her garments were fastened in a respectable manner.

There was no sign of Aragon, but she couldn't blame him for that. She was the one who had left (in or out of her own body) to visit a godly realm.

Still picking granules of sea salt from her sleeves, she stepped out into the leather corridor.

"There she is," she heard. Egg and Clio ran up to her.

"We've been looking for you," said Egg.

"The storm is over," said Clio.

"Thank the gods for that," said Kassa in relief. "Or perhaps not," she added, remembering that the gods had little to do with it. "We were due for some good news."

"Singespitter said you were communicating with a god," said Clio. "Did you find anything out?"

Aragon and I are going to have a daughter, Kassa thought. Or was she a possible potentiality of a daughter? "I found out that Aragon was telling the truth about where he has been all this time," she said aloud. "It's a good start. Let's go and look at some storm damage." They headed along the corridor. "Where is Aragon?" Kassa asked.

Egg and Clio looked at each other. "No one's seen him for a while," admitted Egg. "We thought he was with you."

Kassa's step didn't falter. "Oh, I'm sure he's around somewhere."

~

Further investigation revealed that Aragon Silversword was, in fact, nowhere in the Axgaard encampment. Kassa took this news with a smile and a nod, her eyes gradually becoming glassier. After a while, people stopped mentioning him.

It was lunchtime, which meant that the dining hall was full of bearded, boisterous Axgaard warriors. Meat bones, bread crusts and various kinds of axe-shaped cutlery flew through the air.

Vice-Chancellor Bertie stayed behind in the tents to work on his repairs of the Great Reversing Barrel with the help of Baron Svenhilda's husband, the clockwork man called Doc.

Kassa, Clio, Egg, Sean and Singespitter stood outside the Axgaard encampment, staring across the fields to Cluft and Drak. The sky was blue and calm. Scorch marks and melting shards of ice still scarred the land, but these would fade. The storm was over.

"Is that it?" said Clio softly. "Do we just go back to real life now? Will there be lectures tomorrow and Fish Surprise for lunch and essays to be handed in?"

"I don't know," said Kassa. Singespitter's hand found hers, squeezing it softly. "I really hope so."

"They are going to give us extensions for those essays, aren't they?" Sean said suddenly.

Everyone looked at him.

"What? I'm just saying what the rest of you are thinking."

"We'd better head across," said Kassa. "See what the damage is, send letters home to the parents, that sort of thing."

They all started walking down the hill and across the field towards the Great Mocklore Highway.

"That's probably where Uncle Aragon went," Clio said suddenly. "I mean, he is the Chamberlain of Drak. He would have been worried about the people over there."

"Yes," said Kassa. "That's probably where he went."

"I can't believe the city's still here," said Sean. "Shouldn't Drak have vanished in the storm? It's fictional."

"Some fictions are stronger than others," said Kassa. "You never know if magic is going to be permanent until it is. I think the draklight has gone, and hopefully the influence of Harmony as well, but it looks like the city itself is staying."

"I'm glad," said Clio. "It wouldn't feel right if Drak vanished. Not after everything that has happened." Her breath caught in her throat as they neared the road. She had spotted the warlocks, or what was left of them.

Many of the younger warlocks had tried to make rudimentary shelters, using blankets or bedrolls. The fire and ice and stone and wind of the elemental storm had sliced through such flimsy materials. Many of the warlocks had lost limbs, or were wounded or scarred.

It made very little difference, since the end result was that not one of them had survived. Some were frozen, glassy statues in crumpled poses. Some had been scorched, others crushed. Several had been turned to stone. The High Poppinpoose of the Harvestmoons, the Grand Duchydor of the Silversigils, the Sublime Goanna of the Lizardbloods and the Fat False Idol of the Bronzfetishes were all fixed in identical positions of outrage, their hands outflung at the very idea that their careful magical containment of the Harmony sphere could have failed. Kassa knocked on one of them. It was not glass or stone. It was some other, lighter substance. The master warlocks were firmly glued to the highway, unmovable.

"That's going to affect traffic," Kassa commented.

Clio looked at her accusingly. "None of them deserved this!"

"Didn't they?" said Kassa. "I suppose not. It doesn't really matter now."

Egg stared at the mass of apprentice warlocks, forcing himself to look for an apricot beard and to remember which of the twisted, frozen figures had once handed him a bowl of sausages and peas. "Is this my fault?" he asked in a strangled voice.

Kassa turned and hugged him hard. "Sweetheart, don't think that. We passed the point where this was your fault a long time ago. Everyone's had a finger in this pie, from the Light Lords of Harmony to the Gods of Mocklore to Vice-Chancellor Bertie's damn Great Reversing Barrel. Very little of it has anything to do with you." She held him at arm's length and stared into his eyes. "Do you believe me?"

Uncomfortably, he nodded.

"Good," she said. "Now let's go and see what a mess the storm made of Cluft."

She led the way along the road. Singespitter clapped Egg on the shoulder sympathetically and ran after Kassa. Sean tugged an unresisting Clio away from the horrible sight.

Egg stayed behind, gazing at the bloated figure of the High Poppinpoose. "The question is," he muttered, "can I do something to fix it?"

He placed his hand firmly on the warlock's chest, allowing his magic to do the thinking for him. Orange light flared briefly under his palm. He could feel it working...

The High Poppinpoose of the Harvestmoon Order of Warlocks melted in one big rush, splattering the road with a puddle of hot, sticky goo. Egg jumped back wildly, only just managing to avoid being splashed. He looked around wildly to check that no one had seen him, then ran after the others.

Obviously, he needed more practice.

Drak was a mess. Several of the taller towers had been shattered by the storm. Many people in the outer city lay dead in the streets. Those who had survived now lined the streets around the palace, desperate for some sign that all was not lost; desperate for some sign that the draklight was not gone forever.

Inside the palace, Lord Sinistre ran from room to room. "It must be here. It can't all be gone."

His Chamberlain, who had kept up with him every step of the way, said nothing. The warring personalities within Aragon's brain had reached a strange accord, allowing them both to control their own private thoughts. As Aragon considered how strange Drak was without the ever-present influence of the magical draklight, the Chamberlain was able to think about how to organise the relief effort for those who had lost houses, how he was going to feed a city full of people without the magically-produced food they were used to relying on, how they could turn all this into some kind of positive propaganda, and finally, how he was going to tell Lord Sinistre that the Underground Zoo had been damaged in the disaster, allowing many demonic gargoyles, bats and other dangerous creatures to escape into the tunnels under the city.

"We'll look upstairs," Lord Sinistre decided.

"My lord," the Chamberlain interjected. "Are there not more important things we should be doing? Without the draklight, your people will be confused, hungry. We must help them."

"The best thing we can do is bring the draklight back," Lord Sinistre growled. "Do not play the Chamberlain with me, Silversword. Do not pretend you would even be here if I had not compelled you to follow me."

Aragon took over from the anxious Chamberlain. "That is a matter I would like to discuss," he said, fingering at the metal Compelling Collar that bit into his throat. "This is not particularly comfortable, and is quite unnecessary. I know where my duties lie." *Well, one of me does.* "I am not going to abandon my responsibilities if you give me my freedom."

"Duties?" Lord Sinistre laughed. "Would you have returned to deal with your duties without my intervention? Of course not. You would be with that red-haired witch of yours, worrying about her city, not mine."

He has a point, said the Chamberlain.

No he doesn't, snapped Aragon. *As if I could have stayed away with your nagging voice constantly in my head. Besides, whatever you and your precious Lordship think, I do take responsibilities seriously.*

"I was the Champion of the whole Mocklore Empire once," he said aloud. *Well, twice actually, but let's not get unnecessarily complicated.* "I never once flinched in service to the Empire, even when there was a conflict between Imperial duty and my own family. I executed my own brother as my duty to the Empire. When the Emperor himself became a threat to the Empire, I arranged his death as well."

Lord Sinistre's dark eyes flashed as he stared at the other man. "Is that a threat, Chamberlain?"

"I was merely attempting to illustrate my commitment to duty. I am your man. I belong to Drak. This—" and he flicked the tinny Compelling Collar with a fingernail, "—is an irrelevance."

Well said, thought the Chamberlain, impressed.

Don't you start. I'm going to get rid of you as soon as humanly possible.

Perhaps I'll be the one who gets rid of you.

Either way suits me.

"The Collar stays," said Lord Sinistre. "I do not trust you, Chamberlain."

"I suppose that's fair enough," said Aragon. "I don't trust you either."

The two men stared each other down. "Good," said Sinistre finally. "You should not trust me. No one should trust me. I'll teach them to forget that I am the villain!"

"What exactly are you going to do?" Aragon asked.

Lord Sinistre laughed maniacally, his cackle echoing up and down the staircase. "I am going to lure the draklight back!"

Aragon's inner Chamberlain sighed plaintively. *Now we'll never get anything useful done.*

~

Cluft was a mess. Apart from the Third Lecture Theatre and a section of the square of student residence which had been destroyed (including the hour clock tower but not the minute or second), the thatched roof of the administration cottage had been obliterated, the flower beds were beyond retrieval, an entire wall was missing from the library tower and several marble tiles from the staff room temple had been smashed. Egg and Sean's room was undamaged; Clio's was not.

Professor Gootch was dead. The calmness of the dome of harmonylight had apparently forced him to relax for the first time since taking on the position of Professor with a Special Interest in Assassination, and the shock of having his stress removed had finished him off before the elemental storm even got started. Doctor Wampweed had been carved in half by a burning icebolt while getting students to safety, but both halves of him had recovered quite well, growing all the extra bits necessary to make two identical versions of him. This was convenient, as it meant there was someone to take over Professor Gootch's subjects when lessons resumed.

Doctor Mindette Masters had led her Heroics I and Heroics II classes into battle against the storm, which meant that they were all rather bruised, battered and burnt. There were a few quite serious injuries currently being treated, the rest being minor scrapes, cuts and burns.

Three students were killed when the square of student residence was hit. One of them was Clio's roommate, Lemissa. Clio and Sean were both dealing with this by sitting together, not touching or talking, each trying to figure out how they felt.

Egg felt oddly guilty, for feeling sad despite not knowing any of the dead students, for his own part — however small Kassa insisted it was — in the creation of the elemental storm, and for the jealous twinges at Sean and Clio's new closeness, which had started long before the news about Lemissa.

He dealt with this guilt by waiting until Kassa was busy elsewhere, then finding Professor Incendia Noir who had put a call out for students with magical ability to help with the relief effort.

"Magically able?" she asked briskly, tapping Egg's forehead. "Oh, yes. You've a lot of power in there. Untrained, I suppose."

"I only recently found out about it," he admitted.

"Can you spot magic when you see it, or if it's nearby?"

Egg concentrated. He could feel the earthy magic in the ground, the dark and sharp power contained within Professor Noir's rail-thin body, the aftertaste of the elemental storm in the air between his teeth. He knew without looking that Kassa was on the far side of Cluft, her colourful and lyrical magical abilities held as tightly under control as her firmly-laced bodice. "Yes," he said.

"Fine," said Professor Noir. "We're checking the area for remnants of the storm, to see whether the threat is completely past. Work with Singespitter. Check every rock, ice shard or hailstone you see. If you sense any active magic in the storm debris, call me over."

The group of students dispersed, each clutching a map of

Cluft with an area coloured in for them to survey. Egg joined Singespitter. "Does Kassa know you're doing this?"

"Of course not," said Singespitter with a grin. "Nor you, or we'd have heard the screams already."

When Egg looked at the lanky older man in the sheepskin coat he saw an afterflash of Singespitter the sheep, reflected on the back of his retinas. There was no other hint of magic. "You don't have any witchcraft or warlockitude in you, do you?"

"None at all," said Singespitter. "I'm what you call a talented layperson. Know it when I see it, can spot magic a mile off. Can't help being interested in it. Like a shipwreck victim who gets obsessed by boats."

They moved away from Cluft, peering around for storm remnants. There was a large ice-shard wedged in the guttering of the Stick and Swazzle Cocktail Tavern, on the far side of the administration cottage. Singespitter found a long stick and prodded the ice while Egg gazed at it from the inside out. Apart from a residual memory of being flung from the sky, there was no magic here. He shook his head, and they moved on.

"Still," said Singespitter. "Nice to put this ability of mine into practice. The only other use I've found for it is when I was supervising exams last year. Amazing what those third-year Magic Studies kids try to get away with. You tell them that any magic detected in the exam room will be considered evidence of cheating and there they are, waltzing in with half a dozen Memory Retrieval charms attached to their quill, pentagrams painted on the soles of their shoes and a pencil case full of newts." He grinned. "Hey, that job's going to be so much easier this year now I'm a two-leg again. Won't have to stand on a chair to keep an eye on them all."

"You're very calm about it all," said Egg. "I mean, you were a sheep for years and years because of some big magical mistake. Aren't you angry?"

"Wasn't so bad, being a sheep," said Singespitter. He pointed at a scatter pattern of charred pebbles along the path, and they went to investigate. "I never got cold with all that fleece around me — and I hate getting cold. Having wings was really cool. I'll miss being able to fly. Then there's the added bonus, where I got to hang out with Kassa."

The pebbles felt neutral to Egg. They moved on, finding more ice and more pebbles. The ice was melting fast now, but there was enough of it for Egg to sense the lack of magic. It was just ice. Singespitter nodded to confirm that he felt the same.

"You love her, don't you?" Egg asked as they headed for one of the many neat little rivers around Cluft.

"What's love?" said Singespitter lightly. "I belong to her, that's all."

Egg gave him a sideways look. "Belong?"

"Yeah. She's like one of those old-fashioned queens. People line up and volunteer to join her service. You're one."

"I am?"

"Sure. If the Vice-Chancellor said he would expel you if you left school grounds, but Kassa said it was a matter of life or death that you went to Dreadnought with her, what would you do?"

Egg thought about it. "I'd follow Kassa."

"You see? The hardest thing about being an adoring subject is that it's nearly impossible to distinguish yourself from the others. To be special. Aragon got Kassa's attention by being an evil treacherous bastard. He followed that up with the double surprise move of being absolutely loyal to her and making her fall for him." Singespitter shook his head. "Talk about a trick that's hard to top."

Several small rowing boats were lined up by the side of

the little river. Two had been punctured by large, spiky white boulders and one still crackled with an icy coating. Egg probed them magically and felt nothing.

"Whereas being a sheep — a pet, I suppose — gave me an edge of my own," Singespitter went on, nodding his agreement that there were no magical traces here. "When Kassa had a temper tantrum and didn't want people near her, she didn't mean me. Even after she forced her crew to split up and get lives of their own, I got to tag along with her."

"But you're not a sheep any more," said Egg. "How's that going to work?"

"I can still be a best friend or a brother-type," Singespitter shrugged. "Anything but true love, I suppose. That job is well and truly taken."

Egg wasn't convinced. "If Aragon Silversword is so right for Kassa, why isn't he here with her? Where did he run off to?"

"Off doing something important, I expect," said Singespitter. "Never be a hero, Egg. The hours are lousy."

As the ice melted, a puddle formed beneath the guttering of the Stick and Swazzle Cocktail Tavern. A short while after Egg and Singespitter moved on, four small nubs appeared in the puddle, narrow little bumps forming within the chilly surface of the water. Slowly, the nubs became longer, finger-like. A hand, glowing softly white, emerged from within the puddle, its substance formed by the puddle itself. There was only enough puddle to make a single hand, firmly cut off a few inches up the wrist. The hand, still glowing white, scampered across the path until it reached the charred pebbles. With a soft popping sound, the pebbles became one with the hand, forming long, perfectly-manicured fingernails.

"That's better," said the disembodied voice of Ladybird.

The hand scampered onward, looking for further material.

~

Clio and Sean still sat on the bench in the square of student residence, lost in mutual silence, thinking about Lemissa.

"Didn't like her much," Clio admitted finally.

"Me either," said Sean.

She stared at him. "You slept with her!"

"Don't have to like someone to do that."

"I thought you did."

"Shows what you know." He sighed. "Strange, though. To think of her being dead."

"She was our age," Clio agreed.

"Feel kind of guilty, not being more sad."

"Me too."

They shared a brief, understanding look.

"Where's Egg?" Clio asked finally.

"Don't know. Go look for him?"

"Okay."

~

This was the sorcerer's tower, the tallest and pointiest part of the palace of Drak. The uppermost room was filled with a Dark Lord's most important accessories: torture devices, portraits of ancestors, various doomed weapons, jars of disturbing ingredients for magical concoctions, skeletons of long-dead mythical creatures, scrolls of apocalyptic prophecies and — most importantly — six semi-clad demon priestesses who could pluck, skin and sacrifice a dozen chickens in under a minute, and would perform any spell or ritual their master required, the bloodier the better.

Chicken feathers and wet, fresh blood daubed the floor. The demon priestesses chanted, their straggly hair whirling madly around their heads and their scrawny, half-naked bodies formed the complex, stomping movements of a mad ritual dance.

"My lord," the Chamberlain protested. "This is going too far. You must accept that the draklight is gone."

Maybe you should accept that your Lordship is bonkers, thought Aragon.

So what should I do, assassinate him?

That sounded a lot like sarcasm, Chamberlain. I must be having an effect on you.

You claim to be loyal to our lordship. How can you doubt his wisdom?

It's easy. Just listen to the words that come out of his mouth.

"My people are begging for answers," said Lord Sinistre, far beyond the point of reason. "I must summon the darkest, most malevolent magic I can, to lure the draklight back to its home. When we are powerful again, the puny green fields of Mocklore will bend to the will of Drak!"

Aragon tugged at the metal Compelling Collar which still bit into his throat, forcing him to remain close to Lord Sinistre at all times. "This is not going to turn out well," he muttered.

Still trust that he knows what he's doing, Chamberlain old man?

It's not his fault, Silversword. The loss of the draklight has affected his sense of identity.

I know the feeling.

"Drak will be remembered for all time as the darkest of dark cities," Lord Sinistre cried triumphantly.

"But what are you going to do?" Aragon demanded. The

squawking of chickens made him turn around. "I swear, if those women kill one more chicken I will be physically sick."

What he saw was enough to bring bile to his throat, but it was not another sacrifice. The squawking came from the chickens that had already been sacrificed. They stood on their scrappy little legs, bald without their feathers, throats gaping open from the sacrificial wounds. Some of them had been cut entirely open, their entrails used for an earlier weather-prediction spell.

Some chickens were pecking at the demon priestesses in search of seed. One quite happily gobbled up her own discarded entrails, not noticing when her messy prize fell through the hole in her throat.

Aragon backed away, but Lord Sinistre stood firm between him and the door. "Am I right in thinking you decided this would be the ideal moment in time to raise the dead?" Aragon said hoarsely.

"I told you I was a villain," said Sinistre with a happy smile. "I told everyone. They didn't believe me."

"Well now," said Aragon Silversword. "You showed them."

~

Kassa sat on the steps outside the Mermaid Tower, exhausted. "If you're looking for Singespitter and Egg," she said without opening her eyes, "they think I don't know that they're helping Professor Noir check out the storm remains for magical traces."

"Aren't you angry about that?" asked Clio.

"Why should I be? Somebody's got to do it. Not that it will do much good. Magic is good at lying low." She sighed and opened her eyes, blinking in the bright afternoon light. "How are you two doing?"

"We're fine," said Sean. "Sort of."

"I know that feeling." Kassa leaned back against the door of the Tower. "It's too much to think about. I keep telling myself that I can cope as long as nothing else happens. Not one more thing."

"It's all over," said Clio. "Isn't it?"

"That's a dangerous question," said Kassa. "I'm not up to dangerous questions at this stage of the day."

Sean sniffed the air. "Is that coffee?"

Kassa's smile was beautiful. "Mistress Brim is inside setting up for afternoon tea. She started the clockwork coffee-brewing dripolater about ten minutes ago. It should be just about ready. If I could get my legs to obey me, I'd get myself a cup."

"That sounds like a job for me," volunteered Sean. He headed off to the back of the tower, where the entrance to the Seaweed Dining Room was.

"Boys are awfully useful at times," said Clio.

"That they are," said Kassa cheerfully. "Sit down, enjoy the sunshine for a few minutes. We deserve a break."

"It was my first real magical catastrophe," Clio confessed, joining Kassa on the sunny steps.

"Unusual for someone your age. What are you, eighteen?"

"Seventeen."

"You would have been twelve when the Second Glimmer came through. Where were you?"

"Not far from here, but my grandmother's house is fenced all the way around with cold iron. When she heard about the Glimmer she scattered salt around the house and made me hide under my bed all day."

"Sensible woman," said Kassa. "Folklore is the one true protection against wild magic. Can't go past a good bit of cold iron and a handful of salt."

"At least I don't have to worry if she made it through the storm all right," Clio agreed. "We missed the local Tidal

Puddle because we were holidaying in Zibria when I was eight, Grandmother's chicken and herb soup kept the Purple Plague from even reaching our village when I was seven, and when I was four..."

"The first Glimmer?" Kassa guessed, counting back.

"We never even saw it. We were in the Forest of Aardvaalk at the time, trying to... Grandmother was trying to convince my father that plotting to make himself Emperor wasn't a very good idea."

"It never is," said Kassa. "I only know one person who has done it successfully, and even that remains to be seen."

"I never really believed all the stories about the Glimmer," said Clio. "I thought the stories had to be exaggerated."

"I don't believe half of any story I hear, even about events I've witnessed," said Kassa. "When it comes to Mocklore natural disasters, ballads can never measure up to the real thing."

"But this one is over?"

"I hope so," said Kassa. "I'm not up to saving the Empire any more times today. I'm even too tired to fetch my own coffee." She frowned, looking across the cobbled path. "Do you know that girl? She looks lost."

Clio stared. A girl stood near the hedgerows that surrounded the next building, her back to them. She had dark hair, golden skin and a good figure squeezed into a little knitted red dress.

Sean rounded the corner, cheerfully balancing a tray which held three cups of creamy coffee and a plate of buttered scones. "Mistress Brim said you were probably hungry whether you thought so or not and that if the plate didn't come back empty she would be seriously displeased," he called out to Kassa.

The tray hit the cobblestones a moment later, the cups and scone plate jolting off the tray with a smash. Sean stared at the girl across the path, his eyes so wide they almost fell off his face.

"What's going on?" said Kassa, her voice heavy with the expectation that this was some new, horrible disaster and she would be shortly called upon to save the world without even a cup of coffee inside her.

Clio didn't disappoint. "That's Lemissa. My roommate. She's one of the students who was killed in the storm earlier today."

"She seems fine now," said Kassa.

"Um, yes. I noticed that."

As Singespitter and Egg reached the field near the Axgaard encampment, a huge, burly Axgaard warrior crossed their path. He was seven feet tall, wide shouldered and booming. His beard was so big and bushy that it should have been considered a city-state in its own right. He wore so many foul-smelling leathers and skins that the stench of death clung to him. His skin, beneath the mighty beard, was covered in ugly purple patches. "Are you my heir?" he thundered.

Singespitter and Egg glanced briefly around to check he was addressing them.

"I'm not," said Singespitter.

Egg had a horrible sinking feeling. This was not any old Axgaard warrior. This one wore the same crown that Sven-hilda did — a small wooden helmet with two enormous horns nailed to it — although there was none of the elaborate decoration she had added. A huge wooden necklace hung around his neck, depicting a bear skull. And then there were the purple patches… "Are you Jarl Erik?" he asked tentatively.

"Yaarrrgh!" boomed the Jarl. "Who else would I be, boy? Are you my heir?"

"Um, no," said Egg. "I think I might be your grandson, though." On the hill behind the Jarl, Egg could see Svenhilda, fully armed and accompanied by her axe-wielding hand-maidens. The women marched down the slope towards them. "She's your heir," he said helpfully, pointing.

Jarl Erik's face went pale beneath his beard. "A wench?" he bellowed, drawing a huge axe from his back and running up the hill, straight at Svenhilda. "What cursed gods made you my heir, daughter? I'll take my city back by blade and blood!"

"Try, old man!" she screamed into the wind, quickening her pace down the hill. "I'm a better Jarl than you ever were!"

They met in the middle, screaming and shouting, and tumbled down the slope together in a crash of leather and axe-blades.

"So," said Singespitter, watching the fight with interest. "Grandfather, huh?"

"My dead grandfather," said Egg. "He was killed by the Purple Plague nine years ago."

"Right," said Singespitter. "Something a bit funny's going on."

"I'd say so," said Egg.

18

DAY OF THE DEAD

*U*p close, it was fairly evident that Lemissa was dead. The right side of her body was flattened from where she had been crushed when her room caved in. There was a large hole in her throat where an ice shard had pierced her, although the ice had already melted away. "Do you know what happened to you?" Kassa asked now.

Lemissa shrugged, not overly interested in the topic. "I think I died. Is that right?"

"Pretty much," said Kassa.

Clio and Sean kept their distance from the girl. Sean was quite pale.

"You all right?" Clio whispered to him, nudging her hand into his.

"No."

"Me neither."

"Do you know why you came back?" Kassa asked.

Lemissa shrugged again. "Has something gone wrong? I don't have to go to classes, do I?"

"I'm pretty sure not," said Kassa. "Are you the only one?"

"Um," said Clio. "I don't think she is."

There was quite a crowd wandering through Drak now, dead people of all shapes and sizes. They were well-preserved, with no evidence of decay, but many of them wore wounds that displayed how they had died.

"So the bad news is, we've got zombies," said Sean, recovering himself slightly. "The good news is, they're not rotting zombies."

"Aren't we the lucky ones?" Clio said scathingly.

"Hi, little brother."

Sean whirled around, not letting go of Clio's hand. A taller, blonder, slightly-older version of Sean leaned against the Mermaid Tower. He wore the neatly-ironed uniform of a Dreadnought Blackguard, his boots high and shiny. He also wore a silver collar with an exploding tree motif, which had been the symbol of office for all post-Timregis Emperors until it was stolen by one of the less law-abiding post-Timregis Emperors.

"Tam," said Sean, sounding stunned.

"Good to see you," said his eldest brother cheerfully. "How's the family?"

"Same old stuff, really," Sean said after a moment. "Haymish got married. Angus became a priest. Finnley's on a mountain somewhere. Owen and Roddy joined the Blackguards, no surprise there except it's the real Blackguards, not the ponced-up acting troupe you belonged to. Prissilla's hunting for a rich husband."

Tam laughed easily. "This your girl?"

"Oh, no." Sean brought Clio forward. "This is my friend Clio. This is my big brother, Tam."

"Nice to meet you," said Clio, bracing herself to shake Tam's hand. It felt fine, perfectly normal. Warmer than she expected. "I'm sorry about, you know…" She drew her finger slightly across her throat, indicating where his had been slit open.

"Don't mind that," said Tam. "Easy to be philosophical, this side of the coffin."

Sean glanced around at the various other dead people who were threading their way through Cluft. "Da here?"

"Think he wanted to go visit Ma," said Tam. "He headed off towards Dreadnought."

"Oh, man," said Sean, alarmed. "She is not up to that. She's been having funny turns lately. A sudden shock could bring a bad one on."

"Really?" said Tam. "Reckon we could head him off if we hurry."

"Let's go," said Sean. "See you later, Clio!"

The McHagrty boys ran off in the direction of the road.

After taking a few deep breaths to calm herself, Clio went over to Kassa and Lemissa. "Are you all right?" she couldn't help asking her dead roommate. "I mean, how do you feel about being dead?"

"It's not bad," shrugged Lemissa. "Kind of boring."

"Come on," said Kassa, motioning to Clio to follow her. They headed in the direction of the library tower. "This is not the kind of side effect I would have expected from the storm. I think this is something new."

"Who would do this?" Clio asked.

As they reached the library tower, Kassa slowed. "I think that's our answer," she said. "The who at least, not the why."

Aragon Silversword was assisting Lord Sinistre down from the golden skybridge.

"Ah, Mistress Sharpe," Sinistre said, oh so pleased with himself. "Enjoying my little entertainment?"

"How could I fail to enjoy something so petty and pointless?" Kassa replied with a warm smile.

"Before you start blaming me," said Aragon, "I had nothing to do with this."

Kassa's smile widened, but not in a pleasant way. "Oh, really?"

Clio spotted two colourful pirates approaching, a large black-bearded man with a gaping sword wound in his chest and a red-haired woman with greyish skin — a drowning victim? "Ho, Kassa-girl!" the man said cheerfully.

"Not now, Dad," she said, still staring at Lord Sinistre. "What's this, an evil magic substitute for the draklight, or proof that you're the biggest baddest villain of them all?"

"Both," said Lord Sinistre smugly.

Clio heard the two pirates muttering together. "If she's busy, she's busy. You grab the boy, Nell. Time I had that chat with him."

The pirate woman went to Aragon Silversword, neatly unhooking the Compelling Collar from his throat and pulling him away. "Come on, boyo. We want a word."

"Kassa, your parents are kidnapping me," he warned.

"Hush," said Kassa, her eyes fixed on Lord Sinistre. "Care to explain why you felt the need for this attention-grabbing spectacle? Did you enjoy being tied to a chair so much that you want to repeat the experience?"

Lord Sinistre raised himself up to his full height, sneering down at her. "I am the villain," he declared. "You are the hero. Aren't you going to try and vanquish me?"

"Vanquish?" Kassa said scornfully. "What am I going to do, throw a bucket of water over you and hope you melt like sugar candy? You're not a villain any more, Sinistre. You're just going through the motions."

"I raised the dead," he hissed.

"And a right dog's breakfast you made of it, too. You haven't created an army of bloodlusting zombies. You brought a lot of people back from the dead in their right minds and reasonably right bodies, giving them the opportunity to tie up loose ends with their loved ones. It's practically a good deed."

"A good deed?" Lord Sinistre sputtered.

"Look over there," said Kassa. "My parents died years ago. Your little back-from-the-dead spell has given them the chance to meet the man I'm planning to spend the rest of my life with, assuming he doesn't pull any more vanishing acts."

The pirate known as Vicious Bigbeard Daggersharp had pinned Aragon Silversword to a wall, several small knives keeping him in place, and was talking to him in a low, threatening growl. The pirate known as Black Nell smiled sweetly and smacked a sword back and forth between her hands as emphasis to whatever Bigbeard was saying.

Kassa sighed nostalgically. "They used to do that to all my boyfriends. I should thank you."

Lord Sinistre's mouth opened and closed briefly.

Kassa took his arm sympathetically, leading him to sit on the library steps with her. "You're not a villain, you know," she said quietly. "You never were. You were playing the role that Harmony tried to squash you into. It was the draklight that made you all dark and villainous, but it's gone now. Once you get past that, you're left with a city. An ordinary city that needs an ordinary ruler to look after it."

"I don't know how to do ordinary," said Lord Sinistre.

"Well, you'll need a decent bureaucracy behind you," she conceded. "And you should arrange ambassador exchanges between Drak and the other Mocklore cities, so you can get a feel for what opportunities are out there. Do you produce your own velvet?"

"There are some factories in the Outer City. I don't think they run on magic."

"Fantastic, that's your first export product."

Sinistre gazed at her, his dark eyes like sunken holes. "Are you helping me now? Why would you do that?"

"Because," said Kassa, "Drak is part of Mocklore now. We look after our own."

"As simple as that?"

"We don't get much simpler."

"Would this be a bad time to mention that neither myself nor my demon priestesses know how to turn this living dead spell off?"

Kassa rolled her eyes. "I wouldn't have expected anything less."

~

In the deepest part of one of the many rivers that threaded through Cluft, a voice was babbling. "All dead, not my fault. No one else cares, why should I? Not my fault, not my fault."

Clouds formed within the river as the ordinary water separated from that which had melted down from storm debris. The water clouds swirled, forming face, neck, shoulders.

"Our world is dead," hissed the hopeless voice of Quill-smith, his teeth chattering. "Our world is dead, let's take theirs."

It might have sounded far less mad if he was talking to anyone, but the others were elsewhere.

~

Timmy "Da" McHagrty, former Captain of the Dreadnought Blackguards and 17th Emperor of Mocklore, walked amiably along the Great Mocklore Road, heading for his home city of Dreadnought. He was not walking very fast. If there was anything that made you want to slow down and smell the roses, it was being dead.

The back of his Blackguard uniform, which he had

continued to wear in protest after being forced to take the Imperial throne, was scattered with blood-rimmed holes caused by half a dozen over-enthusiastic knife thrusts, thanks to an annoyingly inept murderer.

The amateurism of it still annoyed him. Why couldn't he have had a dignified death at the hands of a proper assassin, like so many of the chaps who had been put on the throne during the appropriately named Year of Too Many Emperors?

A shout made Da McHagrty turn around, and he saw his eldest and youngest sons running towards him. "Sean! You've grown, my boy. I was just on my way to visit your Ma."

"Great thought," Sean said cautiously, still trying to catch his breath. "It's just — I'm not sure it's a great idea for you to visit in person. You know, with the stab wounds and everything."

Da McHagrty was outraged. "What do you expect me to do, boy? Write her a letter?"

Sean seized on this idea gratefully. "Good plan. Nice long letter. She'll like that. It's thoughtful."

"Seanicus McHagrty!" bellowed his father. "You're not too old and I am not too dead to give you a right whack across the ear hole! If I want to see your Ma, I will see her and that's an end to the matter."

"Da usually knows what's best, Sean," agreed Tam.

Sean exploded. "Considering that I'm the only one in this conversation who hasn't managed to get himself killed yet, you'd think my opinion might be worth something!"

Tam's expression changed, looking beyond his father and brother. "I didn't think we'd be here long," he said in a tone of resignation.

"What?" Sean looked around in alarm. A girl walked slowly towards them, across the field from the Axgaard encampment. She was surrounded by a cloud of coppery hair, and moved so lightly that she seemed to be floating.

"Ah, well," said Da McHagrty. "Look after your Ma, Seanicus. Give her my love if you think she's up to knowing I was here. Use your own judgment."

"Wait," said Sean, suddenly panicky. "You can't go."

The girl with the coppery hair was closer now, close enough to touch Da McHagrty. She did so, her pale hand brushing his shoulder. With a sound like a sigh, he vanished.

Sean turned on his brother. "You can't let her do this!"

"We weren't supposed to be here anyway, kid," said Tam. "Call it a happy accident. A short one." The girl touched his face and he, too, vanished.

Sean stared resentfully at the girl. She reminded him of Clio, although he couldn't think why. "Who are you, anyway?"

The girl smiled sweetly. "I know what I'm looking for now," was all she said to him.

~

Egg and Singespitter pushed their way through the crowd of dead people and the living. "What are we going to do about them all?" complained Egg.

"They're not hurting anyone," said Singespitter. "Which makes a change, as far as local catastrophes go."

Aragon had been pinned to a wall by several knives. The two colourful pirates who were responsible for his predicament now ignored him completely as they greeted Kassa, taking turns to enfold her in bone-breaking bear hugs.

"Vicious Bigbeard Daggersharp and Black Nell Witchdaughter," Aragon said in explanation to Egg and Singespitter. He did not seem overly concerned by his current predicament.

While Kassa's parents were distracted, Clio darted forward to help free her uncle, pulling out the knives one by one and dropping them on the cobblestones. She kept turning around to scan the crowd. "Sean met his dad and brother. Have you seen your parents among the walking dead, Egg?"

Egg blinked. "Mine are still alive, actually."

"Oh," said Clio in a small voice. "That's nice." She looked out at the crowd again.

Aragon, free to move at last, placed a hand on her shoulder. "They're not here," he told her.

Rage sparked in her eyes. "*You* wouldn't want them here."

"Would you?"

The simple question upset her. She moved away from Aragon and slipped her hand into Egg's, squeezing it tightly. "Can we get out of here?"

"Don't see why not," said Egg. "Nothing seems to be happening."

Sean McHagrty pushed his way through the crowd. "Some babe is making all the dead people vanish!"

Kassa pulled away from her father's sixth crushing embrace. "Excellent. That means I don't have to figure out how to do it myself."

Black Nell tugged on Bigbeard's sleeve. "If our time's up, I fancy finding someplace high so we can get one last look at the sea before we go."

Bigbeard chuckled. "Never used to be such a softy, Nell."

"Must be the company I keep," she said dryly. "See you around, lass," she said to her daughter.

Kassa nodded, feeling slightly bereft. "Maybe I'll visit," she suggested, thinking of her vision.

Nell scoffed. "Don't you dare!"

"Yo ho ho, Kassa girl!" Bigbeard yelled as his wife dragged him away.

Kassa looked at Aragon, trying not to smile. "So those were my parents."

"I noticed that."

"Scared yet?"

"Always was."

A new voice broke in on their flippant conversation. "Hello, brother."

Kassa saw Aragon's face change. The stone-faced man she had first met five years ago was back again, harder and icier than ever. His shoulders tensed and his hand moved to where, in his pre-Chamberlain days, a rapier would have rested on his hip.

Clio hissed between her teeth and ducked back into an alcove in the wall, dragging Egg with her.

"Who is it?" he whispered.

"My dad."

~

Aragon forgot Kassa, forgot Clio. He gazed at the approaching figure, feeling a haunting ache in the back of his teeth.

Bleyn Silversword was young. It was obscene that he was so young, but there was no getting around the fact that he had been twenty-one years old when he died. He was whip-thin with long limbs and dark blond hair cut close to his scalp. A small splash of blood over his heart, red on a white shirt, was the only sign that death had left on him. His pale grey eyes burned as intensely as they had when he was alive.

Until I killed him.

You killed your own brother? the Chamberlain said in alarm. *Why don't I remember that?*

You know why. Drak erased the bad memories of my past as

well as the good. A Chamberlain with memories of another life in another world was inconvenient.

But I should be able to remember our past now, shouldn't I? We've broken whatever hold Drak ever had on us, and the drak-light is long gone.

If you had my memories, you would be indistinguishable from me.

What's so wrong with that? If nothing else, we could stop having these dratted conversations.

Perhaps, thought Aragon. *Perhaps having a version of myself who did not remember my past was too tempting to give up. Drak offered me an Aragon Silversword who did not remember Bleyn or Dahla or the mad Emperor I served once upon a time. If forgetting them meant forgetting Kassa and my mother and Clio, I was apparently willing to pay that price.*

But not now?

No, Aragon decided. It had been nice to be someone else for a while, but he was not going to lose Kassa again. *I don't need you anymore.*

He waited for a moment, but the Chamberlain had gone. The whole exchange had lasted only a few seconds. Aragon smiled bitingly at Bleyn Silversword, glad to be finally rid of the voice in his head. "Most useful thing you've ever done, little brother."

Bleyn did not understand, of course, so he simply ignored what Aragon had said. He had always been good at that. "Still alive?" he taunted.

"So far," said Aragon.

"Must be nice." Bleyn prowled towards his brother. "Growing older, having new experiences. I wouldn't know."

A few years ago, that comment would have destroyed Aragon. His carefully built-up hardness would have crumbled. Not now. His head had been messed with by the best of them, and Bleyn was certainly not that. *I'd rather live with my past than waste another moment of the present. Good to know.* "No one blames me for what I did," he said aloud, knowing it to be the truth.

"Is that so?" Bleyn said sharply. "No one at all?"

"Mother said she would have done it herself if she could see through the tears to aim the knife."

Bleyn laughed without humour. "Ouch. That hurts." He touched his finger to the bloodstain over his heart. "Not as much as this did, but still. Nice to know you haven't lost the knack."

"I gave you a choice," Aragon hissed. "You had an army of loyalists who thought you were the answer to all their problems. They were willing to die for you. Did you have any idea how well the Emperor was guarded? How many Blackguards had been brought into Dreadnought to protect the city against your rabble? It wouldn't have been a swift, noble battle, it would have been a war. I offered you the chance to walk away, disband your army, be a father to your daughter. You chose to be a martyr."

"What self-respecting revolutionary would have done otherwise?" said Bleyn, sounding pleased with himself.

It was amazing how easy it had been to feel guilty when Bleyn was dead, and how easy it was now to feel guilt-free when faced with the real thing. How had he forgotten how dangerous Bleyn was, how little he cared about other people?

"You weren't even a very good martyr," said Aragon. "Your loyalists fell apart as soon as your body hit the ground. Not one of them even considered continuing the cause."

Bleyn shrugged one shoulder. "You win some, you lose some. Tell the story any way you like, Aragon. Tell yourself you gave me a choice, that stabbing me through the heart prevented a war, that one death saved hundreds more from dying. Can you honestly say that what you did was just?"

"No," said Aragon. "I can't say it. I killed my baby brother. There's no justice in that."

Bleyn smiled. "That's all I wanted to hear." Knives littered the ground, where Clio had dropped them. Bleyn moved snake-fast, scooping one up and flicking the blade close to his brother's throat. Aragon made no move. "Wonder how many men have killed their murderer?" said Bleyn.

~

Egg gathered a handful of magic, holding it in a clenched fist and thinking furiously about how best to put his power to use. He saw Kassa slide two herb daggers from her belt, but she hesitated to use them.

It was Clio who moved, emerging from the alcove to stumble towards Bleyn and Aragon Silversword. "Father, don't."

Bleyn turned, pressing the blade closer to Aragon's throat. Slowly, he looked his daughter up and down. "You grew up pretty."

"Is that all you have to say to me?" she demanded.

He shrugged, the gesture making the knife twitch alarmingly. "What else is there? Suppose they raised you to hate me, Mother and *him*."

"No. They just raised me. I learned to hate you all by myself."

Bleyn smiled. "Ou-uch. Looks like you inherited the family talent for hurting people."

"Don't kill him. Please don't."

Bleyn looked at Aragon, then back to his daughter. "Think I'm a good man, Clio? Think I'm one of those romantic heroes who does what's right instead of what's right for me?"

"No," she said softly.

"Then why do you imagine you can convince me to spare him? What could you possibly say that would make a difference?"

There was a whisper in the crowd. Out of the corner of his eye, Egg saw Lemissa vanish into a puff of dust that blew away on the breeze. Other dead people were vanishing, one by one. The crowd parted, and the reason for this stepped through, a girl with a coppery cloud of hair lifting in the breeze. As she passed close to another dead person, he also turned to dust.

Egg recognised her instantly as Dahla the ghost. She was no longer translucent, her body now as solid as anyone else's. She wasn't crying, either. She moved with a new confidence. When she came level with Kassa, she stood still, her eyes fixed on Bleyn and Aragon.

Aragon moved, using his wrist to deflect the knife from his throat. He spun Bleyn around, locking his brother's arms behind him and holding them fast. Bleyn did not struggle, too busy gazing at Dahla.

Kassa opened her hand and the fallen knife skittered across the cobblestones, joining its companions in a neat pile within the alcove, out of everyone's way.

"I looked for you," Bleyn was saying in a ragged voice. "I searched the Underworld, but you weren't there. You weren't anywhere."

"I was here," said Dahla. "I never left. I couldn't bear to leave my daughter at first, and I stayed too long. I forgot who I was, forgot everything about myself except that I was looking for something." She turned and gazed at Clio, her eyes lighting up with a lovely smile.

Clio stared back, shocked. "Mama?"

"You couldn't bear to leave her," Bleyn said resentfully. "What about me? I was waiting for you. You were my *wife*. Do you still blame me for the fire? It wasn't my fault."

"Nothing ever was, Bleyn," Dahla said with a sigh. "You always found someone else to blame."

"But the fire really wasn't my fault."

"It doesn't matter now."

"Of course it does!"

A shambling figure walked up to Dahla. "I say, young lady, if you wouldn't mind…" It was Professor Gootch, looking rather the worse for wear since his recent death. Dahla smiled sweetly and reached out, touching the professor's face with her bare hand. At her touch, he dissolved into dust.

Bleyn, nervous now, tried to back away but Aragon still held him fast from behind. "How are you doing that?"

"I was chosen to restore order between the alive and the dead," said Dahla.

"You're not going to do that to me, are you?" Bleyn demanded.

"It's time you returned," said Dahla. "You don't belong here."

His face changed, the brashness melting away. "Will you come with me this time?"

Dahla's face was unmoving, like stone. "You have to find your own way." Reaching up, she brushed her lips lightly against his. Bleyn Silversword dissolved into dust, leaving Aragon's arms empty. Dahla and Aragon exchanged a long look before she turned to greet her daughter.

Clio reached a hand out to her mother. Dahla echoed the gesture, matching Clio's hand with her own. Their fingers entwined for a moment. Dahla glanced briefly at Egg, smiling. "Found what I was looking for," she told him.

"I noticed that," he replied with a grin.

"Glad I got to see you all grown up," Dahla told her daughter.

"I wish I had known you," Clio whispered, blinking away tears.

"Ask your uncle Aragon. I'm sure he remembers a better version than I ever really was."

"Do you have to leave now?"

"I sent all the others back," said Dahla. "I should do the same for myself. It's time I got on with whatever happens next."

Clio sighed, and squeezed her mother's hand.

Without letting go, Dahla turned to Aragon for a moment. He leaned down over her so that she could whisper something in his ear. Then she turned back to Clio and smiled before she herself dissolved into dust.

Clio collapsed. Egg and Sean both leaped forward, but it was Aragon who caught her, holding his niece tightly as she wept.

Kassa stepped back from the scene, glaring at Lord Sinistre. "There you are. You caused some real misery with that walking dead spell of yours. How do you feel?"

Sinistre blew his nose into an over-sized purple handkerchief, and dabbed at his eyes.

Kassa clapped him on the shoulder. "I told you that you weren't cut out to be a villain, you soppy old wet lettuce."

"Do you think I'm too old to retrain?" he asked, tucking his handkerchief away.

"No one's ever too old to try something new."

There was a discreet cough. Kassa looked up, and saw her parents climbing down from the nearest roof. "You two? What are you still doing here?"

"Reckon she missed us," said Bigbeard. "Sorry about that."

Black Nell smacked him. "You were hiding behind the chimney, you goose."

Kassa stared at them both in horror. "How are you going to get back? Dahla's gone."

Bigbeard shrugged. "Better be goin' the long way, I suppose."

"We could try and kill each other," Nell said thoughtfully. "Don't know if that works so well a second time around."

Kassa pulled a long silver chain from around her neck and unclasped it. "Well, if you have to travel the long way, you might as well travel in style." A small ship-shaped pendant dangled on the end of the chain. Kassa handed it to her mother. "I believe this is yours."

"Oh, no," said Nell, trying to hand it back. "You're the one who's alive here. You inherited it."

"I don't need it any more," said Kassa insisted. "I'm all grown up. I have a real job and everything. Besides, who is more suited to sail a ghost-ship than a pair of dead people?"

Nell glanced suspiciously at Bigbeard. "She's being all sweet and generous. Are we absolutely sure that she's our daughter?"

Bigbeard grinned. "Takes all kinds to make the world go around, love." He gave Kassa a smacking kiss on the cheek.

Nell flung the pendant away. The tiny ship grew as it flipped over and over, becoming a huge, silver ghostly galleon. All of the onlookers who had never before witnessed this transformation gazed in wonder. Even Clio lifted her head from Aragon's chest and smiled to see the famous *Splashdance*. "What do you think, old man?" Nell called to Bigbeard in a joyful voice. "One more trip for old times' sake?"

"Thought you'd never ask, witch," he said cheerfully.

Bigbeard and Black Nell ran towards the ghost-ship and climbed on board.

Kassa lifted her voice slightly. "You are going straight back to the Underworld, aren't you?"

"Of course!" Nell yelled back. "Well — maybe via the Seventeen Seas."

"At least seven of them!" Bigbeard yelled.

As the crew of two waved madly, the *Splashdance* sailed

away across the landscape of Mocklore, heading for the sea.

There was a pause. "Right," said Kassa. "Anyone fancy a cup of tea? I don't think I could manage coffee now, my nerves are all jangly."

Egg took her aside for a moment, speaking in a low voice. "Dahla said she was sent to restore the natural order between the living and the dead. Who do you think sent her?"

Kassa gave him an absolutely filthy look. "Egfried Friefriedsson, you are not supposed to ask questions like that during a girl's tea break!"

Two heralds in black velvet tunics came scrambling across the golden skybridge, skidding down the slope of it and landing awkwardly on the cobblestones. "My Lord!" one said, spotting Lord Sinistre. "My Lord, you must come back to Drak immediately."

Aragon slowly released Clio, patting her on the shoulder.

Lord Sinistre stood up, smoothing out his leather suit. "What is it, heralds?"

"Those Heroes of Justice, my Lord," sputtered the second herald. "Those strange bright figures who turned up at the ball? They are destroying the palace."

"They have strange powers," said the first herald. "And they're huge! Three glowing giants. Even the demons can't fight them."

Sinistre headed for the bridge. He hesitated for a moment, looking back at Aragon. "Chamberlain?"

Aragon looked at Kassa.

"Go," she said tiredly. "Of course you have to go."

Do I? Aragon asked silently. His inner Chamberlain continued to remain silent. *Just checking.* "I suppose the job is still mine until I find a replacement," he said aloud, and headed after Lord Sinistre. The two of them scrambled up on to the golden skybridge and followed the two heralds back to Drak.

Kassa closed her eyes for a brief moment, breathing deeply. Just as Egg was about to ask if she was all right, her eyes snapped open again. "Right. Sean, Singespitter, run to the Axgaard encampment. Ask Svenhilda if she can spare some axe-wielding warriors or failing that, some axes. Iron ones, not wood. No matter what she does or doesn't contribute, bring Vice-Chancellor Bertie here now, along with his Great Reversing Barrel in whatever state of disrepair it's currently in, plus all the bits. Understand me? Any leftover planks or nails, even a splinter, make sure everything comes along. Got it?"

Singespitter nodded briskly. Sean, looking less sure, followed suit.

"Now," Kassa suggested. The two of them ran off towards the Axgaard encampment. "Clio, follow Aragon," Kassa continued. "Tell him what I said about folklore. Remember what I said about folklore?"

"Best way to fight magic," Clio said breathlessly. "Cold iron, salt circles, garlands of garlic, saucers of milk. My grandmother's tricks."

"Good girl. Go. Egg!"

Egg moved to Kassa's side. "I'm here."

"Where's Quillsmith?"

The question took him by surprise. "What?"

"Come on, Egg, don't mess about. The Light Lords have rebuilt themselves, probably out of storm debris. I know for a fact that Ladybird is on the far side of the square of student residence, trying to find a last bit of ice or rock to make a second foot out of. I can feel her presence with every fibre of my being. Since Quillsmith has always been the most reasonable, or at least the most talkative of that tribe, I'm hoping to get something useful out of him. Where is he?"

It had not occurred to Egg, but now he found that he knew the answer. "He's in one of the rivers."

"Which one?"

"Um, the other side of the Road. Near the staff room temple."

"Right. Follow Clio now. Listen to what she says about folklore. Make sure everyone else does too, if you can."

"Okay," he said, heading for the skybridge.

"And, Egg? Keep your hands in your pockets."

Egg turned back, surprised at her sharp tone. "What?"

"Don't act innocent with me. And don't tell me that you are more powerful than I think you are, or that you have better control of it than I think you have. Magic is last resort, not first response. If you get the urge, stick your hands in your pockets and keep them there until the urge goes away. Understand?"

"Yes, Kassa," he said.

"Good. I trust you, Egg. Allow me to keep doing so."

～

Kassa watched as the boy climbed up on to the skybridge and headed towards Drak. She wished that she really did trust him. After several deep breaths, she started jogging in the direction of the staff temple.

The crowd was in her way, students for the most part. One of them now raised a hand uncertainly. "Mistress Sharpe?"

"Yes, Clifford?"

"Do you want us to do anything?"

"That depends," she said. "Do you want to fight in defence of Drak?"

"Um, not really," said Clifford. Many other students nodded in general agreement.

"Better get back to your rooms, then. Straighten up, maybe do some readings. First essays for Philosophy of

Magic are due in the week after next." She pushed her way through the crowd until she had a clear field, then started running.

"She wasn't serious, was she?" Brittany Yarrowstalk said after a moment. "About the essays."

Clifford bit his lip. "Want to take the chance that she wasn't?"

～

The palace of Drak was in chaos. People ran around in a panic, forgetting to glide elegantly or pout seductively for dramatic effect. Without the draklight to guide them, the people of Drak were just like everyone else, scared and graceless.

"Three glowing giants?" Lord Sinistre said faintly.

"Yes, my Lord," said the butler, who looked less dark and menacing than ever before. This was partly due to the fact that he had thrown his cowl back, revealing a surprisingly young and chubby-cheeked face, but also because without the draklight, his voice had lost a great deal of its sonorous timbre. "Two of them have besieged themselves in the observatory and a third is rampaging around the sixth floor corridors, smashing his way through walls. Two of your demon priestesses have been killed. The rest are busy summoning extra demons to help in the fight, but without the draklight all they can produce are some small, powerless creatures that squeak and run away at the first sign of danger."

Lord Sinistre looked to his Chamberlain. "Can we evacuate the servants and wall these giants up in the Palace?"

"A noble suggestion, my lord," said Aragon. "It might take a while to evacuate all three thousand, however. The enemy would almost certainly guess that something was up before we got everyone out. Besides, how are we supposed to seal them in here? If they are powerful giants, I don't imagine they pay much attention to doors."

Lord Sinistre stared at him. "I have three *thousand* servants?"

"Amazing, isn't it."

Clio finally caught up with them, gasping. "Uncle Aragon, you run super fast."

"What are you doing here?" Aragon demanded.

"Kassa sent me. I have to tell you about the folklore."

"Slow down," said Aragon. "You're not making sense."

"Yes I am, you just don't know it yet. The most effective way to combat magic is folklore. Like Grandmother always does when there's a magical disaster. Salt and cold iron and saucers of milk. If the Light Lords have made new bodies for themselves out of the scrappy leftover bits of Harmony that came down in the elemental storm, they must be almost pure magic."

"Salt and cold iron," muttered Aragon, as Egg joined them. "We can do that. To the kitchens!"

"To the kitchens!" Lord Sinistre echoed cheerfully.

"Don't worry, my Lord," sighed Aragon. "I'll show you where they are."

Kassa skidded to a halt as she passed the bright white temple which served the professors of Cluft as a staff room. She barely stopped herself from plunging into the river on the far side of the temple, but grabbed on to a nearby tree just in time. "You might as well show yourself," she said aloud. "I know you're here."

The water rippled. A white, frothy cloud floated to the surface, forming a face. Quillsmith, glowing white and larger than life, emerged from the river. "Hello, Kassa."

"It must have been very amusing," she said. "Fooling me into thinking you were the nice one, the reasonable one. Why did they put you in prison? It can't have been for an attack of conscience, I stopped believing that one a while ago."

"I told them the truth," he said calmly. "It sounded like madness to them, so they thought they had better put me out of the way for my own — and everybody else's — safety."

"You mean the truth about Harmony being as fictional a creation as Drak?"

"You've been speaking to Amorata," said Quillsmith. "My muse. Yes, that truth. If I had to live with the knowledge, why shouldn't they? But they didn't believe me. Ladybird was the loudest in her protestations, so they stripped the leadership from me and gave it to her. They've been regretting it ever since, of course. The woman is far more unstable than I ever was."

"So what are you doing now?" Kassa demanded. "Your fellow Light Lords are tearing up Drak for no apparent reason."

"Oh, there's a reason," Quillsmith assured her. "They are looking for the pathway between Drak and Harmony. You found it."

"I'm pretty sure I broke it."

"It doesn't even matter. It's a lost cause, if they would only admit it to themselves. Harmony is gone, destroyed. It's too late to save our world."

"How do you know it's not too late?" Kassa demanded. "Don't you owe it to your people to try and restore the magic of Harmony?"

"People," Quillsmith snarled. "What people? They never existed. Faded mirror-images of people in this world, that's all. It's not my fault," he added.

Kassa thought of Ortsino and Strella, of the earnest belief they had in their cause. She felt sick. "How can you not care?"

"They were fictional characters," Quillsmith grated. "*I'm* a fictional character. Nothing that happens to any of us is remotely important."

"It doesn't mean you can't lead a normal life," Kassa said lamely.

"How? Where? Our city is gone, Kassa. Do we take over Drak? I invented that damned city. It is mine by right. What about Mocklore, are we welcome here? Can your community use an extra five ruling Lords?"

Kassa hesitated. She could think of nothing to say.

"Drak, then," Quillsmith agreed, stepping out of the river and on to land. "Don't worry, we'll let most of them live. We need servants and subjects to help us settle into our new life. We may have to kill a few to make our point, but they'll accept their new rulers easily enough."

"What about Lord Sinistre?" she asked, already knowing the answer.

Quillsmith whipped around, his eyes blazing. "He is a fictional character created by a fictional character, a copy of a copy. Do you really think he has more right to live than I?"

"I'll stop you," she warned. *Don't tell him he's mad, I think he already knows that.*

"Of course you will. You think you're a hero. Stopping people like me is the sort of thing that heroes do. But be warned, Kassa Daggersharp. Every hero has a final story, the tale of how they failed to save the thing they wished most to protect. The story where the hero falls. This may very well be yours."

He vanished in a sharp burst of light.

Kassa swore and started running back the way she had come. If only she had boots with less frivolous heels.

19

FIGHTING WITH FOLKLORE

*W*hen Kassa reached the library tower, the crowd had dispersed. Sean and Singespitter had just arrived, with Vice-Chancellor Bertie between them. He protested loudly at their lack of manners, clutching his newly patched Great Reversing Barrel firmly in his arms.

"That's something," said Kassa as she skidded to a halt near them.

"Look here, Kassa," said Vice-Chancellor Bertie. "Do you actually know what you are doing?"

"As much as you ever do."

"Oh, dear. We really are in trouble, then." Bertie removed his tweed jacket and carefully started rolling his shirt sleeves. "All right, I'm ready."

Kassa smiled at him, then took the Great Reversing Barrel and turned it upside down, shaking hard. A few splinters and stray nails rolled out, then something else. Kassa picked up the something else and put it carefully in one of her belt pouches.

"Baron Svenhilda said she can't send anyone," said Singespitter. He and Sean both wielded large Axgaard axes with iron blades. "Her warriors are superstitious, and the appearance of the late Jarl Erik sent them into some kind of religious frenzy. Apparently each of them have to perform a cleansing ritual which involves drinking three mugs of beer, belching their own name, running up and down a mountain twelve times and then killing four mythical fang-beasts. She reckons it will take at least two hours."

"We can't wait," said Kassa. "I'll just have to trust the legendary Axgaardian ability to sniff out where the fight is going down. Are you with me?"

"Silly question," said Singespitter.

Sean nodded, shouldering his axe bravely. "I'm ready."

"Grr," agreed an enthusiastic Vice-Chancellor Bertie, picking up his Barrel again.

"It's the four of us, then," said Kassa.

"Five," said a crisp voice. Incendia Noir, Professor of Magic, walked towards them. Her narrow figure was clad in an elegant black dress with glowing silver sigils stitched around the hem. She carried a wand of carved birchwood, radiating power.

"Hmm," said Kassa, who had little patience for wands. "Magic won't be much use in this fight."

"Indeed," said Professor Noir, producing two nasty-looking iron horseshoes which hung from her belt on a string. "As you can see, I am prepared for many eventualities."

"Fine," said Kassa. "Let's go."

"Excuse me," said an aristocratic voice. There was the sound of two throats being meaningfully cleared. Lord Ambewine of Teatime and Prince Quenby of the Middens emerged, each wearing their official staff cloaks with the badge of the Polyhedrotechnical College (a quarterly shield displaying a full tankard, a half-full tankard, a quill and a falling fish) entwined with their own coats of arms. Lord

Ambewine's was three teacups rampant with a border of sugar lumps, and Prince Quenby's was a large turnip on a multi-coloured field.

"We'd like to help," said Prince Quenby, his pudgy arms wrapped around a giant sack of salt. "It wouldn't hurt to have the newest Mocklore city-state owe a few favours to the rest of us, now would it?"

"Exactly," said Lord Ambewine. He held a large iron poker in one hand, and a spiked mace in the other. "Shall we go?"

"I think we'd better," said Kassa. "Eight it is."

Another throat was cleared. "Would you believe nine?"

"Oh, this is ridiculous," said Kassa, whirling around and gazing upwards to face the newcomer. "What can you possibly get out of helping us?"

Ladybird stood before her, larger than life, bright-white and glowing. The top of Kassa's head only came up to her waist. "You're going after Quillsmith, sweetpea."

"I'm going after all the Light Lords," said Kassa. "Including you."

"You're not the type to attack," said Ladybird scornfully. "You fight in defence of yourself and others, and I am not attacking you. There's nothing to defend against. You found that Quillsmith isn't the darling boy you thought he was. The loss of Harmony hit him harder than the rest of us, and I'm afraid he's just a wee bit broken, and dangerous. Since I'm the person he hates most right now, it's in my interest to help you take him down."

"Are you any better than him?" asked Kassa.

"I care whether I live or die," said Ladybird. "He lost even that when he saw what had happened to our world."

"Why should I trust you?"

"Silly girl. How were you planning on stopping me?"

Kassa eyed her other self warily. Ladybird hummed with

pure magic. If Kassa cut her head off, she would probably not even stop talking. *So how am I going to stop Quillsmith?* "Move out, people," Kassa said sharply, too tired to argue any longer. "We have a city to save."

~

Lord Dreamer smashed the last window in the observatory at the top of the palace of Drak. She withdrew her white, glowing fingers from the glass. "We have to find a way home," she sobbed. "I hate this place, all the bright colours and strange people."

Lord Invisiblus pulled her into his arms. "We will find our way back, I promise you."

"Why couldn't we have been happy where we were? It's this stupid city's fault." She pushed petulantly at the wall of the observatory with her massive, glowing arms and the entire wall crumpled outwards, falling back and away. With the wall gone, Dreamer and Invisiblus could see the dark, gleaming city of Drak stretched out beneath them. "I don't even know who I am," said Dreamer. "Am I Lord Dreamer the Light Lord, or am I Dream Girl, Hero of Justice? Everything's all foggy and strange. I don't remember."

"You're right," said Invisiblus viciously. "It is this stupid city's fault. None of this would have happened if it wasn't for Drak. Let's take it apart."

Lord Dreamer's eyes glowed adoringly. "Piece by piece," she vowed.

Aragon and Lord Sinistre had gathered a small army in the kitchens. Cooks, kitchen hands, scullery maids, poison tasters, footmen and the boy who cleaned the boots all filled the upper corridor. Each was armed with iron pots, cutlery, packages of salt and various stabbing weapons. After ransacking his memory for other anti-magic remedies his mother swore by, and consulting Sherrie the Head Cook on traditional methods of banishing demons, Aragon also included large quantities of vinegar, brown paper, gin, string and honey.

The demon priestess at the front of the kitchen army touched the door of the observatory and nodded. "There are two inside," she informed them. "The one who can turn invisible, and the girl who walks in dreams."

The corridor shook as a mighty crash resounded from behind the doors. "We're going in," said Aragon.

Egg, at the back of the army, touched Clio's arm. "The Cloak is still around somewhere," he whispered.

She nodded, understanding. "You want us to look for him?"

"Why not? They're not shorthanded here."

"And it would get me away from Dream Girl," she said, giving him a hard look. "Just because she's my counterpart doesn't mean I'm going to switch sides, Egg."

"It would still be a bit weird, wouldn't it? Trying to vanquish yourself?"

"Good point. Let's go find the Cloak."

Clutching a large bag of salt and several iron spoons between them, the two students withdrew from the crowd, hurrying along a velvet-strewn corridor. No one saw them go.

"Charge!" yelled Aragon Silversword.

"Charge!" echoed Lord Sinistre, half a beat behind.

The kitchen army charged through the doors of the observatory, brandishing their weapons.

The entrance hall was empty when Kassa and her merry band crashed through the front doors of the palace of Drak.

"Where's a butler when you need one?" Kassa complained, looking at the many doors that surrounded them. "Should be a shortcut to the ballroom around here somewhere." She started opening doors and peering through.

"Why the ballroom?" asked Incendia Noir.

"This lot like flair and dramatics," said Kassa. She looked up at the glowing giant form of Ladybird, who was having to crawl through the huge double doors to fit herself into the entrance hall. "That, and there's no shortage of head room in there. If the Light Lords are all as tall as this one, it will appeal to them."

"In the mood they're in, they are just as likely to remove the ceilings for their own convenience," sniffed Ladybird. The palace shook as she spoke, the walls shuddering.

Kassa found a door that looked promising and ducked inside. "Come on, you lot."

~

The battle in the observatory was a mad, chaotic mess. Aragon was in the middle of it all, and could see nothing but flying salt, slashing iron and the bright white limbs of Lord Dreamer and Lord Invisiblus. The salt stung them, and they screamed. The iron burned them, and they hissed.

The kitchen staff ran in circles around the observatory, spraying salt in all directions.

Lord Dreamer shrieked, letting a powerful storm of magic flow from her fingers in attack against Aragon Silversword. It reflected off the iron toasting fork he held in one hand and bounced harmlessly away.

Invisiblo vanished from sight before the salt circle was complete, but the head butler threw himself between the invisible Light Lord and the missing wall, chanting an anti-demon nursery rhyme. Flickering visible for a moment,

Invisiblo hesitated as the words of the charm slowed his movements, and a few plucky scullery maids took the opportunity to fling more salt and complete the circle.

It was over quickly, the two glowing giants imprisoned by the basic trappings of folklore.

"What do we do now?" Lord Sinistre asked, his eyes gleaming with exhilaration despite the fact that he had contributed little to the actual battle.

"I don't know," said Aragon Silversword. "I think we're supposed to give them a saucer of milk."

"I have a better idea, Chamberlain," said the Head Cook, reaching into an apron pocket and pulling out a length of rope which she handed to him.

Turning the rope over in his hands, Aragon noticed that it had strands of steel wire woven into it, and that the surface of the rope itself had been rubbed roughly with rock salt. It left a residue on his fingers. "You're always thinking, Sherrie," he said, impressed.

She gasped suddenly, fleeing the room. "My word. I have pies in the oven!"

~

Only one Light Lord had taken up residence in the grand ballroom. It was Quillsmith. He floated above the floor, glowing brightly. He held a long, feathery quill in one hand, and wrote in the air before him.

"Kassa Daggersharp and her friends cannot move," he said aloud as he wrote. Each word appeared briefly, glowing faintly white, then faded away.

The little group stopped short. None of them could move their feet. More than that, their will to step in any direction had been removed. "What were we doing?" asked Lord Ambewine in confusion. No one could answer him.

Kassa's thoughts, at least, were clear. Had her natural immunity to mind control returned? She certainly hoped so. Her life would be quite difficult without that particular talent. She hefted her package of salt. Maybe she couldn't move her feet, but there was nothing wrong with her arms...

"The salt becomes sugar and the iron becomes water," said Quillsmith, smug as his nib traced the shape of the words he had spoken aloud.

The various iron implements Kassa had tucked into her belt suddenly turned into water, soaking her skirts. She tossed the package of sugar away in disgust. Salt had been a protective force against the supernatural for as long as magic had existed, but sugar had little power over anything except dessert pixies. Every piece of iron or steel had melted, leaving the group with a handful of wooden axe handles and a wide puddle at their feet. Even the Great Reversing Barrel had split back into individual planks, its nails transformed into droplets of water.

"What do we do now?" hissed Singespitter.

"Not entirely sure," admitted Kassa.

"Your words can't hold me, Quillsmith," said Ladybird. She stepped over Kassa and the others, making her way to the centre of the ballroom. Her glow was a shade less bright than his.

"Oh, I like this," Quillsmith laughed. "Ladybird wants to be a hero. Who saw that coming?"

"Where are the others?" Ladybird asked.

"Wreaking havoc somewhere. Does it matter? I'm more interested in you, Lord Ladybird. Since when do you play peacemaker?"

"I want to live in this world," she said fiercely. "We've lost Harmony, we're not Lords anymore. But we can still live here! They'll find a place for us."

Quillsmith leaned into her, his eyes holding hers. "Don't

you understand?" he whispered. "We can't live. We don't exist."

"You can't hurt me," said Ladybird.

"Can't I?"

Kassa sensed this was time for an interruption. "Harmony doesn't have to be lost!" she yelled at them.

Ladybird and Quillsmith swung around to look at her. Kassa opened her pouch and pulled out the small object that she had removed from the Great Reversing Barrel. It was the gem that had once contained the cities of Harmony and Drak. The world of the silver sand. It was no longer bright white, but a dull grey colour. "It's here," she said. "The essential magic of it — the harmonylight — was drained out, but you haven't lost that magic. It was transformed into the elemental storm, and then into these bodies you wear. If the five of you joined forces, you could recreate your city as it once was." She wasn't entirely sure how such an operation would work, but it was the only plan she had managed to come up with.

Quillsmith gazed at her for a moment, his face unreadable. He opened the hand which did not hold the quill pen, and the small grey Harmony gem flew to him. He held it thoughtfully between finger and thumb. "Fascinating," he said. "We could go back to how things were before?"

"Why not?" said Kassa Daggersharp.

Ladybird had turned and was gazing at the gem with hope alight in her eyes.

Quillsmith brought his finger and thumb together, crushing the gem into dust. "I don't think so."

Ladybird shrieked in outrage, throwing herself at him. Quillsmith brought his quill pen up in a stabbing motion and embedded it deeply between her ribs. "The time when I was willing to share a city has passed," he said in a low, intimate voice.

The quill glowed fiercely, brighter than the two of them put together. The palace of Drak shook, as if the walls themselves were about to fly apart. Ladybird, the quill still buried in her chest, began screaming and did not stop.

~

It was not all that hard to follow Lord Kloakor's trail. Too tall for the doors in most of the rooms, he had elected to walk through the walls, leaving a tall Cloak-shaped hole in them. Clio and Egg followed one of these holes into a laboratory-style room full of bubbling glass vials and large bowls of fruit.

"This must be where they make the food," said Clio. "They don't grow things, they just make it all by magic."

"Made it," corrected Egg. The smell of rotten fruit was sweet in the air, and many of the work benches were covered in funny-coloured mush. "The draklight's gone. Nothing works any more." His fingers were twitching. Following Kassa's sage advice, he stuck them in his pockets.

"This way," said Clio, spotting another Cloak-shaped hole in the far wall.

The floor began shaking suddenly, violently. Egg managed to pull his hands out of his pockets quickly enough to grab on to a table for support. Ahead of him, Clio skidded to the floor. As the whole room buckled and shuddered around them, the contents of several workbenches slid on to the floor.

"Ick," said Clio, drenched in malformed strawberries and sticky pink juice.

Egg slid across the slimy floor to reach her and pull her to her feet. "You all right?"

"Fruity," she said. "Do you think I'll ever get rid of the smell?"

The room shook again, and this time it was Egg who lost his footing.

Clio held a hand out, grinning. "You all right?"

He had landed in a mess of mutant apricots. "I'll live," he said scraping the pulpy orange mess from his whole left side.

The next room was evidently where Lord Sinistre's costumes were made. There was a wide leather-working table on one side, tailor's dummies everywhere and shelves and shelves of silk, satin, lace, and especially velvet.

Several tailors huddled together at the back of the room. They had to be tailors because they wore aprons filled with tools of the trade: pins, measuring tapes, fabric swatches, spools of thread. They were not, however, people in the strictest sense of the word. They had tight red skin, blazing orange eyes and clawed feet. Apparently demons were responsible for Lord Sinistre's wardrobe. Explained a lot, really.

"Did a large glowing man in a shimmery cloak walk through here?" Egg asked them.

The floor shuddered a little bit and several of the demon tailors whimpered. The loss of draklight had hit them hard, and the quaking of the palace was terrifying them. One of the demons pointed shakily across the room. A large, sweeping black velvet wall-hanging with several paper patterns pinned to it now had a gaping, Cloak-sized hole in it.

"Thanks," said Egg.

Clio hurried in that direction. She was nearly at the wall when the palace shook violently again.

"Who is doing this?" Egg asked in frustration, crawling out from under a pile of collapsed tailor's dummies. As soon as he asked the question he knew the answer.

He could *see* into the ballroom where his other self floated in mid-air, laughing as he drained the power from the screaming figure of Ladybird. Quillsmith was becoming more powerful, and the fierce magic that filled him was shaking the palace almost to pieces...

Egg snapped back to himself just as a long fissure cracked along the floorboards. The floor under Clio's feet sloped dangerously as the crack widened. A huge set of heavy shelving tipped towards her, falling hard and fast enough to break every bone in her body.

Clio gasped. There wasn't enough breath in her to scream. The shelving had stopped only inches from her chest, hovering above her at an unnatural angle. She scrambled out from underneath it, staring at Egg.

He breathed out, lowering his hands, and the shelving dropped the last few inches to crunch against the floor. "You'd better get out of here," he said to the few demon tailors who had not already fled. They obeyed, grabbing precious armfuls of cloth and half-finished sewing projects as they went.

Egg clambered over the fallen shelving to reach Clio. "I think it's my turn to ask if you're all right."

He had never seen her blue eyes so wide. She was trembling a little, still shocked. "Egg," she said finally. "That was magic you used to save me. Real magic. Wasn't it?"

"I'm pretty sure it's the real thing."

"Since when?"

"I was born with it, although it's been lying unused for years. That's why those warlocks were always after me. I think the draklight woke it up, made it impossible to ignore. Then after the draklight vanished, my magic got stronger." He winced a little, thinking of Kassa. *I trust you, Egg.* "Kassa said I shouldn't use it, no matter what."

Clio breathed out shakily, then squeezed his hand. "Glad you did."

"Me too."

~

Tears ran down Kassa's face as she watched Ladybird die. The screaming seemed to go on forever. Ladybird no longer glowed white. Quillsmith glowed brighter than ever. As the white glow of the harmonylight left Ladybird's body, her colour was restored: wild pink hair and candy-striped gown. Around them, the ballroom shook so violently that it seemed impossible that it was still standing.

Finally Ladybird's screams trailed into silence. "If we don't exist," she whispered, "why is power so important to you?"

"It's all there is left," said Quillsmith softly. "Nothing else matters."

Professor Incendia Noir, who had been beside Kassa when the group was frozen to the spot, leaned slightly towards her. "Is it worth mentioning at this point that I am still able to move my feet?" she asked in an undertone.

Kassa stared at her. "What? You are powerful enough to resist Quillsmith's spell?"

"Not exactly," said Professor Noir dryly. "He placed the compulsion on Kassa Daggersharp and her friends. You and I have never been friends."

"Point," said Kassa, impressed. She liked a good loophole. "Get out of here, quick as you can. Fetch help. The Chamberlain of Drak would be particularly useful, but Egfried Friefriedsson is essential. And while you're at it, find me something to write with."

Incendia nodded and slipped back through the group, and out of the ballroom.

Slowly, painfully, the last of Ladybird was pulled into the quill pen. Her body became as thin as tissue paper, then crumpled into nothing.

Glowing with her power as well as his own, Quillsmith

turned and smiled at Kassa Daggersharp, his quill poised in the air. "Now," he said in a friendly voice. "What shall I write next?"

～

"Maybe it was those stories of yours," said Clio. The room they were currently exploring contained a huge swimming pool surrounded by red glass lanterns that sent blood-coloured patterns of light across the walls.

"What were my stories?" said Egg.

"All this magic of yours started coming out recently. Maybe it was prevented from coming out before because you devoted all your energy into writing and illustrating those hero stories. When you stopped doing that, the magic found its way out."

"Maybe," said Egg. "They weren't my stories, though. That other version of me sent them into my brain from another dimension."

Clio made a scornful noise. "How long have you been making up stories and drawing pictures about them?"

Egg thought about it. "All my life. Ever since I could hold a quill."

"So don't tell me it's not a part of you. If you don't want this magic, you could start drawing again. Maybe the power will just settle down, go back to being quiet and occasional."

Egg stared at her. "You said you were glad I used the magic. I saved your life. Why shouldn't I use it, if I'm careful?"

Clio looked at him in surprise. "I didn't mean that. I thought you didn't want to be a warlock."

"I don't," he muttered.

"Well, then."

"It's an interesting idea. Thanks." The idea of getting rid

of his magic was no longer tempting to Egg. It belonged to him, more than his drawings and stories ever had. Why should he give it up?

"There isn't a Cloak-sized hole here," said Clio, examining the intact walls.

Egg pointed towards the glass doors at the far side of the pool room. They stood open, leading to a balcony.

"Oh," said Clio. She hefted her package of salt and her iron spoon. "Do you think we're ever going to catch up with him?"

A tortured scream came from the balcony.

"I think we just did," said Egg, heading for the glass doors. He summoned up the magic within him — just in case — and the iron spoon in his hand felt hot, uncomfortable. Impatiently, he flung it aside, letting it clatter on the floor. Clio was close behind. He could feel where she was. The close presence of the salt she held made the hairs on the back of his neck stand up. He didn't like it, and took another step forward to put some distance between them, stepping out on to the balcony.

Lord Kloakor was doubled over the ornate black spiral pattern of the balcony rails. His grey-white cloak flapped and shimmered around him. "She's dead!" he screamed, whirling around to face Egg and Clio. "What are you going to do to me? Ladybird is slain, Quillsmith is mad, Dreamer and Invisiblus are captured, their cries for help muffled by insultingly primitive devices of folklore. My city is lost, the people we tried to protect are dead. We did not exist, should not exist. Will you blind me with salt and beat me with iron, or have you done enough?"

"You tried to invade us," Egg said hotly.

"My world is dead," Lord Kloakor growled. "Have we not been punished?" He straightened up, glowing with power, twice as tall as Egg. "Should we not take our own retribution?"

Egg felt the magic rise within his own body. He glared blazingly at Lord Kloakor and stretched himself upwards. Kassa had been wrong. He could control this power. Indeed, there was so much of it that he hardly needed to control it. He had merely to will something, and it would come to pass. For now, he willed himself the equal of Lord Kloakor, his body extending until he was the same height and size. He was glowing too, not a bright glow like that which surrounded Lord Kloakor, but dark as Drak itself.

"So," said Lord Kloakor with a snarl. "The draklight did not vanish. It found a skin to hide inside. Do you think you can match me, boy? Harmony created Drak. It is not our equal!"

"Perhaps not," Egg whispered. "But you are just a fifth of the whole of Harmony. All of Drak's power is here, and my own as well." He could recognise the draklight now, entwined with his own magic. *So that's where it went.*

"Stop it!" screamed Clio. "Stop it, both of you. Do you even know why you are fighting?" She threw the package of salt squarely at Egg's back.

He felt it coming, and pulled himself into two halves so that the salt sailed through the gap in his body and struck Lord Kloakor squarely in the chest. As Egg reformed his body, Lord Kloakor was knocked backward over the railings. He clung to them, one hand raised in a threatening gesture against Clio.

Egg reached out and took Lord Kloakor's hand. He had never done anything so easily before in his life. He held the glowing white hand firmly with his own, and squeezed.

It was hard to think of this bright figure as being a Light Lord, a person in his own right. He looked so much like the Cloak, a character Egg had inked on to the page for the first time at the age of twelve. *I created him.* The Cloak screamed, a soundless scream that went on forever. The glow faded from his skin and the pale greyness was bleached away, leaving colourless skin like crumpled tissue paper which simply, a moment later, dissolved in the breeze.

Egg was slammed backwards by the force of the harmonylight he had sucked from the Cloak. His body skidded to a stop in front of the glass doors. Slowly, he brought himself under control, diminishing back to his ordinary form. He opened his eyes, and looked at Clio. She stood over him, her cheeks two red spots of anger. There was something in her cold blue eyes that he did not recognise. Fear? The danger was past. Didn't she know that?

"Did you mean to do it?" she demanded. "Tell me it was an accident, Egg. Tell me you didn't mean to go that far. Tell me you didn't do it deliberately."

Egg gazed at her, confused.

"Don't you even know?" Clio said hollowly. To his surprise, she held her iron spoon out towards him, a threatening gesture. "Move away from the door."

The iron was nothing to him. He was beyond such petty mechanisms now. He could think of a dozen different ways to remove it from her grasp. But this was Clio. He stepped aside, leaving the doorway clear.

She moved cautiously back into the pool room, the spoon pointed at him as if it were a wand or a knife. When she was far enough away from him, she turned and ran.

Clio was afraid of him. Egg stood up, feeling very strange. He had killed the Cloak. No, not the Cloak. He had killed Lord Kloakor. *Did you mean to do it? Tell me you didn't do it deliberately. Don't you even know?* He had killed Lord Kloakor, and Clio was afraid of him.

Egg staggered to the balcony rails and threw up, noisily.

THE BIGGEST, BADDEST VILLAIN OF THEM ALL

*a*ragon Silversword and Lord Sinistre left a gang of kitchen hands and poison tasters in charge of the captured Light Lords while they and an elite team of footmen and scullery maids went in search of the others. They met Incendia Noir on the central staircase that spiralled above the entrance hall.

"Kassa is trapped in the ballroom with the Light Lord called Quillsmith," she said crisply. "She's asking for help."

"She doesn't do that often," Aragon remarked. "Quickest way to the ballroom?"

"Side entrance or grand entrance?" Sinistre returned.

"As sidelong as possible."

Sinistre smiled brightly. It was an unnatural expression on a face more suited to brooding snarls and seductive smirks. "I am rather enjoying myself," he confided.

"So glad," said Aragon sarcastically. "The door?"

"This way."

They back-tracked across a corridor, then down another, passing a wall with a large Cloak-shaped hole in it. Egg emerged suddenly from the hole, wide-eyed and gasping for breath. "Have you seen Clio?"

"Not recently," said Aragon. "Any sign of the Cloak, or whatever he calls himself?"

Egg composed himself. "Um, no," he lied. "Not yet."

Aragon's eyes flicked briefly over him, as if he had spotted the untruth. "That should be our next priority, then."

"Kassa said this boy would be of particular help to her," said Incendia Noir. She eyed Egg. Power rolled off him in waves, crackling across the hairs on the back of his arms and making his eyes shine with a fierce intensity. "Now I see why. I can take over the hunt for the Cloak if you wish. Kassa requires your assistance, Chamberlain, and a quill pen."

Aragon patted his pockets. "I usually carry one on me...ah."

Lord Sinistre had proudly produced a huge, sweeping peacock feather with an engraved silver nib from one of his many pockets.

"Well, now," said Aragon Silversword. "I can't compete with that."

~

"It's a tricky one," said Quillsmith. "Should I make the people of Drak bow to me in subjugation, or should I obliterate them all and start from scratch with people of my own making. What do you think, Kassa?"

She stared at the giant Light Lord. "You don't want to hear what I think."

"Oh, you're wrong. I'm fascinated."

"Wouldn't you rather conquer Drak the good old-fashioned way?" Kassa suggested, to buy some time. "March in, promise them something better than the previous leader did? I can't imagine Lord Sinistre was entirely popular."

"Popularity is irrelevant," said Quillsmith. "But thank you for reminding me that I need to do something about him." He held up the hand which did not hold the deadly quill pen, and made a motioning gesture. The door at the far side of the ballroom flew open and three figures — Lord Sinistre, Aragon Silversword and Egg — sailed over Quillsmith's head, crashing lightly to the floor just in front of Kassa. "Did you really think I wouldn't notice them?" Quillsmith chided.

"I'm bitterly disappointed," said Kassa. At her feet, Aragon held a large peacock quill behind his back. She took it, concealing it in her skirts.

"Lord Sinistre comes forward and bows on bended knee to the new King of Drak," said Quillsmith, writing the words with his pen as he spoke them.

"Mocklore doesn't have kings," Kassa corrected, but Lord Sinistre was compelled to follow the stage direction. He walked across the shiny floor towards Quillsmith, sank to one knee and bowed his head in obedience. "They were abolished more than eighty years ago and replaced by Lordlings because kings had a nasty habit of starting wars all the time."

"That sounds like a good tradition," said Quillsmith. "Remind me to start several wars once I have finished this bit of business. A sword appears before Sinistre, former Lord of Drak," he wrote aloud.

A sleek, silver sword appeared from nowhere, floating in mid-air before the Lordling of Drak, who stared at it in surprise. It was a pale, shinier version of the doomed blade of Dathazarrr.

"You know what I want you to do with that," said Quillsmith. "Shall I write it, or will you do it of your own free will? I can't decide which I would enjoy more."

Slowly, Sinistre reached out a black-gloved hand to touch the hilt of the gleaming sword.

"No," said Aragon Silversword, leaping to his feet. "This will not happen."

"Stay out of this, Chamberlain," said Quillsmith. "There are no dishes to be cleared away, and I can't think what other business you might have here."

"I may be the Chamberlain," Aragon said coolly, "but I am also Lord Sinistre's Champion. No one may raise a hand or blade or pen to him while I live. You go through me to get to him. It is the way these things work."

"That should not delay me too much," said Quillsmith, amused. "Do you actually wish to fight?"

Aragon moved Lord Sinistre's hand away and grasped the hilt of the gleaming silver sword. "If you don't mind," he said politely.

"I could take you apart with a thought or a word."

"I know that," said Aragon Silversword. "Don't you think a duel would be more entertaining?"

Kassa grabbed Egg by his collar, pulling him towards her. "I can't unwrite any of Quillsmith's spells," she whispered, trying to hand him the quill pen. "I've tried, but my magic doesn't work that way. You'll have to do it."

Egg stared at the quill in quiet horror, his mind filled with the soundless scream that Lord Kloakor had uttered before he died. "I can't."

"You must," she hissed. "The rest of us can't move unless you release us, and Aragon is going to need your help. Quietly. Undoing someone else's spell is nearly impossible, but there's a chance if you use the same kind of magic. Quill magic. I'm a songwitch, so anything I do will be loud, musical and call attention to us. It also, quite probably, won't work against that pen of his."

"You said I shouldn't use magic at all," Egg said, starting to sweat. Could he use his power again, knowing what it had done last time?

Kassa rolled her eyes. "Don't you know a last resort when you see one?"

Slowly, Egg took the quill pen. He could see how to thread his magic through it like ink. A thin rivulet of magic, nothing big and splashy. He could handle this. "Kassa and the others are released and able to move as they wish," he whispered, tracing the shapes of the letters to form words with the pen.

"Good," breathed Kassa, testing her feet.

Singespitter came to her side instantly. "What do we do now?"

"Stay still, be calm and prepare to run away very fast," said Kassa.

"As if," Singespitter said impatiently. "Give us some real orders."

Quillsmith and Aragon moved to the far side of the ballroom, giving themselves plenty of space. "Hardly a fair fight," commented Quillsmith, towering over Aragon at twice his height and still glowing with fierce white magic.

"Well, I didn't want to be the first to say it," said Aragon, gripping the sword-hilt and eyeing the pen that Quillsmith still held. "But my weapon is quite a bit longer than yours."

Quillsmith smiled, his body diminishing to human-height. He stood opposite Aragon, still glowing. He extended his quill pen, and it became a thin, white blade. "Better?"

"It'll do," said Aragon. "Let's fence."

The two circled each other carefully, touching blades in a few preliminary strokes before launching into a full, fleet-footed duel.

Kassa turned her back on them. "While they're distracted, the rest of you had better make yourselves scarce."

Egg, hovering at her elbow with the quill pen still shakily grasped in his hand, wished for one desperate moment that she was including him in that request.

"I say," protested Vice-Chancellor Bertie. "We haven't done anything yet."

Lord Ambewine and Prince Quenby added their voices to the grumbles, although theirs were somewhat less enthusiastic.

"Where did Incendia get to?" Kassa asked Egg.

"She went after Lord Kloakor," he said, not meeting her gaze. "The other two were captured by Aragon and the kitchen army."

"Well, then," said Kassa to the professors. "One fearsome Light Lord still at large, to be captured like the others. That sounds like a mission. Off you go." She glared hard at Singespitter and Sean McHagrty. "I don't suppose either of you could be convinced to join them?"

"Wouldn't want to go anywhere we weren't invited," said Singespitter, grinning.

"What he said," said Sean. They were both staying put, with her.

As the door closed behind the three professors, it opened again to admit Clio, who was rather subdued. She looked quickly at Egg, then away from him.

"Ah, Clio," said Kassa. "I wondered where you had got to. You can choose between the mild danger of tracking Lord Kloakor, or the grave danger of staying here with the rest of us."

This time, Clio looked at Egg longer and harder, realising that he hadn't told anyone the truth. "Here, please," she said, turning to Kassa. "Why is my uncle duelling a Light Lord?"

"Oh," said Kassa, glancing at the figures of Aragon Silversword and Quillsmith as they danced backwards and forwards across the floor, their swords flicking in lightning-quick movements. "He gets these ideas from time to time. Not always badly timed."

"Aragon's the better swordsman," said Singespitter, his

eyes darting back and forth as he watched the duel. "But...is Quillsmith getting taller?"

Almost imperceptibly, as he was forced to concede further ground to Aragon, Quillsmith's brightly-glowing body expanded, giving him the advantage of height. If you looked closely, you could also see that his feet hovered a touch above the ground.

"Cheating," said Kassa. "Hardly surprising, I suppose. Do something about it, Egg."

Egg jumped. He had not expected to have his magic called upon again so soon. "What?"

"Stop Quillsmith using his Lordly powers," Kassa said impatiently. "Make it a fair fight."

"Won't Quillsmith notice if I do that?"

"Probably, but I think we've got all the mileage we're going to get out of this little distraction. Oh, wait a minute. Take the compulsion off Sinistre first, then help Aragon."

Egg concentrated, writing a quick sentence in the air to release Lord Sinistre, who still knelt in the middle of the ballroom, his head consistently bowed in the direction of Quillsmith. The darting movements of the duel had meant that his head was forced to flick back and forth so many times that he was in danger of getting whiplash. The moment Lord Sinistre was released from the spell, he keeled over in exhaustion.

Egg turned his attention to the duel. If he placed a spell on Aragon instead of Quillsmith, it might be less noticeable. "Make Aragon's power equal to that of his opponent," he wrote, murmuring the words as he did so.

"Good plan," approved Kassa.

Instead of bringing Quillsmith down to Aragon's mortal level, the spell brought Aragon's power up to meet Quillsmith's. For every extra inch in height, or moment of levitation that Quillsmith took, Aragon equalled him. He, too, began to glow brightly white.

While Egg watched the cut, parry and swipe of the duel, it was hard to put Lord Kloakor out of his mind. Aragon, with the extra height and bright white glow, looked so like his counterpart. It almost seemed to Egg that the glowing figure of Aragon *was* the Cloak, surrounded by that strange, flickering garment…

With a step, twist and slice, Aragon moved in for the kill, finally disarming his opponent. The white sword flew in a shining arc across the ballroom, becoming a quill pen again, out of reach.

Aragon deliberately tripped the unarmed Light Lord, forcing him flat to the ground, with the silver sword at his throat.

Quillsmith laughed, a throaty chuckle which sent a new shudder through all the walls of the palace, and even of Drak itself. The city shook under and around them. "Did you really think I would let you win?"

"I suppose honourable behaviour is too much to hope for," Aragon conceded.

"Not again," muttered Lord Sinistre, struggling to his feet. A dozen mirror tiles from the ceiling smashed around him. "My poor city."

The shaking and rumbling increased tenfold. More tiles fell from the ceiling. The staircase that encircled the great hall shuddered and cracked away from the wall. A fissure opened in the floor. The whole palace was about to come crashing in on them.

They could hear the cries and screams of the people of Drak throughout the city as buildings collapsed and streets began to crumble.

"Stop it," grated Aragon, bringing his sword down in a mighty killing stroke, enough to sever Quillsmith's head from his body. The sword passed harmlessly through the Light Lord's neck, then dissolved into silver sand.

Aragon flung himself away.

Quillsmith floated into the air and hovered above their heads, laughing.

"Stop it," begged Lord Sinistre, tormented by the sounds of his city in pain.

The shaking and crashing and screaming only increased. Quillsmith laughed harder, with greater glee. Every window in the ballroom smashed outward in an explosion of glass.

"Stop it," said Kassa Daggersharp, and everything stopped.

In fact, the crushing destruction of the city continued, it was only the dreadful, dreadful sound of it which had been momentarily stopped by a soft silence. Quillsmith stopped laughing. He turned to Kassa. Everyone was looking at Kassa, wondering what she would do next.

Kassa sang. Her voice was awful and beautiful and relentless. No one could quite make out what words she was singing, but after half a minute of her song, the palace stopped shaking.

The glowing light drained from Quillsmith's face, body, self. He struggled for a moment, not quite understanding what she was doing to him. By the time he did understand, it was far too late to do anything about it. Kassa was draining him.

Her song continued. Every note drained more light from Quillsmith. Kassa swelled with the new power she had taken upon herself, glowing pink and white as Ladybird once had. She fell to her knees.

Aragon made his way to her side. "What's wrong with her?" he demanded, his voice the first sound in the ballroom since Kassa's song had begun.

Egg lifted his head, troubled. "Too much. All of Ladybird's

power is in there as well as Quillsmith's, that's two-fifths of that elemental storm we lived through. Maybe more, those two were the most powerful of the five. I don't think Kassa can drain it all by herself."

"Can you help her?" Aragon asked.

Egg nodded painfully. He raised a hand, and lifted Quillsmith's white quill pen from where it lay on the floor some distance away.

The quill pen flew to Quillsmith, who was immobilised by Kassa's power-draining song. He raised a hopeful hand to the pen as it circled around him, but at Egg's command the quill ducked neatly away from the hand of Quillsmith, plunging instead between his shoulder blades in the centre of his back.

Quillsmith yelled in pain and anger, his magic now being sucked away by two sources. He swayed, but did not fall.

Egg crouched beside Kassa, taking her hand in his. They could do this, together. He had not thought he could ever do such a thing again, raise his magic against another living person, drain their power until they ceased to exist, but if Kassa had chosen to do it, perhaps it was not so very wrong. Quillsmith had to be stopped, didn't he?

Will she do the same to me if I let my power get out of control? Egg was suddenly dizzy, sick with grief for what he had done and was about to do.

Kassa's song ended. For a moment, Egg did not realise the significance, and continued to drain Quillsmith's magic into himself.

"Egg, stop," she said softly. Then, in a more dangerous voice, "Stop now."

He felt a sharp crack across his face, and jolted as if waking up from a tormented night's sleep. The shock made him release his hold on the quill pen, and on Quillsmith. A wild sea of power and magic filled Egg's skin, singing to him, but it was nothing to the intensity he saw in Kassa's golden eyes. "He's not dead," he gasped.

Quillsmith still stood in the centre of the ballroom, swaying.

"Of course not," said Kassa gently. "Did you think I meant to kill him? Only a power-drunk fool like Quillsmith himself would drain someone to death. That's why control is so very important."

Egg shivered. His body was so full of magic and conflicting emotions that he thought he might explode.

Kassa lay a cool hand on his face. "Be calm. It's a strange sensation, holding so much of someone's magic inside you, but it will pass. The power will ebb away into the cosmos, where it belongs. You'll be back to your old self in a few days."

Egg cracked. A tear slid down his face, then another. "Do you promise?"

"What have you done to me?" demanded an equally shaky voice. Quillsmith stood alone, human-height, unglowing. He looked like a normal mortal. "What have you done to me?" he howled.

Kassa stood up. "Congratulations, Quillsmith. We turned you into a real boy."

"He has no magic at all?" Lord Sinistre asked.

"Not a smidgen," said Kassa. "Well, maybe a smidgen. I'm not entirely sure how to measure a smidgen."

"Thank goodness for that," said Lord Sinistre, sounding back to his old self. He raised his voice slightly. "Guards!"

There was a rattling sound and several dozen fully-armoured guards trotted into the ballroom. At Lord Sinistre's imperious direction, they surrounded Quillsmith, drawing their swords.

"Cold iron," Aragon muttered. "You know, we could have used those guards earlier."

"Take him to the dungeons!" Lord Sinistre commanded delightedly.

"Do you really think that will help?" said Kassa.

"It will help me," crowed the Lordling, back his element. "To the dungeons!"

The guards firmly escorted Quillsmith out of the ballroom.

Kassa sighed. "I suppose it's as safe a place as any, for the time being."

"You have other plans for him?" Aragon said.

"Thinking about it. I'll have to speak to the other three Light Lords first. I think I have a plan to send them all home. Ladybird said they were redeemable. Let's see if we can prove her right."

Egg turned away so that neither Kassa or Aragon could see the expression on his face. Clio stood in front of him, though her eyes bright blue and accusing. "Well?" she demanded.

"Well, what?"

"You obviously haven't told them what you did. Why not? Are you ashamed, or just biding your time until you can do the same to the others?"

"I didn't mean it," he insisted, wondering if he sounded as unconvincing as he felt.

Clio placed a hand on his arm, her voice more gentle than he deserved. "You have to tell Kassa."

"Leave me alone," Egg growled, pushing her away. The power welled up inside him, the magic of the draklight and Lord Kloakor and Ladybird and Quillsmith. It was all too much. Any part of it could come crashing free at any moment and incinerate Clio, or anyone else who happened to be in the way. "Stay away from me!"

Sean saw what was going on and came over in a hurry,

pushing himself firmly between Clio and Egg. "What do you think you're doing, mate?"

Egg laughed, a disturbingly similar laugh to that of Quill-smith. "You think Clio needs protection from me?"

"I think a lot of people might," Sean said steadily.

"Sean, stop it," said Clio. "You're making things worse."

"And that would make you a hero, would it?" said Egg, ignoring her to face down Sean. "Protecting people from me?"

"I don't care what it makes me," said Sean. "What does it make you?"

Egg's eyes flashed black, and then white. His hand rose slightly to hit Sean, or worse. Slowly, he lowered his hand and walked away.

Clio let her breath out in one big rush. She turned on Sean, angry. "Do you really think that was helpful?"

"We're not dead, are we?"

"Egg wouldn't hurt us." She hesitated, biting her lip.

"Not so sure about that, huh?" said Sean. "We'd better get Kassa after him."

It was unnecessary. Kassa had seen their little exchange, although she had been too far away to hear much of what had been said. As Egg opened the huge double doors to leave the ballroom, Kassa went after him. Aragon and Singespitter exchanged a brief glance and then went after her.

Clio closed her eyes, exhausted. "Do you think anyone would notice if we just went home?"

∼

Egg climbed the main staircase with steady, even steps. He barely knew where he was going.

"Egg." Kassa hurried up behind him. "I know everything is

chaotic at the moment. Too much magical intake can make you a little crazy."

"You think I'm crazy?" he said in a dull voice, swinging around to face her.

"Maybe," she said, concerned. "Confused, certainly. I know how you feel."

Egg laughed. "You know how I feel? Do you know how it felt to drain Lord Kloakor until he dissolved into nothing? Do you know what it feels like to have a whole city's worth of draklight creeping about in your skin? Do you know how it feels to realise you're the villain?"

Kassa gazed at him, her golden eyes sad as she took in everything he had told her. "Egg, I can help you."

"I don't think so." He punched her in the stomach with all the magic he had readily to hand. It was a lot. Kassa's body was flung backwards, then dropped like a stone to the distant floor below.

Without waiting to see if she survived the fall, Egg turned and continued his climb up, up to the very top of the palace of Drak. A high place was exactly what he needed right now.

～

Kassa caught herself a foot from the ground, and lowered herself to lie flat on the gleaming floor of the entrance hall to the Palace. "Damn it," she whispered. "Damn it, damn it, damn it."

"Are you hurt?" demanded Singespitter, running up to her.

"Of course she's hurt," said Aragon, reaching them a second later. "Can you move?"

"I'm fine, help me up," she said.

They both supported her with their strong arms, dragging her to her feet. "He won't listen to me," she said in frustration. "Why should he? I did everything wrong."

"You weren't the one pushing people off staircases," Aragon grated.

Kassa gripped his arm, then Singespitter's. "You have to go after him, both of you. You have to save him."

"The kid looks kind of all-powerful to me right now," said Singespitter. "Save him from what?"

"Himself," said Aragon, understanding.

Kassa nodded. "If you can keep him alive, I may be able to find a solution to all this. But I need time."

"It's going to have to be a really good solution," Singespitter warned. "What makes you think he'll listen to us?"

"Neither of you has magic, and neither of you is afraid of it."

Aragon raised a hand. "I dispute that."

"Me, too," said Singespitter. "Hello, five years as a sheep?"

Kassa growled at them both. "If either of you have any desire to see that boy survive to his next birthday, get going."

Egg discovered the sorcerer's tower, the tallest and pointiest part of the palace of Drak. With a thought, he unfurled the roof like the petals of a flower and stood at the very edge of one of those petals, gazing down at the city below.

This was a very high place.

There was so much magic under his skin, so much power. Flight would be easy. It was falling that would take effort. He would need forcible control of his motley magic to prevent it from snaking out a tendril to save his life.

Did he have enough control to rein those powers in, to step from the edge of the open roof and fall like any normal mortal? There was only one way to find out.

As he moved a fraction further towards the edge, Egg heard voices nearby. One was loud and huffy: "So many bloody stairs, my legs are so numb they feel like they've been stung by spiders!"

"Hush," said the other voice, cool and clinical. "He can hear us."

"Don't come any closer!" Egg yelled down.

Singespitter crawled into view, collapsing on the floor of the sorcerer's tower among the various demonic instruments and ingredients. "I don't see why not," he wheezed. "We're not much danger to you now. The stairs just about did us in."

Aragon Silversword emerged next. "Singespitter's right," he said calmly. "We're hardly a threat. We didn't even bring any iron with us."

"We didn't?" said Singespitter. "That was careless. Big scary powerful warlock versus us, without even a bit of iron to protect us. We are not the brains of this outfit."

"We can go all the way back down to the kitchens and get some if you like," said Aragon. "Of course, it means climbing back up the stairs again…"

"Ugh," groaned Singespitter. "Don't even suggest it."

"You can forget the clown act," Egg said sharply, his footing beginning to waver a little. "I know Kassa sent you."

"Of course she sent us," said Aragon. "If ever I get into as desperate a situation as you did today, I hope Kassa would care enough to send someone after me."

"Do you think you can help me?" Egg demanded.

"Dunno about help," said Singespitter. "She didn't say anything about help, did she?"

"She said to save him, not help him," Aragon agreed. "Although 'help' could be implied."

"I tried to kill her!" Egg shouted.

"I noticed that," said Aragon. "You and I might need to have a duel about that one of these days."

"Very helpful," said Singespitter. "Can't you go five minutes without challenging someone to a duel? Classic attention-seeking behavior, Silversword."

"Listen, Fleecy, if you can't contribute to the conversation, why don't you go and knit something?"

"Lovely riposte, very witty with the sheep theme and everything. You should be on the stage." Singespitter turned serious. "Egg, what Mister Sword-up-his-butt meant to say is that Kassa is very forgiving when her favourite people try to kill her. This one here has done it hundreds of times."

"Once," corrected Aragon.

Singespitter lifted his eyebrows. "Oh, come on."

"Maybe twice."

"Didn't stop her hopping into a hammock with you, did it?" Singespitter frowned. "Actually, that's a bit disturbing, when you think about it."

"We're getting off-topic," Aragon growled.

"Oh, yeah. Point is, Egg, Kassa is your cousin and your teacher and she cares about you and she's already forgiven what you tried to do to her otherwise she wouldn't have bothered sending us up here, would she?"

Egg stared at the city below his feet, wondering how fast he would fall, and how hard he would hit the ground. "What about Lord Kloakor?" he yelled down to his bizarre rescue party. "Who's going to forgive me for that?"

"It was an accident, wasn't it?" Aragon called up.

Egg hesitated. "I don't think so."

"Oh, boy," muttered Singespitter. He glanced at Aragon. "What do we say to that? It doesn't matter that he killed someone? Of course it freaking matters."

"I've run out of ideas," admitted Aragon. "We need Kassa, she's the one who's best at talking people into submission."

"I can still hear you!" Egg yelled down.

"We know!" said Singespitter. "Shut up for a minute, will you? We're trying to figure out what to say next."

"May I try?" asked a soft, almost-familiar voice.

Aragon and Singespitter turned, half-expecting to see Clio. It was only her in a manner of speaking.

Lord Dreamer, a diminished mortal version of Lord Dreamer in a soft white dress, stepped into the room at the top of the sorcerer's tower. Without the glow of a Light Lord, her resemblance to Clio was even more pronounced, down to the bright blue eyes and fair hair.

"How did you get out of the salt circle?" Aragon asked.

"We stepped through," she said with a smile. "It was easy once we chose to leave our magic behind."

"So you're ordinary," said Singespitter. "Mortal?"

"For now," said Lord Dreamer. She raised her voice slightly. "Egg, would you come with me for a moment? There is something I would like you to see."

Egg hesitated, gazing down at her.

Lord Dreamer held a pale hand out to him. "Please, Egg. You may return here afterwards, if you wish. None of us will hinder you."

Quietly, Egg climbed down from the open roof, and took Lord Dreamer's hand. Together, they left the tower.

"Girls are so much better at this sort of thing," said Singespitter.

"Don't they know it," agreed Aragon.

Lord Dreamer led Egg to the ruined remains of the observatory. Broken glass hung from every window-frame. A cool wind blew in through the missing wall. In the centre of the room was a large circle of salt. Hovering in the centre of that salt was a sphere, a little larger than a watermelon, glowing brightly white.

"My magic, and that of Lord Invisiblus," said Lord Dreamer.

"Where is he?" Egg asked.

"Fetching Quillsmith from the dungeons. We are taking him home."

Egg stared at her in wonder. "Home?"

"We have spoken with your friend Kassa," said Lord Dreamer. "She believes that we can recreate our world, or something like it. All we need is the magic the five of us held, the harmonylight. Kassa has already poured into the sphere what she took from Quillsmith, and that which belonged to Ladybird. I would like you to do the same with the magic you hold that once belonged to Quillsmith, Ladybird and Kloakor."

Egg pulled his gaze away from her bright blue eyes. "You know about that?"

She nodded.

"I'm so sorry," he said, letting the misery spill out of him. "I didn't mean...I don't know what I meant to do, but I am sorry that I did it."

Lord Dreamer's eyes softened. "Our attempt to invade this land caused the deaths of many. We behaved as enemies to you. It is a wonder that your people let any of us live, let alone gave us the means to recreate our world. Kloakor cannot be a part of our new world, but his magic can. Will you relinquish it to us?"

"I have the draklight as well," Egg admitted.

Lord Dreamer looked surprised. "So much power within one boy's skin," she wondered. "It is good. We should take the dark magic as well as the light. This time, we will build a balanced world, a sustainable world of many shades and colours."

"Will you take my magic?" Egg blurted out. "The magic I was born with?"

Dreamer shook her head slowly. "That is yours to keep."

"But I can't be trusted with it!"

"You are young," she told him. "You will learn. I believe you have learned much already." She leaned forward, and kissed him.

Egg felt the walls fall down, releasing the layers and layers of magic he had held for so long. He had expected their loss to be painful, as it had been for Kloakor and Quillsmith, but Lord Dreamer was gentle with him. The magic drained out of him like rain trickling off a roof. He felt an incredible lightness as the draklight left him, and an unfamiliar realness as the last of the harmonylight was taken.

It's over. It's really over.

Lord Dreamer broke the kiss, and breathed the combined magic of Drak, Quillsmith, Ladybird and Kloakor into a second sphere. She rubbed the salt circle away with her foot, and sent the sphere to join the first. They glowed white and then black at the moment of merging, then became a soft, mottled grey.

Lord Invisiblus came through the doors with a sullen Quillsmith. "Time to go?" he said cheerfully.

"Our new life begins," Dreamer agreed. She smiled sweetly at Egg. "You will be remembered, Egfried Friefriedsson."

"I'm not sure if that's a good thing," he said wryly.

Dreamer blew him a kiss, then turned towards the grey sphere. Quillsmith and Invisiblus joined her. The three of them stepped into the sphere of magic, and were gone.

The sphere shrunk to the size of a small cherry plum, fell to the floor of the observatory and rolled towards Egg. He picked it up and put it in his pocket.

Aragon and Singespitter were waiting for him outside. "I

take it we don't need to escort you back up to the sorcerer's tower?" Aragon asked.

Egg managed a smile. "I'd rather not, if you don't mind. Too many stairs."

"Right, then," said Singespitter. "You know what comes next."

Egg sighed. "A conversation with Kassa."

Aragon clapped him on the back in a comradely fashion. "And you thought you'd already had a bad day."

~

Aragon and Singespitter guided Egg to a door in a corridor lined with red velvet. The boy knocked, and entered. The door closed behind him.

"I suppose we could listen at the keyhole," said Singespitter.

"Or we could have lunch," said Aragon.

Lunch won. They wandered along the corridor together.

"So that's an end to it," said Singespitter.

"Looks like."

"Tell me how much you love Kassa." The question came out of nowhere.

Aragon froze. "Any particular reason?"

"Take pity on an ex-sheep who needs to hear it."

"Well, if you insist," said Aragon Silversword. "For a start, I love her boots."

"They are good boots," Singespitter agreed with a sigh.

~

Egg found himself in a study, elegant and mahogany-lined. Kassa sat on a large desk with her back to the door, gazing out the window. "It seems funny to see sunshine over Drak," she said. "It'll probably take them a while to get used to the daylight concept."

"Where is everyone?" Egg asked.

"Well, let's see." She slipped off the desk and into the chair. "I found Sean and Clio asleep at the foot of the Great Staircase and sent them home to Cluft. The professors are still running around on a wild goose chase, except Incendia Noir who has scored herself an invitation to an intimate supper with Lord Sinistre. Both of them, naturally, have gone off to spend a few hours selecting the perfect outfit. The kitchen staff have been thrown into an absolute frenzy, since it's their job to conjure up an entire supper menu in less than four hours. It takes a surprisingly long time to carve pears into slivers, poach poppy seeds and whip up lettuce mayonnaise, you know. Then there's us. Are you ready to talk yet?"

"About how stupid I was, or how dangerous I was?"

"Don't be so hard on yourself, Egg. We're not even halfway through the semester. You can't be expected to know everything yet."

Egg pulled the tiny grey sphere out of his pocket and placed it on the desk. "I gave the magic back. All of it that wasn't mine to start with. I wish they'd taken the rest."

"Why?" Kassa said in surprise. "You can't deny your own magic, Egg. That's like denying your hair colour, or your height."

"But all those lectures about how magic is bad for you…"

"It is bad for you. And dangerous and powerful and perilous and all those other things. But it's yours. You have to deal with it and control it and learn to appreciate it without falling into the trap of obsession or dependence. These are complicated lessons, Egg. Second year stuff, if not post-graduate."

"I got it all wrong," he said miserably.

"I didn't do much better, and I've been around a lot longer

than you. I should have seen that you were in trouble, and I didn't. I got my own magic gradually, in bits and pieces. The first twenty or so times I used it, something went seriously wrong. That's an easy way to learn responsibility. You, however, became practically omnipotent overnight. It was like throwing a toddler into a stormy ocean in the hope that they'll figure out how to swim." She frowned. "To be fair, my parents did do that to me, and I am a pretty good swimmer."

"The worst thing is that I liked it," Egg burst out. "I liked the power, not being ordinary."

Kassa shook her head. "Ordinary is a choice, Egg. Like 'villain' is a choice. Learning to control your magic is the most important choice of all."

"How do I do it?" he asked.

Kassa smiled. "Be yourself. Try not to hurt anyone. Forgive yourself for your mistakes, and learn from them."

"Sounds easy."

"It isn't, believe me. But think about this. Magic is an empty thing to fill your life with. It doesn't give much back. Find something else that you enjoy and spend as much time as you can doing that to balance things out. If magic is not the most important thing in your life, you've already won the battle. Oh, and keep taking my Philosophy of Magic class, I'm looking forward to your mid-semester essay. Particularly if you choose the question about magical ethics and responsibility."

Egg relaxed. "I was expecting you to shout at me," he admitted.

Kassa stood up and moved around the desk. She hugged him briefly. "Only if you don't use footnotes properly. Come on, let's find the kitchens and snaffle some pear slivers."

~

Lord Sinistre sat at a table in the breakfast room, wincing as bands of bright sunlight cut through the gap in the curtains. There was a lot to get used to.

The Chamberlain arrived at the same time as Lord Sinistre's breakfast was brought in on a covered plate. He waited politely until the serving maid had left the room. "Three pieces of news, my lord."

Lord Sinistre was so excited that he didn't even start in on his breakfast. "Nice to be back in the old routine," he said happily.

"As you say, my lord. Firstly, it has taken quite a deal of effort, but almost all the demonic beasts who escaped from the Underground Zoo during the elemental storm have been recaptured. I'm afraid most of the creatures were run to ground in the Hall of Wardrobe. There was a bit of a scuffle, and a lot of collateral damage."

"Never mind that," said Lord Sinistre, distracted by a strange smell that was coming from under the cover on his breakfast plate. "I've worn all those outfits, anyway. Plenty more where they came from."

"Yes, my lord. As it happens, the second piece of news comes from the velvet factories. The workers are so outraged at the thought of making velvet without magic that they have gone on strike."

"I see," said Lord Sinistre, quite dejected. What was that smell? It was quite...intriguing. "And the third piece of news, Chamberlain?"

"I'm taking a day off, my lord."

"Another one?"

"A family matter. Do you have a problem with that, my lord?"

"Oh, no. Why should there be a problem? Here I am in the middle of a complete restructure of our society, and the only person in the city who knows what he is doing chooses to take his day off. I'm ecstatic."

"That wouldn't be sarcasm, would it, my lord?"

Lord Sinistre smiled. "I'm learning from the best, Silver-sword. Off you go."

"Thank you, my lord." Aragon hesitated before leaving. "There is one more thing."

"A fourth piece of news? That's highly irregular."

"More of a warning, my lord. It appears that our Head Cook has been swapping recipes with some of the dinner ladies of Cluft."

"Is that good?"

"I'm not entirely sure. Perhaps you would care to examine the results?"

Lord Sinistre lifted the cover of his plate and recoiled from the contents. "What in Drak is that?"

"Ah," said Aragon. He leaned over the plate. "That would be steak, sausages, bacon, mushrooms, tomato, fried bread and three kinds of egg, my lord."

"I see," said Lord Sinistre. He inhaled deeply. "Cancel all my appointments for the morning, Chamberlain. I think this will require some serious attention."

Aragon grinned as he left. "As you say, my lord."

"You call this eggs on toast?" complained Sean McHagrty, standing at the counter in the Majestic dining hall. He stared in horror at the wafer-thin slice of toasted muffin with a tiny poached quail's egg perched upon it. A faint trace of peach mustard had been drizzled over the yolk of the egg.

"What's wrong with it?" demanded Mistress Pott.

"Oh, nothing much. Could I have another twelve, please?"

Clio was already seated. Her tray held a plate of Mistress Pott's new fruit salad — three grapes prettily arranged on mint leaves — and a tiny goblet of raspberry cordial. She glumly prodded the grapes with her fork, moving them around the plate.

Sean joined her, putting his tray down. "Haven't you cheered up yet?"

"You wanted to be my friend," she pointed out. "That means putting up with me even when I'm in a bad mood."

"I get that, but it's been days."

"That happens to be how long I've been feeling bad."

"So, stop it. It doesn't suit you."

"And you're bored."

"Little bit."

She managed to crack a smile finally. "And you've got something better to do?"

He put his pleading face on. "Imani Almondstone keeps giving me the eye. I've never let an opportunity like that go past!"

Clio glanced across the hall, just in time to see Imani turn her face hurriedly aside. "Go on," she sighed. "Break her heart. I never liked her much anyway."

"You're a gem," Sean said cheerfully, leaning across the table to kiss her on the forehead. He scooped up his tray and moved across the hall, pasting a charming grin on his face. "Imani, has anyone ever told you that you have a beautiful smile?"

Clio shook her head. She still didn't see how that worked for him. He really wasn't that cute.

A shadow fell across her table. Egg stood there. "Can we talk?"

"That depends," she said. "Are you going to buy me dessert?"

"It's breakfast time."

"Don't mess with a beautiful idea."

~

Kassa sat in the deck chair on her balcony, trying to get up the energy to go downstairs and get a cup of coffee, and possibly a bacon sandwich. It was a bacon sandwich sort of morning.

The door opened behind her. "Where have you been?" she complained. "I haven't seen you for days. I know there's not as much room now you're human again, but that doesn't mean you have to move out!"

Singespitter joined her on the balcony and stood at the railings, staring out at the view of the ocean. "That a pirate ship out there?"

"Hard to say. Purple might just be the in thing for ships this season."

"That purple ship just fired a cannonball into the side of the white ship."

"It's probably pirates," she conceded.

"I've been talking to Vice-Chancellor Bertie."

She stared at him, a little confused by the shift in conversation. "About getting your own room?"

"About the Great Reversing Barrel. He's fixed it."

"You mean he's chopped it into tiny bits and buried them somewhere?"

"No, I mean it's now in full working order."

"Should we declare a National Emergency?"

Singespitter looked down at her. Strange, seeing him so much older than he should be, his face creased and his hair greying. *The Glimmer took those years from him,* Kassa thought guiltily. He still had the body language of a teenager.

"Bertie's tested it thoroughly," said Singespitter. "By some strange fluke, it doesn't reverse things anymore, but it does return things that it previously reversed to their original state."

Kassa frowned. "What do we need reversed back? We can't put Harmony in there, not now they've restored their magic themselves. I had a peek at that scroll of yours yesterday, they're doing quite well for themselves."

"Not them," he said simply. "Me. I want to reverse me."

Kassa stood up so fast that the deck chair folded itself up at her feet. "What? What the glory gods are you talking about?"

"I want to go back to being a sheep," said Singespitter.

"But this is your natural form! This is what you are supposed to be!"

"I don't care. The human thing isn't working out for me, Kassa. I've been a sheep too long."

"But you can do anything as a human that you could as a sheep," she protested. "More, because you'll have opposable thumbs."

"They're not all they're cracked up to be, thumbs. Not compared to wings."

"I don't understand," she said, her voice breaking a little.

Carefully, Singespitter leaned forward and kissed her on the mouth. The kiss was long and sweet, and his eyes were sad when he pulled away.

Kassa took a deep breath. "Okay, now I understand. But it's still *stupid*."

"You won't try and stop me?"

"If it's your decision, I have to accept it. But isn't there any other way?"

Singespitter smiled. "Believe it or not, I'm looking forward to it. I won't get cold in winter, as long as I can stay away from those bloody students with the clipping shears during Rag Week. And I'll be able to fly again, Kassa. You've no idea how much I've missed that."

Lost for words, she hugged him, burying her face in his

sheepskin coat. He hugged her back, tightly. "I'll see you soon."

After he left, Kassa lowered herself back into her deck chair and buried her face in her hands for a long time before emerging and taking several deep breaths. "The day is definitely calling for bacon sandwiches," she said aloud. "Possibly three."

~

Outside the Majestic, Egg brought Clio an ice cream cone topped with liquorice curls and pink sprinkles. "Is that enough dessert for you?"

"It seemed like a good idea at the time," she said faintly.

After they had deposited the ice cream in the nearest waste bin, they walked across the square of student residence. "How are you?" she asked.

He shrugged, uncomfortable. "Coping."

"Kassa told me something about what happened. All that magic..."

"It's not an excuse."

"No." Her voice trailed off. Bravely, she tried again. "Have you started on your Philosophy of Magic essay yet?"

"Can't quite face it. Kassa keeps hinting about extra reading, and how she expects more of me than everyone else."

"I could come over to your room this afternoon. We could work on our essays together." A ghost of a smile flashed across her face. "I happen to know that Sean won't be there to interrupt us."

"I'd like that," said Egg.

~

At lunch time, Aragon was waiting for Kassa near the river

that snaked around behind the Mermaid Tower. She regarded him with some suspicion. "Where's the picnic basket?"

"Already set up." He motioned across the river. A red and white checked rug was set out under a sweeping pine tree. An elegant silver-haired lady was busily setting out cups, plates and cutlery.

Kassa panicked as she took in the situation, and tried to run away. Aragon was prepared for this possibility, and grabbed her around the waist. "Oh, no no no," she protested wildly. "This isn't fair! This is the very opposite of fair!"

"I met your parents."

"At knifepoint! Aragon, I can't do this. It's not right."

He squeezed her gently. "I'm not going anywhere this time. We may be living and working in different cities, but you are still going to have to face the fact that you and I are together. It's time you met my mother."

"But she'll hate me," Kassa wailed.

"Remember Bounty?"

"Your ex-girlfriend, the one who wears chainmail lingerie in public?"

"My mother couldn't hate anyone as much as she hated Bounty."

"Say it again," Kassa grumbled.

Aragon could have repeated the comment about Bounty, but he knew that wasn't what Kassa was referring to. "I'm not going anywhere," he said again, slowly and distinctly.

She took a deep breath. "All right, then. I'll meet your mother. But if she says one bitchy word about my clothes, I get to stab her."

"If she says one bitchy word about your clothes, I'll stab her myself."

Bracing herself, Kassa Daggersharp went forward to meet her destiny — or, at least, her destiny's mother.

～

Clio looked at the drawings that were pinned up around the room. She was in total awe. "I can't believe Sean didn't tell me about this."

"I swore him to secrecy," admitted Egg. "I wasn't sure what you'd think."

Every image was familiar, even rendered through Egg's unique ink-heavy drawing style. Clio glanced past images of the Light Lords, the warlocks and the draklighted Cluft to settle on one image in particular, the shadowy confrontation between Aragon Silversword and his brother. She shivered.

"I thought I should give fiction a miss for a while," Egg said apologetically. "Taking a leaf out of the epic poets and chronicling history instead. Do you mind?"

Clio gazed at an image of her mother. Egg had captured Dahla's face perfectly. "I love it," she said. "How's it going to end?"

"Like it did in real life, of course."

"But history doesn't end, it keeps on going. What's your cut off point? What will be the concluding note to this epic of yours?"

"I don't know," he said. "I hadn't thought about it. How do epics usually end?"

"Happily," said Clio. "Or tragically. With a kiss or a death scene."

"There's been enough death," he muttered.

She stared meaningfully at him. "Well, then?"

Egg looked at her, a little excited. "Don't move."

"What?"

"Stand right there." He pulled out his sketching pad and a scratchy pencil, sitting on the bed. "I want to draw you."

"Egg," she said impatiently, giving up on hints altogether. "I was hoping you wanted to kiss me."

He glanced up and grinned at her, his pencil scratching across the page. "I know. And I do. I just want to draw you first."

She rolled her eyes. "Fine. I can wait." A thought occurred to her. "Are you drawing me as a hero or a villain?"

"Wait and see," he promised.

~

As the noon light shone brightly over Cluft and Drak, a sheep took flight out of a window of the administration cottage, his purple wings pumping wildly. He wheeled around in the sky, baaing triumphantly, relishing the glory of flight and freedom.

A few minutes later, clouds passed in front of the sun. Thunder rumbled, and the clouds cracked open. Live salmon tumbled from the sky, spattering over the two cities along with cold, hard rain and the occasional slice of lemon.

In Drak, the population stared in absolute horror at the weather conditions that they were going to have to get used to.

In Cluft, students ran for cover, laughing and screaming. Mistress Brim emerged from the Mermaid Tower, armed with several wide nets and a recipe for salmon pie. Across the river, three picnickers sheltered under the pine tree. None of them had stabbed each other yet, which had to be a good sign.

Singespitter just kept flying, dodging the falling salmon with practiced ease, grinning all over his fleecy face. Things were as they should be. Even the weather was back to normal.

This was going to be a really great semester.

THE MOCKLORE OMNIBUS

Did you miss something? Catch up on Kassa and Aragon's previous adventures with the two original Mocklore novels in one volume!

SPLASHDANCE SILVER (Mocklore Chronicles #1)

Kassa Daggersharp has been avoiding her legacy as the daughter of infamous parents for far too long. But the death of her father, Vicious Bigbeard, leaves her the heir of a precious treasure trove, the Splashdance silver.

All she has to do is form a pirate crew from scratch, dodge the minions of the new Lady Emperor, learn how to control her long-neglected magic, and win the loyalty of the worst traitor in the history of the Mocklore Empire.

No problem, right?

LIQUID GOLD (Mocklore Chronicles #2)

The most seductively dangerous substance in the world is invented by Mocklore alchemists... and promptly stolen by a beautiful troll. This golden goo with the power of time travel causes havok throughout the Mocklore Empire, causing damage to reality and even the Underworld.

It's a problem for everyone, but especially for Kassa, whose unexpected death by trinket leaves her in a prime position to investigate what's going wrong in the land of the dead... while her crew, left behind, have to decide what their futures hold.

Comedy pirates, saucy witches, magical explosions, gratuitous historical trivia and flying sheep... it's just another day in Mocklore.

Buy The Mocklore Omnibus today!

PRAISE FOR THE MOCKLORE CHRONICLES:

"Magical. Such detail. A bloody blast."
—Lisa Gormley

"A brilliantly batty romp ..."

"... delicious high fantasy comedy ..."

"...fun fantasy adventure... brings to mind Terry Pratchett's Discworld..."

BOUNTY: THE NEW MOCKLORE ADVENTURES

It's not easy to make an honest living in the tiny magical empire of Mocklore. Bounty Fenetre isn't a bounty hunter. Delta Void isn't a mercenary. But trouble follows both of them, everywhere they go...

Six stories of adventure, magic, chaos and chainmail lingerie, where fairy tales are bad for your love life, and shoes can solve anything.

Buy BOUNTY today!

SHORT FICTION:

Love and Romanpunk

Please Look After This Angel & other winged stories

NON-FICTION & ESSAYS

It's Raining Musketeers

Pratchett's Women

50 Roman Mistresses

CREATURE COURT

(rerelease coming in 2019)

Power & Majesty

The Shattered City

Reign of Beasts

Cabaret of Monsters

ABOUT THE AUTHOR

Tansy Rayner Roberts lives in a messy house with lots of bookshelves. Sometimes the Tasmanian landscape still looks like Mocklore to her, but she has yet to spot a flying sheep.

Tansy is the winner of Hugo, Washington Small Press, Aurealis and Ditmar Awards. She writes about pirates, witches, superheroes, fairy tale newspapers and magical share houses. When not writing, she runs a literary gift shop on Etsy: Alice & Austen.

You can listen to Tansy across three different podcasts: Galactic Suburbia, providing a feminist point-of-view of the SF publishing world; Verity! six smart women talking about Doctor Who; and Sheep Might Fly, where Tansy reads aloud her stories as audio serials.

Support Tansy's Patreon to receive all kinds of rewards, including ebooks, exclusive stories and more.

Follow TansyRR at:
tansyrr.com/
news@tansyrr.com